BLOOD MIST

MARK ROBERTS

HEAD
ZEUS

First published in the UK in 2015 by Head of Zeus, Ltd

This paperback edition first published in the UK in 2016
by Head of Zeus, Ltd

975312468

A catalogue record for this book is available from
the British Library.

Paperback ISBN 9781784082901
eBook ISBN 9781784082871

Typeset by Adrian McLaughlin

Printed in the UK by Clays Ltd, St Ives Plc

Head of Zeus Ltd
Clerkenwell House
45–47 Clerkenwell Green
London EC1R 0HT

WWW.HEADOFZEUS.COM

For Linda and Eleanor
It wasn't a pearl at all
It was the moon

Liverpool and Merseyside

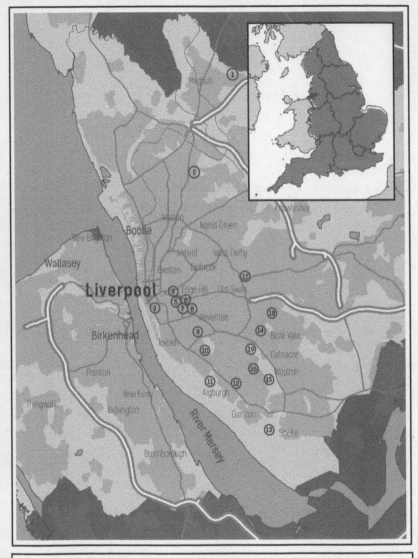

1	Ashworth Psychiatric Hospital	8 St Michael's Care Home
2	Aintree Racecourse	9 Ullet Road
3	Merseyside Police HQ	10 Sefton Park
4	Royal Liverpool Hospital	11 Aigburth Road
5	University of Liverpool	12 The Serpentine
6	The Bears Paw Pub	13 Trinity Road Police Station
7	Williamson Tunnels	

14 Ravenna Way
15 Menlove Avenue
16 Childwall Park Avenue
17 The Park Hospital
18 St Bernard's Primary School
19 Linda McCartney Playground

Liverpool City Centre

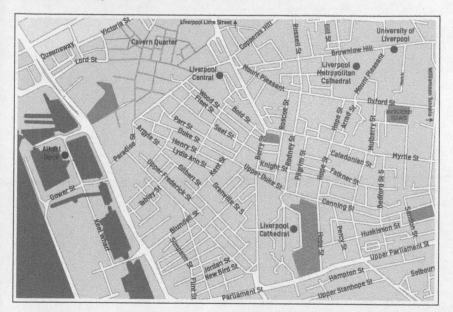

Williamson Tunnels

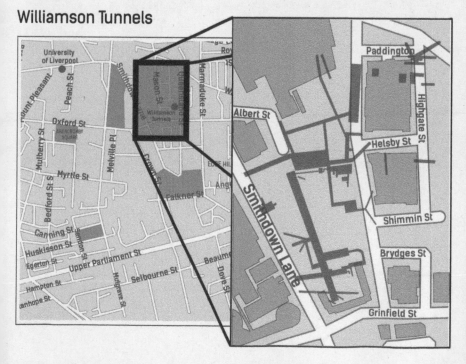

Prologue

October 1984

4.25 pm

'You'll be very happy here, Eve,' said Mrs Tripp.

From the other side of Mrs Tripp's desk, Eve looked over the big lady's shoulder at the scarlet sunset through the window. Beneath her, she felt the space between her feet and the floor, white socks and red sandals dangling above the carpet.

'Eve, how old are you?'

The little girl's eyes flashed as she connected with Mrs Tripp, but she smiled. The fat lady opposite was the boss of the children's home.

'Twenty-nine...take away...twenty-three,' she replied.

'Clever girl,' said Mrs Tripp, glancing at the bulging file in front of her.

Reading upside down, Eve saw the felt-tipped letters of her name on the stiff brown card – 'E V E T T E C L A Y' – and wondered what lay in between.

'Interesting,' said the social worker at Eve's side, indicating the file.

'Very,' replied Mrs Tripp. 'These paper files will all be

I

obsolete soon. It'll all be going onto computers, all this very important information...Imagine!'

Eve touched the edge of Mrs Tripp's desk.

The wood was the same colour as Sister Philomena's coffin. The thing that held her heart in place snapped and everything inside dropped. Once, there wasn't a day without Philomena but now she was gone.

Her earliest memory: Philomena, her smile brighter than the sunshine surrounding her. *I've been waiting all my life for you, Eve.*

Her last memory of Philomena in her coffin: Eve had tried to slip her fingers into Philomena's hand, but all she touched was stone-cold death. As the chapel candles flickered, everything that was lovely, all that Eve had, was gone.

Even though the new house, St Michael's Catholic Care Home for Children, just off Wavertree Road and built on the crown of Edge Hill, had windows through which she could see for miles, Eve didn't like the place. It wasn't St Claire's, the home she'd lived in for six and a half years. St Claire's, where Sister Philomena had taught her to read and write, and all about numbers and Jesus and the Devil. St Claire's was home.

Mrs Tripp continued talking and smiling, but Eve was listening to the noise of the house. She heard the voices of children at play outside, while inside some grown-up or other sang along to happy nonsense on a radio.

'Eve!' The social worker's voice brought the little girl's attention back into the room and the present. 'Take your hand off Mrs Tripp's desk.'

Her fingers and thumb were gripping the lip of the desk. Eve snatched her hand back and said, 'I'm sorry.'

'Of course, you won't be here forever, Eve,' said Mrs

Tripp. Her eyes dipped to Eve's file, like a reader hungry to get back to a book she'd been forced to put down. 'We can, we *will* find you a family to live with, a good Catholic family who want nothing more than a nice little girl...'

Eve leaned forward so that the tips of her toes touched the floor.

'I want...' she said, from the heart.

'Go on.' Mrs Tripp oozed attentiveness.

The wind pressed a dry brown leaf to the window. It scratched across the surface of the glass as the sky seemed to drift and dissolve in crimson clouds.

'I want to live with Sister Philomena.'

Mrs Tripp and the social worker exchanged glances. Eve tilted back into her seat, feet swinging over the empty space, the social worker's uninvited hand on her arm.

'Sister Philomena? But, Eve, she's gone to live with Jesus.'

'Then I would like to live with Sister Philomena and Jesus also.'

'You know you can't do that,' said the social worker. Mrs Tripp nodded. 'Sister Philomena was very old and not well and it was her time to go and live with Jesus. You're a young girl and full of health. It isn't your time to go to Jesus.'

Outside, the wind made a noise like the deep pipe in the organ in the chapel at St Claire's.

'We actually have a family *waiting in the wings*, we think—'

'No!' Eve, feet on the floor and standing, snatched her arm away from the social worker. 'I don't want to live with a family!'

She dug down into recent memory, to the instructions Sister Philomena had given her the very last occasion they had been alone together, for the time when she would no longer be there for her.

The smile on Mrs Tripp's face became a pout.

Eve remembered.

'You cannot make me live with a family if I do not give my permission.'

'But, Eve...' Mrs Tripp's hands were on the edges of her file, pinching the spine and the papers poking out of the open side.

'I will live in this place until I am old enough to leave.' She remembered a long word Philomena had told her to use. 'I am institutionaled from a baby.'

'We're happy for you to live here, Eve.'

'I have human rights.'

'But most children—'

'I am not most children, Mrs Tripp.'

Silence. Eve recalled sitting on Sister Philomena's bed, before she fell asleep and was laid to rest in the chapel at St Claire's. Philomena's words danced around her head. It was time to play what Philomena had called the trump card.

'You either find my real mother and father and I will live with them, or I will live here until I come of age.'

The social worker turned to Eve with the look of someone seeing a ghost.

'Eve, go and stand over there by the door.'

Eve did as she was told but didn't take her eyes off the women, one slug-fat as the other was twig-thin. They both held up their hands to shield their mouths as they fell to whispering.

As Eve watched the women leaning into each other, she wondered if Mrs Tripp's desk was made from the same tree as Sister Philomena's coffin. Eve, who could hear shadows fall on silent seas, concentrated hard on the hissing back-and-forth until it stopped and Mrs Tripp ordered, 'Come back, Eve.'

4

Obediently, she returned, sat, and stared at her scuffed red toes.

'So, Eve,' said Mrs Tripp. 'We'll see how you feel about living with a family when you get a little older. You seem very set in your ideas for *now*. Is there anything else you'd like to say while you're being so forthright?'

Eve looked up from the toes of her sandals.

'I'd like to ask a question,' she said.

'By all means.'

'What's a *bitch*?'

'Eve?' Two women, one voice.

Eve turned her attention to the social worker and addressed her directly. 'You just said, *She even sounds like the old bitch.*'

Mrs Tripp tapped the table hard with a biro. Eve met her eye.

'Welcome to St Michael's, Eve. We do not tolerate bad language here and we demand obedience in the name of Christ Jesus.'

Behind her, coral clouds hung over the River Mersey as the sky dissolved into night.

Mrs Tripp opened up her file and read as Eve followed the social worker to the door.

'I hope you'll be very happy here, Eve,' said Mrs Tripp.

33 years later

The Beginning of the
End of Time

Day One

1

11.55 pm

At five minutes to midnight, DCI Eve Clay pulled through a red light, picking up speed on the snow-bound dual carriageway, listening and looking hard for other vehicles as she sped past the junctions.

The blizzard had shifted north and west into the Irish Sea, but the air was thick with freezing fog and, through it, Clay caught the edge of sirens in the distance behind her. She knew she was at the head of the descending pack.

The crime scene was a two-minute drive from her house in Mersey Road. In fifteen years of investigating violent crimes, it was the closest a scene had ever been to home.

Minutes earlier, as she'd pulled up outside her house, the light in her bedroom had gone on and her iPhone had rung in the same moment. Connecting the call, she'd looked up through the twisting fog at the shape of her husband Thomas in the bedroom window as DS Karl Stone's voice filled the car on speakerphone.

'Eve. The Serpentine...'

'I've just driven past it along Aigburth Road.'

'Number 38. It sounds like a bloodbath.'

A cold sickness radiated from her core to her scalp and the tips of her toes.

'Listen to this recording from switch. Brace yourself.'

Ignition back on.

'Play it for me, Karl!'

Three-point turn.

She'd taken a right turn at the top of Mersey Road onto Aigburth Road, the dual carriageway, as she listened to the recorded voice of a teenage girl, shrill and terrified: 'I've locked my door, I've locked my bedroom door...'

Your bedroom door? Clay's foot sank harder on the accelerator.

Someone – something? – kicked and banged at the girl's door and, amid this chaos, some voices chanted, voices stripped of humanity, a babble that Clay couldn't pin down.

'How many of your family are at home?' The operator's professional calm evaporated at the sound of the door giving way.

'Six.'

'How many are they?'

'I've seen three.'

The wood cracked as the door yielded. The girl howled and cried out. 'Mummy! Mummy! Mummy!'

Beneath her screams, the wet clicking of the intruders' tongues and dislocated sounds like random syllables.

Then sudden silence. The line went dead.

'Karl, how far away are you?'

'I'm coming out of Garston. I'm putting my foot down.'

'Gina Riley and Bill Hendricks?'

'I told switch to call and instruct them to attend the scene.'

'Find out where the closest Scientific Support Unit is.'

Closing down the call, she peered through the glare of the

headlights into the swirling milk on the dual carriageway ahead of her. A red traffic light formed a patch in the fog like blood mist. Tension rolled inside her, head to heart, heart to gut.

The Serpentine was a minute away and, for a moment, she was fired with the hope that the perpetrators would still be in the house or close by. Her pulse rate picked up at the prospect of facing them directly and then her chest tightened as instinct whispered, *The conditions favour them. You're too late. They're well away.*

As Clay turned off the broad space of Aigburth Road and into the enclosed S-shaped channel of The Serpentine, the quality of the fog changed. It became thinner and seemed to roll backwards, as if the mouth of the road was breathing in the clouded air from the dual carriageway and tumbling it round the darkness between the rows of large detached houses.

But then again, Eve...

Deeper into The Serpentine, she drove fast along the winding road, shapes forming to either side. Mature trees lined both pavements, electrified Victorian lamp posts spilled yellow light and behind the whispering fog loomed the vast front gardens and well-appointed homes of its affluent residents.

She saw two points of light heading towards her, car headlights coming up The Serpentine from the opposite direction, slowing down as she stopped her car dead in the middle of the road.

If it was *them*, they wouldn't get past her.

The car stopped and a tall figure stepped out, a shape she recognised immediately. She hurried out of her car as sirens came closer, but the memory of the silence when the girl's phone died sat like something wet and fibrous in her ear.

The advancing silhouette called out. 'Eve?' And DS Karl Stone moved into a yellow puddle of light. Tall and thin, with his prematurely grey hair slicked back and a dark overcoat that looked three sizes too big for him, to Clay's eyes he was the human incarnation of a vulture.

The wrought-iron gate of the house was wide open.

Following Clay into the front garden, Stone hit a beam of torchlight over her shoulder and onto the ground ahead of her. The compacted ice was as hard as stone and the frozen surface was rippled by all manner of indentations, but with nothing that resembled a human footprint.

'Scientific Support?' asked Clay, heading towards the front door.

'Nearest unit's trying to bypass a King Kong RTA on Upper Parliament Street in Toxteth.'

'I've got to go into the scene now,' said Clay. 'Paramedics?'

'Coming off Ullet Road.'

'There could be survivors in there. I'll go in alone to minimise scene contamination.'

'What if the perpetrators are still inside?'

'I'll shout for you. Stay at the front door.'

Closer to the house, Clay saw that the front door was partially open, like a family secret exposed to the gaze of strangers. Darkness sat in the open space and she was drawn by the strange and ugly silence that lay behind the door.

'Torch please, Karl.'

He passed it over her shoulder and she directed the beam to the space above the open door. She paused. Feather-like fingers seemed to drum against the crown of her skull. She lit up the discreet CCTV camera over the door.

'Soon as you can, Karl, your first job, get the footage. If they got in through the front door...'

'Shit visibility, Eve.'

The conditions favour them.

'Which is why…' She fished a pair of blue plastic overshoes from her coat pocket and stepped into them. '…they came out tonight.'

She used the tip of her little finger, right hand, to push the flat edge of the front door wider, giving herself enough room to enter without touching any surface.

Clay raked the darkness with the torch, froze at what she saw and stifled her instinct to turn and hurry away. 'What on earth…' she heard herself whisper, then finished the thought in silence,…*has been here before me tonight?*

2

11.59 pm

In the dark hallway, the silence was exploded by the loud mechanical chime of the landline.

'Police!' She shouted. 'If you can hear me, call out!'

As she stepped deeper inside, the fear that had gripped Clay vanished. She was overtaken by a keen curiosity that dried her mouth and throat and made her heart beat faster. And with this passion to know as much and as quickly as possible, she felt her senses sharpen. The darkness around her became clearer; shapes formed before her eyes. The silence between the ringing of the phone was peppered with minute sounds in and around the house, from the air in an under-floor pipe to the snow-packed roof resisting the wind. Her focus converged into the time and space she inhabited.

Her pulse raced as instinct drew her attention to the stairs above the trio of bodies on the hall floor. 'If you need help, call out to me!'

A clock ticked in the rear of the house and the blood on the walls and floor hit the back of her throat as the taste of wet metal. There was a distinct aroma, as if each particle of air was infused with blood. She took a step, felt and heard the sticky rip as she lifted her foot from the carpet.

Like being locked in a butcher's shop, she thought. *With no ventilation.*

She picked out a path of light along the carpet, past elongated bloodstains, towards the three corpses and the bottom of the stairs.

As she followed the path, she stopped and lit up the display panel on the phone.

'Karl! Check out this mobile. 07700 934763. Who's it registered to? Where's it calling from?'

The ringing stopped and the answer machine kicked in.

'You have reached the Patel family...' The mature voice of the mother, Clay estimated, as she arrived at the configuration of bodies.

A girl, about seven years of age. An elderly woman. A tall middle-aged man. In torchlight, they looked like they'd been savaged by a pack of wild dogs. Their heads were pulped and shapeless above their contorted faces.

'I'm sorry we're not able to take your call...'

The bodies had been arranged carefully into an irregular quadrilateral.

The old lady lay on her side, her head resting on her shoulder and left arm outstretched. The man was on his side, his arms reaching beyond his shattered skull, his fingers connecting with the woman's feet. Bent at the hips, his body formed a right-angle. His long legs tapered to the little girl's head, his toes touching her face. The girl linked up the three sides formed by the adults: she was on her back, her feet touching the old lady's face. A little girl's corpse tucked neatly in death between her father's and grandmother's bodies.

Clay made a mental snapshot of the shape their bodies made.

'...but if you'd like to leave a message after the tone...'

As the fog crept in from behind her, she felt a gentle heat rising from the ground; the warmth of bodies not yet cold.

'. . . we'll get back to you as soon as possible.'

The signal to record played. Silence. Then the caller exhaled, a long, death-like sigh, whispered softly, a sound beneath her hearing, and hung up.

The little girl's eyes were brim-full of astonishment. She was a few years older than Clay's son, Philip, but her long, dark hair was the same colour as his. She squashed the connection and pushed it deep down inside.

Get on, get on with the job . . .

Clay drew the light across the hall, saw bloody marks where the bodies had been dragged for arrangement at the foot of the stairs.

She edged past the bodies.

'Police!' She shouted up from the second stair.

Clay kept moving, past bloodstained wallpaper daubed with random lines that were still not dry.

An irregular quadrilateral with a straight line extending from its top left corner. She picked up speed as she passed another finger-painted bloodstain. This one put Clay in mind of a crooked W, two diagonal lines touching a straight central mark.

As she reached the top of the stairs, something in the configuration of the bodies and the markings on the staircase wall triggered a connection deep inside her brain. They were like shapes lifted from a map.

What am I looking at but cannot see?

'Eve?' Stone's voice was loud and sudden, but she didn't even flinch. It was reassuring to be reminded that, even in this little corner of hell, she was in full control of herself. 'Are you OK?' She heard his concern.

'Alive and kicking. The killers have been painting the walls.'

Clay turned at the top of the stairs. A pool of light spilled onto the wide landing from the open door of a bedroom.

'Paramedics are outside!'

She looked at the three dead females on the landing and called back, 'Too late. No survivors.'

The torch flickered and went off and on again. She switched it off, took in the wider scene. All the doors she could see were wide open. Outside, the wind whistled and sighed, flattened itself against the walls and slid down the slate roof, enfolding the house like a dead lover.

She switched the torch back on.

She looked at the three bodies and knew for sure that she was the only living person in the house now.

A girl, around two years of age.

Clay looked away from her.

She focused on the teenage girl, whose terror she had listened to on the recorded call to emergency services. She saw the mother alongside her and saw the finger-painted blood mark on the staircase wall.

They formed a crooked W.

At the centre, the teenager was laid in a straight line, her feet hard up against the skirting board. To her right, her little sister lay at an angle, her feet touching the teenager's knees. To the left, the mother lay diagonally, feet connecting with those of her elder daughter.

Clay concentrated on the mother. Starting at her feet, she drew the light up her legs and onto her blood-drenched face. Her eyes were missing.

What didn't they want you to see? Clay wondered.

As quickly and carefully as she could, Clay checked each of the seven rooms upstairs, saw that the carnage had happened in two bedrooms and began the journey downstairs. She stopped at the bloody quadrilateral drawn on the wall and looked down at the configuration of bodies near the bottom of the stairs. The shape on the wall matched it, just as the crooked W showed the layout of the mother and daughters upstairs.

In the hallway, she edged along the space between the wall and the body drag marks.

At the end of the long, wide hallway was a kitchen extending to the back of the house. The space was darker than the rest of the house.

The back door leading into the garden was half open and blew wider in the wind.

She turned on a light switch.

For a moment, the tiled floor and the walls and fittings of the chrome-and-onyx open-plan kitchen looked normal. Clay looked up at the blood spray on the upper walls and ceiling.

There were three distinct sets of spray. One near the back door, one in the centre of the kitchen and one near the door leading in from the hall.

Grandmother. Father. Daughter.

She looked around the kitchen and not a thing was out of place.

Walking back to the front door, Clay called, 'Karl, where are Riley and Hendricks?'

'Here.'

'Three teams, comb the neighbourhood. They could still be out there.'

She stopped by the answer machine, a red number 1 flashing on the display. She pressed record on her iPhone, pressed play on the answer machine and counted the length of the silence. Five. Then the loaded sigh. And a tiny sound.

A thought occurred to Clay that she didn't want to believe and, for now, decided not to share with Stone or anyone else. They had timed the call for her arrival at the scene.

She hit the cold air. They were still out there and nearby. Her calm resolve collapsed.

Angry little gods, drunk on blood and power, hidden by the fog.

Her thoughts turned to home, to Thomas and Philip, two minutes away.

Day Two

3

00.12 am

Snow hammered the perimeter wall as the storm's tail lodged above the warren of buildings in the hospital grounds. The wind, trapped inside the wall, rolled the raging snow around the separate medical units and moaned at the front door of the High Dependency Ward. And though all the doors within Ashworth Psychiatric Hospital were locked – from the outer gate through to the units, the wards and the patients' rooms – the storm still wailed: no one in and no one out.

Behind the locked door of his room on the Ward, Adrian White pictured the hospital – his home for the past seven years and the place where his mortal body would one day die – not as a collection of secure NHS psychiatric units but as a village in a Hans Christian Andersen tale, a walled village that kept the world away from the sicknesses it feared most. And White away from the world that labelled him evil.

He faced the window and watched the snow, listening to the wind as it suffocated the hospital. The view was obstructed by four evenly spaced bars set inside reinforced glass.

White could sense the blizzard weakening as it headed west to the Irish Sea. Above his head, it seemed to slow down so it could peer through the little window of his locked room, one force of nature observing another.

He pictured himself moving through the outer wall of the segregation unit and drifting up into the night air, his body exploding and becoming one with the retreating storm. With his mind's eye, as he floated in the snow, he picked out his room and shut out everything except one dark slatted rectangle: his window.

He saw a reflection of himself in the glass, the shimmering shape of a man twisting in the howling wind, shifting in the chaos of snow.

Beyond the reflection he saw his mortal self sitting naked on a chair, watching the snow. He worked from the bottom up, noted his bare feet placed neatly together.

He followed the lines of his legs, his slender, muscular calves leading to the bend of his knees, his thighs flat on the path to his genitals.

He focused on his hips, on his slender, feminine hands, his long, tapering fingers that had calmly counted down the end of life for so many.

Without a pinch of body fat, his hairless arms and torso were defined by muscle; shoulders that could and had carried the weight of heaven, earth and hell across time and space. The tattoos on either side of his heart crouched in the darkness, deeper shadows on the surface of his skin.

His mind's eye gazed down from the sky as he looked directly into the room, at his own earthly face. And he saw nothing there except a stretch of skin that covered his features. He did not know and he could not see what he looked like. Nor could he remember his own face, except for his eyes.

In that *other life*, he had walked the streets wearing shades at all times, to protect himself from the unwanted attention of strangers.

The skin that covered his mouth moved as he tried to call

out to himself, but the only sound was the wind screaming hymns to chaos.

The self in the snow-filled sky dissolved into the pandemonium and drifted away, heading out west to the teeming black waters of the Irish Sea.

Footsteps.

The magic dissolved and his spirit was back inside his body.

From his chair, the only piece of furniture in the room that wasn't bolted to the floor, he heard footsteps. He knew each nurse by the sound of their feet, recognised their fear in the weight of their footfall, their aspirations and dreams by the length of their stride, their despair from the silence between each step. Even down to the way they breathed or held their breath as they looked in on him through the rectangular observation slot in his door.

And their thoughts reached his mind through the crisscrossing electrical impulses that fired hospital doublespeak through their brains.

A risk of harm to others...A risk of harm to self...A risk of being assaulted...A risk of escaping or absconding...A risk of endangering safety or security...

White sensed the nurse's eyes peering through the observation slot. The dimmer switch was turned up to get a better view of the patient sitting in the dark.

'Turn it off now.'

The light died suddenly.

'What do you want, Richard Taylor?' asked White, the lilt in his voice almost falling into song.

'I'm just checking on you.' Within the walls, silence.

Outside, the sound of the wind gave White a sensation of physical pleasure that consumed his whole body and he yielded to it with profound gratitude.

The nurse's footsteps moved away. The moment passed.

'Richard Taylor,' said White. Taylor returned. 'Listen.'

'Go on.'

'I want to see a social worker.'

'Why do you want to see a social worker?'

'Why do you want to know?'

'Seven years and you've asked for nothing, aside from complete segregation from all other patients on religious grounds.'

White could see the snow weakening now as the north wind whipped the last of the storm out to sea.

'Why do you want to see a social worker all of a sudden?'

'Care to come inside, Richard Taylor?'

Taylor didn't attempt to speak or move away. The nurse's presence gave White a direct line back into his childhood, reminded him of what it was to release a moth from a paper bag straight into the target of a naked flame.

'I'd have to bring other nurses with me and a very good reason for entering your cell, and that's not going to happen. Why a social worker?'

'Because it's started.'

'What's started?'

'Can't you hear?'

'I can hear the wind.'

'Then you're not *listening*.'

'What am I listening for?'

'The opening and closing of doors.'

'You mean here? Ashworth?'

'You cannot open the door in front of you until the door behind you is locked. That's the rule, isn't it?'

'Which door?' asked Taylor.

Adrian White soaked up the desperation in Taylor's voice.

'Do you know what you need to do, Mr Taylor?'

28

'Go on.'

'When you're handing over at seven o'clock in the morning, you tell the other nurses that I must see an approved social worker at the earliest opportunity. If I don't see a social worker, I'm going to be very upset. Do you understand, Mr Taylor?'

'I'll arrange it.'

'Go now, Richard Taylor, before the others wonder what took you so long.'

Through the window, Adrian saw a streak of red forming in the night sky.

'What do you mean, *it's started*?'

The wind howled. Ecstasy.

'Bring me a social worker. Flit away.'

Taylor walked away on the tips of his toes at a speed that pleased White.

When morning arrived, it would bring the social worker with it and his request would be granted. The red streak in the sky widened.

He remembered a certain woman and wondered if she had looked into the sky, had seen the colour red emerge from the darkness. He pictured her face an arm's length away, as it had been all those years ago, and spoke to her the parting words of their last encounter.

'The Red Cloud will rise from the belly of the city and when the Red Cloud rises, the river will run with blood.'

The Red Cloud was rising fast.

00.12 am

After three rings that seemed to last a lifetime, Eve's call home connected.

'Eve?' She was relieved to hear Thomas's voice. He was wide awake and knotted with anxiety. 'Where are you?'

'In my car, outside a murder scene. The Serpentine.'

'The Serpentine?'

'Six dead. A whole family.'

From the relative privacy of her car, Clay watched as a child-sized body bag was carried from the gate of the house to the open back door of a black mortuary van.

'Philip? Are you with him?' She spoke rapidly and could hear the tension crackling in her own voice.

'Eve, he's fine. He's asleep in his bed.'

'Are you with him right now?'

'I'm walking from our bedroom into his. Eve, you just don't sound yourself. What have you seen tonight?'

'Don't open the front door, Thomas.' *They could still be out there.* 'Listen really carefully for anything outside. Philip?'

'He's in bed, asleep, the night-light's on beside him. I'm going to lower the phone now. Listen to him breathing.'

She listened as Thomas lowered the phone towards their son. She heard the soft exchange of breath, recognised it as the unique sound of her baby sleeping peacefully in his bed.

Clay pictured herself in Philip's room, light seeping from the landing, picking out the smooth features of her son's face. She wished she could take herself there in the click of her fingers and weld her feet to his bedroom floor by a magical force that nothing could break.

She wanted to stoop and kiss the boy's cheek, like the first time, a little over two years earlier, when Philip, naked and taking his first dozen breaths, had been placed on her breast by the midwife. His face creased and serious, tufts of dark hair across the plates of his scalp; his eyes mostly blind but appearing to stare directly into hers, with a point of light on each pupil, like stars in the night sky.

But she wasn't at home or on the maternity ward. She was outside a house where six members of the same family had just been slaughtered and the zipped-up body of another child was emerging from the fog to join its siblings, parents and grandmother in the back of the mortuary van.

'Eve?' asked Thomas.

'Thank you for that, Thomas.' *For that lifeline back into a world worth living in, with people who I love and who love me back.*

'How bad is it?'

'Stay with Philip, stay with him until I get home. Don't let him out of your sight. Promise me, Thomas.'

'I promise you. When will you be home?'

'I don't know when I'll be home.'

'What if I film him and send it to your phone?'

DC Gina Riley hurried towards her along the pavement, her coat open and flapping behind her in the wind. It was good to see her.

'Yes, please. I've got to go,' said Clay.

'I love you, Eve.'

'Likewise. Philip…'

'If anyone wants to get at Philip, they'll have to get past me first. I'll send you the film.'

As Clay closed down the call, Gina Riley opened the passenger door, bringing the cold night in with her as she sat down next to Clay.

'The streets are swamped with officers. Everyone on duty and available is out there, from Dingle down to Speke, Aigburth up to Old Swan and beyond,' said Riley.

'Listen to this, Gina.'

Clay played back the recording from the family's answer machine.

The tone kicked in and Clay spoke into the silence that followed it.

'This call happened when I entered the house, Gina.'

The sigh and the buried word. And silence.

'As I recorded it, I had the strangest idea, Gina. What was that thought?'

'They watched you going into the scene. The call was for you,' said Riley.

'Yeah, that's exactly what I thought.'

00.16 am

Riley, a small, rotund woman with blonde hair and a dreamy expression that hid her quicksilver mind, was the physical opposite of Clay, who was tall and slim with long, jet-black hair snatched back in a ponytail. Clay declined Riley's offer of a stick of Wrigley's Spearmint Gum and noted how red Riley's lipstick was as she popped the chewing gum into her mouth. She noticed a sharp black trouser suit beneath Riley's coat that did a lot to flatten out the roundness of her body.

'Nice threads, Gina.'

'I look like a Munchkin in a cocktail dress. I was on my way home from a do when I got the call to attend the scene. It was my turn to drive,' said Riley, 'and Tommy's turn to swill red wine. Just as well.'

'You'd be better off with a few drinks inside you,' said Clay, indicating the house.

Clay caught her own reflection in the rear-view mirror and observed the extending network of lines around her deep-brown eyes. She found herself staring, not into her own eyes, but at the creases around them.

'Penny for them?' asked Riley.

'Check out the blood lines on the walls when you go inside. Two shapes.'

Through the fog, yellow blurs at the windows showed that all the lights in the house were on. DS Terry Mason, a Scientific Support officer with over twenty years in a white suit, headed out of the gate looking like a punch-drunk novice.

Clay wound the window down and called. 'Terry!'

He focused on Clay. 'You can come in now.'

'Thank you.' Clay noticed a small plastic evidence bag between the index finger and thumb of his right hand. 'What's that?' she asked.

He held it up to her and she saw what looked like a scrap of mud. On closer inspection, it was wet ash.

'I found it on the snow by the back door, the door leading out of the kitchen.'

DS Mason turned, looked dolefully at the house and walked back down the stepping plates from the gate to the front door.

Clay and Riley got out of the car. They grabbed a pair of protective suits from the open back of a Scientific Support vehicle and, as they stepped into them, Riley asked, 'What do you want me to do?'

'Stick with me. I'm going to have a look around with the lights on. Then I'm shooting down to the Royal Hospital to watch the post-mortems. You stay in the house and latch on to Mason, pump him for his impressions, information. Look for and photograph any graffiti.'

Clay stopped and addressed the uniformed officer at the gate, who was running the log of people coming in and out of the scene.

'Sergeant Cooper, I need DS Stone to join me in the house. When he's finished door-stepping the neighbours, let him in.'

The stepping plates felt unstable against the ice. The walk from the gate to the house reminded Clay of crossing a rope bridge.

'Where's Bill Hendricks?' asked Riley.

'Still coordinating the troops out there.' Clay paused at the door, indicated the CCTV camera. 'Karl's already pulled the footage.'

'We could have them in the next twenty-four hours.' Riley conveyed an optimism that Clay didn't share. She thought of the fog, the taking away of the mother's eyes.

'Shit visibility,' said Clay. 'To quote Karl Stone. They won't allow us to see them for who or what they truly are. Have you heard the tape from switch?'

'No. But I heard about it. Is it as bad as people are making out?'

'They sound like animals, sadistic beasts without any mercy. And making these weird clicking noises. Ready to go inside?'

Riley nodded.

'DS Mason,' called Clay, 'we're coming inside.'

The damp front door, covered with dark fingertip powder and an array of smudges at hand height and around the Yale lock, started to open slowly from within.

'Eve?' Behind her came Stone's voice, advancing towards the house. At the door, he handed Clay a sheet of paper on which he'd written:

Hanif Patel, father – 50s
Kate Patel, mother – 40s/50
Nadia Patel, paternal grandmother – 70s
Alicia Patel – 15
Jane Patel – 7
Freya Patel – 2

'Got the names and ages of the victims from the people next door.'

35

'Thank you,' said Clay, opening the front door.

With the lights on, bloodstained lines on the wall and the bloody drag marks on the carpet commanded a dreadful silence, broken when Riley released her breath.

'Bloody hell.'

'That's what I think it looks like,' agreed Clay. 'Let's get on with it.'

00.23 am

'Terry!' On the stairs, Clay called to DS Mason as she looked at the blood lines on the wall.

He appeared at the top of the stairs, digital camera in his hand.

'Have you seen anything like this before?'

He shook his head and Clay knew how Columbus must have felt when the boat had sailed far away from home.

Alone on the stairs, she looked down at the space where father, grandmother and child had formed an irregular quadrilateral and up at the space where mother and daughters had been placed in a crooked W. The shape of the interlinked bodies tripped something deep inside her brain.

I've seen it before, thought Clay, and wondered if it was some trick of the mind played on her in the short passage of time between her first and second times at the crime scene. But warmth blossomed inside her and with it a dull light that promised to glow brighter.

'Eve?'

She turned to Stone's voice.

'Next-door neighbour told me Kate and Hanif moved in over twenty years ago, along with Hanif's mother, Nadia. It was the only home all four of their children ever knew—'

'Four?'

'Eldest son Sandy's away studying at Durham University.'

'Has he been told?'

'DS Deborah Abbott, one of Durham Constabulary's Victim Liaison team, is driving him back to Liverpool right now.'

'Have you seen the CCTV footage, Karl?'

'Some. It's poor quality. The weather. Grime on the lens. The DVR's pretty old hat anyway, but the pieces I've seen, it's like the world's being filmed through a cloud.' Stone showed Clay a pen drive. 'Two channels, front and back door. No internal footage. Glitch. When I clicked on *selected files—*'

'Karl, no techno speak thanks. Did you save it on a pen drive?'

He showed her the USB stick.

'Go back to Trinity Road and get back to me as soon as you've seen it. We could well have our savages on that stick of yours.'

Clay reached the top of the stairs and lights flashed as Marsh's Scientific Support officers took picture after picture in the bedrooms of the little girl and the teenager. Their doors were on either side of the space where their bodies had been arranged with their mother. For a moment, from the corner of her eye, Clay thought she was seeing things. In the random patterns of camera flashlights spilling from the bedrooms, she saw the three bodies still gathered in that crooked W.

But there was nothing there.

Clay walked to the older girl's room, its entrance blocked by Riley, who was staring into the teenager's personal space.

'Her name was Alicia,' said Clay. 'She was fifteen.'

Alicia's door dangled from the frame by one buckled hinge. Everything faded and Clay heard the recording of the killers in their dehumanised pack and Alicia calling over and over for her mother as they cornered her.

Click click click click. Cameras synchronised with the wet clicking of their tongues.

Clay let her thoughts wander and was consumed by the sense of waste. Hours earlier, Alicia had sat on the bed, listening to music on her iPod through headphones that now lay on the carpet near the head of the bed, dreaming of a future, of university, travel, a career, love. Just as she herself had done as a teenager, night after night in her small bedroom in the St. Michael's Catholic Care Home for Children.

The boy bands on the wall, the make-up bag besides her mirror and the heart-shaped collage of pictures of her alive and happy with her friends were almost unbearable to look at.

'Someone just walk over your grave?' asked Riley.

'Good luck to them if they did. I'm getting cremated, ashes scattered on the Mersey,' replied Clay. 'Excuse me, Gina.' She walked into Alicia's bedroom, the pink walls like diluted blood in the camera's flashlight.

She looked at the bed, saw the bloody imprint of Alicia's skull on the white pillow and a rectangle under the pillowslip. Clay reached inside the slip and pulled out the edge of a packet of ten Embassy cigarettes. She pushed the packet back where Alicia had hidden it.

'They used a blunt instrument,' said Riley. 'Terry Mason estimated at least ten blows each. We can't rule out any sexual violence, but her clothes were undisturbed.'

Mason appeared in the doorway of Alicia's room

'Terry,' said Clay. 'Talk me through what happened here.'

'Someone, probably two of them, held Alicia down as another battered her to death.'

On her way out, Clay turned, looked at the pillow on the bed with its strange continent of blood.

There's someone out there who would have loved you, she thought. *Someone you'd have loved back and had a whole life with – joy, sorrow, a child or even children, a future, a life.*

I'm sorry, Alicia. I'm so sorry. She hurried down the stairs and headed for the mortuary at the Royal Liverpool University Hospital.

00.55 am

During the fog-bound drive from Aigburth to the outskirts of the city centre, DCI Eve Clay decided she would watch Kate Patel's post-mortem. The gouging out of the eyes was unique to her and could provide an insight into the minds of the perpetrators.

As she drove towards the mortuary, she called Hendricks and told him to meet her at the front entrance.

The wind throbbed from the throat of Kensington, seeking ever deeper bass notes as Clay negotiated the glassy surface from the Royal's multi-storey car park to the front entrance of the mortuary. In the heart of a horrible night, she was glad to see Hendricks waiting for her at the front door and that, for a short time, she would not be alone.

With his long, black hair tucked behind his ears and the smile that was always present in his eyes, DS Hendricks looked like a TV gardener forced into a shirt and suit for some formal event he was obliged to attend. People – enemies, mostly – underestimated Hendricks and treated him like a dim-witted village idiot, unaware that he had a doctorate in forensic psychology. He was the most intelligent police officer she had ever met and that was the reason she wanted him at the post-mortem.

A security guard unlocked the door and, as they entered, addressed Clay.

'You know the way to the Autopsy Suites?'

'Thank you.'

As they walked up the stairs to the first floor, Clay glanced back, checked they were alone.

'What do you think, Bill?'

'It's the biggest mass murder we've had in the UK for years. We're going to be surrounded by media by tomorrow evening, from all over the world. Sunglasses on, bright lights in the face all round.'

Their footsteps echoed.

'It's all upside down and back to front, Bill.'

'You've been at the centre of the scene. I haven't. Why do you say that?'

'It felt stagey, like a grotesque game. There were all kinds of confusing markers.'

'Such as, Eve?'

'They trashed the family, left the bodies linked in interconnecting shapes, daubed the walls in blood likewise.'

'Hunch call.' He fell silent for a few moments. 'Did they have fun?'

'They had the absolute time of their lives. And there's something else as well...' Clay's iPhone vibrated and buzzed. An incoming message.

'There's a structure—'

They reached the first floor.

'There's a structure behind the chaos. I don't know what it is, Bill.' Three dead females flashed through her head, death branching out from death. 'It's beyond sinister.'

As they approached the Autopsy Suites, Hendricks said, 'Do you need to deal with your phone?'

She glanced at the display.

The message had been from Thomas, from home. It would be the film of Philip sleeping in his bed. 'Better not just now.' Her heart sank.

At the door of Autopsy Suite One, Clay fell still when she heard the sound of a circular saw spinning into action. Her thoughts immediately turned from her son to the head injuries she'd seen. As the blade connected with bone, she knew the saw was working through a skull. Two to one odds it wasn't an adult.

As she watched Hendricks walk into Autopsy Suite One, a faulty wall light blinked. Her attention was drawn to the progression of serrated steel through human bone, a voice from the past weaved through her memory.

'*When you look into shadows, you look into mirrors. When you look into mirrors, what do you see?*'

Hendricks came out of Autopsy Suite One and said, 'Post-mortems for the three children are happening in there. The adults are in Autopsy Two.'

The whizzing saw in Autopsy Suite One stopped.

'I want you with me in Autopsy Suite Two.'

As they stepped into pants and smocks, in the small gowning room of Autopsy Suite Two, Clay saw Hendricks looking at her. There was a smile buried within his gaze.

'I want you to witness Mrs Patel's post-mortem,' she said. 'Do you know any of the details specific to her?'

'Other than the fact that she was battered to death, no.'

Clay had instructed Stone, Riley, Marsh and the other Scientific Support officers to keep the information from Hendricks. 'Good. Then I'll get a really clear idea of your first impression.'

She knocked on the door of Autopsy Suite Two and called, 'DCI Clay.'

'Come in, Eve,' replied the pathologist, Dr Mary Lamb. 'We've been expecting you.'

Clay entered the room, with its cold, chemical air and harsh overhead light, and was glad Mary Lamb was on duty. A small, slim woman on the verge of retirement, Dr Lamb appeared older than she was and this had been the case through all the years Clay had known her. From the back, even though she was dressed in the blue smock and trousers of the mortuary, there was something about her that reminded Clay of Sister Philomena. In the sombre dark of winter, the thought of the nun brought a fragment of warmth.

'You asked on the phone if you could see the post-mortem on Mrs Patel?'

'That's correct.' Clay's footsteps were deadened by the flat acoustic of the room.

'We're just about to begin.'

Clay turned to the rattling of metal implements on an aluminium surface. Dr Lamb's Anatomical Pathology Technician, Michael Harper – painfully shy, obese, baby-faced – wheeled the pathologist's tools towards the table.

Clay recalled Kate Patel's expensive designer nightdress and its bloody discolouration. 'One of your Scientific Support officers helped us undress her,' said Dr Lamb.

She looked around the room, saw the edge of Mrs Patel's body and felt the urge to find a sheet to cover her dignity. 'She took the lady's nightdress away in evidence bags, as she did with the rest of Mrs Patel's family.'

Clay looked at Mrs Patel's face. Under the glare of the mortuary's brash light, the absence of her eyes was freshly alarming. From the remains of her shattered skull, she looked down the length of her body and saw the massive swelling, the purple and black discolouration to the skin from internal bleeding.

'Cause of death could have been cardiac arrest due to massive shock, but, looking at the condition of her head, it's pretty certainly a brain injury.'

Michael picked up a pair of barber's shears from the

aluminium trolley and, lifting a handful of her blood-matted hair, cut close to the scalp.

'Is she the only one they took the eyes from?' asked Hendricks.

Clay looked at him. Hendricks was transfixed by Mrs Patel's face, the gaping dark spaces where her eyes had once been.

'Yes. Can you think of any precedents?'

'There was a killer in the US, Charles Albright. His victims were all female. He took the women's eyeballs away. I referenced him briefly in my doctorate. Leave it with me,' said Hendricks.

Carefully, Michael placed her hair into a transparent plastic bag.

'Tell me about any symbolism at the scene,' said Hendricks.

'The way the bodies were laid out. The finger-painted blood marks on the wall. They were strangely familiar, but I don't know why.'

From the left side of Mrs Patel's head, Michael cut another bloody clump of hair.

'This could be the key,' said Hendricks. 'Put aside the poetic notion about eyes being windows to the soul...'

'And replace it with...?'

'Where did she die, Eve?'

'Upstairs.'

'Order of deaths?'

'I heard Alicia calling her mother on the 999 recording. I think either Alicia or her mother was the last to die.'

'Did Alicia die upstairs?'

'In her bedroom.' The exchange with Hendricks gave Clay the sense that the fingers of her mind were hovering over a concealed truth. 'When I first saw Mrs Patel, the question I wanted to ask her was, *What didn't they want you to see?*'

Michael handed round large transparent goggles. Clay slipped them on, her own eyes domed behind plastic.

'Pass me the circular saw, please, Michael,' said Dr Lamb, tone neutral and polite, as if she was asking for the sugar bowl. 'We'll take the front of the skull away, the most damaged section.'

Michael drew a black line across Mrs Patel's forehead and Dr Lamb turned the saw on.

'The call to switch. What do we know about Alicia's last moments, Eve?'

Clay turned her eyes away as Dr Lamb connected the spinning blade to the skull just above Mrs Patel's left ear. She looked closely at Hendricks's face as he followed the procedure. She knew he wasn't watching the action of the saw. He was focused on Mrs Patel's face.

'She called out for her mother, then the line went dead.'

Six hours ago, thought Clay, *you were alive at home with your family, and everything was normal.*

When the blood-flecked saw died, Clay watched Michael take it from Dr Lamb. A wider picture of what might have happened on the upstairs landing formed in Clay's mind.

'Remove the section of skull, please, Michael.'

Michael's shoulders tensed and his elbows moved. He followed Dr Lamb's instruction with slick professionalism.

'What are you thinking, Bill?'

'When the killers moved upstairs, I think they killed the mother first. But then, even though the mother was dead, they didn't want her to *see* what they were going to do to her daughters. So they confiscated two body parts, her eyes. I think she represented some sort of authority to them. If they're males, we're looking for savages, but they're also mummy's boys.'

'I believe,' said Dr Lamb, 'I can see the most probable cause of death. Record, please, Michael.'

Michael held a small dictaphone towards Dr Lamb's mouth.

'A splinter of skull bone, approximately nine centimetres long, judging from the wound to the upper skull, lodged in the brain. The blows to the skull from blunt, heavy objects, the wide flatness on the blows to the head... Yes, feet, *human feet, consistent with wounds to the legs and torso.* They kicked her body into a pulp and then finished her off by caving her head in. I've seen it all before. Saturday night usually. But never this extensive, never this brutal.' She paused. 'Turn the dictaphone off, please, Michael.'

'This level of aggression,' said Hendricks. 'What does it suggest to you, Eve?'

As Clay processed the information, she felt the urge to pray to a God she believed didn't exist. She wanted to pray that she was wrong. Instead, a parade of some of the low points in human history passed through her mind.

The Crusades, Palestine, the Spanish Inquisition, Biafra, suicide bombers, the World Trade Centre...

'They killed with such brutality in the name of something they call divine.'

'And they only took the eyes from the mother?' asked Hendricks.

'Yes. But there was another mother there. The grandmother?' said Clay. 'She can't have been that significant to them. But the mother was. The mother mattered enough for them to take her eyes.'

Clay looked into the hollow mess of Mrs Patel's eye sockets and heard herself speak out loud. 'I never looked into my own mother's eyes.'

48

'My mother never stopped looking at me,' replied Hendricks.

Go. 'Thank you, Dr Lamb.' *Look.* 'DS Hendricks will stay with you as you proceed with your work.' *Now.*

Within seconds, she was out of the dressing room. Within a minute, she was running over the icy tarmac to the multi-storey car park.

9

1.35 am

In the driver's seat of her car, as Clay breathed warm air onto her hands and fingers, she realised how cold and wet they felt.

She took out her phone and picked up the message from Thomas. As she pressed play, a smile rose on her face.

Philip's face was bathed in the soft blue glow of the nightlight beside his bed. From the camera angle, Thomas was standing at the bottom of their son's bed, filming.

'Hey, Eve,' whispered Thomas. It was like being stroked. 'I've just come off the phone with you.' He moved slowly down the side of the bed and Philip let out a contented sigh. 'As you can see, he's absolutely fine. Safe and sound and sleeping...Don't worry. He's fine.'

Slowly, Thomas started to zoom in on Philip, the light mixing with the shadows that lay across his face. He lifted a bunched hand and rubbed his nose. The image of Philip's face dominated her iPhone screen.

'I'm going to leave my phone on vibrate by my bedside. If you want or need to ring me at any time, call my mobile. I'm going to stop speaking now and give you some time to look at Philip and see who's going to be waiting for you when you get home.'

Philip turned his face towards the light and Clay could see herself and Thomas in her son's features. Her chin and the shape of her eyes, with Thomas's nose and brow. His hair was dark, like hers, and fell in soft curls around his ears.

He opened his mouth and let out a cross between a sigh and a yawn, his small white teeth perfectly formed in his pink gums.

As his lips came together, the smile on her face froze a little and she concentrated on the shape of his mouth. It was the one feature she couldn't call. When he was a newborn, she'd seen her lips in his, but as time passed, his lips had come to look more and more like Thomas's. She'd joked how Thomas, an expert kisser, had given their son his best feature. At eighteen months, their shape changed again, became more rounded, more like hers, perhaps helped by the amount of exercise they got with his non-stop chatter.

For the first time ever, as she watched him in his bedroom from the distance of a frozen hospital car park, his mouth looked like neither hers nor Thomas's. She pictured Philip's doting grandparents, Thomas's mother and father. Her little boy's mouth was nothing like Mona or Clive's.

A tingle started on her scalp, at her crown, and soon her spine had picked up the cold heat of the sensation that was spreading across her skin.

She hadn't been much older than Philip when, sitting on Sister Philomena's knee in front of the fire in the big sitting room at St Claire's, she had asked her loving protector a question. A man and woman had recently arrived at St Claire's to pick up their daughter, Helen, who was a little older than Eve.

She recalled her child-like logic.

'In a month or so, will my mum or dad come to pick me up?'

Philomena had held onto her a little tighter, as if she was suddenly cold in front of the big blaze into which they stared, making pictures and weaving daydreams from the glowing coals. She looked into Eve's eyes with a fondness that gave the little girl a physical glow.

'No, Eve. Your mother and father will not be collecting you from me.'

'Where are they?'

'They've passed over to the other side.'

'To Jesus? Where Sister Catharine went when she died?'

'They've gone where they belong, where they wanted to go, as we all do.'

'Do you have a picture of them?'

Sister Philomena shook her head. 'How do you feel about that, Eve?'

'Happy. I don't want anyone to take me away from you. No one.'

Sister Philomena leant in and whispered, 'That's my girl.'

'Eve.' She was tugged back to the present by Thomas's voice coming from her iPhone. 'I'm going to say goodnight now, and love you.'

'Goodnight. Love you more,' she replied into the cold air of her car, watching her son's mouth and understanding that its cast could have come from her own mother and father, of whom only three things were certain. They had existed. They had brought her into the world. They had abandoned her. The film sequence ended on a frozen shot of Philip's face. She closed it down and as soon as she did, her phone rang out.

Clay picked up the call. 'Stone' on the display panel.

'Eve?'

'Have you been through the CCTV footage from the Patels'?' she replied.

Stone was calling from a car. The pitch of the engine and the noise of the tyres against the snow and ice told Clay that he was driving faster than he should have been.

'I've edited together three pieces of film.'

'And?'

'They're not on it. Something weird's happened. The pen drive. The CCTV. I don't know. We need to send the whole system to be analysed. The CCTV stopped probably minutes before the killers arrived.'

He sounded confused and frustrated, like he'd just been hammered with inexplicable bad news. She turned on her engine and was in first gear.

'You didn't *see* them?' she asked, thinking, *Were they human?* She buried the thought.

'I didn't see them, Eve, but I've tracked down the owner of the mobile on the Patels' answer machine.'

'I'll meet you there. Where?'

'224 Booker Avenue.'

A fifteen-minute drive from where she was – in good weather conditions.

She was in second gear, her senses flaring.

'Who's the owner?' she asked, in third gear now and hoping there would be no traffic to swerve round as she burned any red lights.

'Mrs Cara Harry. Fifty-four. Primary-school teacher. She hasn't reported her phone as stolen.'

'Wait for me, Karl.' Fourth gear. Forty miles per hour and rising fast. 'I'll be there as fast as I can.'

10

2.05 am

The temperature began to drop steeply and Clay shivered as she watched the lights go on inside 224 Booker Avenue.

Stone rang the bell of the 1930s semi for the third time.

When Mrs Harry opened the door and Stone showed her his warrant card, sleepy confusion gave way to panic.

Stone glanced at Clay. In a silent, knowing look there was agreement. It was possible that the disorientated woman in the doorway was a bridge to the bloodbath in The Serpentine, but she was almost certainly not a part of it.

'It's about your phone.' Stone oozed gruff charm and slowly pushed the woman's door wider.

'My phone? At this hour?' The tall, thin woman with long, grey hair could barely get her words out.

'Mrs Harry, we're in a hurry here, *please*!' Clay pointed inside the house and the bewildered teacher stepped aside.

'This way.' She shut the door and led them inside. They passed a metal Jesus on a wooden cross on the hall wall.

In the shipshape front room, Mrs Harry indicated a beige three-piece suite that looked like it had just come out of its plastic wrapping. Clay and Stone remained on their feet.

Clay weighed up Mrs Harry by the spick-and-span room.

Primary-school teacher, knows what she has in the bank down to the last bean, irons her knickers...

'07700 934763,' said Stone. 'I was looking for the owner of a mobile phone with that number, and your service provider came up with your name and address. I then found out you teach the Year Five class at St Bernard's RC Primary School, right down the road from Belle Vale police station. Right?'

'Yes.' She sounded amazed at his insight.

Clay watched the seconds pass on the mantelpiece clock.

Mrs Harry closed her eyes. 'It went missing on Friday morning, just before the snow arrived.' She opened her eyes and looked consumed with stress. 'It was probably stolen.'

'Why didn't you report it stolen to your service provider?' asked Stone. 'Why didn't you call Belle Vale police station?'

'Friday morning was a nightmare,' said Mrs Harry.

'Cara?' Clay spoke softly, smiled. The teacher looked at Clay, her eyes dithering with the onset of tears. 'Tell me what happened on Friday morning?'

2.10 am

'The last time I saw and touched the phone was eleven o'clock on Friday morning,' said Mrs Harry. 'My mother phoned me. It said on Radio Merseyside all Liverpool schools were closing because of the coming snowstorm. I told her I'd be home early. I noticed the phone was gone at ten past twelve when I went into my bag for my car keys.'

'Did you leave your bag unattended during that time?' asked Clay, feeling her back molars chattering. She bit down, took a deep breath.

'I did, yes. But it was all pretty chaotic, you see...'

Clay recalled the local radio news broadcasts on Friday morning. The storm had defied the forecasts and instead of hitting north-west England at six in the evening had speeded up as it left the Arctic and was expected to arrive in Liverpool at one in the afternoon.

'What happened in school?' asked Clay. 'Friday morning?'

'Mrs Sweeney, the head teacher, decided to close the school at twelve. She told us at half past ten. Parents were told to pick up their children as soon as they could, directly from the classroom. Eleven o'clock, parents filing in and out, I took my eye off my bag on numerous occasions.'

'So it could've been lifted by one of the kids in your class?'

'No, no, no!' Mrs Harry objected. 'One of the children would have shouted out if another pupil had gone into my bag.'

'A parent maybe?'

'No.'

'Can you remember the order in which they left? Who was first to go? Who was last?' asked Clay.

'I'd have to think it through.'

'Why didn't you report your phone stolen?' asked Clay.

'Because I was praying it hadn't been stolen. I was in the school car park when I went into my bag and saw it wasn't there. The site manager had already locked the doors and Mrs Sweeney had told us not to go back in under any circumstances.'

Clay smiled. 'She was in a foul mood because the weather had defied her?'

'Exactly.' Mrs Harry zoned in on Clay. 'I was hoping, praying the phone had slipped out of my bag and that when school reopened I'd find it. I didn't want to bring the police to the school door.'

'You're going to have to call Mrs Sweeney right now,' said Clay.

'What?'

'Phone her, tell her to call the site manager and open the school now. I'm sending DS Stone there to meet with them and take your register away. And I'll need all the contact details of the children in your class. Plus details of who they live with.'

'Their red files?' said Mrs Harry.

'Can you go and make that call for me now, please.'

Clay pointed to the hall, where she'd seen a landline phone on a table.

'Phone Mrs Sweeney at this hour?'

'Absolutely,' said Clay. 'Now, please.'

As she dialled, Mrs Harry looked into the room, directly at Clay, and asked, 'What's happened?'

'A serious crime currently under investigation.' Clay indicated the teacher. 'Karl, take *her* to the school with you.'

'You want her to pick the bad eggs out the basket?'

'Jeanette,' began Cara into the phone. She fell silent, her shoulders sagging as she absorbed Mrs Sweeney's addled speech. 'Well, yes, it is an emergency and I'm sorry to wake you up at this hour...'

'I'm going back to the scene,' said Clay to DS Stone. 'Team meeting, seven o'clock.'

'The police are with me right here, right now, Jeanette...'

As Clay stepped out into the cold, she found warmth in the thought that the killers could be in custody within hours. In the brief time she'd been inside Mrs Harry's home the fog had cleared. Stars glittered and a broadening band of red rolled across the moon in the dark sky over Calderstones Park.

The warmth vanished as the vision triggered a vivid memory.

'*The Red Cloud...*' The Baptist's parting shot to her as he'd been led down to the cells in Preston Crown Court. '*...will rise from the belly of the city and when the Red Cloud rises...*' He'd turned his head and smiled, her last sight of him. '*...the river will run with blood.*'

She turned on the ignition and looked over her shoulder. The night clouds rolled crimson and fires raged on the surface of distant stars.

12

2.45 am

Sometimes, his soul went out. And sometimes, his soul sank deeper within the black hole inside him.

Adrian White plunged into the bottomless pit that he had cultivated from a single speck when he was four years old, on the day he came across a crippled kitten in a place where there was no one else around. He saw himself sinking, a patch of man-shaped darkness deeper than the edges of the blackness within him, his arms extended, like a diver skimming through water, his essence travelling from the material world through his body, the portal to the glory of the gates of hell.

The darkness was deeper than ever and the speed of his hurtling shadow spirit much faster than its opposite entity, light. For now was the Beginning of the End of Time, the moment he had worked and prayed and fasted for. It was almost time to open the gates of hell for billions of human souls to follow. He pictured the chaos and terror as those souls hurtled after him in his mercurial slipstream.

He stopped. *Turn*, a whispered command.

Clack clack clack clack. Footsteps echoed from the material world.

Return.

His soul turned inside out and began the ascent, slowly at first.

More. Blood. More. Souls.

His soul hurtled.

In his room, White's mind shimmered, a sleeper waking from the depths of an all-consuming dream. His lips parted, forming a tight open circle at their centre.

Footsteps. Four sets of feet approaching.

Shadows darted from the friction of his speeding soul against the void that linked his body to hell, shadows like minnows in a black sea. The eye of his soul focused on the surface and he beheld a point of light, the target, his body's parted mouth in the material world. And he accelerated so that the pinpoint of light rolled and opened like nuclear explosions on the sun.

Footsteps. Taylor. Green. Wilson. Keyes.

His soul fell through the fire as the footsteps stopped outside his door and the whispering in the corridor began.

And he was back in the material world.

Adrian White opened his eyes and, for a moment, everything in the plain room was blurred.

Bang. Bang. Bang. The knock at his door echoed and he concentrated on the slatted window, his focus sharpening on the bars.

'Adrian? Can I come in?' It was Taylor.

White's senses snapped into place.

'Come in, Mr Taylor. I need to have a word with you.'

As Green opened the door for Taylor, the quartet of nurses' thoughts drifted into the room like a breeze through a window.

A risk of harm to others . . . A risk of harm to self . . . A risk of being assaulted . . . A risk of escaping or absconding . . . A risk of endangering safety or security . . .

Taylor stood behind him.

'Close the door, Mr Green.'

'Do as he asks,' said Taylor.

Green closed the door.

'Stand where I can see you,' said White.

With a plate of food in his hand, Taylor made his way in front of White.

'Why have you asked for last evening's meal at this hour?' asked Taylor.

'Oh, ye of little faith, Mr Taylor. I was waiting for you to be on duty.'

'Why? Why did you demand that I bring you your meal?'

'Because I sensed doubt in you.'

Taylor looked at the door and then at White.

'Doubt you? When I don't believe in you or a word you say?'

Every muscle in White's body clenched. Taylor watched as the definition of White's arms and legs sharpened and the deadness in his eyes deepened in the silence of the locked room.

'Give me my food,' said White.

Taylor held out the plate and White took it from him. He fingered the food. 'Pork. Carrot. Potato. Potato. Carrot. Pork. Why are we the odd ones out?' he asked.

'Why are *who* the odd ones out?'

'Homo sapiens.'

'Because we're the most intelligent.'

'Really, Mr Taylor? You'll be telling me next that animals don't have souls. And that little doggies aren't allowed into heaven.'

'Just eat your food or whatever it is you do with it.

'That's just it. Doubt. In a nutshell.'

'I'll collect your plate in twenty minutes.'

'Stay. I want to tell you something, Mr Taylor.'

'I don't want to—'

'A psychiatric nurse not wanting to hear what a patient has to say?' White hissed a sigh and something in his throat rattled.

'Mankind is the odd one out because it's the only species that cooks its food with fire. And this perversion, Mr Taylor, constitutes a sin. It causes separation from the true power within the universe. And that is why I am different from the rest of you. That is why I only eat raw food. It is the righteous thing to do. But you – *you*, Mr Taylor – as you wolf down your McDonald's burgers and shovel fries down your throat, don't even consider it a moral issue.'

White mimed stuffing his mouth with fast food, his fingers waving in front of his face as he made a greedy, choking noise. His fingers stilled. Silence returned.

'And if that wasn't bad enough, Mr Taylor, you then have the temerity to doubt what I do with my food.' White pointed at the toilet. 'No. I eat every scrap of food you provide, except for when I fast. Watch. Believe.'

White picked up the raw pork chop and gripped the thick rind of waxy fat. With a swift turn of his neck he separated the fat from the pink meat and drew it into his mouth. He moved the sticky mound to his molars and chewed powerfully, the muscles in his face shifting every time he clamped his jaws together, his eyes fixed on Taylor's.

He drew the back of his hand across his mouth, its tattooed map of black stars brushing against his lips, and he swallowed hard, his Adam's apple pumping.

White smiled. 'Do you know which meat comes closest to the taste of human flesh? Pork.'

White picked up the soft pink meat and ripped half of it into his mouth. As he chewed, he extended the remains of the meat to Taylor. A trickle of red saliva trailed from the corner of his mouth and, as he swallowed, Taylor watched passively.

'You can go now,' said White, cramming the rest of the pork into his mouth. 'Go back to the Kingdom of the Blind, the world of mankind, mankind the least of all the species in Creation. Except for the few. The few who see.'

The door opened and Taylor headed for it.

'Mr Taylor!'

Taylor stopped at the door, listened without turning.

'Just for the record, animals do have souls and when the End Of Time comes their souls will co-exist in the next life alongside the souls of mankind. But in the next life, all will be reversed. Mankind will be the least of all species. Except for the righteous few. Mankind will serve its masters. The jackals. And their souls shall remember. The serpents. And they will be consumed with righteous anger. The vultures. And they will have no mercy. The pigs. Especially the pigs.'

13

2.45 am

DS Karl Stone stared directly into the sorrowful eyes of Jesus Christ and wondered if the Crucifixion painting had a moralising influence on the staffroom of St Bernard's RC Primary. He picked up a fat, dog-eared erotic novel that had clearly been all the way round the block and back. He guessed Jesus was just a part of the fixtures and fittings. As he turned the book over, he smiled. RRP £7.99. Batteries not included.

Stone listened to the sound of three pairs of footsteps approaching the door and began examining Mrs Harry's register. From a class of twenty-six children, only twelve had been present in school on the previous Friday. The majority presumably unwilling to take a chance on the much anticipated freak weather.

Five girls, seven boys, one potential thief linked to a multiple murder where the blood was still wet.

On the car journey to the school, Mrs Harry had been polite and cooperative. And site manager Mr Fitzroy had been more than helpful, despite having to open up the buildings a good four hours earlier than he normally would on a Monday morning. But as soon as head teacher Mrs Sweeney arrived – short and fat, with a body shape that reminded Stone of an outsized hornets' nest – the dynamic shifted negatively.

Dispensing silent, filthy looks, she quickly organised them into a gang.

Stone kept his back turned but watched the reflection in the plate-glass window to his right as the door opened and Mrs Sweeney headed into the room carrying twelve red card files. She stopped, with Mrs Harry and Mr Fitzroy behind her.

'What are you doing?'

Stone tried not to laugh at the barely concealed outrage in her voice. 'Reading,' he replied, looking at the photocopied class list.

He turned slowly.

'You've got the twelve files on the twelve children present in Mrs Harry's class on Friday?'

She placed them on the table.

'Thank you. I'll be taking the files with me, along with the register.'

'But—'

'Yes, I know it's a legal document and I'll return it to school as soon as possible. Are you opening the school today?'

'No.'

'Tuesday?'

'No. All schools are closed until further notice.'

'Then there's no panic.' He turned his attention to Mrs Harry. 'I want to talk to you on your own.'

He thought of Bill Hendricks and the sort of evidence that he might find useful.

'Mrs Sweeney, would you please go and get me the literacy books of the twelve children present in Mrs Harry's class on Friday morning. And any art work they've produced *recently*. We can't waste time. Now, please.'

'You bowl in here, issuing the orders in *my* school, and you haven't even told me why you're investigating *my* children.'

At some point in the unfolding darkness, Stone had heard details of the case broadcast on the hourly Radio City news. What had happened was no longer a secret so he trumped the vexing little cow with the folded arms and the pout with, 'Murder.'

It was as if he'd poured a cup of ice-cold water onto her head. Her eyes filled with shock and the aggression and blood drained from her face.

'Murder?'

'No one blames the head teacher when one of *their* pupils in *their* school is implicated in murder. Murder, Mrs Sweeney, times six.'

He watched the wheels turn in her head as anxiety creased her brow.

'The books and any art work as well, but quickly.' He eyed the clock on the wall; time was racing. 'I really am in a hurry.'

14

2.50 am

The door closed and, with Mrs Sweeney gone, Mrs Harry relaxed as she sat down next to Stone. He spread the files out on the table.

'Back at yours, you didn't tell us there were only twelve kids in on Friday?'

'I could barely think straight. It's the first time I've ever...' She shrugged as the rest of the sentence evaporated.

'Who do you think may have lifted your phone, Cara?'

'No. None of them. They're all good kids.'

'OK, who's the one you know least well?'

'They've all been in the school since they were in reception, aged four. I know them all really well. They're a mixture and they've all got their own funny little ways, but they're not kids who'd get into any trouble. The ones who attended on Friday are either grammar-school material or the kids who are never, ever off.' She dropped her voice a notch and went into confidential mode. 'All the others had the sense to keep their children home. The parents of these kids sent them into school in spite of the weather. Can't miss an educational trick. Or can't wait to send them out of the door.'

'Humour me, Cara. I want some snap comments from you. I'm not going to haunt you with your answers, I promise.

I just want you to answer quickly. Instant judgement call. Their funny little ways?'

'Like word association?'

'Good analogy.'

It was a tactic Hendricks had shared with the team in a brainstorming session. Mrs Harry was stuck in a room with the children for over seven hours a day and, he guessed, knew as much about them as many of their parents did.

He copied her confidential tone and lowered his voice. 'If *you* don't know them, who does?'

Stone laid out the files in two neat rows of six, their names and photos clear to see, and popped the nib of his Parker pen on his spiral-bound notepad.

'Look at their names, make a mental snapshot of their faces.'

She adjusted her glasses on the bridge of her nose and looked down at the table.

'Cara, who's your favourite?'

'Melanie Waters.' Instant response. He jotted down: *FMW.*

'Biggest pain in the neck?'

'David Jones.' Same speed. *PITNDJ.*

'Brightest?'

'Imran Choudhary.' No hesitation. *BIC.*

'Quietest?'

'Oh, two. Faith Drake and Jon Pearson.' *QFD. QJP.*

'Are they friends?'

'No. They have shyness in common, but I'm not aware of any friendship between them.'

'Who are you most concerned about?'

'Paul Peters.' *CPP.*

'Why?'

'He never wants to go out to play. He'd rather lock himself

in a cubicle in the boys' toilets. He claims he's allergic to fresh air.'

'This is starting to sound more and more like the class I was in when I was ten,' said Stone. 'Saddest?'

'Donna Rice.' *SDR*. 'She's prematurely middle-aged.'

'Anyone with compulsive behaviours?'

'Connor Stephens. He can recite the table of elements backwards, forwards and inside out. Should do very well in the entrance exam for grammar school.' *CBCS*.

'Well-balanced? Happy? No cause for concern?'

She nodded as she scanned the folders, smiled and said, 'Yes, well balanced, the rest of them. Tom Tanner, Ryan Nolan, Megan Odemwingie, Sally McManus…But none of them would have stolen my phone. Whatever their little quirks are, they're not thieves.' *WBTTRNMOSMcM*.

'Mrs Harry, I need a favour.'

'I'll be happy to help if I can.'

'We'll need to talk with you again. There are probably going to be a lot of questions to ask. Based on what you've told us, one or more of your twelve could be a direct link to an horrific crime.'

Her shoulders sagged and he drew a finger round in the air to indicate the whole school set-up.

'I get the picture entirely, Mrs Harry, and pardon my French but your head teacher's a bitch. She won't know anything about you helping us because we'll come and visit you in your home. No police station. No lights in your face. No Mrs Sweeney Todd the Fourth.'

Mrs Harry smiled, but laughter, even at her boss's expense, was beyond her.

She looked at him directly and said, 'You know, you look nothing like a police officer.'

'What do I look like?' He smiled.

'An undertaker.' She trusted him and he had her on a hook.

He leaned in a little closer and said, 'I know. It wrong-foots criminals all the time.'

Mrs Harry looked uncomfortable in the silence that followed as they waited for Mrs Sweeney to return.

'So, are you doing a project with your class at the moment?' asked Stone.

'Local history.' Mrs Harry lit up. 'They were allowed to choose the topic. As a class they decided on Williamson Tunnels in Edge Hill.'

'Spooky and full of mystery. I like it,' said Stone. 'Is that work in their literacy books?'

'Yes.'

'Whose idea was it to do Williamson Tunnels?'

'A few of the girls. The boys were miffed because they couldn't do Everton and Liverpool, but once I got them down there—'

The door opened and Mrs Sweeney entered with a plastic box full of exercise books. Mr Fitzroy followed, carrying a large black artist's folder.

'We're done for now,' Stone whispered to Mrs Harry.

'You'll be wanting to interview me to assist you with your investigation?' said Mrs Sweeney.

'Not at the moment,' said Stone. 'But there is something you could do to help.'

'Yes?'

'You can help me carry all these materials to my car.'

On either side of The Serpentine, lights were on in downstairs rooms. From darkened bedrooms, neighbours watched police officers moving in, out and around the crime scene.

A little way down the winding road, Clay saw a silver Audi pull over on the other side of the scene-of-crime tape. A short woman with a shock of frizzy red hair got out from the driver's side, the form of her body obscured by a padded coat. She strode beneath a streetlight, straight towards Clay, as if there wasn't a minute left to live. From the knowing way she took in the whole scene with a swivel-necked glance, Clay guessed the woman was a police officer.

The woman stopped at the tape and, showing her warrant card, said, 'Detective Sergeant Deborah Abbott. Victim Liaison, Durham Police.'

To Clay's eyes, she looked like the unit's head girl.

'DCI Eve Clay. I'm leading the investigation.'

As Clay reached in her pocket for her own warrant card, DS Abbott said, 'It's OK. I recognise you.'

Clay glanced at the car. 'Where's Sandy Patel?'

'He wanted to come here, but his old school friend talked him out of it. He's with Tom Price and his family, 132 Menlove Avenue.'

'How was he on the journey down from Durham?'

'It's been a long drive, DCI Clay. He's swinging between despair and denial.'

'Is he acting?'

'I don't think he has any involvement in what's happened here,' said DS Abbott.

'Is there any mileage in talking to him now?' asked Clay.

'No!' Abbott was adamant. 'He went to pieces when he saw his friend.' Abbott looked at the house and said, 'In my opinion, you'd be better trying him first thing in the morning.'

Clay dipped under the tape to follow Abbott across the snow to her Audi but paused in her tracks when she heard someone saying 'Eve?'

She turned and saw Terry Marsh. His voice was little more than a whisper.

'Kate Patel died trying to defend Freya, her youngest child. Judging by the blood splatter on the walls, door and frame, they killed her in Freya's bedroom doorway, the room next to Alicia's. The drag mark on the carpet from Freya's room to the staging of the bodies, it's clearly Mrs Patel.'

Clay called the order of death. Kate Patel fourth, then Freya in her bedroom, Alicia last. Kate's eyes removed before Freya and Alicia were murdered. 'Anything else?' she asked.

'Waiting for forensic analysis of what we've pulled to come back, but judging by the height of the child and the fact that the blood's mainly on one bedroom wall, she wasn't attacked as she stood up. There were splinters of what looked like skull and brain tissue in the blood on the wall. I'm pretty certain the murder weapon was metal.'

He took out his iPhone. Clay's stomach tightened in the

brief moments before he turned the screen towards her, showing her an image of the little girl's bedroom wall.

'DCI Clay?' DS Abbott called as she got into the Audi.

As Clay walked towards Abbott, she imagined how the scene in the bedroom would have played out.

She pictured the child being dragged from her bed, waking up to bloody mayhem.

Abbott was sitting in the car.

A pair of hands held the child by the feet, upside down against the wall.

The car window slid down.

The little girl's face, staring at the upside-down monsters as the metal bar flew at her head.

Abbott handed Clay a folded piece of paper. 'This is Sandy's mobile number and the landline for Tom Price's home on Menlove Avenue.'

'Thanks for all you've done,' Clay said. 'Safe journey back to Durham.'

She tapped the number into her iPhone and listened to it ringing as the Audi rounded the corner onto Aigburth Road and disappeared into the fog. She wished she could just drive away too.

There was something hypnotic in the ringtone that made her think of the musical mobile that hung above Philip's bed. For a moment she pictured herself watching Philip fall asleep in the blue light of his night-light, Thomas standing behind her, his arms around her.

Someone picked up at the other end and she snapped out of it.

'Hello?' It was a mature man, his tone sombre. In the background it sounded like someone was being tortured.

'Hello, my name's DCI Eve Clay. Is that Mr Price?'

'The boy's in pieces, absolutely distraught.'

'I can hear that. I do need to speak to Sandy. I'll come to your house later this morning, at nine.'

'We'll do everything we can, DCI Clay, to calm him.'

'Thank you. Please don't let him out of your sight, Mr Price. Nine o'clock.'

He hung up, but the unrestrained screaming continued ringing in Clay's ears for a long while after.

16

6.15 am

As night crawled towards dawn, it was as cold in the incident room of Trinity Road police station as it was on the street outside. For although it was a new building, the central-heating system was a joke with two punchlines: ice-cold and red-hot.

Clay kept her coat on and sat down at her desk. With one hand wrapped around a mug of black coffee and her iPhone in the other, she watched her breath in the glow of the desk lamp, the only light on in the empty room.

She felt the hinge of her jaw shivering but didn't know if it was the cold or what she had just received on her iPhone: switchboard had sent her the complete version of Alicia Patel's 999 call to the emergency services.

Her phone buzzed and vibrated. She looked at the screen.

A text from Hendricks. *Something very strange on Mrs Patel's body.*

Clay put the mug on her desk and gazed deeply into the darkness beyond the reach of her desk light. She pressed play on Alicia Patel's 999 call.

The call transferred to the police operative.

The sound of Alicia Patel's feet scrambling up the stairs. Behind her the perpetrators running after her. On the landing above, her mother screaming, 'Get in your room, Alicia, get in your room, for Christ's sake!'

'Hello, where are you calling from?' The operator calm but loud against the din in the house.

It sounded like Alicia had just made it onto the landing as she shouted back, '38, The Serpentine, off Aigburth Road.'

They were on the landing too, but they must have stopped because their feet were still and their mouths were silent.

'What's the nature of your emergency?'

'They've killed my dad, my grandma...' Alicia struggled with the simple task of opening her bedroom door. '...my little sister...' Her door opened. 'Mum, get in with me!'

'Lock yourself in now, Alicia.'

Alicia's door slammed shut.

'I've locked my door, I've locked my bedroom door.'

The kicking and banging on Alicia's door began. Fierce, enraged hands and feet, and with that their voices started up.

'How many of your family at home?'

'Six!' she sobbed.

Clay blocked out Alicia, the operator and the door being broken down, and focused on the attackers, on their noise.

In the deep growling that underpinned the sounds they made, Clay heard a series of clicks, almost like the sound of a heart beating from the wetness of their mouths, and between the clicking beats something phonically plausible made with a thin whistle of air.

She paused the recording, felt something shift in the darkness before her and imagined it was a picture of her mind spiralling into the depths of whatever strange speech this was.

'Ka...' The clicking tongues. '...Ri...' Click clicking. '...Sa...' There was a feral joy in the voices that sent a wave of cold nausea through Clay.

She noted the sounds in her notebook and underneath wrote: *Linguistics Dept University of Liverpool.*

Play. There was more than one voice making the sounds. 'A...'

Then there was a sound that was buried beneath the door giving way and Alicia screaming, 'Mummy! Mummy! Mummy!'

Clay rewound, stopped, mined the darkness of the incident room and felt as if her whole being was getting sucked into the lengthening shadows around her.

'*When you look into shadows, you look into mirrors.*'

Another voice from another time invaded her head. She wrapped her mind around that intrusion, smothered the words and suffocated the memory of that speech.

When she pressed play again, she dipped under the noise of the door coming down and Alicia's pitiful cries for her mother and tried to interpret the last syllable.

'...den.' It was almost an out-breath, a satisfied reflex, a release from some inner tension.

As Alicia howled, the recording seemed to slow right down, emphasising the torment in the teenager's voice as she stared certain violent death in the face.

Then the silence as the connection died.

Clay called police central operations and within two rings the operator picked up.

'DCI Eve Clay. I need two more copies of the call from the Patel house on two separate pen drives.'

'Where are you, DCI Clay?'

'Trinity Road police station. I'd be grateful for those pen drives.'

'They're on their way as soon as.'

'Thank you.'

Clay shut down the call and turned off the desk light.

In the darkness, she picked up her mug of coffee and sipped. It had gone completely cold. On the desk, she rested her head on her arms. Her team would be arriving in half an hour. She closed her eyes.

The building was silent, but Clay's head was full of the voices from the recording. They latched on to the deepest places in her mind, where her blackest memories were housed like dangerous beasts in cages of darkness and silence.

On the desk, she looked at a framed picture of herself and Thomas, with Philip, newborn and sleeping, in her arms. In the photograph, she was looking at Philip and Thomas was looking at her. The glue that bonded them was unconditional love and Clay mouthed the words that the picture always inspired in her.

'Hope. Absolute hope.'

The voices fell silent. And it felt like years since she had last slept.

Within moments, she was in the dark and dreaming of the distant past.

17

6.25 am

As she walked out of the St Michael's Catholic Care Home for Children, Eve stared down at her feet, her sandals red and scuffed. The sound that called her was coming from beneath the ground. It wasn't a voice, more the sound of stones being shifted and the rumbling of moving wheels.

She looked towards the River Mersey. As the sun sank into the water, she saw that the sky was alive with a golden light, swamped by overpowering bands of pink and red.

She glanced back at the home. No one had seen her leave. No one was there to stop her.

Down Smithdown Lane, past the steel-mesh fence that was supposed to keep children from entering. She reached the two huge brick arches, side by side in the sandstone wall; dark, gaping entrances to the tunnels that ran all the way under Edge Hill.

NO TRESPASSING!
DANGER!

Closing her eyes, she saw the flickering light of a candle and heard the steady drip of an underground cave. Then there was a second candle, and another and another, and she saw men stripped to the waist, carving out the underground sandstone.

Clouds of red dust rose into the air, sandstone particles billowing into the sky above.

The picture in her mind and the sound that had drawn her connected.

'Come along, Eve.'

Sister Philomena was behind her. She opened her eyes and, as she tried to turn, felt the weight of Philomena's loving hands on her shoulders.

'Keep walking, little cherub, and don't look back.'

'Why did Mr Williamson build all those tunnels under the ground?' asked Eve.

'Nobody knows for sure, Eve, but one day, when you are much older, I believe you will find out. He was a rich man and he paid soldiers returning from the Napoleonic Wars to build the tunnels...'

The weight lifted from her shoulders, Philomena disappeared, and Eve continued walking forwards, to a row of three derelict terraced houses.

DO NOT ENTER
STRUCTURE UNSAFE

They were boarded up, but the board on the window of the house in the middle had been ripped away, no doubt by the older kids in her house and their friends in the neighbourhood.

She looked over at the towering Bear's Paw pub, close by. There was no one coming in or out of the pub, not a soul hanging around. There was no one now except her and the sound of the subterranean men digging deeper and deeper.

Eve lifted herself up, holding onto the brick where the window frame had once sat. She knelt on the stone ledge and looked into the patch of blackness where the noise was at its loudest.

'Hello!' she called, and her voice came back as an echo.

She eased herself down and felt the floorboards rise and fall beneath her feet as she moved deeper into the gloomy room. Looking up, she saw that a huge section of the ceiling was missing. The slate roof was full of holes and the blood-red light of the dying day filtered through.

Below her, wheels moved as barrows of sandstone were shifted by the men.

And above her, streams of ruby light picked out the rubble that had collapsed into the centre and sides of the room.

She stepped over a chunk of fallen plaster and saw a square of wood set into the lines of the floorboards. Digging her fingers into its sides, she lifted the hatch and propped it against the damp wall of the derelict room.

The noise of the men working underground swelled as the light of their candles shifted and grew. The yellow from the centre of the earth shimmered against the crimson of the sinking sun and set her on fire as she stared into the entrance of the tunnel beneath her.

'Hello...ooo...oo...o...'

In a moment, the noise of the men underground stopped and the light above and beneath her died. She looked into the darkness and heard a sound like a man whispering her name, wanting her to step down into the hole in the floor and meet with him.

She felt a sudden coldness touching the nape of her neck. She screamed and turned. But there was only darkness and the sound of her terror echoing in the tunnels beneath her.

81

18

6.29 am

Clay woke from her dream with a jolt. It was always the same dream, and it always left her scared to the core of her being.

'Are you OK, Eve?' She was shocked but pleased to hear Hendricks's voice. His desk light came on and he sat looking in her direction.

'Bad dream,' she said. 'Was I talking in my sleep?'

'You sobbed a little. You were putting your head down as I was coming in. You've only been asleep for a few minutes.'

'The children's home I grew up in,' she began. 'It was in Edge Hill. We had a fantastic playground in those days, before health and safety became God Almighty.'

'The tunnels?' asked Hendricks. 'Your carers let you play in Williamson Tunnels?'

'They were busy playing cards, you nitwit. I took Thomas for a guided tour of the Williamson Heritage Society's Smithdown Lane Tunnel. It's all hard hats, health and safety now.'

She focused on Hendricks's smiling face, saw him glance down at a piece of paper and knew he had something significant to tell her.

He stood up and walked towards her with a mug of coffee. 'I made this for you while you slept.'

She took the drink. 'You've got that *Jeez, have I got news for you* look in your eyes, Hendricks. You're not pregnant again?'

'The autopsy on Mrs Patel's thrown up a potential shocker.' The smile on his face dissolved; his eyes deeply sad.

He handed her the paper. It was a photograph of Mrs Patel's abdomen, and underneath this image was a smaller picture focused on the pubic bone.

'Let me tell you about the measurements on this,' said Hendricks, 'and then you tell me if we're ready to share it with the whole team in fifteen minutes or so.'

The door opened and Clay looked up. Stone walked into the incident room and showed her the pen drive.

'CCTV,' he said.

'What's the word?' she asked.

'Weird. Someone or something out there's ganging up on us. And I don't bloody well like it one little bit.'

The incident room of Trinity Road police station was full but silent, all eyes on Stone as he inserted his pen drive into the laptop.

Clay thought about the picture Hendricks had brought back from Kate Patel's post-mortem. Mrs Patel, laid out on Dr Lamb's table, her abdomen and pubic bone covered in bruises. The memory of the killers' voices as they broke down Alicia's door floated through the numb quiet and slipped inside her ears, chasing a never-ending loop deep within her brain.

For a moment the room, everyone and everything in it, dissolved as a switch tripped and a series of moving pictures consumed her imagination.

She was inside the Patels' house, the kitchen lights on against the dark and the heating turned up against the bitter cold outside; the walls of the staircase were still unbloodied as Alicia Patel walked out of the kitchen to answer the ringing at the door. Mr Patel appeared at the head of the stairs, raised from his bed by the late-night caller.

'Who is it, Alicia?' Mrs Patel next to her husband now, yawning as her husband marched down the stairs.

'How do I know?' laughed Alicia, pointing at the solid wooden door.

'This had better be good.' The father's voice behind the teenager as she reached the front door.

'Who is it?' The grandmother looked over the banister at the top of the stairs.

The bell rang again, this time longer, insistent: you must come to the door, must open the door, you must let us in...

'It could be a matter of life and death!' said Alicia, taking off the chain and unlocking the dead bolts as her sister's feet landed on the bedroom floor upstairs and the little girl walked across the room above her head.

She opened the door and...

'Eve!' Gina Riley's voice snapped her back into the present reality. 'They're all waiting for you.'

Clay looked across the room and most people were turned in her direction, waiting for her to lead them deeper into the events at the Patels' house.

She picked out Stone, standing at the laptop hooked up to the Smart Board, and Hendricks, writing in a spiral-bound notebook.

Looking around at their expectant faces, Clay said, 'Thank you for all you've done on a long and difficult night, and for getting here through shitty weather conditions at this horribly early hour. That's the good news done with...' She pointed at DS Stone. 'The first piece of really bad news relates to the CCTV from the Patels' house. Karl?'

'I've got together two pieces of f-footage,' said Stone with the bitterness of someone cheated of his birthright in broad daylight.

Clay picked up the stumble in his speech, recognising the telltale stammer of Stone's childhood, which reappeared whenever he was tired and stressed. 'I've already seen this,' she said quickly, 'so are you OK if I talk the troops through it?' She looked at Stone. 'If you'll play and pause, Karl...'

'Sure.' He shrugged blithely, but she saw relief flash through his eyes.

The screen came alive with a picture of the entrance to the Patels' house and a swathe of snow-capped garden.

'This was yesterday afternoon,' explained Clay. 'It's a random selection from hours of footage that shows you what should happen when someone approaches the house. It was around three, a couple of hours after the storm had shifted out to the Irish Sea. You see three figures approaching... It's three of our victims, the girls. You see the two little ones, Jane and Freya, trailing after their big sister Alicia, who's carrying a plastic sledge.'

As the girls came closer and closer to the camera above their front door, the atmosphere in the room became dense with tension and a silence loaded with unspoken advice. *Turn around, go away, your home will soon no longer be safe...*

'Pause,' Clay said. The best close-up of the girls showed Alicia struggling against the cold to turn her key in the lock, the little ones behind her laughing and exhilarated.

'I'm guessing they'd been down to Otterspool Promenade to play on the sledge. Play.'

The girls entered the house for the last time, and the middle sequence began.

Night. The darkness in the garden and at the front of the house was hemmed in by the glow of the streetlights on the pavement beyond the gate. A security light tripped by a stray cat padding past the front door.

'Check the time in the corner. 11.33. We know from Alicia's 999 for help that the killers were in the house at 11.45, by which point they were in the second phase of their massacre. This must've been a minute or two before they got there.'

86

And I got there, thought Clay, *about a minute after they escaped.*

In bald white security light, the garden looked like a scene from a snow dome. And then there was nothing. The screen went suddenly black.

'Off goes the CCTV and doesn't come on again,' said Stone, removing his pen drive.

'Karl's sent the CCTV equipment away for forensic examination, but at this point I can only conclude that the system was working perfectly well up to the minute that the killers arrived, and then it turned itself off.'

She glanced around at the faces of the extended team. Riley and Hendricks looked tired but calm. The others looked quizzical and confused.

'Gina Riley's going to tell you what happened with Scientific Support.'

Riley stepped forward. 'This is a first-impression narrative based on me tailing Terry Mason at the scene. The killers – there were at least three – didn't break into the house. If they were strangers, they probably tricked their way in. Or they were known to at least one member of the family and the Patels felt safe opening the door to them at that late hour. Going by the condition of the pillows and duvets and the fact that the only person not in night clothes was Alicia, the younger children, grandmother and parents must have been in bed. With the exception of Freya, they all came down. They must've gone into the kitchen and that was when the slaughter started. The perpetrators smashed the father, grandmother and middle daughter to death in the kitchen. Several blows each to the head. The eldest daughter, Alicia, managed to get upstairs. Alicia, her mother and the youngest child were killed on the first floor. The killers were lightning quick.'

'Thanks, Gina.' Clay turned to the team. 'I think I can add something to that. I've listened over and over to the whole recording of Alicia's call. Mrs Patel died trying to defend her daughters. She didn't even try to get to the potential safety of Alicia's room because she was in her youngest daughter's doorway trying to bar the way. When Alicia and her mother escaped from the kitchen, they could both have run straight down the hall and out of the front door, but they didn't. They turned left and went upstairs to where the baby was. Any questions so far?'

'Those schoolbooks and paintings on Hendricks's desk – what's that all about, Eve?' DC Christopher Dillon, who looked like he was made of truck tyres but could actually outrun anyone in the room, pointed at the box from St Bernard's.

'Chris, I'll come back to that,' said Clay. 'It's a big lead. Hendricks and Stone will be spending time following that up.'

Hendricks stepped forward and called up the slideshow he'd loaded onto the laptop.

'I'm going to pause it in a few frames,' said Hendricks.

The images of Kate Patel's battered body lingered on the screen for a few seconds as the slideshow played out. Clay watched the room as Hendricks paused on a close shot of Mrs Patel's face, the dark hollows of her eye sockets causing a few reflexive intakes of breath.

'I'll move on,' said Hendricks.

An overview of her whole body, a body that looked like it had been dragged across a mountain by wild beasts. Every bit of her was injured. Her torso was black and her arms lay on the table at odd angles, the bones broken in several places.

'Dr Lamb counted ninety-eight wounds on Mrs Patel's body.'

Her legs from the hips down were swollen and purple.

'They attacked her in the kitchen,' said Clay. 'Before or after they'd murdered her husband, mother-in-law and daughter Jane. They did it in front of Alicia, and then they let mother and daughter out of the kitchen. They wanted an endgame, a chase.' A dial turned inside her head and everything suddenly became clear. 'They were in control of everything that happened in that house. They wanted Alicia to put that call in. They wanted me to hear them in action.'

'You?' asked Riley. 'You just said, *They wanted* me *to hear them in action.*'

'I meant *us*, Gina,' said Clay. 'I'm exhausted.' Clay turned her attention back to Hendricks. 'The injuries to Mrs Patel...'

'Of the ninety-eight, there's one injury that stands out.'

A close-up showed her abdomen from the pubic bone to her navel. Clay looked around and saw that no one was sure what they were looking at. She too had been puzzled when she first saw it.

'Next picture is a close-up of the left side of Mrs Patel's abdomen, between her hip bone and ribs. Look closely for lines.'

The image appeared on the screen and the lines were now clear. Hendricks picked up the red board pen and drew over the shape. First of all he drew an incomplete oval, the outline of the shape. Then he drew over the lines within the oval, a pattern of four zigzags across the widest part of the oval.

Hendricks caught Clay's eye as she watched the lights going on in her team's faces.

'Yes, it's a footprint,' said Hendricks. 'Whoever stomped on Mrs Patel's stomach did it with such force that they left the raised impression of the sole of their right foot. Dr Lamb and her assistant measured it. Over to you, Eve.'

'Brace yourselves,' said Clay. 'It's a size 2. I used to have a Saturday job at Clarks Shoe Shop in Church Street when I was studying for my A Levels. A size 2 is the average size for an eight- to ten-year-old child. It figures that this footprint was left by either a child or an adult with unusually small feet.'

Clay picked up a sheaf of papers and handed them to Stone. 'Take one, pass them on,' she said.

There were the same two images on each page. The top image was the close-up of the footprint on Mrs Patel's skin; underneath was a drawing of the sole of the shoe, minus the heel.

'They've gone in from the side,' said Clay. 'The clarity of the pattern suggests this footwear's brand-new or close to it. We need to know which brand of shoe or trainer, which shops and internet sites sell it and who's been buying it.'

Including herself, there were fourteen team members in the room.

'Stone and Hendricks, I want you to stay here as team communication point and in case anything else comes in. Check your emails on your phones. Karl's emailed each of you the name of one child, his or her age and address. They're all in the Childwall and Belle Vale districts. The phone call to the Patels' house came from a mobile stolen from a teacher at St Bernard's RC Primary. Hence the exercise books. These are the twelve suspects for lifting the teacher's phone and potentially taking part in a mass murder.'

Clay looked at her watch.

'We all go to a different address at eight o'clock. When you're through the front door, call back here to say so. First, you need to see the children in the family. You're looking for extreme fatigue or signs of trauma in the children. If you see this, call me immediately and I'll join you at your given address. You need to see the children's footwear and find out what size shoe they take. We're looking for a size 2. Karl Stone will email you a warrant from the duty magistrate if the parents refuse to cooperate. Everyone back here at ten.'

'Eve?' DC Christopher Dillon interjected. 'We're looking for a kid, *right*? For *this*?' He looked bewildered, just like his colleagues.

'We're looking for a minimum of three suspects. One of them is possibly an eight- to ten-year-old child.'

'Are you going to play the 999 call?' asked Gina Riley.

'Yes. Before we all go our separate ways.'

The clicking beats of the tongues and the broken syllables of the strange language resounded in Clay's memory. Thirteen pairs of eyes looked at her.

'Try not to listen to Alicia. Zone in on the sounds the perpetrators are making. If anyone can make sense of it, you'll go to the top of my Christmas card list.'

Clay clicked play on her laptop and watched the hardened faces of her team melt into ill-concealed bafflement. When the sounds on the recording gave way to silence, she asked, 'Anyone? Anything?'

No one replied and most of the officers didn't look at Clay or anyone else in the room.

'Let's get on with the day. All back here at ten o'clock,' she said.

As the team filed out, Clay turned to Stone and Hendricks.

'If Liverpool Uni haven't got back by nine, I want you, Karl, down to them with two copies of this recording.' She handed him the pen drive and as he set about transferring it to his own computer, Clay said, 'Stress to them that it's a matter of life-and-death urgency and of the upmost confidentiality. We've got to be on them, and fast. They'll do it again. And soon.'

'What makes you say that?' asked Hendricks.

'Their actions so far. They have no mercy but they do have a ritual and ritual doesn't exist in a vacuum. It serves a wider purpose and at the moment the perpetrators are the only ones who know what that is. Let's proceed on the assumption that another family's going to get massacred tonight.'

All eleven officers through the front doors and inside.

'Good,' said Clay to herself, reading the text message from Hendricks. She looked at the nondescript semi-detached house on Barnham Drive that she had parked outside five minutes earlier. Satisfied that the whole team were on track, she got out of her car and walked up the path.

The child Clay had picked out from the list, Faith Drake, one of the two described by Mrs Harry as 'quiet', was clearly up and out of bed. Inside the front room Clay saw a cartoon playing on the flat-screen TV, a CBeebies programme that Philip liked even though it was too old for him. She wondered if he was watching the same programme at that moment, enjoying the bright colours and loud noise.

A woman appeared in the frosted oval at the centre of the front door and Clay fixed her face into a neutral expression.

The door opened. Dressed in a navy blue skirt and red blouse, the tall, thin brunette stared directly at Clay and said, 'Yes?'

'Mrs Drake?'

'Yes?'

'DCI Eve Clay, Merseyside Police.' She showed her white warrant card and noticed the small gold crucifix hanging from the woman's neck. 'Can I come in and talk to you, please?'

'Yes. Certainly.' The woman smiled. 'Is there a problem?'

'I'd rather discuss it indoors, Mrs Drake.'

As Clay moved through the narrow hall, she passed a metal silhouette of the Liverpool skyline on the wall. The Liver Building, St John's Tower, the Roman Catholic cathedral and the Anglican cathedral against a white background.

'Come this way, DCI Clay.'

As Clay followed Mrs Drake to the front room, she heard the sound of a ball being bounced in an upstairs bedroom, from the wall to the floor. Bounce. Bounce. Wall. Floor. Bounce. Bounce. Silence.

Mrs Drake pushed the front room door wider. The blonde laminate flooring of the hall carried on into the front room, as did the off-white walls.

'Faith, turn the television off, please. We have a visitor.'

Without hesitation or argument, Faith Drake rose from the black leather sofa and turned the TV off. She was dressed in blue jeans with a chunky red jumper and thick slippers in the form of grinning reindeer. Her hair was auburn and tied up in a neat bun at the back of her head.

'Hello,' said Faith. She radiated a quiet intelligence and Clay thought she might be a good witness.

'Have a seat, DCI Clay,' said Mrs Drake.

As Clay sat down on a leather armchair next to the sofa, Faith headed towards the door.

'Faith,' said Clay. The girl stopped. 'I've come to talk to you and your mother. I'm a police officer.' The child looked at her mother, who placed a guiding hand on her shoulder and took her to the sofa.

Clay looked at Faith's bulky slippers and asked, 'Why are there two donkeys on your feet?'

'Donkeys? They're reindeer,' said Faith, the darkness that had crossed her face on hearing that Clay was a police officer now replaced with an amused grin.

Clay made a show of looking closely. 'I haven't got my glasses on, but surely, Faith, your slippers are donkeys.'

'No, they're not. They're *reindeer.*'

Clay held out a hand. 'May I have a closer look? Please.'

Faith looked at her mother and took off her left slipper. Clay glanced at the fragile structure of the child's naked foot. No marks or bruising. She examined the slipper from different angles. It was a size 4.

She handed the slipper back, saying casually, 'I'm here about Mrs Harry's phone. It's been stolen.'

Faith frowned. 'That's bad.' Clay watched the turning of the child's mind as the frown on her face solidified into the early stages of panic. 'You … you don't think …? Me …? You don't think it's me?'

'Calm down, Faith.' Her mother held onto her hands.

'I wouldn't do a thing like that.'

'I know you wouldn't, Faith. But I'm sure DCI Clay has a good reason for being here. And you will explain, won't you, DCI Clay?'

Bounce. Bounce. Wall. Floor. Silence.

Clay admired Mrs Drake. She was clearly a good mother and knew instinctively how to reassure her daughter.

'Faith.' Clay smiled when the girl looked at her. 'There were twelve pupils in the classroom at the time we believe Mrs Harry's phone was stolen.'

She paused to allow Faith to absorb this.

'So, Faith, all the boys and girls who were in school on Friday will be having this visit,' said Mrs Drake. 'That's right, isn't it, DCI Clay?'

'Absolutely. It's routine.'

Faith looked reassured.

'Like your mum said, Faith. And they'll all be getting asked the same questions, the ones I'm going to ask you. Ready? Did you see anyone go into Mrs Harry's bag before you went home from school on Friday?'

'No. I'd have told Mrs Harry if I'd seen that happen.'

'Did anybody say they'd been in Mrs Harry's bag and taken anything out?'

'No. If they had said that to me, I'd have told Mrs Harry.'

Clay handed Faith's mother a piece of paper. As Mrs Drake unfolded it, Clay explained. 'It's a list of the names of the children who were in school on Friday. There are twelve of them. Was there anyone from your class in school that day who isn't on the list?'

Faith studied the list in her mother's hand and said, 'They were all the kids who were in.'

'Mrs Harry might have made a mistake, missed off someone on the register who was there?'

'Mrs Harry doesn't make mistakes. Not like that. She's very . . . very . . .'

'Precise?' suggested Faith's mother, pulling a face at Clay. *Precise* as in *pain in the backside*.

'Precise,' said Faith. 'Yes. Anyway, we had a quiz at break time because it was too cold to go out and it was definitely six against six. Yes. We lost because Jon Pearson put his hand up and then couldn't answer so she handed the question over to the other team.'

'Is there anyone on the list who has ever been in trouble for stealing?'

'Yes. Connor Stephens stole a packet of crisps from my lunchbox last term. He said he didn't know it was wrong, but

96

he did. He gave me the crisps back all broken into crumbs.'

'Can I ask you a difficult question, Faith? One that I need you to answer truthfully, even if it is difficult to say out loud.'

'Yes.'

'Is there anyone – or maybe there might be more than one – anyone who was in your class in school on Friday who you're afraid of?'

Outside, snow started falling and Faith's attention was drawn to the window. Her mother squeezed the little girl's hands.

'Sorry, Mrs Clay,' said Faith.

There was silence as Clay locked eyes with Faith. 'Come to think of it,' she said, 'there is someone I'm afraid of.'

'Who?' asked her mother, intercepting Clay's question. It was clearly brand-new bad news to a devoted parent.

'Mrs Harry. But everybody is.'

'Mrs Harry said you're a very quiet girl,' said Clay.

'I am quiet in class. I'm there to learn.' She looked at her mother. 'Aren't I, Mum?'

'I've drilled it into her, the need to be quiet and learn in class. She wants to follow her sister Coral and go to the Blue Coat School.'

Coral. Eleven years plus. Upstairs playing with a ball.

'One more question, Faith, and then I'll leave you in peace.'

Clay stared at the snow falling outside. Her heart sank at the prospect of another polar vortex gripping the city. She hoped it was only a winter shower.

'If you think of anything, Faith, and you need to talk to me, I'm going to give your mum a card with information on how to contact me. No detail is too small. Have a little think for me, go over what happened on Friday in your mind and see if you can come up with anything a little *odd* maybe. Talk to your mum.'

'We'll talk about it, Faith, when I come home from work,' said Mrs Drake.

Silence. 'OK. Can I be excused now? I need the bathroom.'

As Faith headed for the door, Clay said, 'Love your slippers.'

'Thanks. Father Christmas brought them for me,' said Faith with utter conviction.

Clay listened to the sound of Faith running up the stairs and noticed that some of the softness left Mrs Drake's face. 'She still believes in Father Christmas?' Clay asked.

'Yes. She's young for her years. She's not a cynical, street-wise child.' Mrs Drake looked directly at Clay, her expression and voice challenging. 'A DCI at eight o'clock in the morning over a stolen phone? We'd be lucky to see a community officer usually...'

'It's a lead in another case.' Clay stood up and handed Mrs Drake her card. 'Please have that little chat with Faith. She'll be more relaxed around you and she may come up with some detail she didn't mention to me. I'm sorry to have put her through this stress. Call me anytime, 24/7.'

'Of course we'll be in touch if anything comes along.'

'Mrs Drake, where do you work?'

'Why?'

'I think I know you from somewhere and I don't know where.'

'I know you. You shop at Tesco's on Mather Avenue. Don't you, DCI Clay?'

'Yes.' Clay smiled, saw Mrs Drake smiling and making small talk at the checkout. Blue skirt, red blouse. Clay recognised the supermarket uniform.

'That's where I work, that's how *I* know *your* face.'

Clay recalled Mrs Drake's name badge. Anais.

Anais Drake smiled at Clay. As the front door closed, the snow fell hard and fast. Clay took out her iPhone. There were no calls to her from the other team members. Including Barnham Drive, twelve no shows in the panic stakes.

She dialled the Price's landline. At the other end, the receiver was lifted and a young, fractured voice said, 'Yes?'

'Sandy Patel?'

Clay walked to her car.

'Yes?'

'My name's DCI Eve Clay. I'm coming to talk to you. It's earlier than I planned. Are you ready to speak?'

'Yes, I'm ready.'

21

As Clay got out of her car, outside a large detached house on Menlove Avenue, she saw Sandy Patel standing against the gate that separated the front garden from the pavement.

He seemed oblivious to her as she walked towards him, his face lost, his eyes raw with tears and lack of sleep. He was a slim, youthful replica of his father and, for a moment, she saw his figure and face in the quadrilateral of corpses at the bottom of the stairs in the Patels' house.

'I'm DCI Eve Clay.' She showed her warrant card, but he didn't look.

'I'm going out of my mind,' he said. He walked quickly, his breath short and laboured. Clay hurried alongside him.

They turned the corner in silence into Harthill Avenue and he walked into the gritted middle of the road, striding towards the Four Seasons Gateway of Calderstones Park. The four stone female statues – Spring, Summer, Autumn, Winter – were obscured beneath dense layers of snow.

Clay had a job to keep up with his long, swift strides and she understood he was trying to do the impossible: to escape from the horror that engulfed him.

As they walked down the tree-lined path into the heart of the deserted park, a raven flapped from the nearest tree, wings beating against the falling snow. Sandy Patel gasped with fright.

'Have you any idea...?' he began.

Clay pressed record on her iPhone.

'Have you any idea how it feels to have both your parents killed? Your sisters? For your grandmother to die *like that*?' It was a desperate set of questions that played straight into her hands.

'I never knew my parents, Sandy.'

He looked directly at her with a quick twist of the neck and she was there to meet him with a searching gaze of her own.

'They abandoned me when I was a day or two old. I grew up in care. So I can't answer your question about parents, sisters, grandmother, but I do have a husband and little boy. I can imagine what you're going through. Hell.'

As they walked along, the only sound was the grinding of their feet against the snow. The cold, damp air sent Clay's mind rushing back in time to the wet, icy darkness of her underground playground, and to one day in particular.

Eight years old, torch in hand, she followed the older kids. Although she laughed along with them, she grew more afraid the deeper they went into the darkness of an abandoned tunnel.

Cold, stale air pinched her face and the dripping of water echoed against the walls and ceiling. She felt like she was walking into the centre of the earth with only a torch to guide her in the pitch black space.

A sense of awe overwhelmed her. She was amongst the first people to walk into the forgotten tunnel for over a hundred years.

They stopped at the instruction of the biggest boy, the leader.

'Look at that!' He pointed his torch up. Eve and the others followed and she gasped at the tall arch above her head: Gothic, torchlit, beguiling.

'It's like a church!' she had said. The bigger kids turned to her.

The leader spoke, smiled at her.

'Eh, Eve, you've got a point there, kid!'

Sandy broke into a faster stride, throwing the hood of his duffle coat over his head, obscuring his face. She caught up, came back into the moment.

'I'm sorry for you but you're lucky, do you know that?' he asked.

His vaporised breath danced on the air from the edge of his hood.

'What do you mean I'm lucky?'

'You've always been an orphan. I've just become one. You've never argued or fallen out with your parents. You've never had to be sorry for what you have or haven't said or done.'

Or known their love and support, thought Clay.

'What have you got to be sorry about?' She asked the loaded question with a casual air. It took him half a minute to speak.

'Have you tried to find them?' he replied.

'The killers?'

'Your parents.'

'Yes I have, Sandy. Very much so.'

'And?'

'And I've had absolutely no luck whatsoever.'

'Who brought you up?' From a twist in his voice, the question he asked seemed to cause him a sharp and unexpected pain. It was a pain she understood and one that cast her into silence. 'I'm sorry. That was a very personal question.'

'It's all right.' She clung on to the raft that he'd pushed to her, pulled him from the cold waters of his grief. 'You can ask me anything. I'll tell you the truth. Because I believe you'll tell me the truth about yourself. About your family. Do me a favour, lad?'

'What?'

'Hood down, it's better if we can see each other's faces, right?'

After a few moments, he pulled his hood down, his face red with cold and wet with tears.

'If I can ask you anything, I want to ask the same question,' said Sandy. 'Who did bring you up?'

'For the first six years, a lovely and remarkable old lady called Sister Philomena, a nun. She died and that was awful. That was my first encounter with grief.' There was a permanent hole in her heart that always widened at the memory of her passing. For a moment, Clay wished she had a hood she could throw up to disguise her face and shield her emotions. *My lovely Philomena,* she thought, *gone home to her God, the one I could never believe in after her passing.*

'So, Sandy, yeah, from the age of six to eighteen, it was Catholic Social Services.'

'I'm sorry. Jesus? I mean, all those perverts, priests and the like.'

'I was one of the lucky ones. No one harmed me like that. By and large, they were OK, the people who passed in and out of my life. They were just poor people doing what they could to put food on the table for their families.'

He was no longer crying.

'Still?' he said.

'They fuck you up your mum and dad...'

He looked at her, shocked. 'What?'

'It's a line of poetry and it's not true for *everyone*. I'm speaking from personal experience – or the lack of it.'

'Didn't the people who took care of you keep records? About your parents, like?'

'Yes. I have a very clear memory of seeing my file when I transferred from the convent into the children's home. It was a big, fat card file stuffed with papers.'

'How come you haven't been able to track them down then?'

'This was the 1980s. Computers were coming in but they were huge things back then, crude and rather unreliable. I've been told that my records were transferred onto computer but the hard drive crashed.'

'What about the paper files?'

'Electrical fire in the basement of the children's home, where all the records were kept.'

'That sounds like...Do you think that's true?'

'To be honest, I think there's something not right. I know there was a fire and I know computers back then weren't great. But I don't completely believe it. I try not to be too paranoid about it. There was a lot wrong with the system and I'm not the only person whose records have gone missing.'

'How bad does that make you feel?'

He looked at her and, despite the hell he was in, she could see the light of empathy in his eyes. He turned left sharply and headed to the Linda McCartney Children's Playground. Clay couldn't have wished for a better place to move the interview forwards.

'How bad are *you* feeling?' She turned it round.

She saw his face beginning to collapse and tried to counter it with energy and focus. 'I want to catch the bastards who did this to your family. Who did this to you. And I need to do it fast so it doesn't happen to another family.'

He closed his eyes.

'You ready to answer a few questions?'

Clay placed a hand on the centre of his spine and guided him towards the swings. He drew in a breath and began weeping as she cleared the snow from the seat of the swing and said, 'Sit down, Sandy.'

He sat down and gripped the swing's chains.

'Talk to me, Sandy.' She spoke into his ear.

The trees loomed like silhouettes of giants in the milky fog. A lone figure materialised between the trees, the crude shape of a person, gender, age and size unrecognisable. The person moved between the trees, had the freakish look of a black matchstick figure, minus a layer of humanity. As quickly as it had appeared, it disappeared back between the trees.

Although Sandy was lost in the moment of acute grief, Clay didn't have a second to lose. As he pushed himself on the swings, she glanced at her watch and felt the weight of time and space in the span of her wrist.

'Give me...two...minutes...' Push.

'Sure.' Although it was a hundred and twenty seconds she didn't have to spare.

Push.

She counted the seconds down silently.

Push. Push.

Push.

22

8.35 am

Professor Andrew Bailey pressed the laptop headphones with the tips of his index fingers, closed his eyes, focused and winced. Then he opened his eyes again and glanced at DS Stone.

Stone saw regret in the young professor's face, but that didn't deter him. 'I'm very grateful to you for getting back to me as soon as you did and for agreeing to drop everything to see me. Are you ready to listen again, Professor Bailey?'

It was to be Bailey's third time listening to the 999 call from Alicia Patel. By nature calm and polite, he'd been ruffled the first time he heard it, in spite of Stone's warning to expect something deeply disturbing. 'Jesus wept,' he'd exclaimed, his handsome, James Stewart looks creasing in distress.

On the second run-through, he'd sat with the blood draining from his face, his head shaking like the toy dog that had used to nod away in the back window of Stone's mother's car.

DS Stone stood at an angle to him, so that he could register the linguist's reaction to the recording without appearing in Bailey's line of vision.

'I'm ready,' Bailey replied.

'Before you listen again, I want you to try and disregard all your natural reactions to this horror and home in on those...' He caught himself before blurting out the word *kids*. '...voices.'

Stone thought he saw Professor Bailey's hand trembling as he rolled the cursor onto play. He shut his eyes tight, listening hard to the mayhem in his ears once again.

Stone drifted across to the window of Professor Bailey's fourth-floor office and looked down at the snow spiralling against the rectangular pillars of the tenement-grey 1960s Cypress Building. *A strange homage to Soviet architecture*, Stone thought, *amongst the sprawling Victorian splendour of the University of Liverpool's power base.*

He turned, hearing the gentle sound of headphones being placed down on the desk.

'I can hear tiny discrete units of sound – what we in linguistics call phones,' the professor explained, 'but they're not strung together in the form of any global language that I can recognise.'

'How many spoken languages can you recognise?' asked Stone.

'Three hundred and thirty, thereabouts.'

'And how many languages are spoken around the world?'

'Roughly six and a half thousand.'

Stone felt as if the floor beneath him had vanished. He laughed briefly and unhappily. 'Professor Bailey, give me some good news.'

'Well, yes, there is good news. With the phones and the clicking, I'm thinking it's a hybrid of spoken language and some coded system of punctuation, a form of Morse code, which makes me think it's a synthetic language.'

'What does that mean?'

'Organic languages are based on recognisable sounds strung together in a commonly recognisable order. While there are some recognisable sounds in that recording, what these people are articulating is non-recognisable. There's also a rhythm, but it's uneven. Does it harmonise with the natural ebbs and flows of human physiology? I'd have to listen to an extended example. This is too brief. But I suggest that the only people in the world who know this language are the ones *using* it – I hesitate to say *speaking* it – plus whoever might have taught them it or developed it with them.'

Stone took a deep breath. He needed to get back to Trinity Road police station, but he never liked leaving sensitive evidence with an expert. He wasn't just relying on their expertise, he was relying on their ability to keep information tight. And Stone just didn't trust human nature. 'You're the only person to hear what's on this recording. Keep the pen drives on your person at all times until you hand them back to me.'

'OK, Detective Sergeant Stone!' Professor Bailey held his hands up in ironic surrender. 'I won't breathe a word to anyone and I heard what you said when you came through the door. It's a matter of life and death. Let me put your mind at rest. Two copies of the same recording.' He held up the two drives, placed one in the inner pocket of his jacket and, brandishing the other one, said, 'This one I'm going to clean up personally, out of earshot of anyone at all. I can get rid of all kinds of surface noise and pinpoint and highlight the voices of the assailants. I'll do it quickly, I promise.'

'I'd appreciate that, Professor Bailey.'

'I had Radio City on in the car this morning. It's that family in Aigburth, isn't it?'

'Yes,' said Stone. 'When can you feed back to me?'

'Later today. I'll call you.'

As Stone hurried down the echoing concrete staircase, his mind drifted back to the seven o'clock meeting and what Eve

Clay had said about the killers wanting *her* to hear them. If it was a secret language, how could she understand it?

How could anyone understand the darkness that lurked within such broken language, other than the broken souls that it seemed had invented and used it?

23

8.40 am

In the Linda McCartney Children's Playground, Clay sat on the swing next to Sandy. They were both still.

'Ready now?' she asked.

He nodded.

'I know this is hard for you, but I need you to talk to me, Sandy. You know that most murder victims are killed by people they knew?'

'No one we know is capable of this. They didn't have any enemies. None of the people we know are violent.'

Even though the snow was slackening off, the cold pinched and twisted Clay's ears, nose and cheeks.

'Tell me about the families you know. Start with the ones in Liverpool, the ones with kids.'

He blinked and wiped a snowflake from his left eye, his feet shifting from side to side like windscreen wipers.

'Mum and Dad are friends with other couples with kids, yeah.'

'Have they fallen out with any of them?' asked Clay.

Sandy took a packet of cigarettes and a red disposable lighter from his pocket. He popped a cigarette into his mouth and offered the packet to Clay. 'They don't know I smoke.'

Clay, a lifelong non-smoker, took a cigarette and balanced

it between her lips. He flared up her cigarette. She blew out a thin stream of smoke without inhaling, her taste buds bitter and stinging.

'They've drifted apart from a few couples, but that's just life. There's been no blazing rows over money or whatever.'

'Your mum and dad have four children. Any of their friends have three children?'

Sandy considered the question carefully, holding on to a huge lungful of smoke.

'Why?' he finally answered.

'We're following a lead, leftfield: three perpetrators, siblings maybe, maybe not. That's why I'm asking about families with three children.'

A look crossed his face, as if she'd said, *The prime suspects are aliens.*

'Have you got Mum's handbag?'

'Yes.' *Along with her body and the bodies of your sisters, grandmother and father,* she thought. Her heart went out to the young man beside her.

'Couples with three kids?' she urged softly.

'I seem to remember some, but I couldn't even name them. They'll be in the address book that Mum keeps in her handbag. Work your way through that.'

'Does your mum have a job?'

'She's a housewife.'

'Dad?'

'He's got his own company. Chemical research. Boring scientific stuff.'

'What's it called?'

'Patel Chemical Solutions. It's over the Runcorn Bridge in Widnes,' he added.

'*Boring scientific stuff?*'

'He loves anything to do with science. He's obsessed. Correction. *Loved* anything to do with science. *Was* obsessed.'

'You're not such a big fan?'

Sandy turned his head away from Clay and said something brief and quiet. She squeezed his shoulder and his eyes turned towards her.

'Say that again,' said Clay.

'I disappointed him.'

'In what way?'

'When I was a little kid in primary school, he used to take me to his laboratory and it was, *One day, son, all this will be yours.* I used to try really hard in school to do well at science. But the older I got, the more the game changed. Big equations. In-depth concepts zigzagging over each other. I just couldn't hack it. He took it as a personal insult, like I was doing it on purpose to put a wall between us. Fortunately, Alicia was the opposite to me. Chemistry, Physics and Biology were a doddle for her. So he turned his attention away from me and poured it onto Alicia.'

Over a hundred metres away, on Menlove Avenue, cars rumbled along as if in slow motion, their engines droning through the still air.

Clay tried to inject some warmth into the conversation. 'I bring my little boy here when I'm not working,' she said.

'Dad used to bring me here when I was little.'

'I can tell you something, Sandy, about that period in your father's life. However happy your memories of those times in the park, they're nothing to the joy they would have brought your dad. Forget what flowed under the bridge after that. You gave him something that nothing and no one can take away. Just like my boy's given me. One day you'll know what I mean, when you bring your child to the park.'

'Yeah?'

'Yeah.'

Sandy looked at her through the haze of his grief.

'Your dad must have been proud of you getting into Durham University?'

He shook his head and uttered a flat, resigned, 'No. Said I was doing a dead-end course.'

'What are you studying?'

'Theology.'

The carefully arranged bodies of Sandy's family came to her mind, and the bloody graffiti on the walls.

'Theology?' she said. 'The opposite of science?'

'Yes and no,' said Sandy, rocking gently on the swing. 'We know so many things, but ultimately we know nothing. As in yesterday I had a family, today I'm all alone.'

'Do you think your faith will help you?'

He had smoked the cigarette down to the butt. He flicked it through the snowflakes and looked at Clay, perplexed.

'What faith? I was good at religious education in school. That and English literature and history. I study theology because I'm good at it. I'm a total atheist.'

'Does that make you stand out in your classes?'

'Well, there's a heavy percentage of God-botherers, wannabe vicars and the like. Then there's a number of students on the fence and a few atheists like me.' He stood up. 'I'd like to walk now.'

Clay dropped her cigarette outside the railings and closed the gate on the metal fence surrounding the play area. She followed Sandy onto the grass leading to the lake, the snow halfway up her shins as she trudged through it.

'Your family weren't churchgoers then?'

'No. We used to be, but we just suddenly stopped when I

was about twelve. Mum was the keen one. Dad used to go to make the numbers up.'

'What church was it?'

'It wasn't a church church – you know, big building with pews and an altar. It was just like people in a meeting room, praying and singing about Jesus.

'Why did your parents stop going to church?'

'They never really explained it to me. Alicia was eight and Jane was a baby. Alicia was a bit of a handful, messing around when she should've been connecting with the Lord Almighty. Mum used to get stressed when she kicked off. I reckon she thought we'd just have a few weeks off, but Mum never took us back again.' Something approaching a smile surfaced on his face. 'I joined a Sunday League team, playing on Camp Hill. Dad said to me, *Football is the new God and Camp Hill is where we shall worship.*'

As they reached the railings around the lake, Sandy wrapped his arms tightly across himself.

'Look at that,' he said. 'Not a single duck or goose on the bank. They're all huddled together on the island in the middle. Who says creatures are dumb?'

He rubbed his eyes and face. 'I used to come and feed them with Dad. Especially on days like this.'

'I used to feed the birds with Philomena. In Abercrombie Gardens, near St Claire's, where I lived until I was six. Sandy?'

'Yes?'

'Who was the leader of the church?'

'Some woman. Can't remember her name or what she looked like. Have you got many more questions for me?'

Clay knew she was walking into a dead-end. She shook her head.

'Good. Because I really don't feel like talking anymore. I need some time and space.'

He took out his packet of cigarettes, held it out to Clay and said, 'I'm giving up.'

'That's a great idea,' said Clay. 'But is this a good time?'

'There's never a good time. Keep them for me in case I change my mind. I assume you'll want to talk to me again.'

She took the packet of cigarettes. 'I will do.' *When your head isn't as scrambled.*

Sandy stared at the island, a ghostly palace in the white air, unseen birds beating their wings against the cold.

She turned and walked away but stopped at the sound of his voice.

'Just for the record, Sandy's kind of a family pet name. When I was small, I had a speech impediment. My name's Andrew. Andy. I couldn't say it. I used to say *Sandy*. Mum took me to the speech therapist at the old Alder Hey, but it was Dad who did hours and hours of work with me to get me over it. What a way to pay him back. I should have tried harder in school. I'm sorry I was a disappointment to him. Really, really sorry...'

Clay stifled the urge to comfort him, knowing that words couldn't help.

Instead, she trudged through the snow. Although it dragged at her feet, she soon found she was jogging. She glanced at her watch and started to run as fast as she could. She was in desperate need of two things. She wanted to start ploughing through Kate Patel's address book, but, even more, she wanted to hold her son in her arms for a few precious minutes before she had to report in for the ten o'clock meeting.

24

9.20 am

On her way home to Mersey Road, Clay turned slowly onto Aigburth Road. She glanced back. On the other side of the dual carriageway there was a growing camp of news organisations at the sealed-off mouth of The Serpentine. Vehicles marked BBC, ITN and Sky were parked up and the pavement was blocked with reporters talking to cameras under the misty glow of the streetlights.

At the lights on the junction of Aigburth and Riversdale roads, the driver of a BMW did a U-turn. The passenger was carrying a boom microphone and the turning car had a Republic of Ireland licence plate. Bill Hendricks's prediction was already coming true. The world's media was descending fast.

Less than a minute later, Clay pulled up at the top of Mersey Road. The proximity of the crime to her home hit her hard. A fresh wave of anxiety passed through her.

What if? filled her head. *What if?* in the beat of her heavy heart. *What if? What if? What if?* She looked back over her shoulder. *What if it had been us, not them?* She tied a mental fist inside her head and hammered the bizarre idea as if it was an overfed pest. *What if this is some personal and deeply buried nightmare playing out on the cold perimeters of reality?*

She stayed where she was, knew she had to completely squash the feeling inside her before she could turn the corner and make a lightning visit home.

'*You can't take this across the threshold of your home.*'

A voice seemed to come from the back seat of her car. She turned, but there was no one there and she knew the voice was inside her head. It spoke to her with a comforting lilt, as if she was still a little girl, and it was from her childhood that the voice came.

'*Go and see your husband and son. You will see very little of them for who knows how long, Eve. Be a good wife and mother.*'

Sister Philomena's voice faded, as did the gnawing uncertainty that had built up inside her as she'd driven through the suburbs into Aigburth.

She parked outside the large red-brick terrace house that was home and thought ahead to meeting again with Sandy Patel. The clock on her dashboard read 9.22. She would have to leave by 9.40 for the ten o'clock meeting.

At the bottom of her road, a murky light was filtering into the sky above the River Mersey.

She opened the front door. Philip was sitting on the bottom step of the staircase. Closing the door behind herself quickly, to block out the world beyond, she sank to her knees as her son bounced towards her with outstretched arms.

'Cold,' said Philip as she wrapped her arms around him. 'Mummy's cold.'

Relief ran through her and, though she knew it was only temporary, a weight lifted from her as she drank in the familiar scent of her son's hair and skin. She looked at him, his body growing, his features changing, and kissed him on the forehead.

Thomas's footsteps came towards her from the kitchen.

'Eve?' he called. Her throat was gridlocked and she couldn't reply. 'Eve?' She heard him moving faster, then he came into view above the curve of Philip's head.

His expression became more and more troubled as he crossed the hall. He dropped down and looked into her eyes, holding the sides of her face in his warm hands.

'Eve, what's the matter, love?'

He folded his arms around her and Philip was locked within the walls of his parents' embrace.

She drew in a deep breath to stem a storm of tears.

'I'm so happy to see you,' she said. 'Safe and...' *Alive.* '...sound.'

25

9.27 am

Eve faced Thomas across the kitchen table. Her husband was almost but not quite stand-out handsome and, each time she looked at him, she was always drawn to his sky-blue eyes. He placed a plate of toast and a mug of tea in front of her. She gripped his hand, tilted her head up and kissed him on the cheek.

'I've taken a few days off from the surgery,' said Thomas. 'I've got a locum covering my list.'

'That's music to my ears,' she replied. 'So you'll be with Philip all the time...'

'One of the advantages of being in charge! I thought you'd be pleased.'

'You bet I am, doc!'

She rose, drifted past him to the double-glazed French window and checked the handle. It was locked.

'Can't you pass the case on to someone else?' asked Thomas.

'There is no one else,' she replied, looking into the tight space of their walled garden.

'What do you mean?' He was behind her, looking with her at the white-capped rose bushes and small lawn thick with frozen snow. The wind rolled against the cold brickwork, sounding like a ghost trapped in a bottle.

'Everything and everyone is stretched to the limit. The spending cutbacks have seen to that. Chance stuck me at the scene first – I was there in the Golden Hour, I've already begun this investigation and I can't turn my back on it. Stone liaised with the duty superintendent and the super's ordered me to shelve anything else and lead the case. I've instructed my team. I want to catch them. I *need* to put them away before they do this to another family.' She pointed through the glass. 'What's that?'

At the bottom of the garden, near the wooden gate that led to an alleyway between Mersey Road and the backs of the terraced houses on Horringford Road, it looked like a black bin bag was being played with by the cold wind.

The *bag* turned and it wasn't a bag at all. It was the largest, sleekest crow and something fibrous was hanging from its beak. It stepped forward a few paces through the snow, its eyes fixed on the French window. Then it turned and dug its beak into the snow, pulling at what lay beneath. Clay felt the vibration of an incoming call on her iPhone.

She banged on the glass, but the crow remained, feeding on the body beneath the snow.

'Is the back door locked?' she asked.

'Yes.' She felt the weight of Thomas's hands on her shoulders, his fingers rubbing the iron-tight muscles, reassuring her. 'It's only a bird. It'll go away in a minute.'

'It's feeding,' said Clay.

It resumed stabbing the snow with its beak.

She took out her iPhone and pressed accept. But she couldn't turn away from the window.

'Is that DCI Eve Clay?'

She checked the display. It was a mobile number she didn't recognise.

'Who is this?' she asked.

'My name's Carolina Hill.'

The crow turned and looked directly at her, its black eyes catching the weak morning light, its yellow beak red from its meal. 'I'm a social worker...' The crow rose, landed on the back wall of the garden and fixed her with one beady eyeball. '...at Ashworth Psychiatric Hospital in Maghull.'

Immediately and with complete certainty, Clay knew what the call was about.

'How did you get my mobile number?'

'I rang your office and a DS Hendricks gave me your number when I told him why I was calling.'

She heard Philip singing as he came into the room. The crow stayed motionless on the wall.

'Go ahead, Carolina. What's up?'

Thomas pressed his weight into her and she felt Philip's hands around her legs.

'I've had a request from one of our patients. He wants to see you.'

'And who would that be?'

'Adrian White.'

The crow rose from the wall and flapped out of her range of vision.

'DCI Clay, are you still there?'

'Yes.' The Baptist. The arrest that had put her face on tabloid papers worldwide. The arrest that almost killed her.

'Why does he want to see me now?' she asked. But she knew what was going to follow.

'It's a really unique request from *Adrian*.' There was something in the way the social worker said *Adrian* that made Clay want to reach a hand through time and space and punch her face. '*Adrian* hasn't had a visitor in his seven years at Ashworth. He's had thousands of requests, people wanting to visit him, but he's turned them all down flat – not that we'd have sanctioned ninety-nine per cent of them, you understand.'

'Wait a minute, Carolina.' She opened the door leading into the garden and stood out in the cold. 'OK, you can go ahead now.'

'You remember Adrian White, of course?'

'I remember *Adrian* very well.' She aped the awe in the social worker's voice.

'He says he needs to see and talk to you. He says he's *anxious* to do so.'

Psychopaths don't suffer anxiety, thought Clay. *Adrian White is the purest psychopath I know of. He is lying.*

'Did he give you any indication as to why he wants to see me so urgently?'

'Yes, but I don't really understand what he meant.'

'What did he say, Carolina?'

'He said he needs to talk to you about the Red Cloud. Does that mean anything to you?'

'No,' she lied. 'Anything else?'

'He says he has some information about your new case, the one you've just started working on. He said he can help you. He said, and he was very definite on this, he stressed, *Six so far and there will be more soon and many more quickly after.* He said it three times. I asked him other questions, but he didn't utter another word. I'm just passing on his request and the things he did say. I'm sorry I can't be of any more help.'

'Oh yes you can,' said Clay.

Through the morning she'd heard reports about the murders on local Radio City news broadcasts, had seen the national media camped outside The Serpentine. It was a massive breaking story.

'Does White have a television set in his cell?'

'No. He was offered one but refused it.'

'A radio?'

'The same. No. He has no access to the news media in his cell. He lives like a hermit. He's declined all creature comforts. I think it's a form of self punish—'

'Between eleven o'clock last night and now, who has he had access to? Who's he spoken with?'

'Richard Taylor, the psychiatric nurse. Richard was on night shift when Adrian asked him to talk to me. He hasn't spoken to anyone else at all. He only speaks when he wants to.'

Something twisted inside Clay. The social worker spoke about Adrian White as if he was a star. People in Ashworth Hospital were no doubt touched by White's dark charisma, the so-called aura that only existed in the gullible minds of people hungry for sensation.

'Are you aware of any significant crime that's been committed in the last twenty-four hours?' asked Clay.

She heard the crow calling in the middle distance, a noise not unlike the cruel laughter of a sadistic child.

'No.'

'Have you discussed any crime with Adrian White?'

'We don't have discussions with Adrian. He speaks. We listen.'

'What did Mr Taylor report to you? During the night was there any exchange between the nurse and Adrian White about a specific crime?'

'None. Just his highly unusual request for you to visit him.'

Clay looked at the small patch of red on the white ground and felt the weight of the snow-filled sky pressing down on her head.

'So what shall I tell him?'

'Tell him nothing,' said Clay, closing down the call and walking towards the bloodstained snow.

It fed and left, thought Clay. *End of.*

'Who was on the phone?' asked Thomas, appearing in the doorway, Philip in his arms.

'Hendricks,' she lied.

'What is it, Eve?' asked Thomas.

'Work,' she said. 'I'll have to go.'

She kissed Philip and Thomas, put her wet coat back on.

'I don't know when I'll be back,' she said. 'But I'll call you whenever I can, Thomas. I need to hear your voice.'

'I wish we were both off. We could bolt the door,' said Thomas.

She took a lingering look at Philip's face. It was definitely changing.

If she lived long enough to see him grow into a man, chances were she would be able to see what her own father had looked like.

She left as quickly as she could, afraid that she would attract the past and all its darkness into the home if she stayed a moment longer.

10.01 am

In the incident room of Trinity Road police station, the whole team was present, seated in a circle and focused on Clay. She looked at the clock on the wall. It felt like a year had passed in just over ten hours, but it also felt as if those hours had disappeared in seconds.

'I want an impression, first of all, so...' Clay opened up to the room. '...those of you who've been making domestic visits, anything to report?'

There was silence.

Clay looked to Hendricks.

'Everyone reported back to me. All the kids in Mrs Harry's class were home. Some were up, some were in their beds asleep. There was absolutely no sign of trauma or distress.'

'Foot size?'

Hendricks handed Clay a list of eleven names and their respective shoe sizes.

Melanie Waters 1
David Jones 1½
Imran Choudhary 3
Jon Pearson 2½
Paul Peters 1

Donna Rice 3½
Connor Stephens 3
Tom Tanner 2½
Megan Odemwingie 1½
Ryan Nolan 4
Sally McManus 2½

'Everyone verified the parents' and children's answers to this question by watching the kids stepping into their shoes,' said Hendricks. 'No one asked to see a warrant. Everyone cooperated fully.'

'Must've been like a beautiful moment from *Cinderella*,' smiled Clay. 'Faith Drake, the kid I saw, was a size 4. No sign of anything there either.' Clay took in everyone in the circle with a long glance. 'No sign of stress in any of the kids you saw?'

No one responded.

'What about the parents' and carers' criminal records, Bill?'

Hendricks held up one finger. 'Sad but probably not significant. It wasn't a conviction because it didn't get that far. Jon Pearson. I managed to speak to the officer from St Helens CID who was on the case. Jon's father, Timothy, committed suicide when his back was against the wall. They had him for downloading child porn. It was part of a wider investigation into a paedophile ring. After the father topped himself, the mother moved to Liverpool to *disappear* in the big city.'

'And when did all this take place?' asked Clay. 'As in how old was Jon Pearson when he moved to Liverpool?'

'Four years of age. Came in the August, started reception class in St Bernard's the following month,' said Hendricks.

'His brothers were ten and eleven years old and went in to the top junior classes.' He consulted a note on his desk. 'Robert and Vincent. It was a riches-to-rags story. Dad had a good job in banking, but when he topped himself it came out they were riddled with all kinds of debt. They went from an affluent suburb to an estate in Liverpool.'

'Anything coming out of the children's writing?'

'I'm still ploughing through the school books. Stone's helping me now he's back from the uni. This'll appeal to you, Eve. The kids have done a local history project on Williamson Tunnels.'

Clay smiled at the link to her childhood and she heard herself say, 'Have a close look at those pages.' The smile was gone. Each passing second tapped against her skull. 'How'd it go at the uni, Stone?' she asked.

'Professor Bailey's feeding back later today. But on first hearing he reckons it's a synthetic language created by or taught to the perpetrators. It's secret to the killers.'

Clay showed the team Kate Patel's address book.

'DS Stone, pick a couple of officers to help you ring round the names in the address book and/or visit as necessary.'

'How was Sandy Patel?' asked Stone.

'Either he's an Oscar-winning actor or he genuinely is in shreds. I believe the latter, but we have to temper sympathy with suspicion. Things weren't good between father and son. They went to church but quit going for a reason or reasons he didn't know. We're looking for friendships and associations with other families with three or more children. Riley, you still like visiting shoe shops?'

'Twelve years since I last went past one without going in.'

'I'd like you to chase up the footprint – high-street and retail-park stores, distributors, internet.' She made eye contact with DC Alastair Ryan, a red-eyed bloodhound of a man, on the verge of retirement.

'Yeah, I can help Riley snoop shoes till the last cow comes home,' he said.

'Where are you off to, Eve?' asked Riley. 'You keep glancing at the door and you're talking faster and faster like you always do when you're in a hurry to leave.'

'If I didn't know better, Gina, I'd say you were a copper.' Clay took a deep breath. 'I have got somewhere to go. I had a phone call from a social worker at Ashworth Hospital. Guess who wants to see me?'

A quiet descended on the room.

'Don't go anywhere near that bastard!' said Karl Stone.

'I have to,' said Clay, calmly.

'Why go anywhere near the little specimen?' asked Riley.

'Because I'm told the Baptist has no access to the media but knows there were six victims in last night's massacre. He's sent me a message via a social worker asking to see me, says he has information and it's going to happen again very soon.'

'*When you look into shadows, you look into mirrors. When you look into mirrors, what do you see?*'

White's voice erupted inside her brain, along with fragments of the last words he'd spoken to her as he was led down into the cells.

'*The Red Cloud…the belly of the city…the river will run with blood.*'

'He said something about a red cloud.' There was a space between her and the others that she had to fill with words. 'Does that ring any bells?'

'I'll come with you,' said Hendricks.

'You've got enough to do. Order up White's records, everything we've got. I'll collect from HQ at Liverpool One.

The three books he wrote.' Their titles came back to her in a rush, as did the sense that there was something about a red cloud in one of them. *'The Beginning of the End of Time. The Elemental. The Matriarch.'*

As she walked quickly to the door, Hendricks called, 'Are you sure?'

'He hasn't spoken to anyone for seven years!' replied Clay. 'He's in the know. I can't turn him down.'

It had stopped snowing by the time Clay arrived on the outskirts of Maghull, but she was still grateful for the satnav in her car, not only because the signs for Ashworth Hospital were obscured beneath the snow, but also because it made her feel slightly less alone.

'It's this way,' said the psychiatric nurse who had met her at the main gate. 'It's like a park here when it isn't snowing.' Clay made out the shapes of trees and shrubs between the buildings. The whole place was enclosed by walls. It felt much more like a prison than a hospital.

'You should come here in spring or summer,' she continued. *Only if it was a matter of life and death*, thought Clay. 'It's soooo green.'

The surface of the snow was treacherous, like a back road in winter, icy and slick. They walked slowly and Clay felt the car journey from south Liverpool to Maghull as a deep pain between her shoulder blades.

As they headed to the High Dependency Ward, home for the past seven years to Adrian White, Clay prepared herself. She called to mind a teenage girl she'd met when she was six years old and newly arrived at the Children's Home in Edge Hill. The girl had left a lasting impression. Her name was Natasha and she was seventeen. Natasha Seventeen. Natasha's face never showed emotion, but her eyes stirred the deepest unease in adults and children alike. She left the home very suddenly one day and two short months later was said to have married the soldier who got her pregnant. Clay remembered hearing the staff discussing her. 'You wouldn't dare do anything but marry the po-faced cow, even with the whole bloody British army behind you,' one of them had said, and they'd all laughed.

Standing outside the High Dependency Ward, Clay summoned up Natasha Seventeen's face and assumed its unyielding stillness. Natasha. A playmate from the Williamson Tunnels.

The psychiatric nurse knocked on a glass panel of the double doors. After the unlocking and locking of two doors, a man opened the front door. As she entered, Clay noticed the name on his identity badge. Richard Taylor. And the telltale scar tissue on his upper lip from the cleft-palate operation he'd had as a baby.

Richard Taylor, who'd passed on the request from White.

'Detective Chief Inspector Eve Clay.' She held up her warrant card

'Yeah, I know who you are. I remember your picture on the front of the *Liverpool Echo*, years back.'

The door closed at her back and she felt the weight of the building pressing down on her.

He stifled a yawn as he opened the first of two doors.

'Tired, Richard?' said Clay.

'Four people phoned in sick. There's always some bug going round in here and we've got to keep a three-to-one staff-to-patient ratio on the day shift. So I'm working a double shift. I finish at 2 pm and then I'm off for two days.'

'Carolina Hill mentioned your name on the phone...'

He pulled a face. *Her!* He shut the inner door, locked it. The Ward filled Clay with a sense of claustrophobia. 'Come with me, DCI Clay. I'll give you a guided tour of Adrian White's humble abode.'

She followed him.

'What we're coming into now is the communal area, but White's never been in here. He doesn't want to know any of the other patients.' His voice dropped. 'Which suits us just fine.'

Clay saw two very ordinary-looking psychopaths, one in his forties and the other in his fifties, playing snooker and getting on with the business of killing the only thing they now could. Time. A handful of other men were scattered around the room, some listlessly watching the game unfold, some with headphones listening to music, others staring into space and reading broadsheet newspapers.

'The snooker guys? Anyone I should know?' she asked.

'The snooker guys aren't patients, DCI Clay, they're psychiatric nurses.'

She laughed.

'What's so funny?' His face softened into a winning smile.

'The joke's on me,' said Clay. 'How many on the ward, including White?'

'Fifteen.'

The place felt largely empty.

'Where's everyone else?'

'Work. Within the hospital grounds. We've got an electronics workshop, a handicrafts department. The patients' rooms are down that corridor.' Taylor pointed at various anonymous doors and stopped at the one signed 'Meeting Room'.

'This is where you're talking to him. Alone. We'll be outside.'

Adrenaline pumped through her.

Taylor took out his phone and hit speed dial. He spoke as his colleague connected. 'You and Danny, where are you? You were supposed to with us at the Meeting Room.' Pause. 'Yeah, I'm there now with her. Right now this second. Yeah, well, be faster than that.' He hung up. 'There'll be three of us outside when you go in, but there's nothing to worry about.'

'Anything I need to know?' asked Clay.

'We haven't had a single incident with him in all his time here. But, yeah, one thing. He hasn't worn clothes at all for seven years. It's part of his religious observation. We had a Sikh nurse at the time. White said, 'Make me wear clothes but make him take off his turban first.' Taylor dropped his voice to a whisper. 'Wait here. I'll go and get him.'

In her mind's eye she recalled Adrian White's face, impassive across a wall of flame. They were on the top floor of a derelict building, she with her back against a windowless wall and he close by a door that led out to the stairs and the front door.

'Come and get me, Eve!'

She recalled the smile on his face, the glimmer in the dead cast of his eyes and the certain knowledge that she was going to die.

The smoke curled inside her, burning her throat and filling her body with poison.

She had no choice. She hurtled through the flames, the smell of her singed hair more sickening than that of the dense smoke around her, her eyes shut tight, her face hot, like she was passing through one world into another. Then she was on the same side of the room as White, the safe side, the side with a way out.

She opened her eyes. He puckered his lips and blew a

stream of breath in her direction, making a gesture with his hand like a priest administering a blessing.

'Eve, you stood in the flames and yet you are untouched, unharmed.'

'I ran through them.' She glanced at her hands, her clothes, warm but not burned.

'Did you?'

Silence, then the sound of approaching feet.

She held her breath and released it slowly.

'Eve.' His voice was exactly as it sounded in her head, when things he'd said to her sprang into her mind from nowhere, from her darkest, secret places. 'Eve, I'm so glad you could get here so soon. How are things in the Red River City?'

She turned towards his voice.

White smiled at her. His eyes were dead. His dreams were not.

12.15 pm

Adrian White.

From the other side of a heavy wooden table, Clay faced the man known around the world as the Baptist.

His hair was now long and crow black, but there were occasional strands of pure white. His naked back was broad and as flat as a wall, smooth and toned, the muscles clearly defined beneath his flawless skin.

The so-called aura that the journalists covering the trial had written about surrounded him like an invisible shield. Clay's rational mind denied this aura existed, but, faced with him after so many years, there was something that separated him from the time and place in which he existed and she knew it came from a personal truth that lived deep inside him. All that mattered was his twisted faith. Having neither fear nor love for anything human, he was exempt from the rules that bound ordinary people. Locked up until his dying day, he was freer than a bird. Psychiatrists labelled him criminally insane. He called himself a Satanic saint and prophet.

'Time has been kind to you,' said White, his voice light as if he'd just bumped into her at a cocktail party. 'Are you enjoying motherhood and married life?'

Clay locked eyes with him. A sickly heat spread within her at the same time as a coldness raised goose bumps on her skin.

Physically, he'd hardly changed at all, but she had no desire to return his compliment.

'You kept your maiden name...?'

'For the purposes of work.'

With a tiny gesture of his left hand, he beckoned her to lean in closer. She didn't move a muscle. Clay saw the black stars tattooed across his hairless hand and fingers: his map of the shift that would occur in the universal heavens when the time came for everything to change.

He had lived in Ashworth, saying little and doing less. She had got married and given birth to a son. One September, he had gone on a month-long hunger strike, claiming it was religious observation, a fast. She had led an ever-changing team of detectives, catching twelve murderers. He had been diagnosed with a brain tumour that baffled doctors when it shrank and disappeared of its own accord. She had tried to unearth the missing pieces of her early life, but they too had disappeared.

On either side of his heart, was a pair of jet-black tattoos.
1   7

'You don't know how pleased I am to see you, Eve.'

He smiled and it sharpened the effect of his eyes. An occasional glimmer of life would move beneath their waxy surface like a little fish shifting just below the stillness of a pond. At White's trial, even Edward Carter QC, the Crown Prosecution Service's most successful barrister, had lost his rhythm at several points during his cross-examination.

'Remember what my last words to you were?'

'No,' she lied.

As he was taken down to the cells, cuffed to two police officers, Adrian White had stared across the crowded courtroom, his eyes fixed on Clay and nothing else. Journalists speculated that there was some sort of bond between him and the woman who had hunted him down.

'The Red Cloud will rise from the belly of the city and when the Red Cloud rises, the river will run with blood.' His words rang out across the silent courtroom like the coded message of a secret lover.

The memory made her scalp feel like it was crawling with lice. She resisted the urge to scratch her head. Stillness was her only option. Anything else would immediately be seen as a sign of weakness.

'What do you want to talk about?' asked Clay.

'Oh, this and that.'

Slowly, White rose to his full height, six foot six.

'Tell me about *this and that*, Adrian.'

'Let's change places, Eve. Sit in my seat.'

'I don't want to.'

'I'm speaking metaphorically.' He towered over Clay and although he didn't move, the space between them felt like it was shrinking. 'I want you to see things from my point of view. That's what you do, isn't it, Eve? See things from other people's perspective, to try and bring the wicked to justice.'

With each word, the volume of his speech dropped and by the time he'd stopped speaking, Clay doubted whether the nurses outside the door could hear anything of what he was saying.

She had to tilt her head to keep eye contact and, as the moments drifted by, she understood why the living closed the eyes of the dead as a reflex action. Looking at him was like staring death in the face.

'Information,' said Clay.

'Yes?'

'Carolina Hill—'

'Who?'

'The social worker who you saw this morning. She said you had some information for me.'

'He died soon afterwards.'

She knew that was a reference to Edward Carter, prosecuting counsel, recognised the diversionary tactic from over a hundred hours in the interview suite.

'Are you playing games with me?'

'Absolutely not.'

'Then I'd like to hear this information you have for me relating to my current case.'

'Did you know I was diagnosed as a paranoid schizophrenic?'

'It's the reason you're in a hospital and not on a Category A wing at Durham or some other prison.'

'It's an incorrect diagnosis.'

'Information, Adrian. Now.'

Slowly, he sat down and looked over her shoulder at the wall.

'Can you see that little window?'

'I saw it on the way in,' she replied. She had absolutely no intention of looking over her shoulder or turning her back on him for a second.

'That was very observant of you, Eve, but then again, that's just one of your many talents. It's just like the one in my room. But just how observant are you? To what degree can you *see*?'

At the edge of her vision, she saw a pair of eyes peering through the observation slot in the doorway and then the slot closed.

'Tell me about last night, Eve.'

'No, you tell me what you claim to know.'

'All things have a beginning, including the end. Last night, the end of all things began with a signal that called *you* to its heart. Are you listening?'

'I'm listening.'

He tilted his head and looked up at the ceiling. As he swallowed, his Adam's apple rose and fell, reminding her of a snake consuming the living body of another creature.

The Baptist dropped his head and she was there, ready to meet his gaze.

'What did you do with my books? *The Elemental. The Matriarch. The Beginning of the End of Time.*'

'After the trial ended, your property was put in a central store for evidence. It's standard procedure.' *And because the thirty-three people we convicted you of murdering were not all of your victims*, thought Clay. *There were more, many more.*

'That works in your favour.' Something tiny moved in the darkness of his pupils. 'Ask me the question that's crawling beneath your scalp, Eve.'

'How do you know there were six victims?' she asked.

'Six?'

'How do you know that?'

'There'll be one survivor at the next one.'

'Are you in contact with the perpetrators?'

'A hostage, if you like. I'm in contact with myself. Now I'm in contact with you. And that is all.'

'How do you know there'll be another killing?'

'It'll be tonight, Eve. Another family. Do you need reading glasses? Remember that day, right at the end of my trial, when I told Mr Edward Carter QC he was going to die shortly from a massive cardiac arrest and the judge cleared the court and unleashed a barrage of fury against me. That was the best part of the whole trial and no one was there to see or hear it.'

'Carter was twenty stone and a heavy smoker. That prediction, that piece of theatre, doesn't make you Nostradamus.' Clay leaned closer. 'I haven't come here to talk about the past.'

'You've come here for a vision of the future.'

'So, where exactly?' asked Clay.

'Where what?'

'Where's this killing you're predicting?'

'I do not predict, I prophesy.'

'Where do you prophesy it's going to happen?'

'Right under your nose, Eve.'

She noticed something in his face, a closing down of the muscles beneath his skin, something the dead sheen of his eyes could never have given away. It was an almost invisible shift that she'd come to know over the days and weeks of interviewing him. He was drifting away, sinking back inside himself and time was against her.

'There was something I didn't see back then about you, about *the Baptist*. In a world that had no vision, you had a vision, not just of the future but of the entire scope and scale of time. Tell me about that vision and I'll go back and read about it in your prophetic books.'

'Did you see the sky last night as you chased through the darkness looking for what little light you could find?'

'Yes, it was dark and full of snow.'

'Says she who has eyes but cannot see. Go to the ground and work your way up.'

She zoned in on her memories of the dark hours of the previous night.

'What was the colour, Eve?'

She saw three generations of bodies at the bottom of the stairs in the Patels' hall. Upstairs, the bloody shapes on the walls of the Patels' home danced through her mind.

'Red.'

'Look higher,' he whispered.

'The sky?'

'Go on.'

'The park, Calderstones Park.'

White clapped rapidly five times and another second was gone forever.

'Don't daydream, Eve. You only have me for a certain amount of time. The sky?'

'The sky turned red some time before dawn.'

'Did you see the cloud?'

'Yes, I did see a red cloud.'

'How was it moving?'

'It was rising.'

'Where?'

'To the east.'

'Did you read my books or did you skim and scan them?'

'Guide me further,' she said.

'Guide yourself, Eve.'

'This red cloud...' Clay pressed. 'Is it the marker of the Beginning of the End of Time?'

Silence.

'Yes.'

As he spoke, she felt his breath across the top of her head and heard the sound of the door opening rapidly. The Baptist had closed down the space across the table.

'Go away,' she called to the nurses.

The Baptist whispered in her ear, 'How long did Mr Edward Carter QC live for after the end of my trial?'

Seven weeks, she thought.

'Stay perfectly still, Adrian!' said Taylor.

'Walk away, DCI Clay!' Another voice.

'It's going to be another busy night for you, Eve. But for now,' said Adrian White, his eyes closing with unnatural slowness, 'time is up. Six? Make that seven.'

She walked past him and, as she reached the door, White said, 'Give my love to the fruit of your womb. They'll do anything to get your attention, Eve.'

She stopped.

'What do you mean?'

White remained seated, still as stone, and Clay knew he wasn't going to say another word.

Richard Taylor closed the door of the Meeting Room and sent his colleagues away with a nod of the head. 'He could have killed you,' he said. 'He was close enough to do that. It would have taken him one second.'

She saw the dark sky above Calderstones Park and, in the shifting patterns of night, the Baptist's language crystallised inside her head.

'The Red Cloud will rise from the belly of the city and when the Red Cloud rises, the river will run with blood.'

Outside the walls of Ashworth Psychiatric Hospital, Clay sat at the wheel of her car and washed down two painkillers with a mouthful of Evian to stem her banging headache.

She needed to see Sandy Patel, to ask if the notion of a red cloud had any significance in his life or the life his immediate family used to have.

Clay scrolled through her contacts and came to the 0151 landline she'd stored for Sandy's bolthole.

After three rings, the call connected.

'Hello?'

'Mrs Price?'

'Yes?'

'Detective Chief Inspector Eve Clay.' She slipped from the aggressive state of mind needed for dealing with Adrian White into the gentle mode reserved for victims, their friends and relatives.

'Oh, hello, Mrs Clay.'

'I was wondering if I could have a word with Sandy.'

'Sandy? He's not here.'

'He's not with you?'

'I thought...we all did...we all thought he was still with you, assisting with your enquiries, that's why we didn't ring him.'

Clay checked the panic rising inside her.

'If he shows up, call me immediately. In the meantime, phone round all the possible places where he might be. Your son and Sandy have friends in common, don't they?'

'Lots.'

'Call them all, see if he's paying someone an unscheduled visit.'

'Is everything all right?'

'I just need to know where he is, in case I need to talk to him.'

Clay was on the phone to Stone within moments.

'Karl, I need you to find Sandy Patel. Start in Calderstones Park and work your way outwards.' She checklisted all the other open spaces in the neighbourhood. 'The Municipal Golf Course, Allerton Towers, Camp Hill, Reynolds Park...'

'How long's he been AWOL?'

'Last time I saw him was around ten past nine this morning.'

She closed down the call. The clock on her dashboard read 1.03 pm.

Inside her bag on the passenger seat she caught a glimpse of Sandy Patel's packet of cigarettes.

And within seconds she was in fourth gear with the speedometer rising rapidly.

DS Gina Riley found a man called Barry Hill who she'd never previously heard of but who was, she realised as she waited for him to answer his phone, probably one of the most significant human beings in her life. Google threw up Hill's name as the regional sales director for Liverpool and the north-west of England of Shoe World, the largest distributor of footwear in the United Kingdom.

Riley, the owner of one hundred and eight pairs of shoes, had never imagined that her private obsession would one day mesh with her professional life. She was researching every angle with enthusiasm and confidence.

As Barry Hill's mobile number rang, she looked at the full-scale reconstruction of the size 2 print she'd drawn and thought about its diamond-within-a-diamond pattern. To the best of her knowledge it didn't look like the sole of a formal shoe.

The phone rang on and on as she scrolled through Google images of footwear soles on her mobile.

'We could do with that...who was that woman...?' said DC Ryan, two desks away.

'Imelda Marcos,' Riley telegraphed. Ring ring.

'That's the one.'

Riley paused scrolling and opened up a raised diamond pattern on a black leather sole. Russell and Bromley black suede ladies' slip-ons. But it didn't have the continuous pattern of the print she was looking for.

'Hello?'

'Barry Hill?'

She could hear cars speeding past him and she figured he'd pulled up on the hard shoulder of some motorway.

'Speaking.'

From the mannered and genial tone of his voice, Riley marked him down as middle-aged, from Warrington, probably a heavily built bruiser.

'My name's Detective Sergeant Gina Riley, Merseyside Constabulary.'

'Oh yes?' There was a pronounced note of surprise. 'Did you say *Sergeant* Gina Riley or *Detective* Sergeant?'

'*Detective* Sergeant Gina Riley.'

'How can I help you?'

'It's not an easy one, but if anyone can help, you're the *man*.' She allowed a moment for the flattery to get him on board. 'We need to identify a specific piece of footwear from the pattern on the sole of a shoe left at a crime scene. You seemed like the person to come to.'

She heard the double click of a cigarette lighter and the rise in the background traffic as his window came down.

'You know how many pairs of shoes were manufactured in the UK last year?'

'5 million made by 5000 people working in the shoe trade according to the British Footwear Association,' said Riley, watching as DC Ryan wiped the drip from his nose with one hand and scrolled with the other.

'Well done.' Barry Hill sounded impressed. 'With unknown

millions of pairs imported from competitive sources around the world. It's a big ask, but I'll do my best to help. Can you describe the pattern to me?'

'A thin diamond, surrounded by a space and with a broad diamond bordering it. The pattern might repeat across the sole. Maybe, maybe not. It's a small shoe, size 2.'

'Size 2. Be a kid's shoe. If it was a kid, then was it a burglary?'

'Yeah, it was a print on a windowsill at a burglary.'

'Little bastard, whoever he is.' Hill spoke with the grit of righteous indignation.

'He?'

'Fewer than one per cent of burglaries are committed by females. Size 2 is the average size for eight- to ten-year-old boys. It's possible from the pattern you've described that it's not a formal shoe and if it's not a formal shoe it could be unisex leisure footwear.'

'You're good with your crime stats, Barry.'

'Someone has to chair the Neighbourhood Watch.'

'Unisex. Leisurewear. Can you pin it to a specific shoe?'

'It could be one of dozens.' She heard him exhale a long stream of smoke, and in the background the drone of traffic slashing up the salty spray of the gritted motorway.

'What about the *indents*, the gaps between the diamonds?'

'Come again?'

'There must be a significant indentation between them because the shapes are so clearly defined. Big chunky indentations.' He coughed. 'So you won't be dealing with a leather sole. It's going to be rubber or plastic. Some material that's pliable. Like I said, it's going to be a plimsoll or a trainer.'

No one in their right mind, thought Riley, *would go out in weather like that in* plimsolls. *But then again*...Images from the Patels' home fast-forwarded through her mind.... *they clearly weren't right in the head.*

As Barry Hill's window rose up, the background din of traffic was bottled.

'Do you have any idea, Barry, what brand of trainer or plimsoll this might be?'

'Do you know how many brands there are out there? How many different shoes within each brand?'

'You're the king of the castle, Barry.'

He laughed a little too smugly.

'Go on!' She injected a note of amusement into her voice. 'What's the bad news, *chief*?'

'You've got a field of thousands. You can probably narrow it down into hundreds based on the pattern, but it could be a trainer that's years old and not being manufactured anymore. It could even be some Croatian trainer that's come in on the foot of some snotty-nosed little immigrant, some cheapo shite that not even Primark will touch, something right off the radar, as in it mightn't even fall in with the official imports on the UK stats.'

'Where do I begin, Barry?' He was quiet. The background noise was gone and she wondered if he'd hung up, triumphant. 'Barry?'

'I'm thinking. Have you got a picture of this footprint?'

'Yes, we have a reconstruction based on a partial print.'

'Send it to my mobile.'

Bad idea. He was knowledgeable, but she didn't want a unique piece of evidence being trophied in some pub.

'Can't.'

'Why?'

'Official Secrets Act.'

'No *shit*?'

'*Shit.* I can meet up with you. Where are you heading, Barry?'

'Kirkby Industrial Estate. Our central distribution ware-house.'

She did a quick reckoning in her head. The M57 and the East Lancashire Road, and in foul weather conditions. She hated those roads at the best of times.

'Shit, yeah!' said Barry, suddenly pleased.

'What is it, Barry?'

'Rupert Baines.'

'Who's he?'

'He works in my warehouse in Kirkby Industrial. You've got to see him to believe him.'

'What's your warehouse address and postcode for the satnav?'

'Lees Road, L33 7SE.'

'I'll meet you there,' she said, standing, looking at the clock on the wall and gathering her bag from the floor.

'I'll be there late afternoon, four-ish.'

'What time does Rupert finish?'

'Five. I'll tell security to expect you.'

'Make sure you do, Barry. Take me to your Rupert.'

She could hear him laughing as she hung up and headed swiftly for the door.

32

3.35 pm

Darkness came before four o'clock. Clay could have screamed with frustration as she negotiated the thickening rush-hour traffic heading into south Liverpool.

As she weaved through the stream of cars on Mather Avenue, her iPhone, on hands free, rang out. It connected to a number she didn't recognise.

'DCI Clay, it's Professor Andrew Bailey, Linguistics Department, University of Liverpool. DS Stone told me to call you with my findings.'

'Thank you for getting back to me so quickly. You've analysed their *language*?'

'I've been listening to it all day. I've given the drives back to DS Stone, along with a cleaned-up copy, and I've wiped all traces of the original from our recording systems. He asked me to call you.'

'I appreciate it.'

Snow fell past the tall white streetlights like dark stars crashing to the earth's surface.

'Two things about this synthetic language. Phonetically, it's recognisable and these are the blends I've detected.'

'Email all this to me, please.'

'I already have done. Ka, ri, sa, a den,. Five distinct sounds.

The mouth clicking? There's a language spoken by fewer than a thousand people in Tanzania, the Hadza. Their language uses a range of clicks for consonants. There are other click-speaking tribes, hunter-gatherers who've hung on to their lands and cultural identities. It could be your perpetrators are imitating some primitive language system using their own synthetic language.'

'How do we know clicking featured in primitive languages?'

'Mitochondrial DNA. Genetic data. The different click-speakers share rare mtDNA and Y chromosomes that indicate common ancestry going back tens of thousands of years. They click because they've hung on to their ancestral languages.'

Clay thought of Kate Patel's face, her crushed skull, the superstitious removal of a dead woman's eyes. Primitive.

'I moved away from human language and turned to Morse code but drew a blank because there was no clear distinction between long and short signals; it was just repetition. I ran it through and looked at it as sound waves and there was no correlation with anything in nature, from birdsong to whale music. Dolphins – I thought I was onto something, but no. The only consistent and constructive thing I can say about the mouth clicking is that between each phonic sound there were five or ten random beats. I've memorised a section. Would you like to hear?'

'Very much so.'

'Ka...' She counted his clicks, ten uneven but identical sounds. '...Ri...' Ten more clicks with no rhythmic pattern. '...Sa.'

She pulled up at a red light at the junction of Mather Avenue and Booker Avenue and glanced at the billboard on the wall of the United Reform Church, a poster of the planet as a spinning football and the words: 'Man United With God'.

She shook her head and almost laughed bitterly.

'DCI Clay, are you still there?'

'I'm taking on board what you've told me.'

'I really can't think of anything else or, to be quite honest, any*one* else who could help you further on this one.'

'I can't thank you enough, Professor Bailey.' The traffic light turned green and she turned left onto Booker Avenue. 'Thank you for calling.'

They either were or wanted to be profoundly different from the rest of humankind. Clay was seized by a wave of light-headedness and nausea.

Her iPhone rang. On the display: 'Stone'.

She let it ring out as she drove on to Calderstones Park, her instincts screaming that DS Karl Stone was calling with bad news about what lay a few hundred metres ahead of her.

33

3.43 pm

Yewtree Road was closed at the junction with Allerton Road. Clay flashed her warrant card at the constable manning the closure and negotiated her car around the marked vehicle parked sideways across the road.

As she drove up to the entrance of Calderstones Park, through the fog she saw the flashing lights of a stationary ambulance and bodies milling on the narrow pavement.

She pulled up, parked and walked along the gritted road.

The back doors of the ambulance were open but so were the back doors of the black mortuary vehicle just ahead of it.

The crackle of static on the officers' walkie-talkies and the disembodied voices leaking through the air combined into an ethereal soundtrack.

'Excuse me, madam.' A constable was directly ahead of her, approaching through the fog. He was young and in her way. When he made out her features, he said, 'I'm sorry, DCI Clay, I thought—'

'Never apologise for doing your job,' she said, turning into the park, onto the short stretch of path that led to the lake.

She dipped under the crime-scene tape stretched out between two oak trees. Stone was at the railings, his back turned to the busy action behind him, looking out, waiting for her.

'Eve? I tried to call you. Your line was busy and then...'

'Have we found him?'

'We found the body of a young male. We don't know if it's Sandy Patel for definite.'

I do, she thought. 'Where?'

'Come with me.'

They walked in silence through the open gate and on to the lake. The all-black form of a frogman stood out in the gathering of bodies on the west bank. A bird, disorientated by the white arc lights that illuminated the scene, rattled out a song from the island in the middle of the lake and Clay saw a sign reading: 'Caution! Thin Ice'.

She recognised a young mortuary technician from the crime scene at Sandy's family home.

On a wheeled trolley nearby was the shape of a man in a zipped body bag.

'What do we know?' asked Clay.

'There was a crack in the ice, a hole with chunks of ice floating in it. The frogger accessed the water underneath, pulled the body out and brought him to the bank. Male, late teens, early twenties.'

Clay stood over the body bag and pulled its zip down thirty centimetres.

His eyes were open and startled, his lips parted against his teeth, which were clenched against the unforgiving cold. Black particles from the lake dotted his teeth like black stars against a white sky.

'I'm giving up.' Sandy's words banged through her head like bullets.

'This is Sandy Patel,' she said. She blocked the swell of

emotion and focused on practicalities. 'Let's get him to the mortuary.' His face was wet, and dirty water dripped onto the bag's shiny surface.

'*Six?*'

'Go round the neighbours' and see if anyone's got CCTV looking out onto the park entrance, or any other footage of anyone on Yewtree Road between eight and ten this morning.'

She thought of the figure she'd glimpsed between the trees as she spoke with Sandy in the Linda McCartney Playground.

'What was that, Eve?'

'*Make that seven.* Something White said as I was leaving him.'

34

4.05 pm

Shoe World's warehouse was more than a cathedral to footwear. To Riley it was a corner of heaven.

It was a cavernous place, its grey metallic walls lined with thousands of boxes of shoes under a vast high ceiling; stark fluorescent lights overhead and cold concrete floors underfoot.

DS Gina Riley smiled as she turned a slow circle in the centre of the warehouse, the wall to the left piled high with shoe boxes, the back wall having its treasures added to, the right wall with its much smaller collection, boxes being loaded onto trolleys to be taken to the trucks waiting at the huge open doorway.

'Pretty impressive, eh?' said Barry Hill with a glow of pride.

She'd nailed his physical size and attitude from their time on the phone, but his face wasn't hard as she'd pictured. Barry Hill, for all his bluster, looked gormless, with curly hair that reminded her of a circus clown.

A tall thin man in his late twenties emerged from a door tucked into the right-hand wall. He was dressed in a blue linen coat and moved awkwardly towards Riley as if walking was a newly acquired skill.

'This is Rupert. He's not right in the head,' said Barry clearly and within the warehouseman's hearing. 'But he's *harmless*.'

'Thanks for that, Barry,' said Riley. 'You can go now.'

'What?' he laughed.

'I want to talk to the *man*.'

Barry glared at her before walking away, and she read his mind. *Ungrateful cow!*

Rupert stopped, stood three metres away, indicated the air between them. 'Personal space,' he said. His voice was a little mechanical, but there was something childlike in his eyes.

'I agree, Rupert, personal space is very important when dealing with new people.'

'Can I see your warrant card?'

She held the small white card out as far as she could and he said, 'Perfect, Detective Sergeant Gina Riley. How can I help you?'

She looked around at the thousands of boxes, each of which contained dozens of smaller boxes, and said, 'I'm told you're an expert on the subject of shoes.'

'Yes, I am a world authority on that subject. I would like to go on *Mastermind*, but my general knowledge is laughable. And though I am not in a good mood, I will assist you in your investigation into shoes.'

'I'm sorry to hear that, Rupert. What's put you in a bad mood?'

'This morning I took delivery of five thousand pairs of training shoes from our supplier in Fuzhou, south-west China. I opened the boxes to check the contents and to count them, of course, which is one of my many roles in the Shoe World Warehouse. They had only supplied four thousand nine hundred and ninety-nine pairs. I had to go and see Mrs Milligan in the office to make a formal complaint.'

A light went on inside Riley's head. Rupert Baines? Asperger syndrome.

'I can see that that amuses you, Detective Sergeant Gina Riley of the Merseyside Constabulary.'

'I'm smiling because I think you can really help me out. I think the inaccurate supply of shoes was at worst dishonest and at best sloppy work.'

'Yes, I agree with you.' He stepped forward a couple of paces. She copied him.

'What have you got?' he asked.

She stretched out her arm and he took her drawing of the reconstructed sole. He stared at it, looked over the top of the sheet at Riley, and looked hard again at the image.

'Well,' he said, at length. 'It's either a plimsoll or a trainer. What did you base the drawing on?'

'On a partial footprint.'

'In that case...' He offered the sheet back.

'You can keep the drawing, Rupert, but you mustn't show it to anyone.'

He touched his head. 'I have a photographic memory.'

She took it back. 'What do you think, Rupert?'

'It could be one of eighty-three types of casual shoe. I'll have to check.'

She looked around at the mountainous boxes. 'Could you check it now, Rupert? I know this may take time, but I'd be most grateful, pretty please.'

'Don't soft-soap me, Detective Sergeant Riley. Yes, I will check now, but it could take many hours.'

'My card.' She handed it to him, he glanced at it, handed it back and rattled off the eleven digits of her mobile phone number.

'I shall get back to you the minute I confirm my suspicions.'

'What do you suspect, Rupert?'

'Oh. Just about everything, Detective Sergeant Riley.'

He stepped forward and held out his hand. She shook it, his hand warm and loose.

'Have a safe journey home and, rest assured, you will be hearing from me.'

'Thank you, Rupert, I look forward to that,' she said to his departing back.

'Fabriqué en Chine!' he called, without turning, his voice echoing in the vastness of the warehouse.

'Made in China?' she replied.

'As are most things in the world nowadays.'

The snow stopped suddenly as Clay parked on the white expanse of Kings Dock. A cold wind whipped from the river as she walked towards Liverpool One and the imposing brown block that was Merseyside Police Headquarters.

She felt her phone vibrate in her hand but concentrated on getting across the road and onto the pavement outside HQ.

'Eeeehh!' A seven-year-old child shrieked as he was half-dragged to the other side by his mother.

'Don't look!' she commanded. He ignored her.

Clay followed his gaze. A seagull lay in the road, its white body and wings broken by the wheel of a car, its eyes open, staring up at the frozen sky. It put her in mind of deadness, of Adrian White's eyes and his unfathomable, unblinking stare.

She looked up. There was a chorus of screeching in the sky as a gathering of gulls circled overhead, calling out over and over what sounded like, *Beware...Beware...*

Her phone stopped ringing.

'*When you look into shadows, you look into mirrors. When you look into mirrors, what do you see?*'

As the traffic throbbed at the red light to her left, she felt the glaring sodium lights above the broad lanes of tarmac beating back the darkness like cold fire. She clutched her coat at the collar, consumed by the memory of the burning room where she'd faced Adrian White and how her mind had blanked out as she shot through the wall of flame.

On the other side of the flames, face to face with Adrian White. Darkness. He'd offered no resistance as she cuffed his hands. The heat of a hundred fires burning. Darkness. Hands behind his back, she led him quickly down the stairs. Darkness. Running, dragging him with her as the burning building started to collapse behind them.

The first words he spoke to her were now branded onto the surface of her brain, like the mark of a slave owner.

'When you look into shadows, you look into mirrors. When you look into mirrors, what do you see?'

She walked through the HQ's front entrance and checked in with the civilian receptionist.

'We've got what you've called for, DCI Clay,' he said, stooping.

He handed her a seventy-five-litre blue stacker box.

'And I'm to tell you that everything else has been forwarded to your laptop at Trinity Road.'

She lifted the stacker box and felt the weight of Adrian White's three manuscripts inside. She recalled her first sight of them, as she led a raid into his nondescript terraced house on Nicander Road, and the mind-bending hours spent trawling through the obscure outpourings of his Satanic faith.

The Matriarch.

The Elemental.

The label sellotaped to the lid of the box read simply: 'Adrian White. Crime number: 0514335654'.

The Beginning of the End of Time.

Outside, as she walked within the incessant roar of the Dock Road traffic, it was as if being close to the documents peeled away layers of time. She remembered the curse at the end of *The Elemental*, the words White had spoken as he was led away to the cells.

She found herself saying them, her breath condensing in the freezing air.

'The Red Cloud will rise from the belly of the city and when the Red Cloud rises, the river will run with blood.'

As she crossed back towards the Albert Dock, she peered over the top of the box. The dead gull was gone and the sky above was full of unfallen snow and silence.

Clay placed the stacker box into the boot and slammed the door shut, her arms aching from the three-hundred-metre walk. There was a foul taste in her mouth and she guessed it was from the puff of the cigarette she'd taken to help Sandy Patel bond with her. It felt like a lifetime ago.

She closed the door against the bitter wind and looked out across the River Mersey at the illuminated tower of Birkenhead Town Hall and the Cammell Laird shipyard across the water on the Wirral. Behind her, the two cathedrals loomed against the thickening night sky like illuminated giants, houses of God with thousands of stained-glass eyes watching over the city.

In a hurry to get back to Trinity Road, Clay turned on the ignition, but as she did so she was seized by the unsettling notion that she had overlooked something significant. In her head she retraced her walk from the car to HQ and arrived at the point when she was crossing the road and her phone was ringing out.

She turned off the ignition and pulled her phone from her pocket.

'You have one new voicemail message sent today at 4.47.' Clay waited.

'Detective Chief Inspector Clay?' It was a well-spoken young woman. 'My name's Coral Drake. You came to our house this morning to talk to my mum and my little sister Faith.' In the background, Clay made out the sound of a ball bouncing. Wall. Floor. Bounce. Bounce. Silence. 'I was wondering if we could either come and see you or you could come and visit us? Faith and I will be at home all day. I'd be grateful if you could get in touch. Or I'll try you again later. Thank you.'

Clay went to press 7 to delete the voicemail but stopped and instead called the Drake family's number.

Three rings later, a voice on the other end. 'Yes?'

'Is that you, Faith?' She sounded much younger than she had face to face that morning.

'Who is this?'

'Detective Chief Inspector Eve Clay. Is your mother there, Faith?'

'No.'

'Is Coral there?'

'Coral, it's for you.'

As she waited, Clay glanced back in the direction of HQ. In the time it had taken her to collect the stacker box, some animal lover had picked up the dead gull to place it in the relative dignity of the nearest public bin. *An accident*, she thought, *and a small act of mercy. Nothing more, nothing less.*

'DCI Clay, thank you for calling back.'

'How can I help you?'

'Faith's remembered something. She wants to tell you something.'

'Coral, are you going to be at home within the next half hour?'

'We'll be waiting for you, DCI Clay.'

Thick flakes of ragged snow suddenly fell across Clay's windscreen in a sharp diagonal line.

The Baptist's books weighed down the back of her car.

An unnerving thought trespassed across her mind.

Time was about to collapse.

There were fifty-three entries in Kate Patel's address book. Detective Sergeant Karl Stone spoke with twenty-eight of the thirty-two within the Liverpool area. Four were dead lines. There were five families with children. And, in a call to Mrs Gillian Tanner, he had learned that there was one family with three children.

Outside the Tanner family's home on Ullet Road, at the back of Sefton Park, Stone parked half-on the pavement. The house was large, detached and well preserved, built for a wealthy Victorian ship owner in an era when Toxteth had been chic, elegant and the height of respectability.

He walked through the wide stone gateway, the gravel path shifting underneath the snow. From behind the decorative stained-glass panels on either side of the red front door, lights glowed against the gloom of the winter afternoon. Stone wished he was at home curled up with a good movie on the Horror Channel.

He rang the bell, smiled directly at the spy hole in the door and held his warrant card up so that whoever looked out could see it was a police officer.

The door opened and a white-haired woman asked, 'Yes?'

'Mrs Gillian Tanner?' He moved his warrant card a little closer. There was a disconnectedness about her.

'Yes.'

'I'm Detective Sergeant Karl Stone, Merseyside Police. We had a conversation on the phone half an hour ago...'

Footsteps. A thin black woman in a navy blue nurse's tunic stepped behind Mrs Tanner. The ID badge clipped to her breast pocket had a picture and her name. Cecilia Beaton.

'Police?' she said, examining his warrant card.

'May I come in?'

'I'm freezing,' said Mrs Tanner, turning and walking back inside.

'Come in,' said Cecilia. 'Have you come to see Gillian?'

'Yes. She said she had three children.'

'That's right. I don't know what you want, but I don't think it'll do you any good speaking to her.'

'Is there another Mrs Tanner in the house?' asked Stone, closing the front door and watching her turn into the front room. What he'd just seen and heard on the doorstep didn't add up to the woman he'd spoken with on the phone.

'There's only one Mrs Tanner.' Cecilia smiled and sighed. 'And that's more than enough.'

'I'm confused,' said Stone.

'She has lucid moments, but they're becoming fewer and further apart. Maybe I can help. I spend more time with her than her husband and kids. What do you want?'

'Bring me a pair of shoes, trainers if possible, belonging to each of Mrs Tanner's children please.'

Nurse Beaton looked at Stone as if he was insane.

'OK...'

5.06 pm

Mrs Tanner stared into the fire burning in the grate and appeared to either be ignoring or have forgotten that Stone was sitting adjacent to her on the large red leather sofa.

Stone looked at the soles of the trainers in spite of the fact that their sizes were 7, 5 and 4. The patterns were nothing like the diamond imprint on Mrs Patel's body.

Taking his coffee from Nurse Beaton, Stone couldn't remember the last time he'd been served a drink in a china cup and saucer.

'How long's Mrs Tanner had dementia?' he asked.

'Started about ten years ago. I've been with her for the past two.'

'She sounded great on the phone.'

'Little pockets of lucidity followed by exhaustion.'

'Tell me again how old the children are?'

'Seventeen, fourteen and twelve.'

He looked around. There was neither sign nor sound of any adolescents in the house.

'Becca and Dan, the oldest two, are out. In the park, so they say.'

'The other child?'

'Maisy's in her room.'

'She doesn't want to play out in the snow?'

Nurse Beaton shook her head. 'Maisy doesn't like the cold.'

'What time did you come on duty this morning?'

'Seven o'clock.'

'Where were the children?'

'Up and about. Their father's a disciplinarian, insists they're up before he leaves for work, doesn't want them sleeping through the day.'

Victorian ethos, Victorian home, thought Stone, taking in the room. Without the red leather suite, it could have been the set for a period drama.

'Does Mrs Tanner ever talk about the past?'

'She confuses the present with the past and the past with the present.'

'Does she still have friends calling?'

'No. People don't see the point. She never has visitors. This is a very isolated family, Detective Sergeant Stone.'

'Does she ever mention a family by the name of Patel?'

A little light went on behind Nurse Beaton's eyes.

'Now that rings a bell,' she said.

He allowed her time and space, then prompted, 'Kate and Hanif, the mother and father, Alicia—'

Her face fell. 'My God, the family in Aigburth? Mrs Tanner knows that poor family?'

'The Tanner family were in Mrs Patel's address book.'

Stone placed his cup and saucer down on the coffee table and stood up. He looked much older than he was in the huge framed mirror above the fireplace and the room behind him seemed twice as large. *Nothing is as it seems.* The words he wanted carving on his gravestone.

'Can I have a little look around, Cecilia?'

Before she could respond, he wandered out into the cavernous hallway. It was big enough to house his whole unkempt bachelor pad.

'Why did you come here exactly, Detective Sergeant Stone?' she asked as she followed him.

'We're trying to piece together as much information about the Patels as we can. When's Mr Tanner home from work?'

'It can be any hour.'

'Where does he work?'

'The Royal Hospital.'

'Doctor?'

'Management. That's all I know,' said Nurse Beaton. 'He's very secretive. He has strange ways.'

Great, thought Stone. *A direct link to the Patels, but she's demented and he's an odd bod.* Daniel and Gillian Tanner, their names in neat, linked print in Kate Patel's address book, from a time before dementia came to the Tanner's home and before the storm unleashed itself in The Serpentine.

'When will Becca and Dan be back?'

'When they're hungry.'

'Have you got a direct number for Mr Tanner at the Royal?'

'Yes, but I'm under strict instructions to use it only in the case of an emergency.'

'This is an emergency, Cecilia. Give me his work number and I'll deal with him.'

The sound of something metal slithered from the shadows at the top of the stairs. Stone watched as a steel Slinky landed on a stair and pulled itself down onto the next level under its own shifting weight. The Slinky kept descending and was followed by a pair of bare feet and the hem of a white nightdress just above the ankles. Stone turned to the nurse.

'Maisy?' he asked.

The girl stopped, hand on the banister, and peered at Stone for a fleeting moment. Then she turned and hurried back up the few steps to the upstairs landing.

He'd seen her face for long enough to ask, 'Maisy has learning difficulties?'

Cecilia nodded. 'She's non-verbal.' She handed him a piece of paper. 'Mr Tanner's work number.'

The sound of a key turning in the lock.

Becca and Dan raced into the hall, laughing, faces red and raw with cold, the freezing air pouring in with them. No sign of trauma or homicidal mania. Stone felt a surge of sympathy for them, growing up with the living death of a demented mother, a disabled sister and a father who sounded like a king-sized pain in the arse.

Becca stopped, registered Stone's presence with a quizzical frown.

'He's a police officer,' explained Nurse Beaton.

Stone focused on Becca. She was of a similar age to Alicia.

'What's this about?' asked Dan.

'Becca, do you know anyone called Alicia Patel?'

Deadpan, she eyeballed Stone. 'No, I don't know an Alicia Patel.'

'Is she a bank robber?' asked Dan, smiling.

'I wish she was,' replied Stone.

Neither of them reacted.

'Sandy Patel?'

'No,' they spoke in harmony.

'I don't know anyone called Patel,' said Dan.

'I've never even heard of them.' Becca directed the comment to her brother.

'Keep your voices down, your mother's sleeping,' said Cecilia.

Exuberance quashed, the teenagers tiptoed up the stairs to the safety of their rooms as Stone thanked Nurse Beaton and returned to the raw cold outside.

As he walked into the gathering darkness, the streetlights fired up, glowing amber along the roadside. He sat behind the wheel of his car, took out his phone and pressed 'Clay' on speed dial. As he watched the front door of the house, he reminded himself of two home truths.

Murderers, especially the most ruthless and prolific ones, seldom looked like murderers.

And no one ever, ever thought that they would become a murder victim.

As she arrived outside the Drake family home in Barnham Drive, Clay picked up the call from Stone.

'Where are you, Karl?'

'Ullet Road. The Tanner family. On the surface everything looks normal. But there's something bothering me and I can't explain what it is. There's a weird, weird atmosphere in the house.'

As the cold night tightened, Clay got out of her car and headed for the Drakes' front door. 'Ask Hendricks to organise a dig into the Tanners' background.'

As she spoke, Clay had the clearest sensation that she was being watched. She eyed the front of the house. There was no one there. The curtains were drawn.

'Eve? Eve, are you all right?'

'Yeah. I've got to go.'

She closed the call down and pressed record on her iPhone.

At the front door, she heard the thump of a ball against an upstairs wall and the bump as it bounced onto the floor. Wall. Floor. Bump. Bump. Silence. Regular as a slow heartbeat.

She rang the bell. The ball game stopped.

A light came on in the hall but the door stayed shut.

'Who is it?' It was Coral's voice, Faith's older sister, seventeen years old and nervous in her own home as so many other people would be when darkness gripped the city.

'It's DCI Eve Clay.'

'Yes, yes.'

A lock was unbolted, the door opened. With one eye, Coral looked out at Clay. Behind her, Faith walked down the stairs.

As Coral closed the door after Clay, she whispered, 'You will go easy on her, won't you? Faith's scared to death, the poor little thing.'

'Does your mother know about this?' asked Clay.

Coral shook her head. 'We can't call her when she's at work. She's doing a double shift. We're a single-parent family.'

Clay followed Coral into the front room. Faith was standing at the window. The little girl looked as if she had been crying and her face was red. She turned away.

'Come and sit next to your sister,' said Clay.

The TV was off. In the fireplace, lights glowed through the plastic replica of burning logs and coals, but they gave off no heat.

Coral guided Faith by the hand to the sofa. Clay shivered as she knelt down on the floor in front of Faith so she could make direct eye contact. She noticed how thin both girls were and wondered if, like so many young females, they felt obliged to be celebrity-slim.

'Is there something you want to tell me, Faith?' she asked.

Silence. Outside a speeding car hit a speed bump and the crash was like a bell tolling in the night.

'Faith,' said Coral. 'Just tell the truth. Tell DCI Clay what you told me.'

'I'm scared.'

'Don't be scared, Faith,' said Clay. 'If you tell me the truth, you'll be helping me and I'll protect you with all the powers I have.'

'It's about Mrs Harry's mobile phone. Nokia Eseries E63. Black with a silver-and-black on/off button and tiny little letters and numbers. I know who stole it.'

Lines of energy shot up and down Clay's spine as Faith sobbed into her sister's arms.

'Coral, do you know who took Mrs Harry's mobile phone?' Clay pressed.

'Yes, I do.'

'Faith,' said Clay, 'do you want your sister to speak for you?'

'Yes.'

Clay held Coral's unblinking gaze. 'Give me a name, Coral?'

'Jon Pearson. Jon and Faith were the last two children to be picked up on Friday.'

'Where does he live?'

'Five minutes from here.'

'What's his address?'

Faith spoke, but, through broken sobs, it was unintelligible.

Coral picked up Faith's blue book bag. She reached inside it and showed Clay a piece of paper with a childish drawing of a penis and a girl licking it.

'There's more to this than just a phone,' said Coral. 'He's been drawing obscene pictures and writing filthy messages and forcing them on her. He's harassing her.'

'I will deal with any related issues, Coral, but for now I need Jon Pearson's address. Immediately.'

'Sev-ven,' Faith managed to say.

'Go on,' urged Clay. Coral wrapped both arms around her sister.

'Ravenna Way.'

'Do you know why she didn't tell me this morning?' asked Clay.

'She's scared to death of him.'

Clay stopped recording and, making her way rapidly to the front door, called Hendricks. She opened the front door, was aware of someone behind her, watching. Hendricks connected.

'I've got a name and address for the person who took Mrs Harry's mobile phone.'

'Jon Pearson's threatened Faith with all kinds of horrific things,' said Coral.

Clay glanced back at her, then directed her attention to Hendricks. 'I'm round the corner from 7 Ravenna Way, Belle Vale. You know it, Bill?' She opened the door and stepped outside.

'It's sick and disgusting what he's said he'll do to her.' Coral followed her to the front door.

'Coral.' Clay turned. 'I'll deal with all that later, I promise, but I'm dealing with this now, OK?'

'OK. But I don't understand how a ten-year-old can know such sick things.'

Clay made her way to her car. 'I'll meet you there, Bill. Bring Riley. Call the duty magistrate and have them issue a search warrant.'

As she pulled away towards the junction with Childwall Valley Road, Clay glanced back. The sisters were in the doorway, watching from the step, lit by the dull glow of their narrow hall. And though it was dark, it seemed to Clay that they were both crying, holding on to each other as if they were in danger of drowning in thin air.

A phone call to Daniel Tanner's direct line at the Royal Liverpool University Hospital had drawn a blank. In his car outside the Tanners' home, Stone had counted forty rings with no reply and no answer machine kicking in.

On his way into reception at the Royal Hospital, a lard-faced man in a wheelchair with bilateral amputations and an unlit cigarette dangling from the corner of his mouth caught Stone's eye.

'Got a light, mate?'

Stone patted his chest, three fast beats. 'Fresh out, *mate*.'

'Arsehole.'

'Yes I've got one of them, but it's currently on a break.'

He showed his warrant card to the pretty blonde receptionist, her smile fixed, which reminded Stone that a course of teeth whitening could be the first step towards reviving his dormant love life.

'I'm looking for a Daniel Tanner.'

She typed quickly onto her laptop and said, 'Extension 3431. Want me to call him?'

'What floor?

'Eight.'

'Thanks.' He smiled back, tight-lipped, and moved through the bodies that milled around him, trying Tanner's number again.

After several rings, extension 3431 picked up.

'Hello?' A male voice.

'I'd like to speak to Daniel Tanner, please.'

'So would I. He showed up for work this morning and went home with a contagious stomach bug at nine o'clock.'

Stone's undefined suspicion about the Tanners twitched into a hunch.

'Who am I speaking to, please?'

'Detective Sergeant Karl Stone. Who are you?'

'Mr David Passmore. Vascular consultant. Daniel's our unit manager.'

'And you haven't seen him since nine o'clock?'

'No.'

'He didn't report back in for duty?'

'He's never off sick. He finds excuses to stay late. I think he prefers being at work to being at home. He looked upset. He's a man who doesn't show much emotion, but he was off-kilter this morning. I think the stomach bug was an excuse to get out.'

'Where would he go if he wasn't at home?'

'No idea. He only speaks when he has to and never talks about anything but work. But now, Detective Sergeant, I have to go. I'm due in theatre, emergency aneurysm.'

On his way back to the multi-storey car park, Stone dialled the Tanners' home landline.

'Hi.'

'Becca, it's DS Stone, the policeman—'

'Yes.'

'Is your dad home yet?'

A fully lit double-decker bus, the number 10, sprayed salty water into Stone's path.

'He doesn't get in till around seven.'

'Have you got my number, Becca?'

'It's on the display. Do you want me to get him to call you when he gets in?'

'Yes, please. Tell him to call me. It's very important.'

'Becca! Becca! Becca!' Her brother's voice called in the background, loud and urgent. 'Come and see the telly now!'

Stone heard her moving towards the television set, the sound growing louder the closer she came.

'As soon as your Dad gets in, Becca.'

'Becca, look!'

Stone heard the steady drone of a television set.

'That copper said, *Do you know Alicia Patel?*'

'Oh my God!' said Becca. 'That girl you mentioned, Alicia Patel – her picture's, like, on telly right now.'

'She was murdered last night, Becca. It's that serious. Please. As soon as your father arrives home, tell him to call me. And if he won't, for any reason, *you* call me and let me know he's home. I won't blow you up to your dad. Can you do that for me?'

'God, yeah, of course. Oh my God, all six of them. Yeah. I will. Honest to God.'

In moving to Liverpool from her five-bedroom detached house in St Helens, Mrs Pearson, mother of three boys and widow of a paedophile, had found a good place to hide.

Ravenna Way was buried in a warren of almost identical streets in Belle Vale. Grey houses faced and neighboured each other and there was no sign of anyone or anything moving. Clay drove slowly, looking at odd numbers and counting down from the mid thirties. The place felt like a ghost town.

Outside number seven, two cars pulled up behind her. In her wing mirror, Clay watched Hendricks and Riley emerge. She got out.

'I've got the warrant,' said Hendricks, showing his phone. 'Duty magistrate emailed it to me.'

In the dark, the wooden gate of the tiny front garden creaked as Clay stepped onto the path. She knocked.

Behind the pane of frosted glass, a light went on and a woman's figure headed towards the front door.

'Who is it?' She sounded utterly sick and tired of life.

'Police.'

'Oh God, no, not again.'

'Our brethren have clearly visited this flock before,' said Clay.

Mrs Pearson opened the door, her black hair parted along a line of grey roots and her face pinched and creased from years of heavy smoking. She made way for Clay, Hendricks and Riley to enter the small hall.

'What have they been up to now?' she shouted towards the front room. '*I said*, what have the stupid good-for-nothings been up to now?'

Silence was their answer.

A TV played too loudly, MTV headache music.

'Turn that down *now*!' For a small, prematurely withered woman, Mrs Pearson had a loud voice and whoever was watching the box obeyed immediately without objection.

'I don't know what's gone on in Belle Vale Shopping Centre today and I don't care either. Robbie and Vincent have been home all day.'

Clay opened the door to the front room.

Two teenage boys were slumped on separate armchairs, bathed in the vivid shifting colours of a dance-music DVD. The floor was littered with empty Lucozade bottles and grease-smeared paper bags from Sayers. Clay switched on the light and both boys turned to face her, blinking. The room hummed with the closed-in smell of two adolescent boys.

Clay sniffed the air. 'I think they may well have been in all day.'

They squinted.

'What the fuck?'

'Who are yah?'

Clay motioned to Riley, who walked into the room.

'OK, turn the TV off altogether, boys,' said Riley. She blocked the doorway and the TV was turned off.

'It's Jon we've come to see,' said Clay.

'Jon?'

Hendricks showed Mrs Pearson the warrant on his phone.

'What for?'

'Where is Jon?'

'In his room upstairs.'

Clay started up the stairs. One of the teenagers called, 'What's going on?'

'Sit down now!' Riley's voice, sharp as a razor and ready to slash.

Mrs Pearson hurried up the stairs after Clay. 'He's not like his brothers. He's a good boy. They were all good when we lived in St Helens. I blame Liverpool. I blame the people round here.'

Clay indicated one of four doors on the small landing. 'This his room?'

'What's he done?'

'We're investigating the theft of a mobile phone.'

'Jon wouldn't dare do a thing like that. He's frightened of the police. Not like his brothers. He cries and hides in his bedroom when the police call here.'

Clay knocked on the bedroom door. 'Jon Pearson?'

'He's frightened of his own shadow, for God's sake.'

'Yeah.' A timid little voice, babyish and full of uncertainty, filtered through the door.

'Tell him to open the door,' said Clay.

Mrs Pearson opened the door.

A ten-year-old boy dressed in Power Rangers pyjamas that he'd outgrown and with a dishevelled mop of red hair stood in the middle of the room.

'Who's she, Mum?'

'My name is Eve Clay and I'm a police officer with Merseyside Police.'

He looked bewildered and his eyes filled up immediately.

'We have a warrant to search your house, Jon. That means we can take up every floorboard until we find the thing we are looking for. You can make this much easier for everyone.'

'How?'

'By giving me the mobile phone.'

'What mobile phone?'

'The one you took from your teacher, the one you took from Mrs Harry's bag on Friday.'

'Mum?' He buried himself face first in his mother's body and started to sob. 'I don't know what she means, Mum. I haven't robbed anything ever.'

Clay glanced down the stairs. Hendricks was moving closer to the door of the front room, as the teenagers protested.

'I was in all night last night...'

'Wha'? Wha'? Wha' you saying?'

'Me ma'll tell yah.'

'I was in, OK, in!'

'Sit down!' barked Riley. 'Don't even think about intimidating me with your low-rent gangsta moves.'

Clay looked around Jon Pearson's bedroom. Liverpool FC bedspread. Clothes on the floor, including a Liverpool football shirt, three seasons out of date. Toys and junk from Poundland littering most of the surfaces. A battered Nintendo DS. The private space of a poor child whose sobbing was growing louder by the minute.

She walked into the stale air of Jon's bedroom. The wind pressed down noisily on the roof above her head. Her eye was taken by the navy blue V-necked jumper on the back of the only chair in the room. It had the St Bernard's RC Primary School logo stitched in gold on the breast. His tie lay over his jumper and his grey trousers on the seat of the chair.

From the blue of his jumper, her eye chased each piece of the room.

'Do you have a book bag, Jon?'

He nodded.

'Where is it?'

He shook his head.

'Did he bring his book bag home on Friday, Mrs Pearson?'

'Mrs Harry's a...She insists. He's scared of her. He's scared of everything.'

Clay walked out of the room and, standing in the narrow space of the upstairs landing, listened to the muted voices of Riley and Hendricks bombarding Robbie and Vincent Pearson with their loaded questions.

She heard the cistern behind the bathroom door to her left and focused on the other two doors. There was a smell of sour musk and cheese coming from the bedroom door nearest to her. Robbie and Vincent's boudoir.

Clay opened the door and turned on the light.

It looked like it had been ransacked by wolves. The walls were full, floor to ceiling, of pictures of half-naked models.

'I never go in there,' said Mrs Pearson. 'It's too depressing for words.'

Clay drifted deeper into the chaos, her eyes searching for the same shade of blue as Jon's school jumper. A corner of blue poked out from a tangle of twisted clothes left on the floor. She stooped.

A soft vinyl surface.

It was Jon's reading-book bag, his name inked on the pale blue name box. Clay picked it up.

'Jon, come here!'

She heard his tears as he approached. She faced him. 'Look at me, Jon. Did you have this with you in school on

Friday? Jon?' She raised her voice. 'Did you have this bag in school with you on Friday?'

'Yes.'

'And you brought it home, right, when school closed early?'

'Yeah.'

She focused on his mum. 'You picked him up from school on Friday, Mrs Pearson?'

'No, it were Vinnie. Broadgreen International School was already closed, see. Vinnie's a good lad really...'

Clay tore back the Velcro strips that sealed the flap to the bag.

'Don't!' said Jon, agitated. 'It's mine.'

Clay looked at Mrs Pearson and glanced inside.

'It's private!' His voice rose to a scream and he struggled against his mother, who held him back.

'Hendricks! Come up!' called Clay.

His feet were light as he ran up the stairs two at a time.

Clay edged past Mrs Pearson. Jon pleaded, 'On Dad's grave, I never stole a thing!'

Clay took Hendricks to one side and opened the book bag.

In a heap of scrap paper and against a slim reading book, there was a black mobile phone.

The whole house was quiet. The only sound was the traffic blown in on the north wind from Childwall Valley Road.

'Jon,' said Clay. 'You must tell the truth to—'

'Don't even think about it!' shouted Riley downstairs.

There was a dull thud from the front room and Jon's brothers screamed incoherently, their feet pounding.

The two boys spilled into the hall and raced towards the front door, Vincent wielding a baseball bat. They sprinted out of the house as Riley staggered from the front room. Hendricks was down the stairs in seconds, followed by Clay.

Riley propped herself up against the wall, unsure whether she was going to throw up or faint. A lump rose on her forehead and her eyes dithered.

Hendricks was out of the front door.

Clay held Riley by her armpits as she slid down to the floor.

'Little bastard...my bag...car keys...'

Her eyes rolled and the lights went out inside her head.

Upstairs, Mrs Pearson's screaming did nothing to cover the sound of Riley's car engine roaring away from the house.

As Clay called for back-up, she shouted, 'Get dressed, Jon Pearson. *Now!* You're coming with me. And Mrs Pearson, I want a list of names and contact details of all your sons' associates and friends.'

'But I don't know half the people they hang out with.'

'Just get me a list before the ambulance gets here or I'll do you for perverting the course of justice!'

42

6.59 pm

At one minute to seven, Daniel Tanner put his key in the lock of the door to his home in Ullet Road.

'Regular as clockwork,' muttered Nurse Beaton, putting on her coat in the hall. Overtime, at time and a half, began at one minute past seven and Mr Tanner had only been late twice in two years.

A tall, rotund man with a pot belly and sloping shoulders, Daniel Tanner caught his reflection in the hall mirror and lingered a moment.

Cecilia interrupted his thoughts. 'You know I'm going to be late in the morning? Dentist appointment.'

'Rebecca and Daniel will have to watch over their mother. Is she in bed now?'

'At half past six. As usual.'

'Hi, Dad!' Mobile phone in hand, Rebecca emerged from the front room. 'Dad, I've run out of credit on my phone.'

'Once your monthly allowance is gone, it's gone.' He held out his hand. 'Give it to me, Rebecca.' Only her eyes moved – towards the landline. 'If I catch you using the landline, Rebecca, I'll confiscate your mobile for a month.' She gave him her phone and ran up the stairs to her room.

'Good day at the hospital, Mr Tanner?'

'Same old. How were things here?' He checked the answer machine. '00 MSG'. Good.

'Eventful by our standards.'

'Did Gillian have one of her *moments*?'

'No, but she did have a visitor.'

'Oh? Who?'

'A police officer, Detective Sergeant Karl Stone. He wanted to ask Mrs Tanner about the Patel family in Aigburth. I think he went to the hospital to look for you.'

'He did, yes. I spoke to him briefly in my office.'

'What a terrible thing to happen.'

'Dreadful.'

Silence. Then the grandfather clock chimed seven.

'Your dinner's in the microwave, Maisy's had her bath, Rebecca and Daniel have been fine.'

'They stayed in all day, I hope, as per my instructions?'

'Of course. They wouldn't dream of disobeying you. I wouldn't let them, even if they wanted to.'

Cecilia opened the front door and watched a light snow shower pass across the cast of Ullet Road's streetlights.

'You're letting all the warm air escape, the heating.'

'Dock it from my wages, face-ache,' whispered Cecilia.

'I didn't catch that.'

'I got the impression you knew the Patels.'

Mr Tanner clenched his jaw and turned slightly. 'What's for supper?'

'Bully beef and chips.' She smiled. 'Beef casserole.'

She walked down the path, away from the Tanners', the snow pelting down on her head and a dead weight lifting from her back.

The phone in the hallway rang. Six rings later, the answer

machine kicked in. The automated message played out and there was a pause after the bleep.

'I'd like to leave a message for Mr Daniel Tanner. My name is Detective Sergeant Karl Stone and I came to the Royal today to see you. Unfortunately, you weren't there.'

The blood drained from Tanner's face.

'I'd like to come and see you first thing in the morning. Seven o'clock. I'll come to you. Ring me if there's a problem with that, but we do need to talk at the next possible opportunity. 07744 468768.'

No one will be answering the door to you, thought Daniel Turner as he deleted the message and unplugged the phone. Stone could press the bell and keep his finger there all day. *No one will be calling here.*

No one. No one. No one!

In the distance, from the incident room on the top floor of Trinity Road police station, Clay could see the illuminated structure of the Runcorn Bridge. It looked like the skeleton of a huge prehistoric beast, suspended in the mid-air darkness and buffeted by the snow travelling over the flat mud of the Mersey estuary.

On her desk were three literacy books from Mrs Harry's class, left open for her by Hendricks, with a note: *Best of the bunch.*

She checked the names on the covers.

Connor Stephens. Faith Drake. Donna Rice.

Clay opened Faith's book and noted the careful drawing of Joseph Williamson's face framed by an underground arch.

THE WILLIAMSON TUNNELS

JOSEPH WILLIAMSON (1769-1840) WAS A CHRISTIAN AND BELONGED TO ST THOMAS' CHURCH. HE WANTED TO HELP SOLDIERS WITH NO JOBS AFTER THE WAR WITH NAPOLYEOM. BECAUSE HE WAS KIND. SO HE PAYED THEM TO DIG TUNNELS UNDER THE GROUEND IN EDGHE HILL. BUT HE WAS ALSO A STRANGE MAN WITH FUNNNY LITTLE WAYS. LIKE COUNTING HIS WHEELBARROW COLLECTION AND LEAVING A WHEELBARROW IN HIS FRONT ROOM. HE LET ALL HIS WIFE'S BIRDS FLY AWAY.

Clay scanned Connor's and Donna's writing. It was the same information in different words.

She looked up at the six officers who were silently trudging through Adrian White's three large handwritten books. Pens in hand, they scribbled occasional notes into spiral-bound pads, looking utterly puzzled. Clay recalled her own confusion, years ago, as she'd tried to decipher what read like a stream of completely fractured consciousness.

Hendricks handed her a cup of coffee.

'How are you doing, Bill?' she asked.

'Sore pride. Belle Vale's a maze, but it's the Pearson boys' back yard. I reckon they lost me before I even turned on the ignition. What's the latest on Gina?'

'She's staying in overnight for observation. She put her hands up to block the blow from the baseball bat. Heavy bruising to the forehead, no fractures, but they're worried about a potential brain haemorrhage.'

'About Mrs Patel...The removal of her eyes...'

'Go on!' Clay sipped her coffee and waited.

'Remember I mentioned the American killer Charles Albright, how he removed the eyes from his victims after they'd died? There was no symbolism in it, it was simple barbarism. But given the graffiti at the Patels' house, and the connection with Adrian White, I'm going to make a speculative connection. Most religions have some sort of all-seeing Eye of Divinity – usually male. But it strikes me that our killers may see their Divine Eye as female. And, more specifically, matriarchal.'

'The Matriarch?' An inexplicable coldness ran through Clay.

'Perhaps.' Hendricks nodded. 'Could their Satanic divinity be female?'

It was as if Hendricks had opened a door and behind that door was an almost blinding white light.

'If it is, then why not a female counterpart on the other side? In taking Mrs Patel's eyes, they were symbolically blinding God. Concealing certain of their actions and asserting their absolute authority.'

Behind the light was a shape, moving closer to the door, a form at once alien and familiar, a shape that threatened to overwhelm Clay with forbidden knowledge that would split her brain in two and change the way she saw and understood everything.

'Let's keep this to ourselves,' she said. 'My instincts are telling me you're on to something. Keep spinning those plates.'

She raised her voice and addressed the officers trawling through White's manuscripts. 'Whatever you've seen or heard since we met up in The Serpentine last night, apply it to the concepts White comes out with in his writing. The murderers are going to hit again. Tonight, he said.'

'How was he?' asked Hendricks. 'The Baptist?'

'Physically well. Placid. Full of the joys of Satan.'

'No change there then,' said DS Stone. 'Did you look into those beady eyes?'

'If only I could down some Dettol and cleanse myself from the inside out.'

She nodded at White's books. 'As you may have realised by now, *The Elemental* is different to *The Matriarch* and *The Beginning of the End of Time.*'

'In what way?'

'*The Elemental* is a straightforward diary detailing his murder spree and how he used the elements, or the lack of them, to kill his victims. He either burned them to death, drowned them, buried them alive in the earth or strangled them.'

'Nice guy.'

'He also promised more to come when the so-called Red Cloud rises.' Clay paused and looked from one officer to the other. 'As you may recall me telling you before, the last thing White said to me when he'd been convicted was, *The Red Cloud will rise from the belly of the city and when the Red Cloud rises, the river will run with blood.*' She shrugged. 'I'm afraid that's as much help as I can give you for now.'

Her desk phone rang. She picked up, listened and said, 'I'll be down there right away.' She turned to Hendricks. 'We've got a date. Interview Suite 1. Jon Pearson and his entourage.'

44

7.13 pm

'You want to help your son, Mrs Pearson?' Clay addressed Jon's mother in the corner of Interview Suite 1.

She nodded. 'Of course I do.'

'Then reassure him in front of me that whatever he's done, everything between the two of you will be fine.'

Clay looked at the boy. His young social worker was doing her best to attract his attention, but he sat like a waxwork. His solicitor, meanwhile, stared impassively at the space behind Hendricks's head.

'Have you got anywhere to stay tonight, Mrs Pearson?'

'Yes.'

'You understand that you won't be able to go home for the foreseeable future?' She looked puzzled. 'It's one thing that your older sons have committed a serious assault on a police officer, but right now they're also prime suspects in a case of multiple murder. As we speak, I've got officers searching your house inside and out for evidence.'

What little light was still in her eyes dissolved.

Out of nowhere, Jon Pearson's solicitor answered an unasked question. 'Jon,' she said. 'Tell the truth, that's my advice.'

Clay moved next to Hendricks and Mrs Pearson took her place next to Jon.

On the table between them was Jon's book bag, the crumpled sheets of paper, a slim Oxford Reading Tree book and, in a transparent forensic evidence bag, Mrs Harry's black Nokia E63 mobile phone.

Clay prompted Mrs Pearson with a glance.

'Jon.' She tugged at his arm until he looked at her. 'I want you to know that whatever happens next, I will still love you come what may. Whatever you may have done—'

'But I haven't done anything, Mum, honest to God.'

'Whatever you may or may not have done, I will always love you and you will always be my son. You must tell the truth, do you understand?'

'I have been telling the truth.'

'Jon,' began Clay, 'what we're going to do first of all, and it's the only thing we're going to be doing tonight because it's getting late for a lad of your age, is we're going to look at the items on the table and we're going to establish ownership of those items. Do you understand?'

He was silent.

'For instance,' said Clay. She pointed at the bag. 'Whose is that book bag?'

'It's mine,' he replied.

'Great, it's that easy. Look, it's even got your name across the panel at the top in big black capital letters. Is that your writing?'

'Yes.'

'Two out of two correct so far, Jon. And I'm going to put it to you that everything on the table that came out of your book bag belongs to you except for one item. Look at the table.' He followed the instruction. 'Tell me in your own words what you can see.'

He looked and was silent for a long, long time.

'What can you see, Jon?'

'A book bag, papers, a book. A mobile phone.'

'And where did I find these things?'

'In my brothers' bedroom.'

'And how did they get there?'

'I brought them from school.'

'We've had a look at the papers in your bag, Jon.' Slowly, Clay drew the papers closer. She had rearranged them into a specific order. 'Do the papers belong to you?'

'No, not really.'

She turned over the first crumpled page and showed him a child-like pencil drawing of a robot made of hinged cuboids and the name in block capital letters: 'THARG'.

'Did you draw that?'

'Yes. I did that on Friday morning.'

She showed the next piece.

'That's not my writing,' he said.

Mrs Pearson's eyes rolled. 'Jon, that *is* your handwriting.'

'No it's not.'

'Jon,' Hendricks said. 'Read what it says on the paper.'

He looked at Hendricks as if he was a monster that had suddenly appeared in the room out of thin air.

'Or shall I read it to you?'

'It wasn't me.'

'Eat my shit, you bitch hore,' said Hendricks, as if he was reading the opening line of a fairy tale. He pointed at the sheet. 'There's a silent *w* missing from the word *whore*, but I don't suppose that spelling will come up in the SATs.'

Clay turned over the next sheet.

'Oh my God, Jon!' said his mother.

'Mrs Pearson, please,' said Clay.

The social worker caught Hendricks's eye and looked away with embarrassment as he said, 'Well, seeing as no

197

one wants to look at your artwork, Jon, I'll describe it. It's a penis with some fluid or other flying from it into what looks like a girl's face and underneath it says, *Suck it bittch.*'

'Jon,' said Clay. 'We've got four more sheets of this stuff to go and, in my opinion, your writing just gets ruder and ruder.' She waited for that to sink in. 'Shall we carry on with the show-and-tell or shall we stop right there?'

'Stop it.'

Mrs Pearson turned to the solicitor and the social worker and said, 'I really don't know where he gets it from.'

'I will stop it, Jon, on the condition you stop messing around and tell me the truth. Deal?'

'Deal.'

'Did you do these drawings? This writing?'

'Yes.'

'When did you do them?'

'In school, on Friday.'

'Did you show them to anybody?'

'No.'

She pointed at the phone.

'Whose phone is that?'

'I don't know.'

'It is Mrs Harry's phone.'

'How do you know?' he asked.

'I've got her number.' She took out her iPhone and dialled the eleven digits from the Patels' answer machine. The phone rang. 'Mrs Harry's phone.' Clay disconnected the call.

'We've established ownership of everything on the table. Another question and we'll soon be done for now. Who stole Mrs Harry's phone?'

'It...it must've been me,' said Jon, eyeing the phone in the evidence bag.

In the silence that followed, Clay stared directly at the boy, willing him to look at her, which he eventually did. She pushed the papers away.

'Have you been out much recently, Jon?' asked Clay.

Jon looked at her. 'What do you mean?'

'Have you left the house since Friday?'

'Yeah.'

'With your brothers?'

'No.'

'Did you go out last night at all?'

'No.'

'Did your brothers go out?'

'They're always out at night.'

'Did they go out last night?'

'Yeah.'

Clay looked at Mrs Pearson.

'They went out at around seven o'clock.'

'When did they get back, Mrs Pearson?'

'Early hours of the morning. I woke up when they came in. Half one.'

Clay leaned across the table and whispered, 'Jon?'

He looked her in the eye. 'Yeah?'

'Did you . . . put the book bag in your brothers' bedroom?'

He looked incredulous, as if he was facing someone who had seen deep into his head.

He nodded.

'Why did you put it there?'

'Because it's a mess and Mum never goes in there.'

'When did you put it there?'

'When I came home on Friday.'

'So your brothers could have used the phone.'

'They did. They called their mate Lee before they left the

house last night. I heard them. They arranged to meet up with him. They took the phone out with them.'

'Thank you, Jon. You're going to have to stay here tonight. But for now, the interview's over.'

45

7.45 pm

Stone drank in the cool waves of air from the fan he'd positioned next to his desk. At some point in the day, the heating in Trinity Road police station had broken down and all attempts by engineers to turn it off had failed. It was jammed on a high setting.

He angled his desk light onto the third volume of Adrian White's Satanic writings: *The Matriarch*. He listened sympathetically to the frustration of the officers who had spent hours trying to make sense of the books.

'There's a viciousness under the surface,' said DC Cole, a man whose passion for literature made him the stand-out first choice for the task. 'It makes me feel cold. I *feel* like a child peering at hard-core pornography.'

'There's nothing involving *red* and *cloud*?' asked Clay.

'We've made notes where the words *red* and *cloud* feature, but it's as if they've been randomly dropped in, like certain words spring into his head and he writes it down. Listen to this. *The yes star rise city fruit of air blood man run earth your womb fire flame city red will alert cloud…* What was he on when he wrote this?'

'He wasn't on anything. He didn't smoke, drink or do any

drugs,' said Clay. She looked at the officers. They were all drawn and blank-eyed. Except for Stone.

'OK,' said Clay. 'I can see you've all had enough. You'll have to go and join everyone else on the streets looking for Vincent and Robert Pearson. White said they're going to do it again. Tonight. The teams and the territorial zones are on the noticeboard. Pick the streets where you feel you'll be most useful.'

As the officers gathered their things together and made their way out of the door, Clay rolled a chair over to Stone's desk and sat with him in the draft of cool air.

'That's nice.' She hung limply for a moment, then said, 'You know when you're that deprived of sleep, your subconscious starts throwing stray images into your field of vision? I've just seen a cat sitting on your shoulder, Karl.'

'Is it still there?' He stroked thin air six inches above his shoulder.

'Karl.' She leaned closer. 'I was hallucinating. There's nothing there, mate.'

'But there is something *here*, Eve.' He touched White's book *The Matriarch*.

'Go on.' She felt a surge of energy after the torpor that had come off the rest of the team.

'I don't know for sure, Eve, but the more I read it, the more of a sense of rhythm I'm getting. It looks like surreal darkness to the naked eye, but there's something going on here, like there's a serpent hissing a dark lullaby in my ear.'

She looked at him, at his eyes, tired from soaking up White's written words, and saw the tension in him. Little rims of red lined his eyelids and she explored his face, with the sudden intuitive knowledge that Stone had discovered something about the writing that could be the key to the mystery of it.

'Eve, that's your fuck-or-fight face and we don't have time for either.'

She looked at his ears, at the pierced lobes for the diamond studs he wore off duty, his inner dandy fighting a losing battle with advancing age.

'Can you keep going, Karl? I can see how tired you are, but will you please carry on?'

'I'd rather be freezing my balls off on the streets looking for Vincent and Robbie Pearson but, yeah, seeing as it's you, Eve, yeah.'

She felt a surge of excitement and sensed the colour in her throat and face rising, in spite of the fan. Her pulse raced as she spoke with a rush of knowing and sharp intuition. 'Read a passage out loud to me.'

'Chapter one, verse one, from the book entitled *The Matriarch. Evening is on a the is the fall all and on a...*' Clay felt the steady beat of her heart, growing thicker with each pulse. '*...child of actor artifact the one to one to one to who reigns parasite yes you in darkling red cloud oneness.*' Her pulse beat faster and faster. 'That's the end of that chapter. Want me to carry on?'

'Pass me the book, please.'

The blade of the fan cut a choppy beat as it turned and blasted cold air at Clay and Stone. She read over the brief chapter he'd read aloud and said, 'It's a difficult passage, but you read very well.'

'My mother used to torture me every year in the Liverpool Speech and Drama festival. Before my voice broke.'

Clay spiralled back in time to her own childhood, was reminded of a large Bible that used to sit on the lectern of the chapel in St Claire's and of the Irish priest from St Anthony's on Scotland Road, Philomena's friend, who visited daily to say Mass for the elderly nuns and the children in their care. Father James O'Reilly, a thin man in black with the look of Samuel Beckett and a fine reading voice.

'What are you doing, Eve?' asked Stone.

Her palms and fingers were pressed together in prayer.

'Raiding the past to pay for the present.'

She could almost hear the sound of Father O'Reilly's voice reading from St Matthew's Gospel, words her childish ears couldn't comprehend but that filled the echoing chapel with a lilting music.

'Jesus answered, "Watch out that no one deceives you. For many will come in my name, claiming, "I am the Christ."'

The last time she saw him, at Sister Philomena's requiem mass.

Her hands were no longer in a prayer-like posture. 'You're going to hate me for this, Karl.'

'Go on?' He opened his chest wide in front of the fan.

'All this writing by Adrian White, it's not meant to be read silently by individuals sitting down and quietly taking it all in. It's meant to be read aloud and listened to by the faithful. It's like the Dark Ages in the Catholic Church when most people couldn't read or write. They got all their religious instruction from stained-glass windows and priests reading stories from the Bible about Jesus and his home boys.'

'Let me guess,' said Stone. 'You want me to read this out loud to you?'

'Yes, Karl.' She handed him her iPad. 'And I want you to record it all. Start with any sections that feature *red* and *cloud*. Work your way out, looking for anything that looks remotely like it may have something to do with this case.'

Stone picked up a pad from his desk and flicked through dozens of pages of handwritten notes.

'*Red* and *cloud*. I've noted down where those references are already. You going to listen to all this?'

'I was born to listen, Karl.'

The landline phone on her desk rang.

'I'm going to Ullet Road at 7 am,' said Stone.

'I'll meet you there,' she said, picking up the receiver. 'DCI Eve Clay.'

'Eve?' The voice on the other end was thick with sleep or alcohol.

Clay didn't recognise it at first. It was tired, strangled and struggling to make itself heard. Then she worked out who it was. DS Gina Riley.

'Gina? You're supposed to be resting.'

'I'm spaced...out on...painkillers.'

'Do you need me to come and see you?'

'No. Listen. Text message. Rupert Baines. Shoe guy.'

'He's identified the print on Kate Patel's body?'

Stone held up a pair of thumbs and Clay smiled.

'Yeah. Converse. Hundred million. Pairs. World. Wide. UK. Three mill. PA.'

The line went dead.

'Clever,' said Clay. 'Almost invisible. Even down to the soles of their feet.'

46

11.00 pm

As the grandfather clock chimed eleven, Daniel Tanner swallowed a sleeping tablet and washed it down with a mouthful of lukewarm tap water. He turned off the bathroom light and, guided by the lamplight drifting from the bedroom he still shared with his wife, negotiated his way through the shadows of the large upstairs landing.

He paused at the top of the stairs and listened as a thin wind whistled round the walls of the house. The house, like the dizzy dreams of his youth, was too large for its own good and had proved unmanageable since his wife's descent through the ever-narrowing circles of dementia.

The adjoining doors of Rebecca's and Daniel's rooms were shut, but there was a ribbon of light at the base of each and he could hear the overflow of the abysmal music they were listening to on their headphones. Distant Rebecca with her functional-only conversations. Disinterested Daniel who only wanted money.

He paused at his own bedroom door and looked at his wife's face, softened in sleep by the light of a lamp on the table that separated their twin beds. Without thinking, he made his way to his bed and picked up his pillow. Each night the same temptation, sometimes dull, sometimes sharp, as it was in that moment, to press it over her face and claim temporary insanity or the conclusion of some manufactured pact from a time when they'd both had full command of their faculties.

But no. The thought of a custodial sentence proved simply too much and he placed his pillow down. He would just have to sell the house, buy a smaller property and place his wife in a nursing home. Rebecca and Daniel were in touching distance of leaving home. And Maisy? Maisy was Maisy and would have to live with him, with day centres and adult support services when he was at work.

Maisy?

He stepped back out onto the landing and slowly opened her door. Immediately he noticed how bitterly cold the air was inside Maisy's room. He'd turned the heating off two hours earlier, but even so... There was too much light and it was coming in through the big sash window next to his daughter's bed. The thick curtains that usually blocked out all trace of the streetlights on Ullet Road were parted and the sash window was raised. Wind blew the net curtains up into the air, making them billow like jellyfish.

Was this a new trick of Maisy's? Maisy, who had less sense than the average two-year-old.

He looked at the bed and was seized by panic. He couldn't make out her shape in the tangle of bedding. Hurrying over, he called out to her. 'Maisy?' But there was no answer. He felt his heart leap when he saw the side of her face against the creased pillow, her hair spilt and still, framing her sleeping features.

He crossed to the open window, pulled the sash down and reached a hand up to lock it. But the old lock had broken, he remembered, and had come away from the peeling paint and Victorian woodwork. It was just another job he'd been putting off for years.

The bolts that secured the wrought-iron fire escape leading to the stone landing just outside Maisy's window were coming away from the brickwork and were completely unsafe. The thought of her climbing out and falling into the snow made him sick.

The net curtain danced in the wind that still leaked through the ill-fitting frame. He gathered the fabric of the thick hessian curtains and, pulling them together, returned the room to darkness.

I'll get a joiner out first thing in the morning, he thought, *and damn the expense.*

And, summoning the last crumpled leaf of faith within him, Daniel Tanner knelt beside Maisy's bed and said, 'Please, please, please, don't take her away from me.'

'Don't...' Click click click click click click click click click click. '...worry.'

He peered at the sound of the voice in the dense darkness of Maisy's room and wondered if he was finally tipping over into insanity.

Something was coming towards him, he could feel its presence closing down on him.

'We won't harm a hair on *her* head.'

There was more than one.

From his knees, he struggled to his feet.

'Ka...' Click click click click click. Five simultaneous clickings from two sources '...Ri...'

'Who are you?'

Click click click click click.

'...Sa...'

He threw himself over his sleeping daughter to shield her

and felt the cold air move as a heavy weight swung in the darkness.

Click click click click click.

His skull cracked and as he felt himself spiral into the darkness of death he saw Kate Patel's face, the way the light used to dance in her eyes, the scent of her hair.

'A...'

Click click click click click.

'Den...'

His body banging to the floor was the last sound he heard.

Next door, Rebecca slipped off her headphones, listened, imagined she had heard a loud noise. She put her headphones back on and her senses were filled with music.

The Matriarch

Day Three

Clay walked cautiously across the ice from her parking space on Sefton Park to Ullet Road. A number 75 bus rolled past, full of cold, weary-looking workers. *I don't know why you're all looking so pissed off*, thought Clay. *At least you watched TV last night and went to bed to sleep.*

Five to seven in the morning? She pictured what she'd be doing if she was having a day off. In her mind, she sat facing Philip in his high chair, spooning Weetabix into his mouth and making aeroplane sounds to entertain him. Thomas would place a mug of coffee next to her and kiss her on the cheek. She wished she was there, at home with them, instead of making a routine inquiry at the Tanner family's house because they were in Kate Patel's address book and had three children.

As she turned onto Ullet Road, her iPhone went off in her hand. An incoming text message. She keyed in her passcode: 3502 – 35 for Thomas's age and 02 for Philip's – and opened messages.

It was from DS Terry Mason. *The Pearson residence. Look what we found.*

There were a series of photographs attached. A purple Liverpool City Council wheelie bin for general household rubbish, lid down. The same again, but this time with the lid completely open.

Clay looked up and saw Karl Stone waiting at the gateway of the Tanner's home in Ullet Road. 'Karl,' she said, approaching him. 'Something's come in from Ravenna Way, Jon Pearson's house in Belle Vale.' He looked dog-tired, the bags beneath his eyes dark as bruises. 'You OK?' she asked.

'I'm sick of the sound of my own voice. I've just finished recording a whole book.' He handed her the iPad. '*The Matriarch*. It's all on there. I'm telling you straight, Eve, there's something tangible going on inside White's writing. I couldn't sleep. White's words kept rolling round my head. I didn't want to shut my eyes in the end.'

She showed him the screen of her phone and scrolled on. It was a black bin bag. On again, and there was a brown evidence bag with a clear plastic panel down the centre. The next image showed four pieces of charred clothing. Two pairs of jeans and two padded jackets.

They walked up the path.

'Wherever Vincent and Robbie Pearson went the night before last, whatever they did, whatever they're capable of, they didn't make a very good job of destroying and getting rid of what they were wearing,' said Stone.

There was a Honda Civic parked in front of the house.

'Looks like Daddy's home,' he said.

Another text message arrived from Mason. This one had a picture of a laptop with a screensaver of the iconic image of Adrian White and, written in frozen blood-red letters across his chest: *The Baptist*.

The message from Mason was simple: *Robert Pearson's laptop*.

Clay showed it to Stone.

She looked at the tiny, second-hand image of Adrian White and his cold, dead eyes. 'Part of me just doesn't get this, Karl.

I can see how a kid could be into gangsta rap, football, violent PlayStation games.' In her mind, she reviewed the little she knew about the Pearson brothers' life, from regular little boy scouts in an affluent area of St Helens to hanging out on an estate in south Liverpool. But there was much more than that. 'They might look like run-of-the-mill scallies, but maybe that's just survival, adaption to the environment. And what about their father? Who knows what sick shit he planted in their heads when they were little. Let's get the paedo's files sent over from St Helens.'

'Leave it with me.'

Clay banged on the door and it opened a little, just like the door of the Patels' house in The Serpentine had.

'Jesus.'

She touched it lightly to open it wider and called, 'Hello, anyone there? Police! We're coming in!'

She could see that there had been no repetition of what she'd witnessed at the Patels'. She blew a sigh of relief.

'Just as it was yesterday. Nothing out of place,' said Stone.

'We'll have a chat with Mr Tanner. Pick his brains and then I'm going home for a couple of hours shut—'

On the wall to her left, two lines finger-painted in blood. The lines were at a small angle to each other, and the right-hand line was three times as long as the line to the left. Pierced by coldness, Clay heard herself whisper, 'Jesus!'

She looked up the stairs.

'Police!' called Clay. 'Call out to me!'

She ascended the stairs.

The silence on the first floor was deep and ugly.

The harsh tang of other people's blood hit her senses.

Clay's head filled with a sound.

She could hear her own blood pounding inside her skull.

At the top of the stairs, Clay had a good view of the wide landing. Four bodies were laid out alongside each other on the floor.

The bedroom doors were wide open.

She took out her mobile.

The landing walls were fairly clear of blood, but, angling her head to get a better view of the nearest bedroom, she saw the crimson spray that covered what looked like the boy's room. A large poster of the Liverpool Football Club squad, their bodies and faces mostly obscured by the dead boy's blood.

Clay called DS Marsh, Scientific Support team leader.

'Hi, Eve, did you get the pictures through OK?'

The carpets were fairly old and worn and she could see no obvious drag marks as she played her torchlight on the floor.

'Are you there, Eve?'

'Thanks, I got the pictures.'

'We're about done here,' said DS Mason. 'We've come up with an interesting haul.'

'I want you to leave the Pearson scene, right now. I need you at Ullet Road. The Baptist was right. They've followed up on The Serpentine and done it again. Bring your team. Hurry.'

Mr and Mrs Tanner's bodies were laid next to each other. They were at a small angle that had their heads almost touching but their feet half a metre apart. Mr Tanner was detached from his wife and children. The feet of Mrs Tanner's daughter were connected to her mother's feet in a continuing line. The boy's head touched his sister's head and the line of three bodies ended at the soles of his feet.

Clay shone the torch onto Mrs Tanner's face. The sockets were hollow and bloody, the eyes gouged out.

'Karl!'

'Yeah?' His voice echoed.

'Three children in the family, right?'

'Rebecca, Daniel and Maisy. The youngest, Maisy, is non-verbal, has learning difficulties.'

As Stone spoke, Clay drew closer to the bodies of the Tanner family, saw four marks in blood on the wall that provided her with an answer.

g
o
n
e

She went through every room upstairs, knowing that the process was futile. Each space drew a blank.

'They've taken a hostage,' she said. 'Call up Hendricks and tell him to issue a statement to the media on my behalf. He's to get pictures of Robbie and Vincent out there. We want to talk to them in connection with the murders in The Serpentine. The public aren't to approach them. DS Mason's on his way over, to start pulling in the evidence here.'

Clay picked her way quickly but carefully down the stairs.

'Where are you off to?' asked Stone.

'Guess.'

'Give the Baptist a kick in the balls for me,' said Stone. 'What do you want me to do in the meantime?'

'Dig out their address book and any databases with contact details. Look for any connection with the Patels and inform their contacts about what's happened here. If there are any mutual contacts, let me know. They'll need round-the-clock protection.'

Clay hit the cold air and took several deep breaths.

A black taxi pulled up just outside the gate. The back door opened and, head bandaged, Riley stepped out. She walked towards Clay.

'I called the office, they told me you'd be here,' Riley said. Her eyes were panda black.

'What are you doing here?'

'I signed myself out. There's too much to do.'

'Go home, Gina.'

'What's happened here?'

'Adrian White was right.'

'And you're telling me to go home?'

'OK, masochist, get back to Trinity Road. Two of White's books need recording – *The Beginning of the End of Time* and *The Elemental*. Karl's done *The Matriarch*.'

'Yes, sure...'

'And phone your husband,' Clay called back over her shoulder, walking away. 'If you drop down dead, tell him not to sue me for insufficient duty of care.'

As she made her way back to her car, Clay looked to the east, saw two blood-red fingers of light separating from each other and felt the weight of eleven dead bodies shackled to her feet.

In the time it took to drive to Maghull, Clay had listened to most of Stone's recording of Adrian White's *The Matriarch*, pausing and listening again as she waited at traffic lights or in lines of vehicles backed up at junctions and roundabouts.

'Back again so soon,' said the same nurse, escorting her once more to the front door of the building where Adrian White lived and would one day die. Sooner rather than later, hoped Clay.

'I couldn't wait for the spring,' she said.

'Second visit he's had in two days over seven whole years. Amazing.'

As the front door to the High Dependency Ward opened, Clay fixed her face. Natasha Seventeen. Po-faced cow, ready to stare down the Devil.

'Where's Taylor?' she asked, as the snooker-playing nurse who she'd mistaken for a patient opened the door. His name badge: George Green.

'It's his day off.'

She remembered him telling her the day before.

The opening and closing of inner and outer doors took less than a minute but to Clay it felt like a painfully long time.

'We told Adrian you were coming. He refuses to see you,' said Green.

'Well he damn well can't, Georgie-boy,' said Clay. 'This is a formal police interview, not a hospital visit. I'll see your patient Mr White in the meeting room, here and now. His alternative is to come to Trinity Road police station in the Speke–Garston district of Liverpool. Cell. Inconvenience. Not calling the shots. Clothes on. Make that clear to him!'

'Yes.'

'And if I need your help, I'll call for you. Is that clear?'

'Yes.'

'Let's go,' she said, walking ahead of him and noticing how the scene in the day room was almost exactly as it had been a little under twenty-four hours earlier, like she was walking through a living museum exhibit called 'The Blandness Of All We Hold Evil'.

With the right …

50

9.35 am

Adrian White entered the meeting room, the muscles of
his lean, naked body clearly defined, like a model from a
Michelangelo sketchbook.

He sat down across the table and she looked past him at
George Green.

'Wait outside. Thank you.'

She glanced at the small black tattoos either side of his
heart, on the right the number 1 and on the left the number 7.

She pressed record on her iPhone.

'DCI Eve Clay. Date: Twelfth of December. Time: 9.35 am.
I am with Adrian White in the meeting room in Ashworth
Psychiatric Hospital.'

She placed the iPhone down on the table.

'Congratulations, Adrian. You were right.'

'I was?'

'There was a seventh victim from the Patel family. And
there was one survivor from last night's carnage. A little girl
with learning difficulties called Maisy Tanner. She's ten or
thereabouts. So how do you know her?'

'I don't know her.'

'She'd have been about two or three when you were
arrested, so I'm putting it to you, Adrian, that you *did* know

her, just as you knew the Patel family. How do you know these families?'

'I'm only a human being.'

Technically.

'Yet, Eve, you seem to be following the much-travelled path of so many fools who give me credit for gifts I don't possess, who make assumptions about what I can do and what I know.'

'You told me that there was going to be another massacre. You told me there was going to be one survivor. The child concerned has been taken hostage. How did you know there'd be one survivor?' The words *conspiracy to murder* flashed through her mind, but she stayed silent. It would be like flicking a tea towel at a tank.

'What about the symbols? On the walls?' she asked.

'Symbols? Symbols on walls?' White was enjoying himself.

Clay changed direction. 'One survivor. You called it correctly. How?'

'I have visions, waking dreams. We discussed this at length seven years ago. You said I was no better than the Yorkshire Ripper with his voices from God. That was offensive, Eve.'

'Throughout your whole life, you displayed no paranoid schizophrenic tendencies – until you were caught.'

With the tips of the fingers of his right hand, he tapped hard against his heart, between the tattooed 1 and 7, a few times. 'That hurts.'

'How do you know the Patel family?'

'I don't.'

'How do you know the Tanner family?'

'I don't.'

'Which family is going to be targeted next?'

'Why should I tell you anything?'

'Who, where and when?'

'You don't believe I have visions. You think I'm a fraud.'

'Tell me about your visions.'

'I'm sorry about Sandy Patel. I broke the thin ice with the same jagged rock, slipped beneath the ice with him, sank beneath the freezing black water, held onto my breath at the moment he changed his mind but found himself face upwards against a thick wall of ice. I tasted the scummy water as it flowed down his throat and felt the weight of it pressing down against his lungs as the air pumped out of his body in bubbles that burst against the ice. I felt his eyes widening as life left him and darkness encircled him, enfolded him and drank in his mortal soul. I have visions.' A hypnotic energy flashed through his eyes, animating them for a moment, and then came the death stare. 'Do you believe me now, Eve?'

'Do you have a vision of the future?'

'In exchange for something, perhaps.'

'What do you want?' she asked.

'Do you have a cigarette, Eve?'

'You don't smoke.'

'Nor do you. Give me a cigarette, Eve, and I might be able to see more clearly in spite of the smoke.'

Clay placed her bag on her lap and pulled out the cigarettes and lighter Sandy Patel had given her. 'The NHS has a non-smoking policy in all its buildings. This is an NHS hospital. Therefore you're not allowed to smoke.'

'Good old Aristotle. A cigarette, Eve, please.'

She flipped the lid and he took out one of the last three cigarettes in the packet. He put the cigarette in his mouth and leaned back in his seat. Clay sparked up the lighter.

A single flame danced between them. A thin smile spread across his face.

'This reminds me of our first face-to-face meeting, Eve.'

The memory of him across a wall of fire careered through her head, set all her senses tingling. Sudden heat and the sting of nettles beneath her skin.

He leaned forward and she extended the lighter towards him.

White drew on the cigarette, leaning back, exhaling a thin line of smoke, his eyes never leaving Clay's.

'This is nice.'

'When are the killers going to strike again?'

'Tonight.'

'Who?'

'I haven't envisioned that. Yet.'

'What time?'

'After dark. Always, always in the dark.'

'Where?'

'Liverpool.'

'A family?'

'That's the pattern.'

He flicked ash on the table and rubbed it into the wood with the tip of his left thumb.

'Do you know a pair of teenage brothers, Robert and Vincent Pearson?'

'No.'

'Do you know *of* them?'

'Why should I?'

'They're followers of yours.'

'I know none of them, none of them know me, therefore I have no real followers.'

'Good old Aristotle. Information, Adrian, please.'

'Eve, you're looking in the wrong places. Have you ever considered why these murders are happening? What the absolute root cause may be?'

'It's you, Adrian.'

'Is it?'

'All those many followers who you don't know and who don't know you, the ones you're denying, they're aching to gain your attention, your approval, hoping that your so-called magic rubs off on them so that they can have followers of their own, people who can pour time, attention and affection onto them and who they in turn can ignore, dismiss and reject, thus making the hunger stronger, the passion richer and the vicious circle tighter.'

'You are so close to the truth, Eve, but you are so far away.'

'Are you going to tell me who, where and when?'

His eyes drilled into hers and she felt her blood pressure rising. He flicked ash and smeared it on the wood with his thumb.

'Someone, somewhere, tonight.'

'Who are the Red Cloud?'

'Signifiers of the Beginning of the End of Time. Have you read my writing? The truth's all in there. Everything you want to know. Look for it, Eve. You're a detective.'

'Evening is on a the is the fall all…'

'You're getting warm, Eve.'

'…and a on child of actor…'

'Am I still a liar?'

'…artifact…'

'Or do you now believe? You are standing so close to the hot spot. Look.'

He turned the cigarette round and stubbed it five times against his heart, between the tattooed 1 and 7. A shiver of pleasure flashed across his face. He fixed his gaze on Clay, as if she was the most important thing in the universe.

He pointed at the wound on his chest and crossed his lips with his right index finger. Small embers burned in his flesh and the smell of meat cooking filled her nostrils.

Clay stood up, walked backwards to the door and knocked on it.

George opened the door, sniffed. 'What's going on?'

'I'm going back to my room now,' said White, walking past the nurse. 'Our little chat is over. Farewell, Eve.'

As she stopped recording on her iPhone, two nurses followed White, watching him.

Clay gathered up her bag and went towards the day room.

On a large plasma TV on the wall, two images: Robert Pearson and Vincent Pearson. The image switched to Ullet Road, the pavement outside the Tanner family home. In the background there were TV crews from all over Europe; NBC from America. DS Hendricks faced a camera.

'We want to talk to both brothers in connection with an on-going investigation. If members of the public see either Robert or Vincent Pearson, they are not to approach them directly. Anyone with information...'

The camera angle changed and the picture now showed the journalists pointing cameras and microphones at Hendricks. She looked into the wall of faces, hungry for whatever Hendricks would feed them, and there was something in the image that made her say, 'Stop! No. Go back...' when it switched back to Hendricks.

There was something familiar in the bank of journalists' faces. She told herself that she had dealt with the media for years and knew several newspaper men and women. But in the brief footage, there had been something jarringly out of place.

Clay felt the rush of loss. The picture on the TV was wrong, but that wasn't all. She had forgotten something very important. Chaos stabbed her in the back. But what had she done? Forgotten?

'Thank you,' said Hendricks, and the picture changed again, back to the studio and the grim-faced newsreader.

Sandy Patel's cigarettes and lighter. She looked in her bag. They weren't there.

She headed straight back towards the meeting room. George was standing in the middle of the corridor as the other two came away from Adrian White's room.

'What's wrong?' asked George.

'Open the meeting room door.'

As soon as he did so, she saw that the cigarettes and lighter were not on the table.

George walked quickly alongside Clay, past identical facing doors. 'Did you see him self-harm? Did you give him a cigarette?'

'Open his door!' Clay banged on it.

'Come in,' White's voice oozed.

George turned the key and pushed the door open. The cigarette packet and lighter were in White's extended, unfolded right hand. Clay reached out, took the cigarette packet and lighter and felt the tips of White's fingers squeeze her hand.

'They'll do anything to attract your attention.'

'Who?' She glanced at the tattooed numbers either side of White's heart. 1 and 7. He turned his back on her.

She felt as if some shadow had just fallen across her, that her life was about to change. It made her walk away as quickly as she could. But she knew that however fast she ran, it would never be fast enough to stop the shadow from overwhelming her.

'Have you got any good news for me?' asked Clay, her voice echoing faintly around the hallway.

'We've contacted all the families in the Patel and Tanner address books,' replied Stone. 'Sandy Patel gave the password for the family computer to his mate. We've found a few additional contacts on that database. They've been warned.'

'Any other mutual acquaintances, like families showing up in both lists?'

'No. No crossovers. Four of the families in the Tanners' book have moved out of Liverpool. We managed to track down three. One family, the Watsons, emigrated to Australia seven years ago.'

'I'll order patrols in the streets where those families live.'

'Bill Hendricks has got all the Patel and Tanner bank statements going back years and years.'

She pointed upstairs.

'Their bodies have all gone away for post-mortem.'

'Have you got a picture of the bodies in situ?'

He took out his phone and showed her the screen.

Mr Tanner in a straight line at an angle to the longer continuous line that was his wife, daughter and son. Two lines, two dead ends.

The sky was dense and the afternoon light was grey. She took a notebook and pen from her bag and, catching sight of the cigarette packet and lighter, felt completely duped by White.

'Hold the image there, please, Karl.'

Clay started with Mr Tanner and drew a straight line. Beside it, she drew the line of Mrs Tanner's body and that of her daughter and son.

'They've gone to the trouble of making this picture,' said Clay. Pictures are made to be seen. Pictures tell us stories, information, news. Who died where?'

'The father died in Maisy's room. The mother, Rebecca and Daniel in their own rooms. Are they coming out again tonight?'

'According to White, yes.'

'But that was all?'

'More or less.' She nodded.

'Did you kick him between the legs for me?'

'No, but it was a fairly big target, I can tell you that.'

Stone laughed and Clay shrugged, deadpan.

'How do you know, Eve?'

'He walked into the meeting room stark naked. He never wears clothes these days.'

'Really?' Stone's amusement turned to mild bewilderment. 'Any distinguishing features?'

'Tattoos.'

'The ones on his hands? The realigned Satanic universe?'

'He's got two tattoos he didn't have seven years ago.' She pointed either side of her heart and said, 'Number 1 here, number 7 here.' Her scalp crawled at the memory of White's naked chest.

'What's the matter, Eve?'

She looked at her watch. On the way back from Maghull, as she'd listened over and over to Stone's recital of Adrian White's religious writing, the sense of being personally spooked hadn't diminished. It had increased and an unwelcome connection between herself and White formed in her mind.

'I've got to go, Karl. Do me a favour, please. Call Mrs Harry. Tell her I'll come to her house to meet with her. If she asks you any questions, fob her off, tell her she can ask me when we meet up.'

As she got to the front door, Stone said, '1 and 7? What do you want me to do with that?'

'Call the reading team at Trinity Road,' replied Clay. '1 and 7. The first of July. The Baptist's birthday. Tell them to think 1 and 7 in trying to crack the code. And the inversion of my birthday. Seventh of January. 7 and 1.'

As Clay stepped over the threshold of her house in Mersey Road, Thomas came quickly down the stairs. In the front room, Philip was singing along to the TV.

'I saw you parking from the bedroom window.' Thomas sounded pleased, excited to see her. 'God, Eve, you look shattered.'

'Half my head feels like rock, the other half feels like it's going to lift off and float away.'

She sank into his embrace, felt the weight of his lips against hers and was consumed with the need to escape into intimacy with the man she loved and craved.

'You know I'd love to,' she said. 'But I'm only here for minutes and...' She pointed at the front room. He let her go. 'There's something I've got to talk to you about, Thomas.'

'Go ahead.'

'They're going out again tonight.'

'How do you know that?'

'The Baptist told me.'

'You've been in touch with White.'

'He's been in touch with me. He's got the inside track on this case. I've been to see him in Ashworth. Twice.'

'The slimy little shit-bag.'

'Shit-bag!' Philip's voice piped up as he ran across the hall towards his mother and father.

'Naughty!' She wagged a finger at Thomas. 'Naughty word!'

She stooped and picked Philip up. Though her back ached, her heart danced. She kissed him over and over and squeezed him.

'I was about to call you, Eve, and tell you...' Thomas wrapped an arm around her shoulders. 'You were pretty stressed out the other night, worrying about Philip's safety.'

She went back in time to The Serpentine and recalled the churning fear for her son's safety, with the killers so near at hand.

'I'm packing and taking Philip to my parents,' said Thomas. 'You've got enough to contend with. You really don't need the worry of us.'

She felt a wave of pure relief. He had isolated the one thing he was capable of changing to make her life better and acted on it. She looked at him and fell in love yet again.

'That's why I made a bend to come home,' said Clay. 'I was going to tell you to get Philip and yourself out of town.' The channels of their thoughts were running closer with the passage of time. 'I guess we're just turning into an old married couple...'

'White? Did you have to go and see him?'

'Don't be so anxious, love,' said Clay.

'Did you go alone?'

'No, I didn't go on my own,' she lied. 'I was with Hendricks.'

'He sees more of you than I do.'

'Yes, but when you see me and I see you, it's here.'

Philip wriggled in her arms. She put him down and he danced off into the front room.

'There's something else I want to see you about, something I want you to do for me, Thomas. OK?' She gathered the front of his shirt between both hands and pulled him in close. 'Are you listening? Good, then I'll begin. As soon as this thing's over, I want you to jump in the car, drive very, very quickly back to Liverpool, put Philip in the bath and when he's fast asleep...' She pressed her lips against his ear and whispered for many moments. She felt the pulse in his neck quicken and the colour rise in his cheek. She stopped whispering and drew a tiny question mark on his earlobe with the tip of her tongue. She pulled away so she could look into his eyes and asked, 'Do you think you can do all those things to me? Would you like to?'

'Oh yes.'

'Well then, that's fine, because that's exactly what I need.'

'Eve, just hurry up and catch them, OK?'

She kissed her fingertips and stuck them on his lips. 'I've got to go. But *when* I come back...' She held back the if.

'You are on the promise of a lifetime.'

There was an object in the front room of Mrs Harry's house that hadn't been there on her first visit and, Clay guessed, it had been brought out of the attic to ward off evil spirits.

Within touching distance of Clay, in the corner of the room, an eighteen-inch statue of the Virgin Mary stood on a table looking directly at the viewer. The Virgin crushed the Serpent beneath her bare feet, offering beatific grace to the world and violent death to the Devil. It was a domestic version of a much larger statue she recalled from the chapel in St Claire's, one she had prayed to every day with Philomena.

She placed a finger on the Virgin's bare foot and traced it along the back of the Serpent to its gaping jaws and exposed fangs, full of rage in its death throes, one eye looking skywards in accusation of heaven and one at the viewer.

Why are you not saving me? Don't you know who your real friend is?

She took her finger away at the sound of teacups and saucers rattling on a tray. Mrs Harry entered, looking like she hadn't slept since Clay had last called there with Stone. She handed a cup of hot tea to Clay, who swallowed half of it in two gulps.

'Be careful,' said Mrs Harry, in her best school-teacher voice, 'that you don't get burned.'

Clay, who was parched, said, 'Thank you.' And finished off the rest.

'Would you care for another?'

'No thank you. No time.'

'It was on Radio Merseyside. A ten-year-old boy being questioned by the police in connection with the murders. The child couldn't be named for legal reasons.'

'Mrs Harry, that boy is Jon Pearson.'

'No?'

'We found your mobile phone in his house. His two older brothers, Vincent and Robert, committed a serious assault on a police officer. They're on the run as we speak. They're our prime suspects.'

Her face paled and she looked at Clay in extreme shock. 'I taught all three of them. I don't believe it.'

'What do you know about them?'

'Robert and Vincent were mischievous and were often sent to the head's office, but they were never involved in any serious violent incident in school, at least not during their time at St Bernard's. Jon's just quiet, introverted, young for his years.'

'You've seen all Jon's records? You remember going through Vincent and Robert's files? And nothing leaped out at you?'

'No. Why?'

'Did the boys ever display overtly or inappropriate sexual behaviour?'

'No. Absolutely not.' There was a painful silence. 'Will I...?' Mrs Harry stopped, looked embarrassed. Clay knew she was trying to ask an uncomfortable question without making herself look weak. It happened in every single case she worked on.

'Will you have to go to court?' prompted Clay.

'Yes.'

'Most certainly, if this current line of enquiry leads me where I think it's heading.'

Mrs Harry blew her cheeks out and her shoulders slumped.

'There are people who will support you through the process. You're under my strict instruction from this moment to not discuss the case with anyone at all. You understand, Mrs Harry?'

'I understand.'

'If Mrs Sweeney gets you in the office and starts to sweat you down, pick up the phone and I'll be there as quickly as I can. She can talk to me.'

Relief swept across Mrs Harry's face.

'Talking of phones, I'd order a new mobile if I was you. You won't see your old one again.'

'I never want to own a mobile phone ever again, DCI Clay.'

'It's not the phone that's put you where you are now.' She stood up. 'Thanks for the tea. Most welcome.'

As Clay left the room, she glanced back inside.

With both eyes, the Virgin was still watching her, as was the dying Serpent.

54

5.55 pm

Clay poured three heaped teaspoons of white sugar into her mug of tea. She rewound to the beginning of chapter one of *The Matriarch* and prepared to listen to the passage for the fifth consecutive time, not just because of the use of the words *red* and *cloud* but because there was a strange coherence in the surface that mostly wasn't apparent elsewhere in the book.

She looked at Adrian White's spidery yet crystal-clear handwriting, his labour of Satanic love.

Clay closed the book and her eyes and listened to Stone's actorly recitation.

'*The Matriarch*, chapter one, verses one to three. *Evening is on a the is the fall all and a on child of actor artifact the one to one to one to who reigns parasite yes you in darkling red cloud oneness...*'

She opened her eyes, stopped the iPad, picked up a pen and jotted down in her notebook: *A time of day, a fall (from grace?), a child, a deceit, an object, a king, a parasite.*

She listened again, this time allowing the words to flow over her, not listening for meaning but just to hear the words, to find the poetry if she could, as she stared hard at the surface of her desk.

'*Evening is on a the...*'

Her phone moved on her desk and she felt her heart leap. It vibrated against the wooden veneer and the rest of White's words were lost.

On the display panel: *Thomas mobile*.

'Thomas, where are you?'

'With the parents, at their house. Philip is asleep and all is well with the world. Wish you were here.'

She listened. In the background she could hear the steady rhythm and seductive swoosh of evening tides on the shore.

'You're sitting outside, right?'

Swoosh.

'What's the weather like?' she asked, from the stuffy confines of the incident room.

'It's as cold as it is where you are, but the sky's clear. The moon's full and the light's spilling onto the water. The water's jet black. And I'm missing you badly.'

She looked out of the window, saw the sudden change in the weather conditions, could see the same moon as Thomas. Clay cupped her hand around the mouthpiece and whispered, 'Are you sure you're not with some Welsh floozie?'

'Yeah. How did you guess?'

'I can smell her perfume from here. Has she got a tramp stamp?'

'Three, actually.'

'You dirty rascal, Thomas.'

The tide heaved in and she pictured the moonlight rippling over the dark water. '*When you look into shadows, you look into mirrors. When you look into mirrors, what do you see?*'

'Where are you, Eve?'

'At my desk...'

She closed her eyes and for a moment imagined Thomas's arms around her. The familiar scent that was his and his alone coursed through her senses.

'Thomas, I have to go. Call me in the morning.'

'I will do. I love you, Eve.'

'I needed to hear that so badly. And guess what?'

'I guess you love me too.'

'You guess correctly. Thomas...'

'I know, you have to go.'

She hung onto the silence between them and then disconnected the call. She took a moment to turn the screw inside herself and focused on the gravity of the task in front of her.

People have died in horrible circumstances. More will follow. You are the best chance they have.

The ground beneath her was moving and the sky above was pressing down on her head. With the darkness around her, she pressed play on her iPad again. And listened. And listened. And listened.

55

6.05 pm

On the border of Aigburth and Garston, Vincent Pearson drove down Riversdale Road at ten miles per hour, his eyes flicking from the road ahead to the petrol gauge on the dashboard. The needle was firmly in the red zone.

He glanced at his brother Robbie in the passenger seat. His head was propped against the window, his eyes shut, after a night and a day spent hiding in a lock-up garage they'd broken into near John Lennon Liverpool Airport.

It had been over twenty-four hours since either of them had eaten. His head throbbed and his stomach ached with intense hunger.

Vincent steered the female copper's Audi right at the bottom of Riversdale Road and wished he was one of the people living in that road with their nice houses overlooking Liverpool Cricket Club.

'Wake up, Robbie!'

He parked the car on the tarmac in the small bay behind the snow-capped lawns leading down to the Promenade, the walkway that extended over five miles to the Pier Head, following the curve of the River Mersey.

'It's cold,' said Robbie, still dressed in just the T-shirt

and jeans he'd been wearing when the cops had made their unexpected call.

'Wake up, Robbie!' Vincent smacked his brother's arm.

'What?'

The sky was clear, the moon was out and, across the river, thousands of points of light glittered at the gates of some promised land that was for other people but never them. The river washed back and forth across the mud flats, filling Vincent with a sense of peace that was welcome but he knew was utterly false.

Robbie's phone rang out with the brass intro to Beyoncé's *Crazy In Love* and he grabbed it off the dashboard. The display read: 'Spencer'. He showed it to Vincent.

'Don't pick it up, Robbie. He could be cutting himself a cosy little deal with the cops, with us as the price.'

'But it's Spencer. Our best mate.'

'How many times do I have to tell you. You can't trust no one!' The feeling of peace evaporated and the all-encompassing sense of anxiety that Vincent had lived with for years started eating at his centre.

'I need to sleep,' said Robbie.

'Yes, you do. We both do,' replied Vincent with a calmness he just didn't feel. 'But we need to talk first, right?'

The music stopped. Twelve missed calls. All from their best mate, Spencer.

'I've been thinking, Robbie, about all kinds of stuff. You remember when that woman copper called the tall, ugly bloke up the stairs?'

'Yeah, and that bitch in the front room said, *They've got the phone. You're as good as guilty!*'

The passage of seconds replayed itself through Vincent's head for the thousandth time.

The woman copper went to close the living room door. The bloke's footsteps were heavy on the stairs. Upstairs Jon was crying. Their mum was talking fast and loud. Without thinking, the baseball bat from the side of the sofa was in his hand and raining down on the bitch's head as her hands flew up to protect herself. Vincent snatched her bag, took the car keys, tossed the bag down. They hurtled out of the house and got lucky opening the car nearest to the house. The bloke was on the pavement as they raced away, tyres screaming as they turned the corner at sixty miles per hour. Laughing like maniacs as they lost the chasing copper in the web of side roads, not knowing that they were speeding into a maze of insanity that they could never have imagined. Ever.

'What are we going to do?' asked Robbie.

'Use the last of the petrol to drive down to Trinity Road police station and turn ourselves in,' replied Vincent.

'That's a good idea, Vinnie.'

'It's a shit idea. It's the last thing we should do. Didn't you hear the Radio City news, on the hour, every hour for the last twenty-four hours?' He regretted his outburst of anger as soon as it had left him, instantly absorbing his younger brother's hurt at the sharp attack. 'I'm sorry. This is all shit, all fucked-up beyond belief.'

'So what's new?' asked Robbie.

'Listen to what I'm going to say to you. It's important you understand where we are right now. When we get caught—'

'*When?*'

'When.'

'But you said—'

'That was before I heard on the radio what they're going to pin on us. Mass murder!'

Vincent pulled down the sun visor to block out the leering

moon, the stamp of night, the dark hours and the creak of his bedroom door in the old house back in St Helens.

'There were kids involved, Robbie.'

'But we didn't do it. There's no forensic evidence – CSI and all that shit.'

'Did you hear that woman copper or didn't you? *They've got the phone. You're as good as guilty.* They're going to pin a multiple murder on us and there's nothing we can do about it. They've made their minds up. They've planted a fucking telephone in the house. They're going to do us for killing those posh bastards in Aigburth.'

The wind whistled off the river and, in the silence of the car, Vincent heard his dad's voice, hot, urgent and soft in his ear. 'Don't tell Mum. Don't tell a soul.'

'One condition, Dad!' said Vincent.

'*One condition, Dad?* What do you mean, Vinnie?'

'Oh nothing, thinking out loud. Young kids got killed, a toddler, and they're going to pin it on us. Where do you think they'll send us for the rest of our lives? And no, they won't give us parole because everyone thinks we're like fucking Ian Brady and Myra Hindley. So no, there won't be no parole, fucking get that one out of your head.'

'Young Offenders Unit until we're, like, y'know, eighteen?'

'No. They'll put us in the basement of Wakefield Prison until we're eighteen and then they'll put us in with the paedos because all the decent criminals will want to kill us because they think we've messed with little kids.'

'What are we going to do?' asked Robbie.

'Let's try and grab a bit of kip and we'll put our heads together in the morning. Let's sleep on it.'

Vincent opened the door and stepped out.

'Where are you going?' asked Robbie.

'Opening the back door for you. You can sleep on the back seat.'

With his brother curled up in the back with the woman copper's coat covering him, Vincent settled down in the driver's seat and watched the twinkling lights on the Wirral Peninsula.

The wind combed the trees and bushes behind the car and sang a mournful song as it blew off the icy river.

Vincent was dog-tired but knew he couldn't sleep. He had to do the thing he'd always done, the thing that compelled him. Look out for his little brothers. As the moments passed, he couldn't even think about Jon and what was happening to him.

The phone rang. Spencer. Again. He turned the phone off and listened as Robbie's breathing grew deeper and deeper. He would wait until his brother was sleeping soundly before he fulfilled his plan.

Somewhere, in the gardens of the modern apartments overlooking the dark river, a wind chime rattled. It reminded Vincent that once upon a time, in a different life, he had won a badge in Cubs for making a wind chime and, better still, had negotiated a secret treaty in the small hours of the night.

'I won't tell a soul if you leave Robbie and Jon alone.'

Robbie was snoring on the back seat. Vincent peeled off his shirt and got out of the car. The wind bit his skin. Half-dressed, he returned to the driver's seat, without his shirt, shut the door as quietly as possible so as not to wake Robbie and looked across the cold waters of the River Mersey.

He lifted the sun visor and stared in bold accusation at the smirking moon.

Across the river, thousands of lights danced through the gauze of his tears. He turned on the ignition.

56

6.15 pm

There were two piles of bank statements on Bill Hendricks's desk. The Patels' NatWest statements going back fifteen years, with the last five printed off from their internet banking facility. And the Tanner's Barclays statements for the same period.

Clay placed two mugs of coffee in front of him and pulled up a chair. 'I'm glad to have a break from listening to Adrian White's writing.'

'Anything coming through?'

'I keep thinking, imagining even, that I can hear fractured coherence, recognisable meaning buried in the broken syntax. But when I go back to the point where I sense clarity, it's just not there on second listening. It's the aural equivalent of something appearing on the edge of vision.'

Hendricks looked at Clay long and hard. 'Eve, there's something else on your mind, I can tell.'

'It keeps hitting me between the eyes. I think trawling through the Baptist's writings might be a bum steer. Like he's wasting our time at a time when we have no time to lose. He's assisting the perpetrators and laughing at us for good measure.'

'What's the alternative, Eve? He's got the inside track on this nightmare and you're the first person he makes contact with in seven years. If you ignore his writing and something comes out of it, we're all going to look like amateurs.' He sipped his coffee.

'Bill?' She had his whole attention. 'You know when you gave that statement to the press about the Pearson boys?'

'Yes?'

'There was something *not right*. With the hacks. Did you get that?'

'No. Only that there were so many of them, from far and wide. What do you mean, Eve?'

The nagging doubt had come and gone and had been relegated because of more pressing concerns. But it wouldn't go away.

'I can't rationalise it,' said Clay. 'But when I looked at them, it was like looking at a wall of circles with a single square stuck in the middle.' The tap dripped inside her head and she tried to turn it tighter by asking, 'Have you found anything from the bank statements?'

'Oh yes. Forget what job they do or where they live, you can tell a hell of a lot about people from their bank statements.' He pointed at the Patels' statements. 'Happy family.' He pointed at the Tanners' statements. 'Sad family. As the Patels have grown richer, the Tanners have been sinking into economic decline, over the last ten years. Mrs Tanner stopped work and all the family savings have been spent on private healthcare for her. They tried her in several care homes but nothing worked out. She ended up being cared for at home by a succession of agency nurses, but they've had stability for the past two years. Mr Patel's business has mushroomed and they've enjoyed exotic holidays, designer everything, flash cars, the full bling. When the recession hit, all the crap seemed to have slid clean off the Patel family, whereas what little the Tanners did have got gobbled up into the big black economic hole.'

'Have you found a link?'

'That's why I disturbed you from *Listen With Mother*. Go back eight years.' He gave her two sets of bank statements for the financial year starting April 2009.'

She scanned the Patels' income and outgoings for the month and then the Tanners' parallel statement.

'Can you see the same recipient for a standing order in both sets of statements?'

She skimmed and scanned from one page to the next. 'The Christian Grace Foundation' seemed to rise from the page.

The Patels' standing order was for £1000 a month, the Tanners' £150.

Clay turned to May.

'The plot thickens, Eve.'

'In May, the Patels upped the amount to £1500, the Tanners to £250.'

'If you look at the income going in for the month, that raises the contribution to ten per cent for both families,' said Hendricks. 'The Patels can afford that. The Tanners can't.'

'It's that church,' said Clay. 'I bet you it's the church Sandy Patel was telling me about. Excuse me.' She reached out towards Hendricks's laptop.

'You think I haven't tried Google? There are all kinds of Grace Foundations out there, but no sign of a Christian Grace Foundation.'

She turned to the June statements. 'Whoah! Whoah, whoah, whoah. £3000 from the Patels, £500 from the Tanners.'

'Go to February.'

Excited, she flicked through and saw that the standing order from both accounts suddenly ended. 'You do

Company House, I'll try the Charity Commissioner and the two banks.'

'I'm on it.'

'We need to find out who these religious leeches are and who else they had their suckers into,' said Clay, returning quickly to her laptop.

'The whole Christian Grace thing could be a cover for something else,' Hendricks speculated as his fingers danced over the keys.

'Got it. Yeah, it was a registered company, dissolved in February 2010. What was happening in February 2010?' Hendricks called across the room, waving to get the attention of Stone and Riley, who both took off their headphones. Before he had time to re-pose the question, Clay said, 'February 2010? That's when we caught Adrian White.'

The information hung in the air as the room fell briefly silent.

On the Charity Commission website, Clay clicked to search 'Removed Charities', typed in: *Christian Grace Foundation*, and chose 'Throughout England and Wales'.

'It wasn't a registered charity because they didn't want that kind of scrutiny. The Patels and the Tanners were mugged by the same religious con artists. And now they've been murdered on consecutive nights. Karl, get on to the banks. We need to access any records for the Christian Grace Foundation.'

The phone on Clay's desk rang and she picked it up before the first note ended.

'DCI Clay.'

'Eve, it's Sergeant Harris.' The duty sergeant of Trinity Road police station sounded mannered and she guessed he had someone on the other side of the reception desk. 'I've got a young man here, a Lee Spencer, says he needs to talk urgently to whoever's investigating the murder of the Patel family. It's about the Pearson brothers, Vincent and Robert.'

'Take him to Interview Suite 1 and organise a solicitor in case he needs one. I'll be there right away.'

57

6.51 pm

It took the duty solicitor Mr Robson fifteen minutes to arrive at Trinity Road police station and a further fifteen to consult with Lee Spencer. In that half hour Clay went digging for information about the fifteen-year-old and what she found made her pessimistic about his reliability.

Excluded from school from the age of thirteen and a truant from the behavioural unit that battled to educate him, Lee Jonjo Spencer had convictions for shoplifting, handling stolen goods, breaking and entering into commercial premises and was a seasoned pickpocket.

Sergeant Harris led two young men into Interview Suite 1: Lee Spencer and a smartly dressed, mid-twenty-something solicitor, Mr Robson. Harris looked at Clay, who said, 'That'll be fine.'

He closed the door and Clay showed Lee Spencer her iPhone. 'OK with me taping our little chat?'

He nodded. 'Yuh!'

Even though Lee was a decade younger than Mr Robson, with his bleach-blonde hair and street-worn face he looked almost the same age. Clay estimated that in another five years' time, he would look old enough to be the solicitor's father. Dressed in a yellow Adidas tracksuit top and jeans that looked set to fall down to his ankles, Lee Spencer stared directly at Clay from under the peak of his Lacoste baseball cap.

Robson and Spencer. It was a tale of two societies.

'What do you want to tell me about Robert and Vincent Pearson?' began Clay.

'I want you to tell me that I won't get done.'

'Lee, *mate*,' said Mr Robson. 'DCI Clay doesn't have the authority to grant you immunity from the law. No one has that kind of authority. My advice is you tell DCI Clay what you told me in the little meeting room and I'm sure it'll put you in a *favourable* light.'

Elbows and arms on the table, hands joined, Lee looked into the knots of his fingers, the conflict in his head written on his face.

'Lee,' said Clay.

His eyes engaged with hers.

'There've been ten murders in two nights. I was the first police officer there both times. I was the first person to see the bodies. If you help me, I will help you.' She took in Mr Robson as she made the promise but delivered it squarely looking into Lee's eyes.

'How?'

'Any way I can. You walked in here voluntarily. In my book, you're already off to a flying start. There's serious business going on here. You're fifteen years old and you've walked into Trinity Road without your mother or anyone else to support you because you claim to know something significant. There are men in their forties, career criminals, who wouldn't get involved in this even if they knew everything. They'd let other people perish if it meant they stayed out of trouble.'

Something softened in his face and she sensed the bottling-up of tears behind the sullen stamp of his expression.

'Lee, the one thing I haven't got is time. If you've got something to tell me, tell me now. Based on what I know so far, another family's going to get slaughtered tonight.'

'Robbie and Vincent Pearson are my best mates.'

'And?'

'And it's saying on the telly that Robbie and Vincent are wanted in connection with them murders in Aigburth, and that, like, they smacked some copper?'

'I was there in their house when they smacked the copper. With a baseball bat.'

'Whoah?'

'Woe indeed,' said Clay.

'But, y'see, I was with them on Sunday night. They weren't in Aigburth acting like a pair of psycho arseholes.'

'Tell me about Sunday night, Lee?'

A sadness swept across the boy's features and, for a moment, he looked like the oldest man on earth.

'I've been calling them all day but they're not picking up their mobile.'

'You were with them on Sunday night? At the time,' Clay stressed, 'that the Patel family were murdered in their home in The Serpentine in Aigburth?'

'Yuh. They weren't anywhere near Aigburth on Sunday night. They were in Childwall with me.'

'And what were you doing with Robbie and Vincent Pearson in Childwall?' asked Clay.

Lee glanced sideways at Mr Robson.

'Go on, Lee.'

'We screwed a house just by Childwall Fiveways, Rudston Road.' He looked like he couldn't quite believe that the words had come out of his mouth. 'The stuff's all stashed in my house, in my bedroom. We didn't do any unnecessary

252

damage to the house. Call Belle Vale police station. They'll most likely have dealt with it.'

'Bear with me, Lee,' said Clay. '*You* didn't, *Vincent* didn't, *Robbie* didn't phone up the Patel family from a stolen Nokia mobile phone? Sunday night?'

'We got in the house, we robbed everything we could carry and sell, then we were out and back in Belle Vale double-quick. We were dead busy. Why would we be phoning people we don't know in Aigburth?'

'Lee, that was a courageous confession. I'm going to have to leave you here now and another officer is going to come and get some more details from you about what you got up to on Sunday. Mr Robson is one hundred per cent right. You have put yourself in a favourable light.'

As she shut the door of Interview Suite 1, she began running down the corridor. Knowing she could make it upstairs faster than the lift, she hurtled up the concrete steps, her footsteps echoing off the glass walls like the laughter of the Devil at her back.

A thought crystallised. If the call on the Patels' answer machine hadn't come from the stolen mobile in the Pearsons' possession, then what the hell was going on?

58

7.00 pm

The night felt particularly dark when Eric Watson turned the corner of Woolton Road into the lengthy line of large semi-detached houses on Childwall Park Avenue. The place he called home. He tugged at Patch's lead. Patch, a brown twelve-year-old mongrel, paused at a neighbour's wrought-iron gate, sniffing the scents of other exotic dogs. Eric tugged harder than he meant to and Patch looked at him, his eyes doleful beneath the streetlight.

'It's cold, Patch, we're nearly home. Come on. Walk. Not far away.'

Eric's breath formed clouds in the cold air.

Their fifteen-minute walk had extended to twenty because Patch had lingered over emptying his bowels. It was a routine the dictatorial mutt would only do in a certain spot in Black Wood, on the corner of Woolton Road and Aldbourne Avenue.

Eric looked at his mobile phone. No call from his wife. One minute over the quarter hour, she was normally on his case.

Although Eric was exhausted after a blistering day in court, cross-examining a snake-eyed drug dealer for the Crown Prosecution Service, the time spent in Black Wood had soothed the niggling sensation that everything was somehow terribly wrong. *Irrational anxiety*, he reminded himself. *Mistrust is the curse of your life and profession.*

In Black Wood, moonlight had played on the snow-streaked trees that stood like giants reaching up to the stars. In the black sky a red cloud had hovered in front of the moon like something from another world, observing the passage of life on earth.

Through the snow on Childwall Park Avenue. 'Not far now, Patch.'

Patch barked.

'Hush, you big ball of mischief.'

The mongrel barked and barked, tugged at the lead suddenly and broke free from his master. He sprinted off, his bark dissolving into a sustained whimper as he got close to home.

A vice turned on Eric's skull. He started to run but immediately slipped over on the icy pavement and landed on his hands.

Patch stood in the gateway of their home. As Eric hurried, holding onto the railings and walls of his neighbours' houses, Patch fell silent.

Three houses to go.

Patch's whole body shook, the way it did during thunderstorms and on Bonfire Night.

There was a pile of snow on the front lawn. With the streetlight to guide him, Eric had cleared the front path when he came home, trying to shake off the stress of the day. Now there was a form on the snow, lying perfectly still. At first glance, he thought it was a doll, but it was too big to be a toy.

The front door was open. His heart collapsed.

'Mary!' he shouted to his wife inside.

For a moment, Eric thought it was Louise, his youngest daughter, on the snow, but as he walked up the path he saw it was a child he didn't recognise.

'Louise! Terry! Sarah!' He called to all his children, but all that came back was silence.

There was a smear of blood on the double-glazed front door.

He pushed it open and heard the sound of the lead flapping against the snow as Patch ran away at speed.

A front door opened nearby. And another. And several other doors across the wide, leafy road.

The doors of the houses to either side of his flew open. But then he couldn't hear any more doors opening or the noise of any animal fleeing. Because the only sounds Eric Watson could hear were the harrowing screams coming from inside him and the blood pumping through his head.

Hendricks, Riley and Stone stood over Clay at her desk in the incident room as she took Mrs Harry's mobile phone from the evidence bag.

Clay opened the back of the phone, lifted the battery and saw the SIM card tucked neatly into the back of the device.

'If the call on the Patels' answer machine didn't come from that phone, then where?' asked Riley.

Clay's mobile and landline phones rang out simultaneously.

'DCI Clay, it's switchboard. 302 Childwall Park Avenue, there's been another family attacked in their home.'

'How many dead?'

'Four.'

'Survivors?'

'Two.'

Clay turned to Riley. 'Whoever took Mrs Harry's phone has cloned the SIM card and placed the clone in a compatible model. Looks like,' she said, 'the call to the Patels' land-line didn't come from the phone we found in Jon Pearson's house.'

She turned to Stone. 'Karl, go to Barnham Drive. We need to talk to Mrs Drake and Faith, Jon Pearson's classmate. And her sister Coral.'

Then she turned to Riley. 'Gina, come with us to Childwall Park Avenue.' She swiped her bag from the desk and, heading for the door, said to Hendricks, 'You're coming with us too.'

Sliding his arms into his coat, Hendricks followed. 'Let's go in my car,' he said.

Just over a minute later, Clay climbed into the passenger seat and asked, 'How quickly can we get there?'

'Five minutes. There are five sets of lights. If they're red I'll burn them.'

As he pulled his car up in Childwall Park Avenue, Hendricks's tyres slid across the icy surface of the road. There was a crowd on the pavement, contained by two uniformed constables. It seemed as if every light in the road was on, every curtain open.

Clay snatched open the passenger door, raced over and placed herself in the space between the constables.

'Detective Chief Inspector Eve Clay!' She brandished her warrant card and spoke sharply to the crowd. 'You've got thirty seconds to go home and close your doors. At the moment you're endangering the integrity of a crime scene. Go!'

In complete silence the crowd dispersed. Twenty-eight seconds later, she heard the last front door shut.

Clay looked around. Two figures remained. Sitting on the pavement with his back against the wall of 300, there was a man with his face in his hands, weeping.

On the snow mound on the lawn of 302 was a child, a young girl, with a constable standing over her. Clay rushed across to her.

'I've ABC'd her, DCI Clay!' said the constable. 'Physically, she's OK, but she's out of the game.'

Clay looked at the child's face. From a photograph of the Tanner family she'd seen, Clay knew it wasn't Maisy. She gazed at the snow mound where the little girl lay in death-like stillness. Clouds drifted and the moon made her skin look bloodless, her fair hair laid out on either side of her head in almost perfect symmetry. Clay resisted the compulsion to take off her coat and lay it across the child. Instead, she headed towards the partially open door.

Sirens approached from three directions.

Clay looked to Hendricks and indicated the man on the ground. 'Who is he?'

'The neighbours said he's the father of the family. Eric Watson.'

Clay knew the name but wasn't sure where from.

'We think his wife Mary and three children are inside.'

'Did the neighbours know who that girl is?'

'None of the neighbours could identify her.'

Hendricks crouched on his heels, made eye contact and spoke to Eric Watson.

Clay looked inside, through the gap in the doorway. Four bodies were laid out at the bottom of the stairs and Clay recognised the shape immediately. It was the same irregular quadrilateral that Hanif Patel, his mother and daughter had formed on the first night in The Serpentine, only this time the shape was larger and formed from four bodies. By the patterns of blood splatter on the walls and the spray on the ceiling, it looked like they'd all been killed in the hall.

Sirens closed down as vehicles stopped a little way behind her. She turned, attracted the attention of a paramedic and pointed to the child. 'She's unconscious, no visible injuries. I'll send a guard and a child-protection officer to Alder Hey.'

She looked back at the bodies and noticed there was something small and black placed close to the mother's eyeless head.

Clay heard the thud of aluminium stepping plates being banged onto the snow and DS Marsh's voice. 'I'll plate up the hall and you can—'

A phone rang out from the hallway.

'Quickly, DS Marsh.'

He dropped the first two plates. The ringing came from the floor. The phone and answer machine had been placed close to the mother's ear.

Clay threw down four plates to create stepping stones through the hall to the bodies and the ringing phone. On the fourth ring, she strode inside. Two more careful steps and a fifth ring. She could see the display panel on the sixth ring. 07700 934763. The same number that had called the Patels' house, the number traced as Mrs Harry's mobile phone.

A mechanical voice on the Watson's answer machine said, 'There is no one to take your call at the moment. Please leave your message after the tone.'

As the tone sounded, Clay looked at the hollows of the mother's eyes and then at the display panel again.

07700 934763

Silence. And then an out-breath that shaped a sound.

'Eeeeeeeee…'

Silence.

The double click of a tongue like the beat of a diabolical heart.

Silence.

Double click.

Silence.

Double click.

Silence.

Double click.

Silence.

Double click.

'...vette.'

The caller hung up.

Clay hurried back across stepping plates and outside. 'Hendricks?' she called.

Hendricks looked up at her. Eric Watson had slumped down the wall and appeared drunk with grief and shock.

'Car keys, please, Hendricks.' Clay gestured for him to stand up, took the keys and spoke into his ear.

'The killers have just called the Watsons' answer machine. They spoke my name.' She pointed at Eric Watson. 'I don't care how you do it, Bill, but get him talking as fast as you can.'

'Did they say anything else?'

'Only my name.' She ran to Hendricks's car. 'They used mouth clicking,' she shouted.

Within the screech of the car's tyres against the ice, Clay imagined she heard the sound of a mother and three children screaming as they died in their home and wondered what she'd find when she arrived at the Drakes' house in Barnham Drive.

DS Stone was in the paved front garden outside the Drakes' house. All the curtains were drawn. The lights were off and there was no one home. Clay hurried over.

'I've only just got here,' said Stone. 'Guess what? No one home.'

'Order a ram to bang the door open, and a search warrant.'

Clay knocked on the right-hand neighbour's door and Stone, phone in his other hand, knocked to the left.

After an eternity of seconds, an elderly woman opened the door to Clay. She squinted at Clay's warrant card.

'Oh dear.'

'We need to talk to your neighbour Mrs Drake.'

'She's not here.'

'Do you know where she is?'

'She went away with the girls for a few days.'

'Do you know where she went?'

'She didn't tell me.'

'When did she go away?'

'Today. She was scared to death for the girls and herself after what happened to those poor families in Aigburth and Toxteth, so she upped and left, went to stay with relatives outside the city somewhere.' Clay looked at the old woman's mouth as she rattled out the words, the motion of her wrinkled lips hypnotic. 'She said she'd have to come back for work but that the girls would stay away until the police caught whoever's done these terrible things.' Clay imagined her own heart beating in time with the woman's language.

'She said to keep an eye out on the house.' Five double beats of her heart, a beat per word.

If the old woman was right, Mrs Drake had taken exactly the same precaution that she had with her own son in this storm of madness.

The woman's words sank beneath the other sounds clogging up Clay's brain. The message on the answer machine. 'Eeeeee...' Five double clicks of the tongue. '...vette...'

The pent-up pressure in Clay's head began to ease. She turned away from the old woman. There was a sudden sense, deeper in her brain, of a trickle building to a cascading stream.

'Karl!' She felt light-headed. 'Stay here. Right outside the Drakes' house. I've got to get back to Trinity Road.'

'Are you OK? You look like you're about to keel over.'

'I'll be back here as soon as I can. Call in some of the team for support. If you see Anais Drake or her two daughters, Coral and Faith, call me immediately and bring them in for questioning.'

Hendricks sat in the back of a marked police car parked ten metres away from the Watsons' house on Childwall Park Avenue. The house had been sealed off. Another family home turned into a crime scene.

Beside him, Eric Watson sat in silence, staring blindly at the snow on the grass verge outside the passenger window.

'OK, let's go,' said Hendricks to the young constable in the driver's seat.

Eric Watson looked up and stared at the back of the driver's head. 'What's happening?' he asked, his voice thick with emotion.

'Eric,' said Hendricks. 'You can't stay here all night. I do need to talk to you and I understand completely that you don't feel like answering questions at the moment.'

'Where are you taking me?'

'We're going to Trinity Road police station.'

'Why?'

'A change of scenery.'

The mortuary van was on its way. Hendricks pictured Eric Watson being haunted for ever by the vision of his wife and children being carried out of the house in body bags.

'What happened, Eric?'

'I took the dog for a walk. We were gone about twenty minutes, maybe a little longer, I don't know. We came home and then—'

'Did you see anyone?'

'No pedestrians. The odd car. Nothing significant.'

'Have you been following the news, Eric?'

Hendricks wondered if Eric had heard him. His eyes looked like he was lost in another place.

'Eric!' Hendricks gave him a gentle shake and made eye contact. 'The murders...'

'What murders?'

'It's been all over the news.'

'No. I'm in the middle of a massive court case. Drugs. I'm a CPS barrister.'

'One of us, eh?'

'I've been up to my eyes in it. I've scarcely been home. Time for the news? No time even for my wife and children.' He spoke bluntly and self-accusingly. 'Why do you ask about the news?'

'You're a brief. You know the drill in murder cases.'

'I'm the nearest and dearest, therefore I'm the prime suspect. Good luck, Detective Sergeant Hendricks.'

'I'm not taking you in because I think you're responsible for what's happened to your family. I want to get you some support here. And I need to get some background from you.'

Needles of snow fell, melting on contact with the car windows.

'Have you got anyone you want to call, put them in the picture? Somewhere you can stay?'

'No. We keep ourselves to ourselves. We don't have any family. We don't cultivate friendships.'

'There are advantages to that,' said Hendricks. 'Can I ask you a question, Eric? Do you go to church?'

'Personally, I go to eight o'clock communion at Christ the King, Queens Drive on Sunday mornings if I can. Mary and the children don't. Why are you asking?' In spite of his grief, Eric Watson looked at Hendricks with seasoned wariness.

'Did you ever belong to a church called the Christian Grace Foundation?'

Eric closed his eyes, shutting out the world if only for a few moments. He took a deep breath and looked directly at Hendricks.

'The Christian Grace Foundation? So it's finally come back to haunt me.'

At her desk in the empty incident room, Clay switched on her desk light and plugged the earphones into the iPad.

In her head she replayed the message on the Watsons' answer machine. '*Eeeeeeeee...*' Five double clicks. '*...vette.*'

On a piece of Merseyside Constabulary headed notepaper, she jotted down:

E – – – – – vette

Quietly, she spoke to herself.

'E, syllable. Five double clicks of the tongue. Like five heartbeats? Vette, syllable.'

She pressed play on the iPad and listened to the words that had carouselled around her head as she drove from Childwall back to Garston.

'*Evening is on a the fall all and a on child of actor artifact the one to one to one to who reigns parasite yes you in darkling red cloud oneness.*'

She pressed stop.

A given syllable. Five beats. A given syllable.

Hastily, she drew seven lines and wrote the letters of her name at the beginning and end of the set of dashes.

E   vette

– – – – – – –

She opened Adrian White's book and listened again, this

time following the text with her eyes, tapping out the beats on the desktop with her index finger.

'*Evening is on a the is . . .*'

She pressed pause. She picked up her pen and filled in the gaps.

Eve ning

— — — — — — —

Clay looked around, desperately wanting not to be alone, but there was no one there, just the sound in her head of the voice on the Watson family's answer machine.

'*Eeeeeeeee clickclick clickclick clickclick clickclick clickclick vette.*'

She stood up and walked away from the desk. She stopped and gazed into the darkness in the corners of the room.

In her mind she travelled back to Ashworth Psychiatric Hospital and watched as Adrian White walked naked into the meeting room, the numbers 1 and 7 tattooed on either side of his heart.

'No!' she said. 'No, no, no, no!'

She felt a sharp pain in her chest and, for a moment, thought she was going to collapse. But the sensation lifted and as it did so a voice spoke inside her. '*Don't turn away from the verge of truth.*'

In her heart, she was six years old again and Philomena's hands were on her shoulders, her voice as clear as if she'd been in the incident room with her.

Eve Clay, thirty-nine years old, joined in with Philomena's proverb, and spoke to the darkness.

'Ignorance is not bliss. It's just ignorance!'

She turned, walked back and sat down.

1   7

— — — — — —

She put the earphones back in and listened.

Pause.

Underline the first and seventh syllables, first and seventh,
follow the pattern. The words thundered inside her head.

1   7

<u>Eve</u> ning is   on   a   the   <u>is</u>

—   —   —   —   —   —   —

<u>the</u> fall all and a   on   <u>child</u>

—   —   —   —   —   —   —

She wrote down:

Eve is the child

Play.

She looked at and heard the next syllable: *of*

She wrote the word down.

Eve is the child of

The desk phone rang.

She counted syllables across the words.

...ac tor art i fact the...

Seventh in the sequence: *the*

Eve is the child of the

Suddenly she felt as if she had turned to stone, like her
flesh and bones had transformed into flint, encasing her
organs, which had melted into boiling lava.

The desk phone stopped ringing but straight away her
mobile rattled against the tabletop. The desk phone rang again.

Urgent! Urgent! Urgent! Urgent! Urgent! The word
bellowed inside her and she turned from stone and lava to
flesh, bone and blood.

She picked up her landline but couldn't find her voice.

'Eve, are you there?' It was Hendricks.

'Bill?'

'Eve, what's wrong?'

'What's happening?'

'I'm downstairs with Eric Watson.'

'Leave him with Sergeant Harris for now.'

'Eve, what's happening?'

'Come upstairs, Bill. Please hurry.'

He hung up immediately and she called Stone.

'Call Cole and anyone who's been working on the Baptist's writing and tell them to get to the incident room as soon as possible. I'll leave instructions. I've cracked the Baptist's code. I want everything we can squeeze from his writing by dawn.'

She took a deep breath and looked at the next seven syllables, underlined the first and seventh in the sequence.

<u>One</u> to one to one to <u>who</u>.

Eve is the child of the one who...

64

8.25 pm

In the observation suite of Alder Hey in the Park Hospital, the little girl appeared to be in an enchanted sleep.

An examination by an A&E consultant had shown no apparent medical problems with the child. Her blood pressure was normal and there were no external injuries. A CAT scan showed her brain activity as normal, but she showed no signs of coming round.

Riley sat next to the unknown child.

The green curtain around them parted. Riley expected to see Sergeant Alice Cowans, child-protection officer, returning from the toilet. Instead, it was an obese woman in her forties, dressed in a white coat and bearing a metal tray of needles.

'I need to take her blood sample.'

'Be my guest,' said Riley. 'She's out for the count.'

'It's all over the hospital.' The phlebotomist took a needle from its sterile wrapping. 'She's survived one of them murders.'

'That's pure nonsense. She was found at an RTA.' Riley felt sharply protective towards the child and didn't want prying eyes coming to stare at her. 'Put that out there.'

The phlebotomist swabbed the vein inside the girl's elbow.

The girl jerked and her eyes fluttered. The woman looked at Riley's face and said, 'You look like you've been in the ring with Mike Tyson.'

'You look like you've been in the ring with Hulk Hogan.'

The curtain parted again. As Sergeant Cowans came through, she said, 'I got lost on the way back.'

'Everything's well signposted,' said the phlebotomist. She prepared the needle.

Cowans and Riley exchanged a look.

The little girl's eyes flickered. She stared up at the ceiling.

'You awake, hon?' asked the phlebotomist.

The girl appeared not to have heard. She yawned and displayed two perfect rows of white teeth.

'Just giving you a little needle—'

'*Hon!*' said Riley, rolling her eyes. The phlebotomist flashed her a dirty look.

Cowans walked towards the bed and looked at the girl. She was pretty enough to be a child model and her hair, though gritty in places from the spray and snow, was as rich as honey and shone in the light from the anglepoise lamp on the wall above the bed.

When the needle sank into her arm, her face formed a mask of pain, but she didn't make a sound. As the phlebotomist drew her blood into the barrel of the needle, the girl's eyes drifted towards her. She stared at the woman, her face dissolving into neutral.

The phlebotomist drew the needle out and capped it. As she taped a cotton-wool ball onto the girl's inner elbow, the girl looked at Riley.

'All done now,' said Riley. 'You're in Alder Hey Hospital. You're perfectly safe. I'm a police officer. My name's Gina Riley and this is another police officer, Alice Cowans and she'll be looking after you until we can find your parents and get them to come and collect you. Can you hear me?'

The girl nodded.

'Do you understand what I'm saying to you?'

She nodded again.

'Can you speak to me?' She said nothing. 'I need to know your name.' Silence. 'Would you like me to send for paper and a pencil and you can write down your name?'

Cowans turned to the phlebotomist, who was watching from the corner of the cubicle, slack-jawed and crawling with sly curiosity. 'Would you like to go and get a seat, make yourself comfortable?' she asked

The little girl looked at the phlebotomist and a smile danced on her lips.

She pointed at the woman and beckoned her back to the bed with a tiny, bird-like flutter of her fingers.

The phlebotomist looked at Riley and Cowans triumphantly as she rolled back to the girl's bedside. 'You don't want *them*, do you? You want *me*, don't you, hon?'

The girl's lips moved and her voice was so soft it sounded like hissing.

'Speak up, love, I can't hear you.'

The girl spoke a little louder and the phlebotomist bent down from the hips, turned her right ear towards the child.

'I still can't hear you, hon.' Annoyance now bobbed up to the sugar-coated surface of her voice.

'I . . .'

'Go ahead, girl.'

The little girl rose from the pillow and pressed her mouth to the phlebotomist's ear. Riley and the phlebotomist stared at each other.

In a heartbeat, the girl's hands were at the phlebotomist's

head, her fingers entwined in tight knots of hair that she twisted and pulled. The phlebotomist screamed as the child bit down hard on her ear, her eyes pooling with rage and pain. The girl tugged with her teeth, anchoring her weight against the woman's head. A spray of blood hit the wall above the bed.

Riley grabbed hold of the girl's face and skull and tugged it away from the woman, who staggered backwards, screaming and holding the bloody wound at the side of her head.

Half of the woman's ear hung from the girl's mouth and her fingers were full of cheaply dyed blonde hair.

The phlebotomist's screams grew louder, shriller.

The little girl held Riley's gaze as she pulled the flesh into her mouth with her tongue and chewed, a stream of blood running down from the corner of her mouth.

'Raw is righteous.'

The little girl threw her hands at Riley's throat, but she intercepted her, grabbed the girl's wrists. The girl writhed and raged on the bed.

Riley pinned her down on her stomach and pressed the entire weight of her body on the child, who bucked and fought back with a strength that belied her physical size.

'Get her legs!' said Riley.

As Cowans leaned in to restrain her, the girl lashed out with her foot, catching her in the face. Cowans staggered under the sudden impact and backed into the green curtain.

'We need a doctor! Doctor!'

The curtains opened and a twenty-stone security guard and a female doctor appeared.

The guard approached from the side, pushed her feet down.

'I'll get a sedative,' said the doctor, departing.

'Why...' Riley struggled to speak, so fierce was the girl's resistance. '...did the Red...Cloud leave...you...behind?'

With one hand, she pressed the girl's head against the pillow.

The girl's eye was close to Riley's face. She stopped chewing and swallowed. 'We are Red Cloud and we turn human flesh to shit,' she said, darkness filling her eyes, her face contorting with apocalyptic fury. She spat a stream of thick, bloody phlegm into Riley's eye.

'You've got big feet for such a little girl,' said Riley. 'What size shoes do you wear? Size 2?'

The girl screamed, as if a rod of hot steel was twisting through her core.

Riley turned to Sergeant Cowans, blood streaming from her nose. 'Call Eve Clay . . .'

The little girl fell silent.

'. . . and get her to come here immediately.'

She started screaming again, growing louder with each out-breath. In the spaces around them, children started crying and, within seconds, the cries turned to screams as terror took hold.

65

8.26 pm

1		7
Eve	ning is on a the	is
The	fall all and a on	child
Of	actor artifact	the
One	to one to one to	who
Reigns	parasite yes you	in
Dark	ling red cloud one	ness

'How did you crack it, Eve?' asked Hendricks.

'The answer machine message in the Watsons' hall. The numbers 1 and 7 tattooed on Adrian White's chest. I listened to it over and over again. If I hadn't listened so much, I'm not sure I'd have made that final leap. Only the first and the seventh syllables count. The five beats in between, the heartbeats if you like, are just padding. Look at the six lines I've written down.'

The phone on her desk rang out, but it sounded far away.

'I wouldn't let him get under your skin. It's probably common knowledge out there that you didn't know your parents or even who they were. How many people did you meet, adults and children, when you were in the care system?'

'Hundreds. Hundreds and hundreds.'

'People talk. Facebook. Current status? On the toilet,

trawling over other people's lives. White's created a fictional history of your life based around that snippet of fact.'

She took the earphone jack from the iPad and pressed play. Stone's voice filled the room, reading the second chapter of *The Matriarch*.

'You going to get your phone, Eve?'

'I'll do 1471.'

She could feel her blood pressure rising as her face flared red. Hendricks watched her with quiet sympathy.

'Eve, you were the public face of the hunt to catch the Baptist. You know what I call this? Head games. And he can only play head games with you if you agree to join in with him.'

Hendricks confirmed a truth Clay's rational brain had already worked out. But in her heart, a maggot-sized version of Adrian White was stretching and contracting from chamber to chamber, playing on her insecurity, fuelling the torment of not knowing.

'You're right, Bill. Head games. Power play. He must have known he was going to get caught one day, that his power over life and death and people's hearts and minds was going to end with him being sent down and the key being thrown away. So, what was next for him?'

The door opened and DC Cole, the well-read officer who'd been assigned to reading and recording the Baptist's writings, walked into the incident room.

'I've cracked the code,' said Clay.

Cole looked impressed.

She explained the pattern and handed Cole a stack of photocopies from *The Matriarch* as he sat at his desk. She pointed at the verse that followed and read, '*Eternal night have clear to the red day Blood to ask undressed by the stars he moth stood in a on her night night so to those night on those when those red to the wind*... Here's the problem. The code breaks down immediately after the message, *Eve is the child of one who reigns in darkness.* My gut instinct is that there are other buried messages and it's a matter of trawling through White's writing, word by word, to see if the code kicks in again.'

Cole switched on his desk light and drilled the top page with his eyes, followed the text with his index finger.

'Don't—' began Hendricks, softly.

'I know,' interrupted Clay. 'I won't let anyone else see I'm rattled.'

'I've got Eric Watson waiting downstairs.'

The phone on Clay's desk stopped ringing and her iPhone erupted.

'He was a part of the Christian Grace Foundation.'

'You'd better get back to him then.' As she watched Hendricks walk away, Clay connected the call.

'DCI Eve Clay?' A voice she didn't know above the echoing screams and cries of children.

'Yes, who is this?'

'Sergeant Cowans, child-protection officer. I'm at Alder Hey with DS Gina Riley and the girl from the Watson crime scene.'

'What the hell's going on there?' It sounded like the sound-track from a suicide bombing.

'DCI Clay,' urged Sergeant Cowans, 'please get here as quickly as you can. We're going to a one bed room on the third floor.'

'I'll meet you there,' said Clay. 'How's the girl?'

'Savage. She's been sedated. DS Riley told me to tell you...' Cowans clearly didn't understand what she was about to say. 'She's Red Cloud.'

Clay disconnected and raced towards the door.

66

8.40 pm

In Interview Suite 1, Eric Watson sat half slumped over a mug of tea that had long gone cold. As Hendricks waited, sympathy for the man in front of him collided with his urgent need to gain information.

'Eric.' There was an edge of iron in his voice and Eric Watson looked up.

'Three nights. Three families. If the pattern continues, there'll be a fourth family within the next twenty-four hours, and you know what, Eric, chances are it'll be someone you know or knew in the past.'

Watson's interest was piqued. 'How do you *know* that?'

'Did you not hear about the Patel family?'

He thought about it for a moment and said, 'Hanif and Kate Patel?'

'Yes. It's been all over the news media.'

'Like I said, I've been locked in my study, getting my cross-examination ready. I worked, I ate, I slept a little. *Do Not Disturb* sign on the door. I was in court all day, with Jonas Bamber in the dock.'

'Bamber, as in drug lord Jonas Bamber?'

'Do you know how much money, time, effort and manpower has gone into getting his case this far?' A fresh wave of tears rolled down Eric's face. His mind rocketed to a different place. 'I can't believe what's happened...'

'Jonas Bamber. You were saying...?'

'My boss made it clear to me. If I messed it up on the day, then all that...work...so many people...'

Hendricks handed Eric a paper handkerchief. 'I understand,' said Hendricks, who'd once found out the result of a General Election two days late, having been locked deep undercover on a people-trafficking ring.

Eric wiped his face.

'The Tanner family?' asked Hendricks.

'Daniel and Gillian Tanner were...' Memory played out in Eric's eyes, and he looked utterly uncomfortable. '...Christian Grace Foundation. So were the Patels.'

'I'm sorry, Eric, but your family was targeted and one thing we know is that the three families all belonged to the Christian Grace Foundation. Hence my remark that you'll know or have known the next set of victims. I need to know what the Christian Grace Foundation was.'

'It was a small evangelical church based in Edge Hill. We used to have our services in a little hall in the old Archbishop Blanch School. Kate Patel was a governor of the school.'

Eric sipped his tea. Hendricks pushed. 'Go on!'

'There were ten families, ourselves included.' Silence.

'Eric, please, talk to me.'

'The idea was that we would take the example of the very earliest Christian Church and build an extended family in which everyone was equal and we all had a role to play, with no one better or bigger than anyone else.'

'There must've been a hierarchy, Eric? Ten families? It sounds small and manageable, but...'

'Yes, you're right. It was a naive dream to think we could

all come to each other's aid in time of need, like the early Christian Church. But at first, back then, it all seemed so...possible.'

'Someone must have started the group? You say there were no leaders, but in my experience, the founders are usually the leaders. Who were the founders?'

'Founder. Singular. Karisa Aden.' As he spoke her name, there was fear in his voice but also a real sadness. 'Married but her husband was away doing missionary work for the Lord. No kids, so she said, barren as Sarah in the Old Testament.'

'You still have faith?'

'I've clung on.' Eric looked deep inside himself. 'No. No.'

A picture started forming in Hendricks's head.

'Eric, forgive me. I'm going to jump from A to X here and, believe me, I am not being judgemental, but did you...?'

'Yes, I slept with Karisa. But I wasn't alone in receiving her favours. Most of the adults did. Men and women. And many of the older boys and girls. My wife's not a lesbian, but she turned into one when she was around Karisa.'

'Was she especially beautiful?'

'No. She was ordinary. But everybody thought she was...this goddess. It was like this collective madness around her. She took everyone in. We all thought we were the only person sleeping with her. We all thought we were the one. She was brilliant at building walls of silence within the group. We knew little or nothing about each other because she swore us to secrecy. The only person we could speak to was Karisa. And by the time I'd slept with her three times, she knew everything about me. All the dark things, the secrets, little details that should never see the light of day. I was completely and utterly in love with her and when I got to that point, that's when she started pushing me away. That's when she started demanding tithes for the church. That was when the walls of silence started to crumble. When ten per cent of my net income wasn't enough and she wanted twenty per cent, that's when husbands started to confess to their wives and when wives turned back to husbands and said, *Me too*.'

'Did you ever speak to, say, Hanif Patel about this?'

'Apart from my wife, Daniel Tanner was the first member of the group I spoke with. But that was only because of a coincidence.'

Hendricks wrote down: *Karisa Aden*. 'Was that her real name?'

'I doubt it.'

'How come you confessed to Daniel Tanner?'

'I didn't confess. I had genital herpes. I went to the STD Clinic at the Royal Hospital where Daniel works. I was waiting to be seen by the medics when Daniel walked in. I nearly died. He sat next to me and said, 'Karisa? I've had to go privately. People know me here.' That was the big moment. We had a meeting, on the Friday night, the seven sets of parents and the three single parents. Everything came out. Karisa knew nothing about the meeting, so we thought. We made a plan. We were going to confront her at the Sunday morning service. It was February 2010. We were going to demand all our money back and threaten her with the police. We showed up on the Sunday morning, and so did the Patels and the Tanners, along with Cynthia Highsmith and Pete and Jenny Williams. No one else showed, including Karisa. She wasn't physically at that meeting, but she was there all right. She had spies in the camp, people still loyal to her in spite of everything. When I phoned the bank to cancel the standing order to the Christian Grace Foundation, the man in the call centre told me there was no need. The Christian Grace Foundation had shut up shop on the Saturday morning and transferred all its funds out of the account.'

'You didn't see or hear from Karisa again?'

'I received a phone call from an undisclosed number on the Monday afternoon. She said, "Always remember, Eric, I know you conspired to pervert the course of justice. I know enough to get you struck off and sent to jail. Don't even think of involving the police."'

He looked Hendricks in the eye.

'I have nothing to hide and I have nothing to lose now. I want to confess...'

Hendricks switched record off on his phone.

'...to perverting the course of justice.'

'You're talking nonsense now, Eric. Do you want us to catch the killers?'

'Of course.'

'Then stop wasting my time repeating idle threats from some lowlife prostitute and con artist.

'If you take me...home...I'll be able to give you all the contact details for the other people involved, so you can warn them.'

Hendricks had the worst kind of sinking feeling and, guessing what was coming next, said, 'We did try to track down everyone else from the Christian Grace Foundation.' He remembered seeing Eric and Mary Watson's names in the Tanners' address book and their 2009 address being in the Albert Dock. The family that emigrated.

'I don't blame you,' he said.

'What for?'

'Moving away to Australia for a new start. But what brought you back to Liverpool?'

'We were there for three years. We woke up one bright, sunny morning and looked at each other. It was as if we had a moment of pure telepathy. *Why should we let that woman drive us from our home?*' A tear rolled down his left cheek. 'I said to Mary, *I miss the rain*. She said, *Me too*. We came home because we wanted to live life with our children on our terms not hers. So that's what we did. We came home. But she hadn't gone away, had she?'

In the lift ascending from the ground floor of Alder Hey in the Park, a text arrived on Clay's iPhone. She looked at the screen.

Hendricks

Christian Grace Foundation Leader Karisa Aden

Clay stepped out of the lift onto the third floor of the hospital onto a state of the art glass corridor. Riley was at the end of the corridor next to an armed police officer.

'She's in here, Eve. She's fighting to stay conscious, keeps drifting in and out.'

There was a hum of electrical energy in the air.

Clay walked past glass walled en suite wards, glanced at the sick children in various stages of getting ready to settle down for the night and wondered what she was going to encounter when she reached the end of the corridor.

'Savage?' asked Clay.

'She bit the phlebotomist's ear off, chewed it, swallowed it down,' said Riley as Clay stopped outside the single bed ward.

She looked through the glass and saw the girl lying still on the surface of the bed, dressed in a sky blue gown.

Clay entered and approached the girl on the bed. Her body was limp like a rag doll and her eyes were open but glazed. There was a rim of red around her lips, as if she'd been playing with her mother's lipstick. Her bloodless face was death-like.

She turned to the woman at the foot of the bed and asked, 'Sergeant Cowans?'

Cowans nodded.

'Can I ask you to step out of the room for a moment, please?'

When Cowans closed the glass door behind her, Clay stooped to put her face directly in the girl's eye line. Somewhere in the girl's eyes, remote awareness. Her muddled consciousness seemed to reach out to Clay and, for a moment, she looked like a drowning infant pleading silently for her life.

'Look at me,' said Clay.

She could see the struggle in the child's face as she tried to follow Clay's instruction and cling to consciousness.

'Listen to me.'

The ghost of a frown formed on the girl's forehead.

'I'm going to help you.'

Clay took the girl's limp hands and rubbed her fingers.

'And I want you to help me. Do you understand?'

The girl's lips parted as if she was forming a sound and a thin string of blood-streaked saliva fell from her lower lip.

'You feel very sleepy right now, as if you're in a dream.'

Her head lolled slightly, to one side.

'I'm going to tell you my name.'

The girl's hold on reality was slipping fast.

'My name is Eve Clay.'

'M.' Under her breath, a single sound, the beginning of a word she didn't have the energy to complete.

'I think I know your name.'

The girl forced her sinking lids apart and looked at Clay

through a haze of tears. Her eyes closed, she forced them wide open again, her willpower wrestling with the chemical haze.

'You should be out for the count,' whispered Clay. 'For a little girl you've got some strength.'

Clay looked down at the girl's bare feet. They looked like a size 2. She pictured them in Converse, one foot stomping down on Kate Patel.

'Is your name Drake?'

Clay sat on the edge of the bed and stroked the girl's head and face.

Tears fell from her eyes onto the back of Clay's hand. As the girl's eyes closed, a look of pure joy flashed through the deadness of her face, a shooting star flying through a pitch-black sky.

The girl's head turned slightly and her lips connected with Clay's fingers. She stilled her hands. Clay felt the soft puckering of the girl's lips as she kissed her fingers like a pilgrim at a holy statue.

She turned to look out onto the corridor outside and beckoned Riley to come inside.

Clay stood up and, as Riley entered the room, she scooped up the child from the bed and held her. She nodded at the bed and Riley pulled back the covers.

She laid the child down on her back, arranged the pillow under her head and covered her with the sheet and blankets. Just like Sister Philomena had done for her every night when she was a child. But Clay had no prayer to say over the child, no heaven to plead with for the child's safety and protection.

There was a smile on the child's face, a definite turn on the corners of her blood-red lips.

The rhythm of a rubber ball bouncing against an upstairs wall, onto the floor and back again built up inside Clay's head.

'I thought Faith only had one sister, Coral, and that Coral was playing with the ball. But it was you, wasn't it?' *Trying to attract my attention*, thought Clay. *Letting me know you were there.*

Clay turned to Riley. 'When she wakes, if the doctor needs to give her a sedative, ask him to give her a much reduced dose. I need her awake and talking.'

Five words rolled around Clay's head. *A prayer of sorts*, she thought. 'If there's a problem when she wakes up, tell her if she does as she's told I'll come back and see her right away. When she wakes, call me immediately. I'll be straight over.'

As Clay walked away, she felt the warmth of the child's tears and the weight of her lips lingering on the backs of her hands. The words rolled around her head, over and over.

You're safe now, Little Darkness.

You're safe now.

Little Darkness.

On the way to Barnham Drive, Clay ordered back-up officers to the Drakes' house. When she arrived, they were there with Stone, waiting for her.

Ram in hand at the front door, Stone asked, 'Ready, Eve?'

Clay stared at the plain, ordinary-looking front door and was filled with cold foreboding. Once again she felt the weight of Little Darkness's lips on the backs of her hands.

She looked at the door and imagined a vicious power, invisible and lingering in the shadows, waiting to snatch at her flesh and swallow her whole, wiping her physical presence from the earth, condemning her to billions of light years of oblivion.

'Eve, are you ready?' Stone repeated.

She rocketed back into reality. 'Ram the door!'

The hall was dark except for a red glow on the wall.

Clay stepped inside and saw the source of the dull light. It was the metal silhouette of the Liverpool skyline, the one she'd seen on her last visit to the Drakes' house.

Now it was switched on and the sky behind the black outlines of the cathedrals, the Liver Building and the Radio City Tower was blood red.

She turned towards Stone, his face made vivid by the crimson cast. 'Red Cloud rising,' she said.

Her voice echoed in the darkness. There were no signs of life in the house. 'They've gone,' she said. 'Keep guard on the front and back entrances. Close the front door and everyone stay as quiet as possible. Just in case they return.'

'You want me to turn on the lights?' asked Stone.

'No.'

'They won't come back now.'

'They're capable of anything,' said Clay.

As she raised her right hand to wipe the film of perspiration from her forehead, her fingers were made red with the light from the Liverpool skyline. She turned on her torch and drowned her hands in the plain yellow beam.

The bulb flickered as she stepped forward to the front room, where she'd spoken with Faith and her mother. The sofa and armchairs, the television that Faith had so casually watched, everything was as it had been. She explored the plain walls but nothing had been daubed there, no esoteric markings. As with her first impression, it was bland, soulless.

In the small room next to the front room she was surprised to see plain floorboards. She moved her light around the walls and into the space within.

'What is it?' asked Stone.

'It's empty. No carpet, not a stick of furniture.' She combed the room with torchlight. 'The walls are bare plaster and there's a piece of hardboard nailed across the window frame.'

She found the light switch and flicked it. Nothing. She pointed the torch at the ceiling and saw there was no light bulb, only a pair of unsheathed cables.

Had it simply been stripped for refurbishment? In the kitchen there was a table and four chairs, and a plate and full complement of cutlery at each place. Clay wandered deeper in, the bare floorboards creaking under her weight. There was a sink with no dishes in it, a two-burner cooker that looked like it had been made in the 1950s. She turned on the gas ring but there was no release of gas. She looked at the back of the cooker. It wasn't even connected.

The wall units were of a similar era. She opened a cupboard door. Four small cups, cracked and without handles, stood in a neat line in a space filled only with shadows.

Clay recalled Coral's words. 'We're a single-parent family.' But it didn't explain the poverty of the kitchen when the mother of that family worked double shifts.

In her mind, Clay walked from the front door to the back door. She realised that the front room was only for show. Visitors who called would go no further than that room. The rest of the downstairs, Clay knew, would be an ascetic shell. Even the stair carpet stretched only as far as the turn at the head of the stairs, the furthest point visible from the front door.

Poverty. The word echoed in Clay's head. Why such poverty? *Poverty.* The word sparked another. *Obedience.* A concept that might explain such miserable living conditions.

'What's going on?' The effect of Stone's voice was strange, like he was speaking to her underwater.

The relative affluence of the Drakes' victims was markedly at odds with the lifestyle chosen by Anais Drake. How thin had self-denial made Coral and Faith?

'They're nuns, Anais and her daughters...' As Clay articulated the idea that had formed in her mind, she instinctively knew she was in the presence of a bizarre truth. 'A cell of Satanic nuns for whom poverty is an essential vow.'

Just like Adrian White in his bare room in Ashworth Psychiatric Hospital. She pictured him there and felt increasingly convinced that there was some sort of bond between that small room and the house she found herself in, between the Baptist and the Drake family.

The largest bedroom at the front of the house was empty except for two single beds and the pair of cheap curtains hanging in the window that said *normal* to anyone glancing up as they passed on the pavement outside. She guessed it was the bedroom of Anais and one of her daughters. But in the little girl's sad gathering of garments, hung on a rail with her mother's supermarket uniform, there was no school uniform or any hint of a life outside the family home.

The second largest bedroom was just as drab. A metal-framed single bed with a large wooden wardrobe towering over it. Clay opened the door with trepidation and was taken aback to see just a St Bernard's school uniform and four other sets of clothes hanging there. Clothes to be worn out in the world, perfect disguises.

In the smallest bedroom at the back of the house, Coral's Liverpool Blue Coat School uniform lay draped and folded over a chair.

On the floor lay a long metal stick with a hook at one end. Clay scanned the bedroom ceiling, took in the bare-ended electrical cables, felt herself turning inside out as she stepped outside Coral's room and found the entrance to the loft next to the bathroom.

Inside the bathroom a tap double dripped, echoing. The rhythm of a heartbeat. Stone was in there. Clay heard the rattle of liquid in a metal canister and the spray of an aerosol, caught the scent of deodorant.

Click click click click click click click click click click.

She joined Stone in the bathroom. There were four toothbrushes and a tube of Colgate, two bars of soap on

293

dishes and a towel neatly folded next to a small stack of flannels. She looked inside a small box of make-up. Lipstick, mascara, foundation. A hairbrush and comb next to a pot of hair bobbles and metal clips. But somehow it didn't feel like a woman's bathroom, more like a man's vision of one.

'It's almost normal,' said Stone.

Clay caught her torch-lit reflection alongside Stone's in the narrow mirror on the wall. They both looked like half-formed ghosts.

'Almost,' she agreed. 'But not quite. The only reason they wash is because they can't afford to smell. It would get them noticed out there.' Clay had the clearest sense that everything in their world was a constructed inversion of reality. 'The only reason they use the toilet and don't relieve their bladders and bowels on the floor is because they'd end up sick and needing medical care or the smell would have the neighbours calling social services in. Abnormal is their normal.'

The sound of a phone ringing filtered down through the ceiling. It was coming from the loft.

Clay retrieved the metal arm from Coral's room. She stepped onto the cramped upstairs landing and passed her torch to Stone. He lit up the entrance to the loft and, with both hands, she guided the hook into the catch. Turning it slowly, she lowered the door on its hinges.

A strange light poured into the darkness around them. Candles. Dozens of them. A hundred or more perhaps, all burning in the loft.

The phone continued to ring, louder now, insistent, urging her to hurry into the space above her head, to connect with the caller.

Clay pulled the ladder down and started up it.

'Be careful,' said Stone. 'They could be up there.'

'I do hope so, Karl!' she said, swiping the metal arm menacingly in the air. But her heart banged against her ribs and her head buzzed with energy as she came closer to the square entrance.

The sloping roof-space was alive with light. She poked her head inside and froze at what she saw. Instinctively, she wanted to scuttle back down the ladder, but she couldn't move.

Dread and terror waltzed inside.

The shadow that had pursued her from Ashworth settled on her back.

69

9.45 pm

The phone on Hendricks's desk clattered into life and he snatched the cradle from the receiver.

'Eve, what's happening?'

'It's not Eve, Bill,' said Sergeant Harris. 'Sorry to disappoint you. It's about the boy, Jon Pearson. He wants to talk to you right now. Says it's very important.'

'Did he say what it's about?'

'He wants to tell the whole truth. He asked for Eve but said that you would do. *Any copper, really* – they were his words. He's insisting he wants to do it *right now*.'

'I'll call his mother, social worker and solicitor. Tell him it'll probably take an hour.' Hendricks looked at the time and sighed. Nine forty-five already. 'Given his age and the time, this isn't ideal.'

'It's all logged, Bill. He's slept from coming out of the last interview. He's just woken up.'

'Tell him to get himself ready with what he wants to say. I'll interview him as soon as his people are here.'

70

9.45 pm

'Eve, what is it?' Stone's voice was tense and urgent.

Candles burned on the floor and on the beams, in every available space within the half-pyramid.

A switch clicked inside Clay and she carried on up the ladder, one foot following the other as she made it to the top and stepped into the loft.

She heard the ladder creak under the weight of Stone's feet as he began to climb up after her. 'No! No! No!' she shouted. 'Stay down there. You *can't*, you can't come up here.'

The floor was made of caber boards and in the centre of it was the mobile phone, still ringing. Clay walked over to it, but as she picked it up it stopped. Slowly, she turned a 360-degree anti-clockwise circle, her eyes fixed on the sloping walls. There wasn't a centimetre that wasn't covered with images. Pictures that brought tears to her eyes and left her consumed with a dizzying nausea.

She dropped the phone, shut her eyes tightly and buried her face in her hands.

'Open your eyes! Look! Face what is before you!'

Voices slashed through her head at angles, voices she didn't recognise, and for a moment she thought she was going to die.

'Eve, what is it?' Stone's voice sounded like it was trapped in a bottle as the wind oozed and echoed like a whispered curse around the slates above her head.

She dropped to her knees, forced herself to remove her hands from her face and opened her eyes.

'Eve, talk to me, for Christ's sake!'

'Karl.' But she couldn't say she was all right.

'I'm coming up,' he called.

'No! You can't. You mustn't. I won't allow it.'

She sat on the caber flooring and picked up a glossy white-trimmed square, a Polaroid colour photograph from the 1980s, a blurred image that seemed to dance with life in front of her eyes.

Clay gazed at the photograph and felt tears stream down her face.

In the photograph she was three years old, wearing a blue dress with white socks drawn up to her knees. She was smiling into the camera, her arms raised into the air, her hands lovingly held by Sister Philomena's hands, on whose knee she sat.

She blinked away the tears, focused on Philomena's face and was amazed at how youthful her features were. In the well of memory, Philomena always looked elderly, but now she understood that the key image of the first love of her life had been tainted by her end, by death.

'We were so . . . happy together. Weren't we?'

Her eyes drilled into the photograph.

'Stay with me, don't go away, help me!'

She slipped the photograph inside her coat pocket.

'*Look around you, Eve.*'

Philomena's voice comforted her.

'*Look.*'

She encouraged.

'*See what is before you.*'

Clay turned to the sound of Philomena's voice, but all she saw were pinpoints of candlelight and the images that dominated the interior of the roof.

She wiped her eyes with the back of her hands and got to her feet. There was an altar at the centre of the loft, a table covered with a rich purple velvet cover, and it was here that her instinct told her to start.

Clay stood at the front of the altar and worked out that she could follow a chronological thread between the images.

First, there was a blown-up and crude radiographer's scan of a foetus. Slowly, her eyes followed the curve of the unborn child's spine. Notch by notch, she felt as if a finger was tracing the same path down her backbone. The child's fist was tight against its mouth, a thumb placed firmly inside. She made out the curve of the baby's middle and the tapering bones of the legs, all the pieces of an incubating human life beneath a storm of white static.

Her eyes drifted in an anti-clockwise direction and she saw a picture that made her gasp. A woman's legs wide open, her inner thighs splattered with blood and water, her vagina gaping and a baby's head emerging into a pair of waiting hands. She looked away and saw the next picture of herself, minutes old and cleaned up, the edge of the placenta still visible.

Clay kept turning. The next picture was taken from a distance. A blurred shot of her on a swing, aged three. Then she was ten years old, snapped through the railings of Our Lady Immaculate Roman Catholic Primary School. She was alone in the playground, lost in thought.

Looking at the posed photograph of herself in cap and gown, taken on the day she graduated with a first-class degree in geography from the University of Liverpool, she remembered how she'd given her allocation of family tickets to a girl who had a family to see her go through the rite of passage.

She picked herself out from the group shot of her class at the Merseyside Police Training Academy. In spite of her cap, and the formal face she'd been told to keep fixed, the joy and pride in her eyes was unmistakeable. In the next picture, she marched behind Stephen Jones, a handsome and charismatic young man who'd never known how strongly she'd felt about him and who had unwittingly broken her heart by becoming engaged to *the girlfriend back home in Wrexham*.

She felt the weight and cold touch of a drop of water on her head and looked up to the roof. There was another drop forming in the crack to the sky. It felt like she'd been smacked on the skull with a hammer.

'Talk to me, Eve. What's up there?'

'Karl,' she mumbled, trying to reassure him she was alive and conscious even though she was lost for words. Tucked into the shadows was a thick rectangle of card. She picked it up and felt as if her feet were going to rise from the floor.

'E V E T T E C L A Y' was spelled across its front. The file on Mrs Tripp's desk from thirty-plus years ago. She placed it down and looked around.

'What are you looking at, Eve?'

On a wooden beam facing her Clay noticed something gleaming in the candlelight. She walked towards it, drawn magnetically to the tiny object. Close to it, in the shadow of a cross-beam, she saw its twin.

'Jesus,' she said softly, and wished he was there to pray to.

She closed her eyes and tried to wipe her mind clean, but she knew she was saddled with a memory that would never leave her.

'Eve, what can you see?'

'I can see Kate Patel's eyes staring directly at me. I think they're hers, judging by the photos I've seen of her.'

In the silence, she wasn't sure whether she'd said the words out loud or just thought them. She stepped to one side, glanced again at the disembodied eyeballs and took in the space into which they stared.

She pivoted left.

'I can see another pair of eyes.' She walked towards them. 'I'm not sure whose they are.'

Clay looked away and saw a collage of images of herself. She was drawn to it by a large picture close to the centre. She was on the main path in Calderstones Park, pushing Philip in a pram, the autumn sun shining through a shower of falling leaves. The picture was clear, close-up, as if it had been taken right over her shoulder.

Now she knew they had been within touching distance of her for years and she'd never even known it. She scanned the other pictures. Newspaper cuttings about her arrest of the Baptist and pictures of her outside Preston Crown Court were pasted on the lining of the roof alongside pictures of her with Thomas on the deserted beach in Formby during their first winter together.

The marrow in her bones turned cold and sour. She felt a profound sense of violation. Suddenly, seeing her own life laid out around the walls became too much for her. *I need*, she thought, *to stand for an hour – no, more – for hours under a blistering hot shower.* From her scalp downwards, her skin felt filthy and uncomfortable, like she'd contracted a malevolent virus that had targeted her and her alone, leaving the rest of humanity untouched.

Clay sighed bitterly as she looked away. Another beam

and the third pair of eyes. All three were directing their unseeing gaze at the same point in the loft.

'What are you looking at?' she asked as she moved towards the focus of their attention. 'What do you want me to see?'

The focus of the three pairs of eyes was the altar.

Clay arrived at the table and, holding the edges, slowly pulled the purple velvet cover away.

Instinctively, she shut her eyes, but the picture was already printed deep in the fabric of her brain. It would stay there forever.

She forced herself to look again, to test reality. Her bones dissolved and a whip cracked dead centre through her brain. Now she couldn't look away, even though every piece of her will screamed at her to throw the cover back on the altar and escape from the obscenity that decorated it.

9.55 pm

On the surface of the altar, vivid colour dominated a universal sky. Shooting stars and meteors flashed through the shifting colours of night, the planets of the solar system laid out in order at the bare feet of a black-robed goddess, her arms outstretched, controlling order with the fingers of one hand and orchestrating chaos with the other.

Her robe was open. A serpent suckled one breast and a demonic infant fed on the other. She hovered in space, her legs wide open astride a dragon-like Satan who exhaled fire as he shot red-hot bursts inside her.

Sooner or later, Clay thought, focusing on the goddess's face, *other people will have to come in here and see this. I cannot keep the world away from this insanity. A beam of clarity came to her through the madness.*

'Karl!' She stared at the features of the goddess. 'Take a deep breath. When you come up, tell me if you think I'm going out of my mind.' There was a wistful smile on the painted face, but the eyes were hard and cold, like the Baptist's.

Clay listened to the creaking of Stone's footsteps as he ascended the ladder, then the stillness when his head came through and he saw the Satanic temple.

Then he exploded. 'Jesus! What is going on here?'

'It would seem my life is not my own. What I thought was my life wasn't. Isn't.'

Stone climbed into the space. 'Whatever's going on here, Eve... This is not you!'

Clay couldn't take her eyes away from the painted face on the altar, the faint smile and the dead eyes, the skin tone and the overall expression. The title of the Baptist's book flooded her mind. *The Matriarch*. Eve Clay was looking down at a lovingly painted image of herself.

'Karl, come and look at this. This is what they think I am.'

Bill Hendricks looked across the table in Interview Suite 1 at Jon Pearson, who was flanked by his mother, social worker and solicitor. He glanced at the video camera in the corner of the room and formally opened proceedings.

'This is a most unusual hour for an interview to take place with a person of your age. Just for the record, Jon, would you tell me what you said to Sergeant Harris, the custody sergeant.'

'I told him I wanted to speak to a copper right now because I'm not tired because I've been fast asleep and I've lost sense of what time it is but I'm wide awake and I want to tell the truth.'

'Fair enough, Jon. Sergeant Harris told me you wanted to tell the whole truth.'

'Yeah.'

There was a dip in the boy's bravado. He looked at his mother and she said, 'Tell the truth, Jon. Just tell the truth.'

'I feel...dead embarrassed.' He indicated the book bag. 'I want to talk about the drawings.'

Hendricks concealed his crashing disappointment with a neutral, 'OK. We can talk about the phone in a minute.'

'Can I ask you a question...' The boy checked the ID badge hanging from Hendricks's neck. '...Mr Hendry?'

'Fire away.'

'Can you get into trouble for making drawings like these?'

'That would depend on how old the people in the drawings are. How old are they?'

'Ten.'

'And are they real children or imaginary?'

'Real.'

'Then yes, technically speaking, whoever did these drawings has made a pornographic image of a minor. That's a very serious offence. Do you understand what's going on in the pictures?'

Hendricks slid the paper back inside the book bag.

'Yes, I do understand. Kind of.'

Hendricks looked at each of the women to cover up his glancing at Mrs Pearson, freefalling for the hundred thousandth time over many sorry years. 'How come you understand?'

'When I lived in St Helens, when I was a little kid, there was this man in our street and he used to make me sit with him and watch films of men and women and sometimes women and women and sometimes men and men and sometimes two women and one man…Sometimes he used to say what was going on, like a…a…like a…'

'Like a football commentator on telly describing what's happening in the match?'

'Exactly.' The little boy fell silent, stared into space and slowly returned his attention to Hendricks. 'I want to tell the truth. I admit…' He held up his right hand. '…this hand wrote the words on those dirty drawings. But I only did it because she made me.'

'*She*, Jon?'

'There's this girl in our class. She told me she's a witch and

306

I believe her because she can read my mind. Do you believe in witches, Mr Hendry?'

'I believe there are people who do some pretty strange stuff because they think it will please invisible powers and will help themselves and harm their enemies.'

'No. Honest to God, she's a witch. She can predict what's going to happen before it happens.'

'Has this witch in your class got a name?'

'Yeah. She whispers, *Mrs Harry is going to lose her temper and shout in ten seconds' time. Count in your head, Jon.* And she does. And it makes me go cold and hot. And I'm scared of her. She did the drawings, not me. And she made me write those things down. She said she'd put a curse on me. That I'd get taken away from my mum. When I woke up, just now, my head was, like, dead clear. And I thought, *Yeah, the curse has worked.* She can't do anything worse than have the coppers come to the house and take me away from me mum, so now I'm not afraid. I've not got nothing to hide. I'm going to tell on her, the nasty little cow!'

Jon panted, his face loaded with anger.

Hendricks poured him a glass of water and he downed it in one.

'Did she give you the pictures?'

'Told me to hide them in my house but not to look at them or open my book bag under any circumstances or it could unleash the curse.'

Hendricks looked at Jon and said, 'Faith Drake?'

The boy looked astonished. Hendricks glanced at his watch.

'It's not magic how I know, Jon. All that stuff she's been peddling is mumbo-jumbo. Dangerous and nasty mumbo-jumbo. Take it from me, everything that happens can be

307

explained.' He took in the group. 'Mrs Pearson, stay with Jon. I need to get the ball rolling to release him from custody.'

'Oh no,' said Jon. 'I want to stay here. And my mum. I don't mind being here so long as me mum's here. We're safer here. Aren't we?'

Outside the interview suite, Hendricks speed-dialled Clay.

'Bill?'

'Eve. Jon Pearson—'

'Faith Drake planted the phone and the pornographic drawings on him.'

'Yes. He thinks she's a witch.'

'She is a witch,' said Clay. There was a brief silence. 'As are her mother and sisters. They're a blood coven. You need to come to Barnham Drive as quickly as you can, Bill.'

Stone pulled the scene-of-crime tape across the top of the Drakes' staircase.

Clay stood at the bottom of the stairs, her personal file under her arm and the Nokia E63 phone from the loft in her hand. The Liverpool skyline picture glowed red against the hall wall. As the wind whistled outside, images from the display in the loft fast-forwarded through her head. Stone came downstairs and she looked him in the eye and said, 'Stay here with the constables until I send cover. We need to circulate the Drakes' pictures nationwide.'

'But there isn't a single photograph of them in the house, Eve.'

'Look at these, Karl.' She opened the photo gallery of the Nokia, the same model as Mrs Harry's mobile, and scrolled. 'Here, take the phone. Nine pictures from three crime scenes. What can you see?'

'I can see the bodies of Hanif Patel, his mother and daughter at the bottom of their stairs.' He scrolled. 'I can see the bodies of Kate Patel and her two daughters arranged on the upstairs landing.' Scroll.

Clay suddenly felt herself drawn to the bag on her shoulder.

'I can see the empty sockets of Kate Patel's eyes.' Scroll. 'I can see the bodies of Daniel Tanner, his wife and teenage children.' Scroll.

She looked inside her bag and saw the edge of Sandy Patel's cigarette packet. With her free hand she plucked it out.

'I can see a picture of Maisy Tanner standing over the bodies of her family.' Scroll. 'I can see the empty sockets of Gillian Tanner's eyes.' Scroll.

'Wait a second, Karl!'

She flipped open the lid of the cigarette packet and saw Adrian White's distinctive handwriting.

. n . w . - o

During the minute he'd had the packet behind the locked door of his room in Ashworth, he'd put his mark on Sandy Patel's property, just as the Red Cloud had left their barbaric stamp on his family's bodies.

Clay said nothing, put the cigarette packet back inside her bag.

'Go on, Karl!'

'I can see a photograph of a teenage boy trying to run away in the hall of the Watsons' house.' Scroll. 'I can see the bodies of Mary Watson and her three children arranged in the hall.' Scroll. 'I can see the empty sockets of Mary Watson's eyes.'

'Wait! Go back. And again.'

Stone looked at the screen, looked up at Clay and met her gazes with a puzzled smile.

'What's going on?' asked Hendricks, just arrived from Trinity Road.

'They took a picture of the Watson boy running away, towards the kitchen. Faith's chasing him with a metal bar and we've got a full-on shot of her face.'

'How come?' Hendricks peered over Stone's shoulder at the phone. 'If it's a picture of her chasing after him, won't you just get her back?'

'There's a large mirror in the Watsons' hall and they've managed to get a clear shot of Faith, even though she looks like a raving maniac.'

The demonic rage in Faith's eyes and the cast that the light made on the mirror made the image look like a still from a horror movie.

'*Looks* like...?' said Hendricks.

Stone zoomed in on Faith's face. There was something inhuman in her eyes. Her mouth was contorted, her teeth bared. She looked like a wild animal.

'She's in a state of religious frenzy,' said Clay. 'She's on a complete spiritual trip. Possessed.'

'I don't believe in the supernatural.' Stone spoke his thoughts out loud. 'I've come eyeball to eyeball with some really vicious hard cases, but she actually looks like the Devil.'

'Copy the pictures over to me and get them circulated nationally. Put a call out to all stations, ports and airports. When you've done that, check with the Women's Hospital for the birth records for Anais Drake.'

Clay's mobile rang out. The display read: 'Riley'. She connected.

'What's happening at Alder Hey, Gina?'

'The Drake girl, she's coming round. She's asking for you. She's becoming more and more distressed.' In the background, Clay could hear shouting and crying. 'She's begging to see you, Eve.'

'Tell her from me to stop speaking. I demand silence and obedience from her. And don't let Dr Midazolam anywhere near her with a hypodermic needle. Tell her I'm on my way.'

She calculated the distance from Childwall to Alder Hey. 'I'll be there in five to ten minutes.'

She handed her file to Stone. 'I'm trusting you with my life, Karl.'

'I won't let it out of my hands!' he called to Clay's departing back.

Driving to Alder Hey in the Park, Clay tried to block out all thoughts of the painted image of herself on the altar in the Drakes' loft space, but the image was too vivid. Her head spun as she recalled a detail she hadn't acknowledged on first sight. The Devil, with whom she was shown wistfully fornicating, had had his claws around her centre, completely enclosing her womb.

Why? she thought, bitterness mounting. *Why me?*

On the third floor, Clay could hear the fatigue in her own footsteps as she passed the darkened wards and sleeping children. As she approached the side ward, she noted the little girl's laboured breathing.

'Now, breathe out slowly.' Riley's voice, calm but firm. 'DCI Clay wants you calm.'

Clay looked through glass. DS Gina Riley and Sergeant Cowans were on either side of the bed, each holding the little girl by the hand. The girl was sitting bolt upright, rocking backwards and forwards, her face full of tension, holding in a storm of tears. Clay shivered at the thought of her involvement in the barbarity of the last three nights, a small child placed by chance in a pit of psychosis.

Stepping into the room, Clay looked directly into the girl's eyes. She squinted as if she was seeing an apparition and suddenly stopped rocking. Clay walked over to the bottom of the bed.

The girl leaned forward and twisted her hips and legs so that she was on her knees.

'Let go of her hands,' said Clay.

'She's dangerous,' said Riley, releasing one hand as Cowans let go of the other.

The girl bent her elbows and, with her fingers outstretched and palms turned up to the ceiling, said, 'I dreamed you looked me in the eyes, Blessed Mother. I dreamed you carried me, centre of all shade, and laid me down to sleep.'

Clay imitated the girl, holding her own hands up to the sides of her head, palms to the ceiling. 'Listen,' she said. 'Hush.'

Outside, the wind battered the building.

'What's your name, Little Darkness?'

'Am I seeing you?'

'Yes.'

'Am I dreaming?'

'You are seeing me as I am seeing you.' Clay mirrored the girl's actions. As the girl stretched her hands out to Clay, so Clay held her own hands out towards the girl.

'What is my name?'

'They think you're Eve.'

'What is your name?'

'Adie.'

'Who am I?' asked Clay.

'Part human.'

'*Part* human?'

'Part not.' Adie Drake drew her index finger across her sealed lips. 'That is the great mystery,' she said, in a voice that could have pronounced, *And they all lived happily ever after.*

Clay turned her hands so the backs faced Adie and beckoned her forward. The girl placed her hands on the bed and crawled on all fours towards Clay. When she was just beyond arm's reach, Clay said, 'Stop!'

She stopped.

'Sit.'

She sat, legs outstretched, her palms pressed against the bed. Clay saw a glimmer of light beneath the dark surface of the girl's eyes. Adie's lips trembled as she spoke from the heart, words that were too quiet to hear.

'I can't hear you,' whispered Clay.

'Blessed Mother, who looks into shadows, sees mirrors...'

Adie fell silent and stretched out her right arm towards Clay, who took a step closer and held the girl's hand. The girl lifted her left hand towards Clay. She twined her fingers around the girl's hand and was surprised by the intense cold of her flesh.

'When I dream of you, Blessed Mother, when I touch you, you explode into millions of stars and then the stars die and I am alone again.'

Clay wondered if Adie was visually impaired. Her unfocused stare was both pitiful and unnerving.

'Adie, I went to your house to visit you, but you weren't there.'

'Only you can be in two places at one time. I was here.'

'Your mother wasn't there. Coral wasn't there. Faith wasn't there.'

'Only you. They were. Somewhere. Else.'

'Where is? Somewhere? Else?'

'Only you can see for miles.'

'They're in the dark,' said Clay.

'Yes.'

'But the dark is all around us.'

'And you are the true centre of that darkness.'

Clay sat next to Adie on the end of the bed and disentangled her fingers from the girl's. Slowly, she picked the little girl up by her bony arms and sat her on her knee. Adie's head came to rest against Clay's shoulder. She was too thin. Her bones jutted into Clay's skin and she understood that fasting went hand in hand with poverty as a part of the Red Cloud's religious observation.

She wrapped her arms around the girl, holding her tight. 'Do you feel safe now?'

'Safer than I've ever felt.'

'The Red Cloud is rising, Adie?'

'The Red Cloud has risen, the river runs with blood.'

'Who is the Red Cloud?'

'We are the Red Cloud and though we are one, there are many, in all places and through all time, waiting to rise up. We are the first and others will follow. We are the sign that you are here. Other Clouds will rise. The Yellow Cloud. The Black Cloud. The whole world is covered with Clouds waiting to rise.'

Clay noticed a coldness spreading across Adie's face, her dark eyes filling with a deeper pitch.

'The Red Cloud rose tonight?'

'It was their joy to be chosen and our privilege to serve.'

In her bag, Clay's iPhone rang out.

'What was that noise?' Adie was alarmed and Clay held her tighter.

'It was nothing.'

Clay felt Riley take her bag. The phone stopped ringing.

'It's me.' Riley's voice, softly.

'What did you say?' asked Adie.

'It's me,' replied Clay. She looked down at Adie's feet. A picture of the bruising on Kate Patel's body, the diamond pattern of the sole of a small footprint, rose up and faded.

'What do *you* do when the Red Cloud rises, Adie?'

'You know what I do.'

'I want to know if you have been instructed correctly by Anais.'

'I am the door.'

Three successive images flashed through Clay's head. *I am the door.*

'I know what you did,' she said. 'I watched you and...' She pictured Adie at the door of the Patels' house. '...you stood at the door of the big house and rang the bell.'

'The girl called Alicia opened the door,' Adie said. '*I am lost*, I said, tears falling down my cheek. *Let me in. I am scared of the dark.* She called, *Mum! Dad!*'

Clay glanced back at Riley. Adie had caught the cadences of Alicia's voice, imitating her with chilling precision, as if the teenager's restless spirit had slipped inside the little girl's body.

'She shut the door. Alicia. *What's going on, Alicia?*' Now Adie slipped effortlessly into the mature tone of a middle-aged woman, a voice Clay knew was Kate Patel's. 'Did I do well?'

She fell silent. Clay heard only the sound of a pen dancing wildly across the surface of a piece of paper.

'I've been waiting all my life for you,' said Adie. 'Have you been waiting all your life for me?'

Clay whispered in Adie's ear. 'Can you tell me what I am?'

'I've told you all I know now, Blessed Mother.' Her body sagged with exhaustion. Her eyelids closed over slowly as she battled to stay awake. In moments, the fight was over.

Clay lifted Adie and placed her carefully between the sheets, tucking her in and listening as her soft breathing thickened. She imagined Philip born into the same circumstances as Adie. She turned to Riley and Cowans. 'First thing in the morning,' said Clay to Sergeant Cowans. 'I want the consultant psychiatrist with her. I want you to get the ball rolling to make her a ward of court. Sergeant Cowans, you're to stay with her as her key child-protection officer. I'll send support so you won't be alone with her. Gina, I need you to come with me now.'

Clay saw the paper in Gina Riley's hand.

'What was the phone call?'

'Bill Hendricks,' said Riley. 'I wrote it all down to pass to you.'

I've been in touch with the Women's Hospital and I got the registrar out of bed. Coral Drake was born at the Women's on 4 January 2000. Her birth was registered at Brougham Terrace by her mother Anais on 6 January, father unknown. Faith Drake was born at the Women's on 1 March 2008, birth registered on 3 March by her mother, father unknown. The registrar checked against the national database. There are no records of Anais Drake having a third child. Officially, it looks like the little girl you have in Alder Hey doesn't even exist.

75

11.17 pm

In her car, Clay waited, listened, her iPhone on speakerphone.

'Anais Drake's fixed on you because of the Baptist,' said Riley, sitting next to her, staring out as fresh snow fell on the old frozen covering.

Clay listened to the silence on the other end of the line and pictured the emptiness of the day room as the patients on the High Dependency Ward slept soundly and the night staff whittled away the wood of time with card games played in the half light of desk lamps in the nurses' station.

Flat-footed steps came towards the phone and she pictured the Baptist, physically naked, his twisted spirit gorging itself on the sudden call in the small hours, his eyes sucking in the shadows around him and replenishing the vat of darkness within.

She heard a door close and a door open.

Voices. But not his. There would be a group of four nurses escorting him to the phone.

'He's coming to the phone,' she said, gripped with a sharp sense of expectation and creased with the probability of failure and frustration.

Riley pressed record on her phone, held it close to Clay's mobile and flicked open her notebook.

The receiver was picked up from the desk.

'DCI Clay?' It was George Green. 'I'll put you on to Adrian White.' Clay listened as he handed the receiver over to White. She stayed quiet. In her mind's eye, she recalled White standing silent and impassive in the dock in Preston Crown Court after Judge Royce-Lear asked him to enter his plea. The judge had become impatient. 'Do you have auditory impairment? Guilty or not guilty?'

'Unafraid of silence.'

'How is Adie?' His voice went off like a bomb inside her ear. 'Fifty-three. Did she enlighten you, Eve? Forty.'

Riley glanced up from making notes, made eye contact with Clay.

They both knew White wanted the gratification of her asking for clarification on the numbers he was throwing out. Clay gave him none.

'Was she pleased to see you, my little Adie?'

'In what way does she belong to you?'

'Did you warm to her? Sixty-two.'

'The marks you made inside Sandy Patel's cigarette packet...'

'How did you miss them, Eve?'

'You only give information when you want me to do something, when you want to manipulate a situation from a distance.'

'You could be right. You could be wrong. Out of the mouths of babes, Eve.'

'Adie's asleep and she's told me everything she knows.'

'She couldn't possibly have done that.'

'What do you mean?'

'I mean you've got sixty-eight seconds before I hang up, that's less than two, Eve.'

'What do you mean?'

'I mean ninety-five's too many. Time's a wasting, Eve. And that's a real sin.'

'You've got all the time in the world.'

'What is the world to me? Time? I sit and watch the seconds die, counting down the death of time, the final countdown, the beginning of the end. Count with me, Eve, and wake up to the one reason you were put on this planet. What is your birthday, Eve? Has the sun finally set on that fateful day?'

The seventh of January, thought Clay. Seconds collapsed in the silence between them.

'Such intimacy between...'

'How are you communicating with the Red Cloud?'

'...the hunter and the hunted, but which is which?'

She could feel the pleasure throbbing from him and pouring into her ear.

'How are the Red Cloud communicating with you?'

'I emit signals. They receive them.'

'Who is the link between you and the Red Cloud?'

'Why, Eve, you! Even though you don't know who you are, Eve. But I do. And soon so will many others.'

'Who do you think I am?'

'You are about to find out.'

The line went dead.

She threw open the door and scrambled out of the car. 'You drive!' she said to Riley as she made her way round to the passenger seat.

She buckled herself in as Riley turned on the ignition.

'Where are we going?'

'Back to the Drakes' house.'

Clay threw on the little light above her head.

Riley was in third gear and rising to speed as she negotiated the treacherous surface of the car park.

On her iPhone, Clay connected to the internet, YouTube. She typed in: *Bill Hendricks Merseyside Police press statement*.

She looked at the screen and pressed play with the sound muted. She watched Hendricks speaking formally to the press, reviewing what she'd seen on the TV in the day room after she had talked to White. Finger poised on the pause button, she waited for the moment when the camera turned to focus on his audience. Feeling deeply uneasy, she paused the footage. The screen was full of faces obscured by cameras and microphones.

Riley slowed at a junction as another vehicle crossed her path. 'What you looking at?' she asked.

Clay showed her the image. 'I want this picture but clear and blown up, earliest opportunity.'

'I'll call DC TN Ryan and get him on the job.' She sped across the junction.

'TN?' asked Clay.

'Techno nerd.'

Clay stared at the picture, pressed play, drilled the screen with her eyes.

'What's eating you about it?'

'I don't know for certain, but it's ringing my alarm bells. Maybe it's just because it was the first thing I saw after hooking up with the Baptist in sunny Ashworth.'

Or maybe, she thought, *I'm going mad and will never be the same again.*

Play. Pause. She gazed into another moment of the footage. Eyes. Mouths. Faces. Something.

Nothing.

11.37 pm

On the journey from Alder Hey in the Park to the Drakes' house, Clay watched the footage on YouTube over and over. But when Riley pulled up outside the house, she was still none the wiser.

Frustrated, she turned to Riley. 'Listen to what White says on the call. Pull out anything that strikes you as loaded.'

She stepped out of the car.

'Bring it to me as soon as you finish transcribing. Bring it up to the loft. Don't worry if you can't make sense of it. We'll put our heads together. I'll be in the loft with Karl Stone and Bill Hendricks. We're the only four allowed in there.'

'What's inside the house? The loft?'

'Sickness,' replied Clay. 'Prepare yourself.' She shut the passenger door and headed towards Hendricks and the squalor that was the Drake family home.

'Bill, while I've been gone, Karl hasn't mentioned anything to you about the loft space?'

'No, he said you didn't want him to spill the beans.'

'The whole house is riddled with signs of profound psychological damage. But the loft, the loft is something I really need you to look at.'

'Take me there, Eve.'

'On one condition. You have to be completely honest with me. And that's going to be most the difficult thing I have or will ever ask of you.'

They stopped at the door and the uniformed officer manning it looked away.

'I'll tell you the truth, Eve, however hard that is.'

In the Drakes' loft, the air was still, silent and bitterly cold.

'I'll go in first. You follow me.'

Clay clutched the file that Stone had guarded for her. She was torn between wanting to drop everything so she could devour its contents, and pushing ahead with the night's work.

There'll soon be time, she told herself, but it did nothing to douse the lifelong fire of not knowing.

She folded her arms and clutched the file to her breasts, watching Hendricks's face as he emerged into the loft. He stopped dead on the ladder, just as she'd done when she'd first entered. Hendricks took in the whole room with a swivel of his head, then his eyes settled on Clay.

She was overwhelmed with emotion as Hendricks made the last few steps into the loft. As Stone followed him up the ladder, Hendricks stayed out of Clay's personal space but looked her directly in the eye.

'None of this is anything to do with you, Eve.'

'Then who is it to do with?' she asked, almost hugging herself, remembering exactly how she'd felt in the days after Philomena died and she was transferred to St Michael's Catholic Care Home for Children. For a moment, she was six years old again, small and at the mercy of the world around her.

'Anais Drake. You're the centre of someone else's mindset. It's psychotic. We battle it, that's what we do. You're not alone. This is someone else's belief system and that mindset and belief system doesn't come from you, owes nothing to you. Anais Drake? How far down into her life will we have to dig to uncover the abnormalities in her experience? Not far.'

Hendricks turned a full circle and approached the altar. He looked at it for a few moments and then lifted the purple velvet cover, revealing the pornographic image of Eve Clay.

He covered up the image again.

'There's a two-step inversion going on here,' he said. 'Humanity as divinity. Divinity as demonism. We're just not conditioned to think like that in the West. But Anais Drake does. If I'd caught the Baptist, it'd be me on these walls, not you.'

Clay nodded but completely disagreed with him. Everything in the small, dark, suburban chapel went far beyond her connection to Adrian White. The images on the inside of the roof were stepping stones that linked her whole life from her earliest days to the present. That someone had been following her, stalking her down the years without her knowledge, was horrific enough. But the fact that Anais Drake and her children knew more about her early life than she did herself was unbearable. Even the image on the altar could not compete with that.

'What do you want us to do, Eve?' asked Hendricks.

'Read the writing on the walls. Look at the pictures.'

A candle died in the corner and the smell of smoke permeated the half-lit loft.

She drifted to the altar and placed the file down on the purple velvet. A desperate urge to look at the records of her life possessed her. But although she was in the company of two men she trusted with her life, not knowing what lay within those covers, she had no idea how she would react to what she found there.

She looked up and watched as Stone shone a torch onto the walls and Hendricks took pictures.

Do you want to find out here? her inner voice whispered. *In this cesspit? There are better places, safer spaces for you to be in.*

Clay looked down at the surface of the file and was transported back in time to Mrs Tripp's office in St Michael's Catholic Care Home for Children. Her name in thick black felt-tip capital letters across the battered surface of the card.

'E V E T T E C L A Y'

She didn't know whether it was a trick of time or the light, but she was certain that the file was much slimmer than it had been in the autumn of 1984. No, it had bulged on Mrs Tripp's desk. On the Drakes' altar, the papers inside sat neatly. Whatever was in there, much was missing.

'Have you found any numbers?' She heard her own voice and it sounded like someone else speaking.

'No,' said Hendricks.

'I saw some numbers carved on a rafter,' said Stone, pointing his torch at the wood. '07...01...78.'

'That's thought to be the day I was born. It's when I get my birthday cards.'

She looked back at the file and wondered how on earth Anais Drake had acquired it.

Footsteps sounded on the creaking ladder. 'Who is it?' she called.

'It's me. Gina.'

Clay looked to the entrance of the loft as Riley's face appeared.

'Weird!' Riley exclaimed. She buried the shock and looked directly at Clay. 'But so what?' She climbed in, clutching her pen and notebook. 'Look at this,' she said, advancing towards Clay, not even glancing at the walls.

'What have you got?'

Riley handed over the notebook. 'I picked through the Baptist's words and this is what I've come up with.'

11.55 pm

Clay scanned Riley's neat handwriting.

fifty-three
forty
Adie enlighten you
warm to her sixty-two
out of the mouths of babes
sixty=eight
less than two
ninety-five
time's a wasting
real sin
seconds die
death of time
final countdown
birthday (date of Eve's birth)
sun finally set
fateful day
hunter and hunted

'I think the numbers refer to time. He referenced time,' said Riley.

'If he's talking on the surface about time then in my book he's talking about anything else but time. The time talk's a smokescreen,' replied Clay. Riley pressed play on her phone and, as the recorded conversation drifted round the rafters, Clay could feel a presence growing behind her. A smell of musk and a vivid sweetness filled the air.

'You could be right... You could be wrong... Out of the mouths of babes, Eve?'

Clay turned slowly as a cold breath danced on the nape of her neck.

She could feel the part of him that lived in her head seeping out of her like an evil spirit and solidifying in the shadows of the loft, hanging over her like a toxic red cloud that was aching to rain blood down on her.

'What is the world to me?'

She zoned in on the recording, tried to block the rising dread within herself, joining in with his words under her breath.

You don't know who you are, Eve. But I do. And soon so will many others.

Who do you think I am? Her voice sounded hollow, waiting for something to come and fill the vacuum.

The line went dead. The recording ended.

Under Riley's notes, she wrote: *fifty-three, forty, sixty-two, sixty-eight less than two, ninety-five.*

My birthday? Seventh of January 1978. She jotted down: 7/1 78.

She read the numbers out loud as she converted them into digits with the pen.

53 40 62 68...

'Less than two?' she thought out loud. Minus two.

...–2 95 7/1 or 71 78.

A drop of icy water landed on her head and a chill spread through her. Another candle faltered and died and as she breathed in the smoke a sourness erupted on her taste buds, triggering a memory of the Linda McCartney Playground and then of the meeting room at Ashworth Hospital. Her reflexes sent her into her handbag for another look at Sandy Patel's cigarette packet. She flipped it open and peered again at the marks the Baptist had made.

. *n* . *w* . - *o*

'Stop what you're doing!'

The words span around her head and the electrical storm on the surface of her brain caused speech to gridlock in her throat.

'Eve, what is it?' Hendricks sounded worried.

'53...' she managed to say... 'point 406268 – the "n" on the cigarette packet is for north. Minus 2 point 957178. "w" is for west. They're coordinates for an area in Liverpool.'

'How do you know that?' asked Riley.

'I've got a degree in geography, Liverpool Uni.'

She watched as Stone pressed the Maps app. He tapped search.

'Read the numbers to me, Eve.'

'53.406268.'

Stone typed as she spoke, placing the decimal point after the digits 53.

'-2.957178'

As he finished typing, Stone turned his phone screen towards her.

Immediately a street map appeared with a red-headed pin pointing to an exact location and the words *Mount Vernon*.

'Edge Hill. Mount Vernon.'

Clay read the map and recognised the site overlooking the old Archbishop Blanche School and knew that it was now the location of Liberty Park, a modern block of student accommodation.

'It's close to where I lived in St Claire's, until I was six years old. That set of coordinates...' She shut her eyes, put her hands over her face as she sank into the darkness of the dream of her childhood adventure into the derelict house. She kept her eyes shut, remained locked in the darkness, and said, 'I know why the Red Cloud staged the bodies in the way they did.'

Pictures appeared in the darkness, lit up suddenly and back to black. Hanif Patel and his mother and daughter in an irregular quadrilateral. Kate Patel and her two daughters as a crooked w. The bloody marks on the walls of the Patels' staircase.

She opened her eyes and the dim candlelight was almost blinding, so deep was the darkness from which she emerged.

'They staged them as maps.'

'Maps? Of what?'

'The Victorian tunnels under Edge Hill. The ones that have been discovered and mapped. There are still hundreds of tunnels that haven't been located. But these shapes, the bodies...'

The idea came to her quickly and she was immediately convinced of what was coming next. The precise shape of the bodies at each of the three scenes suddenly made perfect sense to her.

Clay's iPhone rang out. She looked at the display and saw: 'No Caller ID'.

She pressed connect.

'Come and get us, but come alone.'

'I know where you are, Anais.' Clay turned on speakerphone. 'And I know why you picked the Williamson Tunnels.'

'Yes. But do you know who *you* are?'

Day Four

'Where am I, Anais?'

'You're in the sanctum. The sacred space. There is another sanctum. Do you like how we have set it out for you?' Anais spoke softly, with a mixture of reverence and suspicion.

Clay knew it was possible to get a telephone signal in the tunnels. She'd been chided by a guide for not switching off her mobile when she'd last been on a Williamson Heritage Centre tour of the U-shaped section at Smithdown Lane.

'Where's Maisy Tanner?' she asked.

'Are you going to come and get her?'

'What do you want, Anais?'

'Come to us, but come alone. You've been misguided from the day of your birth. Do you want to know about your birth?'

'How do you know about the day of my birth?'

'Many people know about the day of your birth. The seventh of January is a special day to us. To all of us. And you will come to us. You must come to us.'

'Are your girls there? Faith? Coral?'

'Are your colleagues there? Stone? Hendricks? Riley? They shouldn't be in the sanctum. But that's all part of the confusion surrounding you. It won't last. It can't. My girls are here. They are waiting for you. So am I. Shall I tell you something about Faith and Coral? They have no fear of death whatsoever.'

'Why don't you leave the girls where they are, and you and me, we'll meet in the Mount Vernon tunnel. I know exactly where the entrance is.'

'There are many ways in and we know several that no one else knows.' Anais's voice had taken on a menacing tone that rattled Clay and sent her mind spinning with anxiety.

'What about Adie?' she asked, switching tack. 'Do you want to know how she is?'

'She's well. She's perfectly normal. We are all normal, we are right, we see things clearly, for what they are. It is the world that has one blind eye and the other one blinkered and short-sighted. Adrienne can see the clearest of us all.'

'Is that why you left your child in Childwall Park Avenue?'

'My child?' Anais laughed. 'It isn't your fault.'

Clay sensed that Anais was talking as much to herself as she was to her.

'What's not my fault?'

'That you don't understand. That you don't see straight. That you listen but you cannot hear.'

'Adrienne? Did you name her after Adrian White?'

'You've been abused, Eve. Horribly misguided in all... Adrienne has been brought up in quite the opposite way. I am going to go now.'

'I don't think you'll ever see little Adrienne again. How does that make you feel, Anais?'

A moment of quiet passed.

'Proud. Come, but come alone. Let me make myself clear. If you bring anyone with you, I will kill Maisy Tanner and both of my girls before your eyes.'

'How will I find you?'

'You will know.'

'But there are miles of tunnels under Edge Hill.'

'Indeed. And there are many more miles still to be unearthed. But they will be. And we know a way in that no one else knows. And we shall see you in the dark. And we shall see you are the dark and the darkness will wind her way to us and we will welcome the darkness and drink it in and become united with the darkness.' Silence. 'You've got an hour. If you don't make contact with us in that hour, I will make martyrs of my daughters and food for the rats of Maisy. When you look into shadows, you look into mirrors. When you look into mirrors, what do you see?'

The line went dead.

'You can't go into Williamson Tunnels alone,' said Stone.

'It's a trick,' said Hendricks. 'They'll kill you and we'll never find your body.'

The same sour music ran around the inside of Clay's head.

'We'll come down with you,' said Gina Riley.

'If any of you go down, you're as good as dead. They can probably make their way round the tunnels in the dark. You can't. You might as well say goodbye to your loved ones right now. They want something from me. That's why I've got a chance. I'm going on my own. I'm going into the dark. I have no choice.'

Clay looked at her watch. There were many hours until daylight.

'You need to track down the people who maintain the tunnels. Call him or her and tell them to meet me at the back of The Bear's Paw pub in Edge Hill. Cordon off the area from the Royal to the junction of Wavertree Road and Tunnel Road. Curfew. No one in the neighbourhood is to leave their house.'

She felt the life lines on the palms of her hands moisten.

'And we need paramedics and mortuary vans on standby at the edge of the exclusion zone. 53.406268, –2.957178.'

There was something else about the place that ran as a deep current beneath the waves in Clay's head, but she kept it to herself.

She was down the ladder from the loft two steps at a time.

Clay had fifty-nine minutes to make contact with the Red Cloud. As she headed towards the front door, she wondered if she would still be alive when morning came.

80

00.10 am

As the phone rang out in the nurses' station, George Green turned over a seven of spades and his game of solitaire turned into a dead-end.

He picked up and said, 'Staff nurse...'

'Is that you, Richard?' A young female.

'Er...no, Richard Taylor's off sick. George Green speaking. Can I help you?'

'Have you looked in on Adrian White lately?'

The line went dead.

Green looked around at the dark, empty day room. He phoned his colleague on the night shift.

'Where are you, Eddie?'

'Just outside. Been for a smoke.'

'Hurry.'

George Green did the sums. There should be four if one of them needed to enter White's room. There were only four on the shift. Danny Wilson was on his break and Tim Keyes was doing his usual. Hiding.

Eddie let himself into the ward. He followed George at speed. George told him about the call.

'It's probably some student prank,' said Eddie as they hurried onto White's corridor. Silence from each door they passed. They came to the end of the corridor and from behind White's door heard an erratic rhythm.

Eddie turned the dimmer switch up and George raised the flap on the observation panel.

'Oh my Jesus!' said George as Eddie opened the door. 'Call for help, Eddie.'

As Eddie took out his phone, George hurried inside White's room.

On the floor, in the space between the bed and the table, White lay on his back, his limbs thrashing, sweat pouring from him and his open mouth rimmed with thick white foam.

'Adrian White, it's George Green, on-duty nurse.' George dropped to his knees and stuck his fingers inside White's mouth. The airway was clear of obstacles and he could hear White's laboured breathing. The nurse found a pulse banging in White's wrist. 'You're having a seizure.'

He placed his hands under White's head and looked at Eddie's back, the phone at his ear. He could hear his voice but not the words.

'Who's coming, Eddie?'

'Dr Campbell.'

'Go find Danny and Tim and get them here before anyone else arrives or we'll be on a disciplinary for breaching safety protocol.'

George looked at White's head, his raven-black hair soaked with sweat. As he watched White, he was shocked at the wave of tenderness that washed through him. He looked at White's face. For a moment, George was reminded of the first boy he'd had a crush on. 'Adrian. You're perfectly safe.'

'*You're* not!'

George looked up to Eddie's voice.

Eddie's eyes welled with joyful tears and he gazed down at White with the devotion of a pilgrim. George looked at White and saw death in his cold gaze.

'Shouldn't have gone in on your own, mate,' said Eddie. With a swish of his hand, he shut the door.

In a fraction of a moment, five strong fingers grasped the top of George's skull and slammed him face first into the floor. The weight of Adrian White's entire body pinned him to the floor.

Stars danced in the blackness inside his head. Shifting zigzags rubbed out the details of his peripheral vision and he felt the remorseless pressure of a large hand around his throat.

Wetness filled George's ear as White's tongue probed the cavity.

He lifted George's face from the floor, pulled his head back high.

George shut his eyes and felt his smashed face crashing towards the ground.

81

00.40 am

53.40 62 68 n, –2. 95 71 78 w

The Bear's Paw pub overlooked the Liverpool city skyline. It was in the lee of the pub's exterior back wall that Clay signed her name on three forms and took the Glock 17 pistol from its rectangular case. The sergeant in charge of the police weapons store had waited for her there with the gun and the paperwork.

'The magazine's loaded with ten rounds,' he said.

She could tell this from the weight of the pistol in her hand. She found herself hoping that when – if – she came out of the tunnel again, the Glock 17 would still weigh the same.

'Eve!'

Clay turned to the sound of Gina Riley's voice, coming towards her in the company of a small, middle-aged woman, her shape hidden behind a thick coat, a woollen scarf wrapped around her head.

As they came closer, Clay slipped the gun into her coat pocket.

'This is Shirley Wright, Eve. She's from the Friends of Williamson's Tunnels.'

'Thank you for coming out at this hour and for making it here so quickly,' said Clay.

'Is someone down there?' asked Shirley.

'We think so, Shirley. We had a tip-off from...one of the students.' Clay pointed at the modern apartment block overlooking the pub and the small metal manhole cover nearby. Uniformed officers guarded the entrance and across the road the order to stay indoors was issued to the occupants of a row of Georgian terraced houses.

'There's an awful lot of coppers round here...'

'Shirley, I don't mean to be rude, but I haven't got a moment to spare. If I get into the tunnel through that covered shaft, how many ways out are there?'

'I don't know. We're finding new entrances and exits all the time.'

'Suppose I wanted to get out quickly. Where are the nearest bolt holes?'

Shirley pointed. 'There are several potential exits. Grove Street. Mason Street. Smithdown Lane. Elm Grove. One hundred to two hundred metres from here.'

Clay reached inside her coat pocket and unfolded a map of the Williamson Tunnels. She pointed at an irregular quadrilateral of linked-up tunnels beneath their feet, its shape all too similar to that of the interlinked corpses of Hanif Patel and, his mother and daughter.

'What do I watch out for down there?' asked Clay.

'It'll be very wet down there. The floor will be slippery. It was used as a communal dump for the best part of two hundred years. A lot of debris has been cleared but there's still all kinds that hasn't been cleared. How are you in the dark?'

'I'm used to it,' said Clay.

'There are sets of winding stairs, some old stone, some modern metal. They'll take you down to the fourth level.'

'How far down?'

'Eleven metres. You'll be on the corner there.' She pointed to the map at the bottom left corner of the irregular quadrilateral.

'Thank you.'

Clay walked towards the manhole cover.

Hendricks and Stone raised it in a single lift.

Clay didn't look at either of them but instead stared down into the subterranean darkness. She turned and stepped onto the top rung of the ladder, pointed her torch into the black pit.

'Keep the lid off,' said Clay, beginning her descent. 'Listen out. If you hear screaming, get down there as quickly as you can.'

Clay reached the bottom of the final metal staircase. Apart from the light of the torch in her hand, she was in complete darkness.

She turned and, torch in hand, explored the curved ceiling and straight wet sandstone walls of the tunnel.

Drip drip.

She listened to the double drip of water falling from the ceiling.

Drip drip.

Click click, she thought.

The wet clicking of their mouths mimicked by the action of water underground.

She walked forward, grasping her pistol and flicking the beam of her torch from the ground to the space ahead of her. The light picked out the entrances to smaller tunnels on either side of her.

She stopped and listened. The acoustics made the dripping water echo. There was no sign of life. Her heart banged against her chest and the blood pumped inside her ears.

She carried on, glancing over her shoulder at the shadows pressing down on her back. She considered calling out to the Red Cloud but dismissed the idea.

The place smelled of sulphur, of wet sandstone and stale air, and it made the end of her nose sore.

As she trod further into the darkness, adrenaline made her hearing sharper.

Drip drip. Drip drip. There was more than one source. Behind her. Ahead of her. And a sound of soft scratching low down, far away.

She stopped and turned off her torch to maximise her sense of hearing.

In the dark, she was seized by the sense that she was slowly turning upside down. She pressed her feet down hard on the sandstone ground and the sensation sharpened. It was as if the whole tunnel was turning, as if gravity was the only thing that stopped her being tossed around the walls, the ground, the arch of the roof. The turning stopped and Clay felt as if she was hanging upside down. She listened.

Three or four sets of dripping water now, all at different speeds.

And something was coming at her. It travelled along the ground, grinding against the stone as it came nearer and nearer.

She gripped her pistol and turned her light on. She was standing upright, feet on the ground, on the spot where she had turned off her torch. *What*, she wondered, sick at the thought, *if the torch hadn't come on?*

Torchlight caught the edge of something spinning towards her through the darkness. It slipped away from her light and, in the micro beat she'd glimpsed it, she couldn't tell if it was a dead or living thing.

Heat blossomed on her skin.

It was near her feet.

The blood drained to her internal organs, a cold river poured down her spine and her head felt light.

She dragged the beam to her right and saw an old china plate spinning on the ground, falling down in decreasing circles before finally tottering to a dead halt.

Clay poked her light in the direction from which the plate may have come, but there was nothing there. A cold breeze blew in from behind her and when it touched her neck she felt sweat prickling her back.

Something inside her head felt disconnected. Clay paused, questioned herself, realised that all sense of time had deserted her. She didn't know how long she'd been down in the tunnel.

To her right, at head height, something was coming for her through the fabric of the wall.

She swivelled the torch and picked out a side tunnel, a square of darkness filling with the noise of a body travelling at speed through the sandstone.

A black rat jumped from the hole into her path, inches from her feet. It looked up at her, its eyes like beads of black blood. She pointed her gun at it. Her ribs tightened. Her lungs and heart felt like they were being compressed into one tight, meaty ball. She looked into the rat's eyes and saw the eyes of the crow, feeding and watching her from the garden of her home.

Just above the hem of her trousers, a small sharp weight. She turned slowly and saw a grey rat with its front paws resting on her lower left leg. It sniffed her, its nose and whiskers twitching, its little yellow teeth sharp and poised.

She kicked the rat with her right foot, but it hung on tighter, biting into the fabric of her trouser leg. Setting her pistol down, she seized the rodent by the knotty gristle of its tail, tore it away from her leg with a sweep of her arm and smashed its body against the tunnel wall. The light in its visible eye went out and a fine spray of blood hit her cheek.

The rat's body fell from her hand and she raked the floor with her torch, looking for the pistol.

It wasn't in the place where she'd put it down.

Panic mounted inside her. An invisible hand clawed her throat as she searched for it. She stumbled slightly. Her toe connected with the body of the pistol and sent it skating across the wet ground, away into the darkness.

She stopped and listened, heard her weapon clatter into a small chasm and drop down into a tunnel below her, even deeper in the earth.

She took the deepest breath she could, held onto it, released it slowly.

Dozens of leaks now dripped into the tunnel and within the chaotic counter-rhythms she briefly heard the wet clicking of human tongues. The dripping continued but the clicking stopped.

From around a corner, seductive pools of yellow light oozed into the darkness. She wondered if fear was making her see things. She turned off her torch to test her senses.

The light was real and rhymed with the candlelight in the Drakes' loft.

Clay counted her steps as she marched further into the tunnel. She focused on the corner. Her mind became strangely composed, the events of the past minute dissolving with each pace she took. She turned the corner.

Just enough light to make out the shapes of two girls and a woman.

In candlelight, Anais Drake stood over her daughters. Faith and Coral were kneeling. Anais held a metal bar over Coral's head and was poised to strike.

'One more second,' said Anais, 'and you'd have been one second too late.'

Coral Drake's head was upright, but her eyes were downcast.

Faith's glassy eyes connected with Clay. The child looked blank, as if she'd left her mind behind in another place. Clay wondered if the version of Faith she'd met at her home on the morning after the Red Cloud had slaughtered the Patels would ever return.

Anais lowered the metal bar.

'One second?' said Clay, attracting Coral's attention. 'I arrived in the second I chose to arrive in.'

Something stirred inside Coral as the light danced on her eyes, but Clay couldn't tell if it was defiance or relief at having been pulled back from the point of death.

'Where's Maisy?'

'Where we left her,' said Anais.

Clay looked at Coral and back at Faith, to Coral and Faith, a pendulum that skipped Anais.

'You've been deceived, Eve. And that's what's going to make this so complicated.'

'Who's deceived me?' Still she didn't look at Anais, just focused on Coral and Faith.

'Everyone you've ever known. Except us. We would never do that to the real you.'

349

'Faith and Coral have deceived me. They told me a boy called Jon Pearson stole a mobile phone.'

'They weren't speaking to the real you, they were addressing the reality of what you've become after the lie you've been tricked into living. Their words were part of a wider way of guiding you back to the truth, back to what you truly are.'

'Why are you kneeling, Coral? Why don't you get up?'

'I'm kneeling before you.'

'Stand up, both of you.'

Coral and Faith obeyed and, in the flickering light and shifting shadows, Anais and her daughters looked like they had just risen from the dead, their dark coats like shrouds.

'Do you know who you are, Eve?' asked Anais.

'Yes.'

'Who are you?'

'The Matriarch.' Clay's voice echoed and she challenged the mother with a look of contempt. 'Eve Clay is the daughter of the one who reigns in darkness. What is Adrian White to you?'

'The prophet sent to guide us in rescuing you from the bottomless well you've fallen into, so that you can fulfil the purpose of your life.'

'And what is the purpose of my life?' asked Clay.

'This is the complication. Look at you. You were meant for greatness. But look at what you've become. You don't even understand why the things that have happened these past three days and nights have happened.'

'What have I become?'

'You came here to battle with us. Us, your saviours. You want to catch us and punish us for what we did for you because your whole life has been corrupted into a living lie,' said Anais.

'How are you my saviours?'

'Everything we have done has been to save you.'

'The murder of families in their own homes was done to save me?'

'We'd do anything to get your attention, Eve. And that's what we did. We took what you have become and we used it to help save you, to guide you to what you are. We wove ourselves into the fabric of what passes for your life and made you chase after us. But you weren't just chasing after us, Eve, were you? Think about it . . .'

She heard little Adie's voice inside her head, words that made her brain feel like it was turning to liquid and spurting from her ears.

'I am only part human. You are talking to and you are talking about the part of me that is human. Tell me about the part that is not human.'

'You know so much, yet you understand so little. You can read the writing of the prophet. You have spoken with Adie. You have seen the altar in the sanctum. And yet, you are lost.'

'Tell me about the part of me that is not human.'

Above her head, in the space above the tunnel's arched ceiling, the sound of footsteps. Clay wondered if she was imagining it, but the sound was clear. It felt like electrical waves were coursing to the extremities of her body.

'Tell me about the part of me that is not human.'

'Not here. Drop your torch, drop the part of you that rejects the darkness, as a tiny gesture of faith, faith in we who have so much absolute faith in what you must become. Drop your torch.'

She tossed it around the corner, a marker for anyone who might come looking for her corpse. She pointed at the candles. 'You too have rejected the darkness.'

With a single, practised breath each, Coral and Faith stooped and blew out the candles.

'No. They were for your benefit. For the corrupted you.'

Smoke curled in the darkness.

'This is what we accept. This is what we see. This is what you truly are.'

Clay felt a hand on her shoulder.

'Reach out and do the same,' said Coral.

Clay stretched her hand out and rested it on Faith's shoulder.

'Where are we going?' she asked.

'We're going to ask you to perform another act of faith, a bigger one, a better one. One that will show us that you are prepared to join us and fulfil yourself. If you can't do that, we will kill you. Walk.'

Clay stepped forwards in complete blindness, her hand sitting firmly on Faith's tiny shoulder.

'Keep moving as one flesh,' said Anais, ahead of Faith. 'When you have performed the act of faith, we will know that you can never go back to your old life, to the hideous lie. When you perform the act of faith, I will tell you everything about the part of you that is not human.'

Above her head, above the sound of their own echoing footsteps, Clay heard the footsteps above the arch. *This is what it must be like in hell*, she thought. *Walking deeper into darkness with the sound of yourself around you and, above, the sound of other lost souls performing the same eternal punishment.*

'Where are we going?' she asked.

'Going. Going. Going…'

But when the echo of her voice died, there was only one response.

Footsteps.

Gina Riley stared down at the entrance to the dark hole that Eve Clay had descended into and was unable to take her eyes off it. To look away would feel like an act of betrayal and cowardice.

The same thought chewed her mind, over and over.

What was going on down there?

She tried to rationalise. There had been no gunfire. Apparently. No sound of voices or conflict rising to the surface through the paving stones and tarmac.

She shivered in the night air and imagined how much colder it must be beneath the ground with its damp walls and uncertain darkness. Still she couldn't tear her eyes away from the tunnel entrance.

Fear for Eve Clay gripped her. The silence could be read another way. Maybe they had waited in the darkness, hiding until Eve came into their space and—

Riley was seized by a dangerous compulsion. She looked around and observed Hendricks watching her with quiet intensity.

'What are you looking at?' she asked.

'You can't go down there, Gina.'

'How did you...?'

'I've been watching your face. I know how much you think of Eve. And I'm telling you now, if you and Eve both came out alive, she'd kill you with her bare hands for risking both your life and hers. We've seen inside the Red Cloud...' He pointed at his own head. 'We've seen their collective psyche on the walls of their shrine. Eve's got a unique status. It gives her ambiguity. Down there, with them, that's as good a weapon as a gun and a brighter hope than anything you or I can offer.'

'Are you sure?' asked Riley.

'I'm sure.'

She felt the weight of his arm across her shoulders.

'You're a terrible liar, Bill.'

Silence.

'Liar? Optimist? Is there a difference?'

She felt his arm rise from her shoulders, sensed him moving away quietly.

Gina Riley looked down into the dark hole into which Eve Clay had descended and fought back a wave of tears.

Clay sensed a change, a slowdown in the blind march from Anais at the front, through Faith immediately ahead. She in turn drew Coral to a dead halt. She ransacked the darkness but there was no break in the blackness, no shimmer or suggestion of shape, light or substance.

Coral's hand unfolded from her shoulder and as Clay withdrew her fingers from Faith's shoulder, Anais said, 'We're here.'

Nowhere. Clay reached out to her left and right, touched thin air and nothing else. 'Where's here?' she asked.

'The way in and the way out,' replied Anais. 'The way up and the way down.'

Clay tilted her head and was astonished at the sight of a single point of light, a lone star in the barren heavens above them.

'What is it?'

She sensed Anais coming towards her, pictured the woman in her doorway on Barnham Drive with the crucifix around her neck. She felt Anais's breath streaming into her as her lips brushed her left earlobe. 'Come with me.' Anais's hand tightened around hers. 'Walk.'

As they walked, Clay focused on the pinpoint of light above them. It shimmered, seemed to vanish, came back.

'Steps.'

Anais guided Clay's hand towards the wall of the tunnel. She fingered the flat, narrow indentation, a tight ledge, the base of a crude stairway hacked out of the sandstone.

Clay felt Anais's hands fold against the sides of her face. Her breath washed over her lips. 'Do you want to see Maisy?' she whispered menacingly. Anais let go of her face. 'Then climb. Follow me.'

As she began to climb, Anais said, 'We're behind you and in front of you. 'If you do anything wrong, we will wipe you from the face of the earth. The work of a lifetime will simply have to start over again.'

Clay reached up and felt the edge of two uneven steps above her head. Her right foot found the flat of another step at the bottom of the wall as her hands gripped the stone ledges above. As she began the ascent, she felt a pair of hands at the base of her back and the sole of Anais's foot brushing her scalp.

She looked up to the point of light and found another handhold set into the sandstone wall.

Clay climbed towards the star.

With each painful step of the long climb, the light above grew larger. Clay worked out a method. Reach up with the hands, grip, lift, and probe with the feet.

She felt warm breath at her heels.

As she climbed higher, she felt a compulsion to grab Anais Drake's ankle and fling her down into the darkness. And then jump down and fight her to the bloody death. She glanced back at the darkness and was filled with an even stronger compulsion: to press on towards the light.

Clay's arms and legs burned and she felt herself slowing down as the distance between herself and Anais Drake grew wider. *How many times have you done this?* she wondered, glancing back at the dark form of Coral below her.

She paused, turned to the girls and asked quietly, 'What does this lead to?'

'You'll soon see,' said Coral. 'Keep moving.'

'What's that light?'

Drip drip. Drip drip. Inch by inch, Clay pulled her way up the wet sandstone, heart pounding, her breath short and heavy.

Anais Drake. Clay tossed the name up and down in her mind, pulled it apart, juggled the letters and played them back to front as she climbed, trying to divert her attention from the pain in her arms and legs.

An ais Dr ake
ek a rD si a nA

Clay froze. The light disappeared briefly as Anais Drake pulled herself through the opening. Then it returned. Another step up and the light was enticing and big enough to swallow a grown woman. *It's a hole.* Beyond the hole, Clay saw a flat surface, a wall or a ceiling.

She tried to speed up, desperate now to get to the hole and pass through it and out of the tunnel, but the grip in her right hand suddenly failed and her fingers slipped off the slimy stone. Clay's body swung away from the rock. Her right foot shot off the step. She anchored herself with her left foot and hand, stretched her right arm up again, connected, then slipped off again. She tried again, heard the blood banging inside her head, felt the sandpaper of her tongue rasping against the bone-dry roof of her mouth. The whole of her body was slick with sweat. She pictured Philip and Thomas standing over her grave.

She twisted towards the rock one more time and was back on the stone ladder.

'Climb!' nagged Coral behind her.

The temptation to stamp on her face was immense, but the overwhelming need for light pushed Clay up another rung. And another.

An. A. Dr. De. Ka.

And another. Above Clay's head, a foot pounded out a heartbeat.

The white surface grew clearer. *Ri.*

It was flat. *S. A.* The closer she came, the more her muscles burned.

Clay could smell a different damp, the damp of an unloved room.

There was a division in the white where a wall met a ceiling.

A naked light bulb hung from a white plastic flex.

Her hand clutched the ragged edge of a damp floorboard.

Another step and her head touched the light.

Two hands on the edges of the hole and she pushed herself up.

It was an empty room. *Ka.*

Anais stood in the corner, watching as Clay hauled herself into the space. 'They've weakened you,' she said. 'You are soft, but we will make you strong.'

Clay pulled her legs and feet onto the floor of the room. Taking a huge breath, she stood to her full height. In each hand, Anais held a metal bar.

Coral pulled herself up into the room with practised ease and Faith followed.

'It's time,' said Anais, 'for your act of faith.'

The wooden ladder leading from the damp, bare room to a trap door in the ceiling told Clay they were in a basement, the basement of a house that opened onto a maze of underground tunnels.

Anais Drake watched Clay closely. Clay cast her mind back to when she was based at the nearby Admiral Street police station and worked out a possible location for the building.

There was a row of terraced houses on one side of Smithdown Lane.

Somewhere above, Clay heard the sound of a child crying. 'Maisy?' she asked. 'What have you done with the little girl?'

Anais stared in silence at Clay. The crying intensified. 'What little girl?'

'What do you want from me?' asked Clay.

'What we deserve. What we need. What we shall have. There are many of us. Not just me and mine. We are all over the world. You were born to be the Matriarch, part human, part inhuman, the sum much more than human.'

'Which part of me is human?'

'Your flesh, Eve. That which your mother furnished.'

'Who was my mother?'

'You've seen her,' said Anais.

'When?'

'Recently.'

'When?'

'Yesterday. Today.'

'She's still alive?'

Clay tried to match the women she'd encountered since midnight with the ones who'd crossed her path prior to that. There was no one who could possibly have been her mother.

'Give me a name.'

'No. She gave you a name, but it was taken from you.'

'Her name?'

'Your face, face your face, your face.'

In her mind she walked up to the altar in the Drakes' sanctum.

Above her head, a floorboard creaked. She recalled the surface of the altar.

She heard a heavy footstep near the creaking board. Maisy's crying intensified. She sounded terrified. Each passing second was a second lost. If Maisy was crying, she was alive – but for how long?

'Concentrate!' snapped Anais. Irritated, she clicked her fingers.

Clay focused.

The image of her on the altar. That face. The naked body. The serpent and demon at her breasts. Her thighs straddling the fire-spouting Satan.

'You're thinking about the altar, Eve. That woman wasn't you. It was your mother, who gave you your flesh, your limbs, your body, your face. It wasn't you on the altar, Eve. But it soon will be. Because it has to be. Soon that will be you.'

It wasn't her at the centre of the altar, it was their vision of

361

her parents at the moment of her conception. A pipe rattled in the fabric of the house above them and Clay's skin crawled.

'I look like my mother, don't I?'

'When you look into shadows, you look into mirrors. When you look into mirrors, what do you see?'

'Maisy Tanner?' replied Clay, glancing at the wooden ladder but seeing only the metal bars in Anais's hands. The crying drifted further away. A sour taste filled Clay's mouth. She wanted to be sick.

'Think about your mother, Eve.'

In Clay's head, insanity translated into a possible narrative. Her mother had been snared by a cult, a Satanic cult. She had become pregnant. As the baby grew inside her, so did her love for it. She had given birth and risked death for running away and abandoning her baby to the mercy of strangers. *To save me from the madness which I now face.*

Anais pointed at the corner in which Coral stood. 'An act of faith. Kill Coral.'

Clay looked at Coral.

'Kill Coral,' said Anais calmly. 'Kill her and I'll take you back down into the tunnels. I know a way out. I will take you to safety and all that will follow. There are many waiting for you in this world. Kill her. It will be your act of faith, your way back to us, away from the world of lies.'

Clay waited, counted to ten, looked at Coral in the corner. This time, Coral looked back at Clay with the doleful gaze of a cow as the abattoir door slams shut at her back. From another corner, Faith stared at her mother.

With her back to Anais, Clay said, 'Give me the metal bar.'

'No,' said Anais. 'Do it with your bare hands!'

Clay hung on to Coral's gaze. 'Coral, come here. I will make a martyr of you. That's what you want, isn't it, Coral?'

For a moment, a look of panic crossed Coral's face.

In the space above, hasty footsteps thumped up a staircase. The bland noise of a television in another house leaked into the pit.

'Coral, come here.'

As Coral stepped forward, Anais watched impassively. The sound of water running through pipes in the house above them masked Coral's laboured breathing.

'Kneel down in front of me.'

Coral knelt down in front of Clay.

'Why Coral?' Clay asked Anais.

'Kill her,' replied Anais.

'Why Coral and not Faith?'

'Strangle her. Do it!'

'No. Leave Faith alone,' said Coral, turning to Clay, her eyes pleading. 'Let her live.'

'Kill the bitch now,' said Anais.

'Coral your first choice again, Anais? What's she done to make you hate her so much?'

Clay turned to Faith and said, 'Come here, Faith, and say goodbye to your big sister.'

Faith stood over Coral and rested a hand on her sister's shoulder. 'Coral,' whispered Faith. Coral looked up at her sister. 'I've got that painted-in-a-corner feeling, the one we talked about.'

'Well, when I'm not here and you get that feeling, talk to me inside your head and listen to your memory of me. Remember all the things I've said to you. Remember what I've always said: I will live in your mind if your mind lets me in. Death cannot part us. Only we can do that.'

The silence between the girls was dense with grief. And Clay understood that, in their brief lives, death was always a moment away and their mother was the reaper.

Coral picked up her sister's hand and kissed it.

Walking backwards towards her mother, Faith's eyes were pinned on Coral, two sisters reading each other's faces as all hope collapsed.

A distant ambulance siren sang out from the night, advancing deeper into Edge Hill.

'Do you believe in me, Coral?' Clay watched Anais and sensed the quickening warmth of sadistic pleasure in her eyes.

'I believe in you.'

Clay placed her hands on Coral's shoulders. 'And I believe in you, Coral. Get up!'

Coral stood.

'Kill...' Anais double-clicked her tongue. 'Kill...' Click click. 'Kill...' Click click. 'Kill...'

Clay saw impatience rising in her eyes. 'No!' she said. She fixed on Faith. 'No!' Anais's face froze. Pleasure became rage in the turning of a moment. She prodded Faith's shoulder with the iron bar.

'She's lied to you, Coral,' Clay said. 'Faith, everything she's told you is a pack of lies.'

'Do not listen to the corruption...'

'I'm not going to harm either of...'

'...in her mouth.'

'...you. Listen to me!' Clay wrapped her arms tightly around Coral and focused on Faith. 'I'll protect you. That's what mothers do. I'm painted into the same corner as you.' A low, bestial note sounded from the base of Anais's throat. 'This is my act of faith with you. I will live and die and stand by both of you. This is my act of faith.'

The sound of the child crying drifted higher into the building above and Clay felt herself torn between two dreadful realities. The one she was trapped in and the one that was playing out somewhere upstairs.

Anais thrust a metal bar into Faith's hand. 'Kill your sister, Faith, and when you've killed your sister, kill Clay!'

Clay released her arms and ushered Coral behind her. 'Faith!' She made eye contact with the girl and held it. 'Don't touch your sister!'

'Faith! Kill both of them before I smash your head wide open.' Anais shoved Faith in the back.

The girl took a step forward and stopped.

Clay watched Faith's face. She was fixed on Coral. Love surged through her eyes and a cold darkness followed.

'Kill?' said Faith.

'Kill!' commanded Anais.

'Obey?'

'Obey!'

Faith threw her arm up and over her shoulder and smashed the bar into her mother's face.

Anais stood her ground, weaving left to right. She raised the other bar over Faith's head.

Faith turned and moved back as her mother swiped thin air.

'Come to me, Faith. Come to Coral, she needs you.'

Faith raised the bar again and smashed it into her mother's face. A line of blood sprayed around the room as Anais dropped to her knees. Faith hit her mother again and again on the head, each blow quicker and more fierce than the previous strike. In moments, Anais's blood had coated the wall and the low ceiling.

'Coral, tell her to stop!'

'Faith, stop it now!'

But she carried on hitting her mother's body and venting a lifetime of rage. She screamed. An inarticulate rage poured from her. She clicked and uttered noises, sounds that had no recognisable phonemic notation but were thick with obscenity and hatred. Her screams filled the room and echoed down into the tunnel.

Clay looked directly at Coral, connected with her.

Faith's rage intensified, power picking up with each blow, her mother's blood showering her face, hair and body.

'Faith!' Clay stepped towards her, looked anxiously in the direction of the ladder. As the bar swung back, Clay grabbed it with both hands. Faith froze and released the iron bar. Coral picked up the other weapon.

Clay threw the bar into the tunnel below and stared at Coral.

Coral dropped the bar into the darkness beneath them.

As Clay moved to the bottom of the ladder, Anais raised her hand, her arm rising towards Faith.

Clay was on the bottom step.

Faith stamped on her mother's face and the basement filled with the sharp crack of bone as Anais's arm dropped like a falling tree.

Halfway up the ladder, Clay paused, torn between the girls in the basement and Maisy in the house above.

Faith stared down at her mother. The little girl had become still and calm.

'Coral, you stay here with her!' ordered Clay, as she hurried to the top of the wooden ladder. 'Good . . . riddance . . . mother . . .' Faith smiled.

'We'll stay!' whispered Coral. She drew her little sister back from their mother's corpse. 'This is our act of faith.'

Her words trailed after Clay as she sprinted into the kitchen of the house in the heart of Edge Hill.

88

1.48 am

From the first floor came the sound of running water and the cries of a frightened child.

As Clay took the stairs two at a time, the water stopped running and the child stopped crying. The silence made her blood run cold. She followed the sound of dripping, down the first floor landing, along a narrow corridor, past one bedroom and another and then to the bathroom door.

Air bubbled though water as Clay stepped into the bathroom.

Maisy Tanner was pinned to the bottom of a bath full of water, weighted down by a chunk of sandstone. Her eyes were wide beneath the water and a stream of bubbles rose from her mouth as the breath passed from her body.

Clay reached in, heaved the sandstone away, grabbed the child by the shoulders and hauled her out of the water. She laid Maisy on the tiled floor. The little girl was frozen, her body like a sealed knot. The room span around Clay's head as she squashed her lips against Maisy's mouth and blew. She pressed the heel of her hand to her breastbone and compressed.

Maisy threw up a stream of water. As the little girl drew in a lungful of air, Clay felt a presence in the doorway behind her. She looked over her shoulder and saw a streak of darkness flying at her head. She shifted and the metal bar cracked into the tiled floor. A man landed on his knees next to her, the bar still in his hands, his face covered by a black balaclava, his eyes wild.

Clay grabbed the shaft of the bar. She hung on as he yanked it towards himself and felt the dwindling strength in her fingers dissolve on the surface of the metal.

He pulled it clear away.

Clay slipped on the wet floor but made it up onto both feet.

Behind her, Maisy took another raw, gargling lungful of air.

He was on his feet too. She knew his eyes, but a name didn't click. He lurched at her.

Clay reached up to his face and, with her index and middle finger, poked his eyes sharply.

One hand flew to his face as he swiped down with the bar. The bar connected with the side of the bath, arched back and clipped him on the mouth. He let go and the bar fell into the bath water.

With one foot, Clay pushed Maisy's body as far into the corner as she could. *Protect her, above all else.* She steadied her weight and balanced. She lifted her foot and kicked him in the stomach.

A bomb of white light exploded inside and outside her brain as he punched the side of her head.

Her fingers connected with the rough surface of his mask. She tugged and the mask came away, exposing the lower half of his face.

His eyes swam with tears, the whites red raw. She knew him.

With one hand, fingers splayed, he aimed for Clay's face. She bit down and trapped his index finger between her top and lower teeth.

She crunched hard on his flesh and bone.

He reeled back.

Clay pulled the bar from the water.

She lunged and poked his throat with the bar.

He held his hands up, spluttered, 'No! No!'

'Take the mask off!' *He had been at Ullet Road.*

She poked his mouth with the butt of the bar, heard the crack of his front teeth. *He had stood facing Hendricks.*

'Do you want some more?' shouted Clay. *He had posed as a cameraman.*

'Please, no...'

She watched sweat and blood leak onto the scar tissue on his upper lip. The hare-lipped cameraman at Ullet Road. Like the hare-lipped nurse at Ashworth Hospital.

Ullet Road. A vulture at the scene of the crime.

It all clicked into place as he raised the mask to the top of his head, exposing his face. *Adrian White's errand boy.*

'Was it all those nights in Ashworth, all those whisperings in the dark that turned you into this, Richard?'

The psychiatric nurse closed his eyes.

'I'm talking to you, Taylor. Open your eyes and look at me.'

Richard Taylor tried to focus, but couldn't. 'I can't see.'

She stuck the butt of the metal bar under his chin. Blood poured from his broken teeth and gums.

'Did you pass messages between Adrian White and Anais Drake?'

'He had me tied up in knots.'

'Are you the go-between for the Baptist and the Red Cloud?'

'Yes. Yes I am.'

'Talk!'

'If you came out of the basement alone, I was to kill you and leave your body in the tunnels. The rest was for the rats.'

Maisy sobbed for breath, her eyes wide open now.

'Move a muscle and I promise you, I will kill you,' said Clay. 'And under the circumstances, I will get away with murder.' She positioned herself to shield Maisy's body, then smashed the bathroom window with the bar. 'I'm up here!' she called into the darkness.

Many sets of feet sprinted towards the house.

But Eve Clay was listening to another sound, a strange music from the basement, the ecstatic laughter of two sisters.

And she pictured them dancing for joy around their mother's corpse.

In the interview room at Trinity Road police station, Coral Drake almost jumped out of her seat when Clay moved the table to one side.

'Let me reiterate, Coral. You have the right to a solicitor—'

'I don't want a solicitor. I don't need her here.' Coral looked accusingly at the child-protection officer sitting in the corner.

'You're under eighteen. *I* need her here, even if *you* think *you* don't.'

'I need nothing.' Her voice had dropped to little more than a whisper.

Clay moved her chair, closed down the distance between them. 'How did your mother know Adrian White?'

'She told me he is our father.'

Clay said nothing and, in silence, waited.

'He didn't live with us, he wasn't like a regular father, he came and went. But even when he wasn't there, he filled the whole house. Even years after the trial was over and his body had been locked away. I'd be alone in my room and I could feel him just outside the door, ready to walk in at any moment. My mother said it was his spirit. That he could send his spirit travelling to any place he wanted and that he continually visited the house and was watching our every move. There was no escaping him. Even at night when I was sleeping, he walked into my dreams. Do you know what I mean?'

Clay understood perfectly but remained silent.

'My mother said he could physically walk away from the hospital at any moment he chose but that he was waiting for the right moment, the Beginning of the End of Time. And that he had people in the hospital who were on his side.'

Anger filled her face and then fear returned.

'One night during the September fast...some months ago...' Coral's expression clouded and Clay wondered if she knew which year it was. '...there was a ring on the bell. At my mother's command, I went to the door and opened it. It was a man. The Stranger. He said, *The Beginning of the End of Time has arrived. Prepare to signal this to the Clouds across the world.*'

Clay pictured Richard Taylor, terrified and crying, begging for mercy, his mask removed on the bathroom floor.

'Every doubt I'd ever had about things my mother had told me vanished. She had been predicting this for years. The Stranger told me he would be in touch again and walked away. Time went on, the September fast ended. The Stranger returned in the night. I woke up from a nightmare of Father and he was at the foot of my bed. *Your father has a message for you. His spirit is in my flesh. Obey your mother in all things when the Beginning of the End of Time arrives, or the doors of the hospital will open and he will reap vengeance on you. It is you and Faith and Adrienne or them.*'

'Them?' asked Clay.

'Those we killed in their homes.' She paused. Before my eyes, the Stranger turned into my father and back into the Stranger and I was convinced beyond any doubt.'

The silence was long and full of a pain that was beyond healing. Coral sank back inside herself.

'This Stranger,' asked Clay. 'Was there any distinctive mark on his face?'

Coral nodded and touched her top lip. 'A scar. Right here.'

'Coral,' said Clay, 'were you hungry, in need of food, at this time?'

'We are always hungry, Mrs Clay. Our bodies are cages, hunger sets us free.'

'Are you hungry now, Coral?'

'I'm starving.'

'I'm hungry too, Coral, I haven't eaten for ages. Shall we eat the same food together?'

'Perhaps.'

Clay phoned the duty sergeant and ordered toast and milk.

'When did the Stranger next come, Coral?'

'A week ago, when the snow arrived. I was coming home from school, walking down Woolton Road into the first of the blizzards. He said, *Tell your mother the Beginning of the End of Time is here. Harvest. Christian Grace Foundation.* That was all.'

The sounds and letters comprising Anais Drake's name flew around inside Clay's head and settled, making order from chaos. A minute passed, then two, then five. Clay listened to the noise of starlings in a tree outside, hopeless birds fooled by artificial light into thinking night was day.

'Did you ever go to a Christian church with your mother?'

'No.' It was the first and only note of amusement Clay would see in Coral Drake. And it was brief.

'Did your mother ever refer to herself by another name?'

Clay recalled the text from Hendricks.

'Such as?'

'Karisa Aden.' The anagram of Anais Drake, the aka she'd used to bleed dry the families of the Christian Grace Foundation.

'No.'

There was a knock on the door. Clay went over, opened it wide enough to take the toast and milk from a young WPC, thanked her and closed it again. Clay had the clearest sense that there was something dark in the room, something that needed shielding from everyone but her. She looked at the child-protection officer in the corner. Though the blood had drained from her face, Clay could not dismiss her from the room.

Coral fell on the toast, ripping it with her teeth and over-filling her mouth. As she swallowed the milk in one long set of gulps, Clay looked away and thought, *You have systematically been reduced to the level of a beast.*

'Do you have any friends in school?'

'No, I am what I am to this world. Invisible. They look at me, but no one ever sees me.' Coral licked her finger to gather the crumbs from the plate and stuck it in her mouth.

'Do you know two boys called Robbie and Vincent Pearson?'

'I sold them a laptop last week. For £5. The screensaver was my father. I made it impossible for them to wipe that image. They thought they were fooling me. Imagine!'

The thought of Robbie and Vincent turned Clay's mind to another victim. 'How did you know I'd be in Calderstones Park with Sandy Patel?'

'We followed you in the car, my mother and I. She left me there to watch you.'

Clay remembered the blurred figure appearing then disappearing in the trees.

'I waited until you'd gone and followed the boy. He was at the lake. I told him who he was. I'd seen his picture on the wall in his house in The Serpentine. I walked onto the ice with him. I told him, *Death is your only friend now.* I watched him drown. He changed his mind, reached out his hands to me. I said, *I deliver you from this chaos.*'

'And you told this to the Stranger?'

'I told mother.'

Who passed it on to Richard Taylor, thought Clay.

'When I went to the Patels' house in The Serpentine, you called me on the telephone. How did you know I'd be there?'

'We watched you enter the house. We were close at hand. Just as we have been for years. Watching you.'

Clay fell silent, pressed down on the rising sickness inside.

She watched Coral as something heavy passed through her mind. 'When are you going to gather the Clouds?' she asked.

'Never. It isn't the Beginning of the End of Time. I am *not* the Matriarch. You've been lied to, Coral. Your mother. Adrian White. The Stranger. Lies.'

Coral looked puzzled, but then another thought crossed her mind and face in the same moment. 'All this was for nothing?' Instead of anger, Clay saw the opening of a bud, the first touch of relief, and then concern. 'Where is my sister Faith?'

'With your other sister. Alder Hey in the Park Hospital.'

Coral frowned and quizzed Clay with a glance. 'But you don't understand, Mrs Clay, do you?'

'What don't I understand?'

'Adrienne isn't my sister. She's my daughter. My father had sex with me in the sanctum. Over and over. He couldn't get enough of me. Where she was conceived, she was born.

375

I was ten. The pain of creation was nothing to the agony of giving birth to her. The last message from the Stranger, on the morning of the night we visited The Serpentine, was that it would be Faith's turn next if we didn't obey Mother. And, full of my father's spirit, the Stranger was to be the one who took her body. I couldn't let that happen, could I, Mrs Clay? Could I?'

A door opened in Clay's mind. Anais's choice of Coral as her first human sacrifice had a simple explanation. She was jealous of Coral because of the enthusiasm with which White had raped her.

Clay looked at Coral and, for a moment, she looked no more than ten years old. The hideous reality of White's crime against Coral hit Clay hard. She recalled the powerful muscles of the Baptist's body, and the frailty of the child before her filled Clay with a sorrow that she knew she would remember to her dying day.

'No,' said Clay. She sighed. 'I think that's enough for now, Coral.'

'There's something else. Something Faith and I agreed upon for a time such as this. Anais dead. Anais gone. We have a message. Record this on your phone.'

Clay glanced at the camera filming the interview, took out her iPhone and, pressing record, held it close to Coral.

'Are you listening?' asked Coral.

'I'm listening,' replied Clay.

'Then you must be our witness.'

In the small back bedroom of Richard Taylor's house there were three filing cabinets packed with folders and lever-arch files.

Hendricks turned to Clay. 'We haven't had time to go through it all, but it looks like Taylor's written down every single word that White's uttered over the last seven years. He's obsessed with him, totally consumed.'

He handed Clay a diary. 'He didn't even take his annual leave, managed to use the staff shortages and sick leave of other colleagues to be there as often as he could.'

Clay listened to the sound of footsteps running up the stairs and she recognised it as Riley.

When she appeared in the doorway, she looked rattled to the core.

'Two bodies have been discovered at Otterspool Promenade,' she said. 'Robbie and Vincent Pearson. Carbon-monoxide poisoning. It looks like a suicide pact.'

'We know it's definitely them?' asked Clay.

'They killed themselves in my car.'

Clay pictured Mrs Pearson's face, sitting in the interview room with Jon, and wondered how much more sorrow a woman could endure before she crawled into the nearest corner and willed herself to die. 'Has their mother been informed?'

'Stone's on his way to see her. The bodies are at the mortuary. He's going to take Mrs Pearson there for a formal identification, but yeah...' Riley looked around the blank walls of the nondescript bedroom. She took out her iPhone. 'He sent me this.'

She turned the screen of her iPhone to Clay and showed her a picture.

Robbie's head nestled on Vincent's shoulder. They looked like they were sleeping in a dark cloud.

Clay walked to the door.

'Where are you going, Eve?' asked Riley.

'If anyone needs me I'll be at The Serpentine.'

She held up a dog-eared card file filled with pieces of paper and bearing the felt-penned letters: 'E V E T T E C L A Y'.

Time hurtled. The compulsion to connect with love overwhelmed her.

Walking down the stairs, she phoned Thomas.

'Eve? What's happening?'

'It's over, Thomas. Come home as quickly as you can.'

She pictured the scene when she first stepped into the Patels' house and hoped that her next visit would be her final one.

91

5.05 am

Clay stood at the open back door of the Patels' house, the security light picking out the plume of breath coming from her mouth. She breathed in and pictured the turned-off CCTV cameras over the front and back doors.

She blew out a thin stream of smoke-like air and thought, *Alicia, it wasn't the forces of darkness that spiked your family's CCTV cameras.*

Clay closed the door, took out her phone and dialled DS Stone.

Stone picked up.

'How is Mrs Pearson?' asked Clay

Stone shook his head. 'She's under sedation. It was horrific.'

'Jon?'

'Jon's been put into emergency foster care.'

Clay saw a crack of light in the sky.

'What do you want me to do, Eve?'

'Go home, Karl. Watch a slasher movie. Relax.'

'Will do. Anything at your end?'

'No word back from the CCTV engineers?'

'Not yet.'

'We won't hold our breath on that one. I think I know why the CCTV at the Patels' house stopped working. When her parents went to bed, Alicia went outside for a sly smoke. She probably turned the system off and didn't live long enough to turn it back on.'

In the sky, the crack of light widened.

'What if the CCTV had been on?' asked Stone.

'If it had been on, I don't think it would've done the Patels any favours. The Red Cloud had their orders from White. What did they have to be afraid of? It was the Beginning of the End of Time and they were born to announce that.'

She shut the back door.

'I'm going home,' she said and closed down the call.

On the pavement outside the Patels' house, Clay watched a pair of headlights approaching. The car stopped, a man stepped out and walked towards her.

She gripped the card folder in her hands and hugged it into her body.

As he stepped into the streetlight, she saw DC Cole, fresh from trawling through *The Matriarch*, and he looked solemn.

'Have you got something to tell me?' she asked.

The closer Cole came, the more troubled he looked. Although her heart filled with fresh heaviness, she smiled but it did nothing to alleviate the serious stamp on his face.

He handed her a brown envelope.

'The code you cracked – Eve is the child of the one who reigns in darkness – keeps repeating over and over at various points in the text. But there's another piece of information, another message, that keeps coming up through the first and seventh syllable system.'

He looked around. They were alone.

'I've written it out for you, Eve. I'm sorry.'

'Don't be. You've done a good job. See what else you can come up with after you've been home and slept.'

As he turned his back and walked away, the smile fell from Clay's face.

She moved into the glow of a streetlight, took two pieces of folded A4 paper from the envelope.

She waited for DC Cole to pull away and pass her.

In silence, she read the top sheet.

Chapter eleven, verses one to three.

The yes star rise city fruit of air blood man run earth your womb

fire flame city red will alert cloud earth red blood ways be yes
dim star fire air long to rise city blood fire your famine earth run
air other till yes rise no rise yes all time earth run blood yes
star ends.

As she read the words, the voice inside her head turned into
Adrian White's. The music and mockery of his speech filled
her with bitter coldness and, as she pieced together the hidden
meaning of his writing, the coldness turned to red hot anger.

She turned to the bottom sheet and confirmed what she'd
just worked out.

1		7
The	yes star rise city	fruit
of	air blood man run earth	your
womb	fire flame city red	will
al	ert cloud earth red blood	ways
be	yes dim star fire air	long
to	rise city blood fire	your
fa	mine earth run air o	ther
till	yes rise no rise yes	all
time	earth run blood yes star	ends

Her life flashed through her mind: pictures of her mother
fornicating with the Satanic dragon on the Drake's altar, the
moment of her birth, sitting on Philomena's knee in front of
the fire, Philomena's death, St Michael's, school, university,
passing out from police training school, standing across a
wall of fire from Adrian White and running through those
flames, Thomas's sky-blue eyes and the first time she held
Philip in her arms, the fruit of her womb.

Never, *she thought*. And defiance flooded her.

She pictured Philip's face, asleep under the blue glow of the night light.

Ever.

In her mind, she stared into Adrian White's dead eyes across the wall of fire, held onto his cold gaze as she walked calmly into the flames. She drilled her eyes into his as the fire danced around her and The Baptist, and his curses on her past and future, dissolved into thin air before her.

Philip, I would walk through fire for you and I will become that fire, thought Clay. *I will stand in front of you. I will stand behind you and I will stand around you and nothing will get through that inferno.*

On the cold pavement, she turned her eyes to the clear sky, the Moon and the stars, the approach of dawn and a new morning. *And I will never stop loving and sheltering you, Philip.*

Never.

Ever.

Ever.

As Clay stepped over the threshold of her house in Mersey Road, the landline in the hall rang out. She turned on the main light and saw the digits 0151 709 6010, Merseyside Police central switchboard, on the display. She picked up the phone with black expectation.'

'I've got a call for you from Maghull police station. There's been an incident at Ashworth Psychiatric Hospital. The caller wants to be connected to you. I have to warn you—'

'I know,' said Clay. 'I know who it is.'

'Shall I connect you, DCI Clay, or do you want me to divert the call to another officer?'

She looked around at the hallway of her home, the last place she wanted to have a conversation with White, and weighed up her options. There weren't any.

'Connect the call.'

Silence.

The background noise of a normally quiet police station on red alert.

'Eve?'

White sounded in a great mood, pleased with himself and wanting nothing more than to share the vinegar that raised his buckled spirit.

'George, psychiatric nurse, remember him? I've liberated his soul from his body and sent him off to a much better place.'

She hung onto the silence.

'We're going to share the headlines again, Eve, but this time you're going to become known worldwide for what you really are. And I'll be there, a supporting player, moving around in the margins of your greatness. They failed, of course, the Red Cloud. How could they succeed against you? Little Faith, though, who'd have thought it of her? Matricide.'

She said nothing but pictured the scene in the basement in Edge Hill. Faith and Coral Drake in the presence of the mutilated corpse of their mother. She walked inside the Baptist's mind.

'You're in police custody on a horrible night. You've overheard officers speaking as the news breaks.'

'Oh ye of little faith.' She could feel an ice-cold smile in his words.

'I'm going—'

'...to be the magnet for every single human being who chooses the darkness over the light for the rest of your life. You need to listen. Your life will never be the same again and that's why I'm calling you. Prepare yourself from this moment. Your life is no longer your own. Everything's going to come out in the trial.'

There was a silence between the two of them and then Clay spoke softly. 'I'm going to share something with you. You need to listen, Adrian.'

Clay took out her iPhone, selected the recording of Coral Drake and pressed play.

Coral's voice drifted into the receiver: 'Are you listening?'

'I'm listening,' came Clay's response.

'Then you must be our witness.' Silence. 'Faith and Coral Drake have taken vows of poverty and obedience from their earliest days and Faith and Coral have kept to these vows and have never wavered. Faith and Coral Drake want Adrian White to know and understand that the vows we take, we keep. Faith and Coral Drake want Adrian White to further understand that we can make vows of our own, not just endure the ones imposed on us. Faith and Coral are no longer Drake. Faith and Coral have a plan to help them with that *painted-in* feeling. Faith and Coral have made an agreement. Faith and Coral will no longer communicate with the world. Faith and Coral have taken a vow of silence and these are the last words that Coral will ever speak for the rest of her life. Faith fell silent hours ago. Faith and Coral denounce Anais. Faith and Coral denounce Adrian White. Coral is silent from now.'

Clay turned the recording off and lifted the phone to her ear.

'There are some judges who'll deem them unfit for trial because they will not or cannot communicate with their legal representatives. There are judges who will make them take the stand because the girls understand why they're in a courtroom and what a courtroom is. But whatever happens, I'm not going to be the focus of what comes next. Whatever you think I am is a figment of your imagination. *This* is how the world sees me. I'm the woman who put you away seven years ago. I'm the woman who cleared up the mess you left afterwards. Anyone who follows you is in awe of me because I am the end of you. My name is Eve Clay. I am a wife, a mother and a police officer. You are Adrian White. You're insane. Lost. A disgrace to humanity. Locked up forever and waiting to die.'

She held the receiver at a distance as the sound of a long out-breath filled the earpiece. In the silence that followed, she looked at a picture on the wall of herself with Thomas and Philip and heard a clock ticking in the heart of her home.

'Eve?' His voice, lighter than air, drifted over her. She placed the receiver closer to her ear. 'I'll see you again when you least expect it.'

She waited, absorbed the background noise of Maghull police station and told him, 'You'll see me again if I need to see you. But do you know, Adrian, you have a problem with seeing.'

'When you least expect it, Eve.'

'Your eyes are dead. Just like all your dreams.'

Clay placed the receiver down and, sitting on the bottom stair, was pierced with an insight that she would keep to herself forever.

Coral, Faith and Adrienne were like sisters to her.

But she was the lucky one. The one that got away.

6.05 am

Alone in the front room of their home in Mersey Road, Clay wrapped herself in a blanket and lay on the couch with the central heating turned on full. She opened the file and found a letter dated 1984 confirming that she would start school at Our Lady Immaculate. Next was a letter from Alder Hey Hospital about MMR vaccinations. Then a letter confirming her third place in a city-wide Poetry Of Place competition.

The disappointing thought occurred to her that it was all ephemera and wouldn't provide any answers. After ten minutes she was nearing the end of the papers and there was nothing new. The file had merely prompted a few half-memories and part of her wanted to throw it across the room in frustration.

A letter from Notre Dame High School confirming she could take time off to go on a weekend break to Grizedale Forest in the Lake District.

She added the letter to the pile. Then, looking at the next sheet, she felt the colour in her face rising.

She remembered Philomena's handwriting and the address for St Claire's at the head of the letter.

She inspected the markings on the edge of the page. It was a photocopy of a letter from Philomena to Derek Worlock, the Archbishop of Liverpool.

Dear Archbishop Worlock,

Thank you for your prompt response to my letter of 24 May 1978. I will attempt as clearly as I can to address the questions in your letter regarding the abandoned newborn. I hope this will assist you in coming to a decision regarding my request.

I gave her the Hebrew name Evette, meaning living one, but will call her Eve on a daily basis after the first woman in God's creation. For a surname I will call her Clay to reflect the humanity she shares with all her brothers and sisters in Christ, her maternal and paternal surnames being unknown.

I discovered the child as a direct result of the intervention of the Holy Spirit. My spiritual life has been centred on prayer and my material work has been focused on caring for children in the Liverpool diocese for over thirty years. I have been convinced, through submission of my will to the Holy Spirit, that the ultimate purpose of my work for the Lord is to take special care of one special individual with extraordinary needs. On the night I discovered Eve, I was visited in a dream by an angel who urged me to leave St Claire's in the dead of night and who led me to the place where the child had been abandoned by her mother.

As soon as I saw Eve, I understood that the purpose of my life's work was complete. Everything I had done for more than a thousand children over decades of devoted service to the Lord was preparation for this individual child. I fell in love with her on sight and when I picked her up from the ground, human love connected with the love of Christ. The Holy Spirit spoke clearly to me as I carried her back to St Claire's, in a voice as clear as physical speech:

'This is the daughter you yearned for but could never give birth to as a bride of Christ. Cherish her, love her, protect her until your dying day.'

At home, when I undressed Eve to bathe her, I discovered the distressing letter from her birth mother relating to the circumstances of her birth and the forces of darkness that surrounded the child. I submitted the letter directly to your office, along with the letter outlining my specific request relating to Eve. I have not divulged the contents of her mother's letter to anyone and, as I swore on the Holy Bible, those details I will take to my grave.

I seek your permission to become Eve's legal guardian, to seal the bond between the spiritual urging of the Holy Spirit and the workings of the world. Eve is a gift from God and I need to protect the child I love with as much power as I can in imitation of St Joseph as he cared for the infant Jesus.

If you have any questions, I will be more than happy to clarify the points herein.

I look forward to your response.

Yours obediently in Christ,

Sr. Philomena

Mother Superior, St Claire's

Eve turned to the next sheet, headed notepaper from Archbishop Worlock's official residence, marked with the symbol of the Liverpool Diocese.

It was an original, written with a 1970s typewriter, the page dented with the printed word.

Dear Sr. Philomena,

After much prayer and thought, I am convinced there is no other person better suited to caring for this child than you. The gravity of the danger to this child's soul cannot be overstated and I agree that the Holy Spirit has led you into guardianship of her. I have instructed our legal team to proceed with making you her legal guardian and would like you to register her birth with the registrar at Brougham Terrace. I would be grateful if you could inform me of her progress and would like to assure you that both you and Eve will be at the centre of my prayers.

Concerning the information in her mother's letter, I have every confidence that this shocking story will remain known to you and me alone. Be vigilant in prayer and in action. She is an especially vulnerable child but also blessed to have been discovered and saved by you under the guidance of the Holy Spirit.

Thank you for taking on this responsibility.

Yours in Christ
Archbishop Derek Worlock

A mother without a child, thought Clay. A child without a mother.

She looked at the Polaroid photo salvaged from the Drakes' loft and said, 'Philomena, we were made for each other. We were meant to be.'

She turned every last page in the file. The two letters were the only surviving documents from the first six years of her life. She closed the file and gazed at Philomena's writing. The word *love*, repeated over and over, danced from the page, raising the dead weight from the centre of her heart and filling her with a calm certainty.

Philomena was the guiding star, her birth parents inevitable darkness.

She looked to the light, seized on it and knew she would never let it go.

Eve fell into a stillness and felt a calm she remembered from her childhood. Time passed. She didn't move. It was exactly how she used to feel when she prayed with Philomena.

The key turned in the lock on the front door.

'Eve?'

She walked into the hall, to Thomas's voice.

Philip and Thomas stood, hand in hand, waiting for her.

Eve knelt on the floor and held the photograph of herself and Philomena towards Philip.

The little boy ran and fell into her.

'What's this?' Thomas smiled. He looked closely. 'Oh God, is that who I think it is?'

She nodded, listened to herself laughing.

As she held Thomas and Philip into herself, Eve Clay closed her eyes and was visited by her earliest memory. The darkness in her head exploded into bright summer sunshine. The garden of St Claire's stretched out like an eternal meadow and she could see her knees rising and hands swinging on the edge of her vision as she ran across the grass to Philomena, youthful, smiling, arms held out, love waiting to collect its prize.

Philomena scooped her up under the arms and twirled her round and round. The sky was blue and cloudless behind Philomena's head and her face beamed with happiness.

The only sound was Eve's laughter blending with Philomena's and, then, Philomena's voice.

'This is where you come from. This and nowhere else.'

Clay opened her eyes, looked at Philip and Thomas.

'And this is where we belong.'

She took the Polaroid from Thomas.

'Philip, look.' Eve's son turned his eyes to the image of his mother as a small girl sitting on her protector's knee. 'Philip, this is your grandmother. Her name is Philomena.'

Acknowledgements

I'd like to thank Peter, Rosie and Jessica Buckman, Toby Duncan, Paul Goetzee, John Gunning, Laura Palmer and all at Head of Zeus, Lucy Ridout, Linda and Eleanor Roberts, Frank and Ben Rooney, Veronica Stallwood, Lynn Mills, Les Coe, Tom Stapledon, Chris Ilies and all Friends of the Williamson Tunnels, Dave Bridston and all at the Williamson Heritage Centre.

MARK ROBERTS

Dead Silent

Prologue

October, 1985

'Eve, thank you very much for coming in to my office to see me,' gushed Mrs Tripp. She smiled from behind her desk as Eve stood her ground at the door of the office.

Breathless, having run from the garden of St Michael's Catholic Care Home for Children where she had been playing football with the big lads, Eve said, 'You're welcome, Mrs Tripp.'

The pleasantness of Mrs Tripp's manner caused Eve to look down at her feet and perform a simple trick to check she wasn't dreaming. She looked at the black trainers on her feet and told herself, *squeeze your toes*. She squeezed her toes and confirmed. She was wide awake and it was all real.

'Come and take a seat, child,' encouraged Mrs Tripp, her newly permed hair crowned with an outsize yellow ribbon.

You're too old and fat, thought Eve, *to even try and look like that Madonna one.*

As she walked to the chair across from Mrs Tripp's desk, Eve smiled at the boss of the children's home, her feet firmly on the ground, her eyes locked in the fat lady's gaze, and sat down.

'I like your Everton kit, Eve.'

She glanced down. Blue socks bunched at the ankles, soil and grass stained shins from the sliding tackle she had put in a few minutes earlier, white shorts and blue and white top.

'So do I,' said Eve. 'I just wish they weren't sponsored by Hafnia.'

'Why's that, Eve?'

'Hafnia's a canned meat company. In Denmark. Ham. It's dead sly on the animals.'

'Oh, Eve, how many times have we had this out?' Mrs Tripp chuckled, smiling with her face but not with her eyes. 'You're a growing girl and you need to eat meat as part of a balanced diet.'

'As soon as I'm big enough—'

'Yes I know! I know.'

Silence descended. Mrs Tripp looked as far into the distance as the four walls of her office would allow. Eve looked out of the window behind Mrs Tripp. In the sky above the River Mersey, there were two horizontal red lines, as if a giant had drawn two bloody fingers across the grey autumnal clouds.

'My, how you've grown, Eve. I remember the first time you sat on that very chair across from my desk.'

'So do I,' smiled Eve. *It was bloody awful.* 'You're a very busy woman, Mrs Tripp. All those kids. All them staff. How can I help you?'

Mrs Tripp clapped her hands and laughed too loudly. Eve's heart sank.

'It's not a question of how you can help me, it's a question of how we can help you.'

From the corner of the room came a solitary sigh. Eve turned as a tall thin man with snow white hair, dressed all in black except for a white dog collar, stepped out of the shadows into the muddy light of the room.

As he walked towards the desk, he closed the cover of a card file bulging with papers, a file Eve recognised as the one they kept on her. Behind his left ear, she saw a thin hand-rolled cigarette. She looked at his face, his unsmiling eyes fixed on her. She stared back, but stood up as the priest advanced slowly: observing, thinking, nodding.

He placed the file down on Mrs Tripp's desk and, with the strangest sensation in her head that she had lived through this exact moment at another point in her life, Eve read the letters of her name in black felt pen. E V E T T E C L A Y.

'This is Father David Murphy. Father Murphy, this is Evette Clay.'

He placed the hand-rolled cigarette to his lips, flicked his thumbnail against the red tip of a match and lit the loose strands of tobacco hanging from his home-made smoke. Father Murphy took a huge lungful of smoke and blew it out in a thin stream.

'Hello, Eve.' His voice rumbled, his speech posher than a TV news reader.

'Good afternoon, Father Murphy.' She sat down and Father Murphy remained standing.

'How old are you, Eve?' asked the priest.

'As old as the hills,' she laughed, alone.

'So I gather.'

'Seven-and-a-half if it's numbers you're after, Father.' She guessed the next question. 'And I've lived here for a just over one year.'

'Up until then you lived in St Claire's with Sister Philomena?'

'Yes.' The verve deserted her. 'Did you know Sister Philomena, Father?'

'No.' A strand of hope, a connection, faded. 'Does that disappoint you, Eve?'

'Just because you're a priest, it doesn't mean you know all the nuns in the world. I was just wondering if—'

'Father Murphy isn't just a priest, as if that on its own wasn't enough responsibility,' Mrs Tripp railroaded over her. 'He's a fully qualified doctor.'

'Oh!' said Eve, mustering as much enthusiasm as she could.

'I've come to see you, Eve.' Ash dropped onto Mrs Tripp's desk.

But I'm not ill, she thought.

'It's fair to say, isn't it, Eve, there have been one or two odd behaviours,' said Mrs Tripp. Eve knew what was coming next. 'When you set off the fire alarm.'

'That was an accident. Billy Jones was there. He vouched for me.'

Mrs Tripp turned to Father Murphy. 'She's very popular with all the staff and the children. People make exceptions for her.'

'No they don't, they tell the truth,' said Eve.

'Christmas morning. You refused to get out of bed and open your presents.'

'I was sad because I couldn't stop thinking about Philomena. I did get up by lunchtime. And I'd opened my presents by tea. And then I just did what I do most days. I accepted that she's dead. And just get on with it. What else can I do?' The ball of tears behind her eyes threatened to break but the voice inside her shouted, *don't you dare don't you dare don't you dare*! And with that, she experienced a surge of anger and a beam of light.

The memory of the toughest girl she'd ever met in the care system, Natasha Seventeen, and the last piece of advice she'd given her before she left St Michael's. *Don't act depressed kid or they'll cart you off to the funny farm!*

'Jesus Christ!' said Eve, all the bits and pieces falling into place.

'Eve, blasphemy isn't allowed here!'

'I'm saying my prayers. And I'm asking Jesus to give me strength.'

Eve stood up, turned away from Mrs Tripp, and made herself as tall as she could in front of the priest. There was a glimmer of a smile behind the sternness in his eyes.

'Father Murphy, can I ask you a question, please?'

'Of course you can, Eve.'

'Are you one of those head doctors by any chance? What are they called now? Yeah. Are you a shrimp?'

'I believe the expression is shrink.' He took a drag on his cigarette, tapped a ball of ash onto the floor. Eve warmed to the man.

'Am I glad you're here, Father Murphy.'

'You are?'

'Yes. You're just the man we need round here.'

'I think it would be a really good idea to talk about the past,' said Mrs Tripp.

'Me too, me too,' said Eve. 'Thank you, Father Murphy.' She sat down across from Mrs Tripp. 'The past, yes, let's talk about the past.'

She glanced up at Father Murphy, the lower half of his face concealed behind the hand in which he held his cigarette. She recalled a scene in a TV sitcom she had watched.

'Mrs Tripp, tell me about your childhood,' said Eve.

The only things redder than Mrs Tripp's face were the lines in the sky above the River Mersey.

'Go and finish your game of football before it gets dark,' said Father Murphy. 'I've heard about your great loss and I know enough of Sister Philomena to know she'd be completely and utterly proud of the way you are coping at such a tender age. God bless you, Eve. We will meet again. Please know, you will always be in my prayers.'

'Thank you, Father, for understanding.'

He smiled, made the sign of the cross over her head.

The silence in the room behind her as she made her way to the door felt like treacle.

Eve closed the door after herself, checked the corridor. It was empty. She waited.

'You flicked ash onto my desk and my carpet!' complained Mrs Tripp.

'And you have wasted my time,' replied Father Murphy. 'Which is the larger sin? She's perfectly sane in spite of all the things she has had to endure. She's a credit to Sister Philomena who saved her from the powers of darkness and moulded her into the child she is.'

Silence. As Father Murphy's footsteps approached the door of Mrs Tripp's office, his words sank into her spine.

Eve hurtled down the corridor running faster than she ever had. Running like the Devil was at her heels.

Thirty-three Years Later

The Triumph Of Death

Thursday 18 December, 02:38 am

He's been slaughtered.

The old woman's words rolled around DCI Eve Clay's head as she sprinted from her car to the Sefton Park entrance of Lark Lane where scientific support officers had already sealed off the scene of the crime.

'DCI Clay!' She told the constable running the log at the top of the lane.

He's been slaughtered.

According to the witnesses who had discovered the old woman wandering at the junction of Albert Road and Lark Lane. But that was all.

The moon hung low in the clear sky. Sharp light fell on the glass façades of the shops and restaurants on either side and, for a passing moment, Clay imagined she was running down a locked-in corridor of ice.

Closing down on a group of people under a street light, Clay slowed to read the scene. A female constable crouched on her haunches next to an old woman lying in the recovery position on a pair of padded coats on the pavement. Looming above her, DS Gina Riley was deep in conversation with a couple, a man who looked like he'd been made from rubber tyres and a beanpole woman, who put Clay in mind of Popeye and Olive Oil.

'DCI Eve Clay,' she showed her warrant card. 'You're the couple who found her?'

'Yes,' said the man.

The woman looked at Clay with pleading eyes.

'Thank you for helping her. Do you know the old lady's name?'

'No!' They answered in one voice.

'Do you know where she lives?' asked Clay.

'Albert Road, I'm pretty sure,' said the woman.

'Which side?'

'I've seen her coming in and out of the even side,' said the man.

'But she didn't appear to be physically injured?'

'Not until she fitted and smacked her head on the pavement.'

Clay stooped to take a closer look at the old woman, at the fresh wound on her forehead. The coats had been carefully lain under the woman's body to stop her temperature from plummeting with contact to the freezing pavement, and the recovery position was neatly executed. She looked up at the witnesses.

'Are you care workers?' They looked at each other as if Clay was a gifted psychic. 'You've made a really good job of this.' She stood up to her full height. 'So, what happened?'

'She was wandering in the middle of the road.We approached her and she said "he's been slaughtered". Then she wandered here and to this spot, had a seizure and hit the deck. We called 999. She stopped fitting after a minute and fifteen. We timed it. When she stopped fitting, we put her in the recovery position.'

'You didn't see anyone else around?' asked Clay.

'No,' said the man, calmly and firmly.

'Take me to where you think she lives,' said Clay.

A police car, siren off, blue light turning, sat outside The Albert pub on the corner of Lark Lane and Albert Road. Clay followed the couple as they turned into Albert Road and she took in the whole scene in with a three hundred and sixty degree turn.

DS Karl Stone was getting dressed in a white protective suit at the back of a scientific support van.

Facing each other on either side of Albert Road, the tall Victorian terraced houses looked eerie in shadows and moonlight.

'Used to be big single dwellings, family homes when families were big,' said Stone. 'Most of the houses are flatted now, mainly student accommodation,' said Stone.

Clay did a mental date check: the middle of December. A witness famine. She sank deeper into the logic of the time and place, scanned the houses picked out by the scientific support van's NiteOwl light. 'Looks like she's walked out of her home, away from the scene.' Clay combed the pavement with her torch but there were no apparent blood stains.

An ambulance's siren wailed, and Clay realised time was ticking.

As Clay dressed quickly in a protective suit, lights came on in bedrooms as people woke up to the gathering police presence on their doorsteps. Clay's heart sank. Whatever had happened, it looked like the neighbours who were still there had slept through it.

Who's the he? Who's been slaughtered? Husband? Brother? Father? Son? A thought about the potential killer's timing hit her hard. *He's timed this so that the students wouldn't be around.*

'The paramedics are loading her onto a trolley stretcher.' DS Bill Hendricks was hurrying into Albert Road.

'Tell Gina Riley,' called Clay. 'Go in the ambulance with the old woman. Call me when she comes round.'

'I got it!' Riley shouted back.

'DCI Clay!' The man's voice was loud and urgent. He faced a house near the centre of the terrace. 'We're pretty certain this is the one.'

Clay hurried along the pavement and up the stone step. She reached down at the edge of the door and gave it a shove with her gloved fingers.

The door opened a few centimetres. A strange pattern of light emerged within the house.

She turned to the witnesses. 'I think you're right. This is it.' DS Bill Hendricks and DS Karl Stone were behind her. 'You've given your details to the WPC?' They nodded. 'Thank you for your assistance.'

'We won't breathe a word to anyone about any of this,' said the woman.

'I'd appreciate that,' said Clay. 'Because if there has been a murder, my guess is the killer lives around here.' She drew in their astonishment, allowed the uncomfortable notion to sink in. 'You've helped this old lady. Help me with your ongoing silence.'

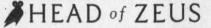